21/10/21

D1313351

By Naomi Miller

Imperfect Alchemist

a&b

IMPERFECT ALCHEMIST

Naomi Miller

Allison & Busby Limited
11 Wardour Mews
London W1F 8AN
allisonandbusby.com

First published in Great Britain by Allison & Busby in 2020.
This paperback edition published by Allison & Busby in 2021.

A CIP catalogue record for this book is available from
the British Library.

10 9 8 7 6 5 4 3 2 1

ISBN 978-0-7490-2627-1

Typeset in 11/16 pt Adobe Garamond Pro by
Allison & Busby Ltd

Printed and bound by
CPI Group (UK) Ltd, Croydon, CR0 4YY

For Chris, who completes the double ouroboros

Opus alchymicum is the alchemical process of transmuting base into precious metals or distilling liquid for refinement over three stages:

Nigredo (*mortificatio*): the initial, black stage, representing the plunge into chaos, darkness, ash; descent, dying.

Albedo (*solutio/ablutio*): the pure, white stage, representing cleansing, washing, purification.

Rubedo (*projectio*): the final red stage, representing completion and release, synthesis, unity of masculine and feminine.

PRELUDE: THE STILL-ROOM

Lady Catherine Herbert

Alchemy is no better than superstition. At best, a fond hope; at worst, heartbreak. Even when the goal is something less ambitious than turning dross into gold.

Catherine sets the lantern on the landing and places the fingertips of one hand against the oak door for balance. Her breath comes in short gasps, her chest tight with bands of pain from climbing the three flights of stairs to the top of the house, lifting feet that seem weighted with lead.

She has been disappointed so many times, she has all but abandoned the quest. Yet, once again, even as her head swims from the dizzy spells that now afflict her, she pulls a ring of keys – brass, silver and gold – from the muslin pouch hanging from her girdle. She turns the lock with the largest one, of brass, and with an effort pushes open the heavy door.

The still-room is bathed in moonlight at this hour, its shelves and tables edged with black shadows, bearing no resemblance to the heated hive of concoction and distillation that has occupied so many of her daylight hours. Now, its cool, eerie silence is forbidding.

She lifts the lantern and enters the room with unsteady steps, inhaling the musky odours of spices and minerals. Her shaky grip sends blades of light and shadow spinning around her until she places the lantern on the worktable that stretches almost the length of one wall. Glass bottles of herbal syrups and cordials, tinctures and balms line the shelves above it, alongside ointments and lotions in pewter pots. Dried herbs from her own garden rest beside costly minerals and spices from abroad, all carefully labelled and separated according to their potential to heal or harm. Stored along the wall beneath the table are chests of ingredients ready to be used once she is well enough to resume her work – if that day ever comes.

Her husband, Henry Herbert, Earl of Pembroke and master of Wilton House, has spared no expense in support of her activity in the still-room, where she has prepared and perfected chemical and herbal remedies for the health of Wilton's large staff and that of the farmers and villagers in the Wiltshire countryside neighbouring the estate. But Lady Catherine has not made this nocturnal visit to obtain syrup for a servant's cough or a tincture to ease a village wife's labour pains. Nor to seek once more the elusive remedy for her own ailments. With such skill to treat others, why is she unable to heal herself?

For years now, her production of medicines has gone hand in hand with the chimerical search for a cure – not for her persistent weakness, but for infertility. Her husband hasn't reproached her for her failure to bear a child, yet at twenty-two and still childless after nine years of marriage, she is all too aware that the absence of an heir to the earldom blocks his hopes for the Pembroke line. She herself is beginning to lose her capacity to imagine an infant in her arms. It is the child she longs for, not the line.

Impatient with these thoughts, Catherine moves purposefully to the cabinet at the far end of the room, past the open shelves holding all the alchemical vessels essential to her work: glass aludels and retorts, silver still pots and copper pelicans. The aludels, known by alchemists as 'eggs' for their ovoid shape, always make her think of her womb, empty and waiting to be filled. Setting the lantern beside the cabinet, she selects the small silver key, unlocks the inlaid door and inhales a muted medley of exotic fragrances. The lower shelves house an array of small bottles and flasks containing specialised tinctures and cordials. Another shelf bears pots of precious spices from faraway lands: cardamom, ginger and saffron from India, nutmeg and cloves from the Spice Islands, cinnamon from Ceylon. When she lifts their lids and closes her eyes, the distinctive note of each aroma mingles in complex harmony with its fellows, intoxicating her senses. The topmost shelf contains the rarest as well as the most dangerous substances, to be used only in small doses for extreme ailments.

The open shelf at the heart of the cabinet is lined with varied pieces of coloured stone, from crimson-veined marble to a large piece of crystalline rose quartz, the queen of her collection, attended by a handful of small gemstones cut from the same quartz – tumbled crystals, smooth and translucent in the flickering light. She rubs one between her fingers and slips it into the muslin pouch.

From the bottom of the cabinet, Catherine removes the object of her quest: a black walnut box, her husband's gift for the safekeeping of her medicinal recipes. She runs her fingers over the alchemical symbols engraved in the lid and sides: crossed lines beneath a circle with horns for *silver*, a circle around a central dot, bearing a sideways crown, for *gold*. She never tires of touching these lines, which seem imbued with the power of the substances they represent.

Unlocking the box with her smallest key, of gold, she lifts the lid and fingers the sheaf of papers. She hopes to pass this precious box along to a daughter. But the collection of recipes is not yet finished. The most important remedy still eludes her. Despite her unending failures, her mounting scepticism of alchemy's powers, she knows that if her strength ever returns she will continue the search, however hopeless.

Rosemary, sage, pennyroyal, angelica, juniper, rue. She whispers the names as if casting an incantation or calling upon spirits to fill her body – or naming the girl child she imagines instructing in the art of alchemy one day.

But now, to the task at hand – not a recipe, but a message.

Placing the box beneath her arm and lifting the lantern, Catherine turns. Moving swiftly, she passes so close to the shelves of vessels that the sleeve of her gown catches on one of the glass aludels. The vessel slides over the edge of the shelf and shatters against the floor. She freezes. Then she closes her eyes and breathes out.

Not all accidents are signs.

Catherine moves to a desk facing the moonlit window and sets down the walnut box. She sinks into the chair fronting the desk, pulls a sheet of paper from the drawer and dips her quill into the inkpot. As she writes, her narrow shoulders relax and her breathing steadies. The words come slowly in the lantern's flickering illumination, but now her hand is firm. At length she sets down the quill, rereads her words and folds the paper. Taking up the sealing candle on the desk, she lights it from the lantern flame, drips crimson wax onto the sheet. With assurance arising from long practice, her fingers find the small silver pendant, blackened with use, that hangs from a thong around her neck. She pushes the circlet firmly into the wax to complete the seal. As the image hardens in the cooling wax, she replaces the pendant around her neck.

She lifts the engraved lid of the box to place the paper inside, then pauses and, dipping her quill once more, writes with a flourish –

To the next Cleopatra

PART ONE: 1573–78

NIGREDO *(mortificatio)*: the initial, black stage, representing the plunge into chaos, darkness, ash; descent, dying.

CHAPTER ONE

Rose, 1573

My mother was a witch.

Or so they said when they dragged her from me. I knew only the truth that she was the centre of my world. But that was why she sent me away.

I was nine years old.

'The lady in the great house will teach you what I can't,' she said. 'Give you tools no one will question – reading, writing, making remedies. None can challenge her learning.'

She gripped my forearms, hard, her mouth twisting like she tasted something bitter, and I scowled to hide my dread.

'Learn all you can, Rose.' Her voice was urgent. 'But don't use it unless you have to. Special knowledge scares folks. That's why—' She broke off with a gulp. I could see her throat working as she swallowed her words. Her once-plump cheeks, that I so loved to kiss, seemed to have become thinner, but I could still breathe in the heady mix of herbal fragrances from her garden and the storeroom, sharp and sweet.

'Mum, *you* can teach me all I need.' My voice cracked with desperation as I tried to burrow into her chest. All I wanted was never to leave her. To stay home with Mum and Da and my little brother. Not to be shut away in the great house to serve a lady I didn't know.

She shook her head, once, that was all.

There was no use arguing. And nothing else I could give her.

Mum was born a farmer's daughter, but it was from her mother that she learnt her skills, like knowing the berries on the hedgerows – which to taste, which to toss, and which to press into cordials that could heal. It was her knowledge of herbs that made my father, Martin Commin, a cloth merchant with a market stall in Salisbury, want to marry her.

I loved that story, and asked Mum to repeat it so many times that I could tell it myself. 'The word is that your daughter Joan knows herbs and grows in knowledge every season,' Da told Mum's father, a sheep farmer. 'I believe there's a market here for herbal medicines, which I can offer at my stall along with the cloth – to keep my customers healthy as well as clothed. I want your Joan for a wife.' My father was never slow to get to the point.

Mum told me he dreamt big. 'That's what appealed to me when he came courting. He was eleven years older than me, but his dreams seemed as new as my own – to make his way in the world, just like I wanted to.' I liked this part of the story, for already I had dreams of my own.

'So we were married in the parish church and set up housekeeping here in Amesbury,' Mum told me, offering my little brother, Michael, a biscuit and me the story, to keep us both satisfied.

'I built up the herbal side of Martin's business and trained his new apprentice – a lad named Simon. Folks soon came from all over Wiltshire for my remedies. At that time, the lord of the great house had taken a first wife he couldn't abide. And she was no healer. When workers fell ill or came into harm's way, his lordship sent them to me.' Here she sighed and fell silent a moment, her sinewed hands smoothing a pleat in her skirt. 'Simon loved the stars. He taught me the cycles of planets while I taught him the cycles of plants.' When I frowned, Mum explained the difference between *plants* and *planets*. 'Planets look like stars in the night sky.' As I listened I scribbled pictures on the hearthstones, as I had ever since I was big enough to hold a stick of charcoal. I drew plants budding with starlight instead of flowers, and Mum smiled. My drawing during her stories kept us both happy.

'Together, Simon and I, we made cures to sell that brought as much business as your father could handle,' she continued. 'Ah, we taught each other so much! And your birth during those years of learning brought me more joy than any cure I could make.' When she fixed me in her calm, brown gaze, I knew no one would ever love me more.

But one day the storytelling stopped, and the happy pattern of our days was broken.

'There's been some trouble,' Mum explained as she hurried into our cottage. Taking a deep breath, she fixed me with a steady gaze. 'Your father's not home until nightfall from the market, so I need you to listen carefully so that you can tell him what I'm telling you.'

I wondered why she couldn't wait to tell him herself. But her voice didn't sound alarmed, so I curled up at her feet, my cheek pressing into her sturdy wool skirts.

'Last market day, when you were with your father, I spent the time with Sally Hutchins, helping to prepare her for childbirth. Sally had many fears about it, as she'd already lost a child. I brought Michael with me, wrapped in a sling across my chest, because I expected it would be hours before her baby arrived. It took until daybreak, but finally I brought that baby into the world. His left arm was withered, but his mother didn't care, so long as he lived and breathed. Or so she said, weeping her thanks and pressing a shilling into my palm. But her husband blamed me.'

That was when I heard voices at the front gate, then pounding on the door. I sprang to my feet and Mum lifted little Michael into my arms. Before she opened the door, she looked back at me and said, very clearly, 'Don't be afraid.'

When the door swung open, I heard the gasp a crowd makes, for it was a crowd outside. Then one shrill woman's voice, crying 'Witch!' What came next was like the shower of sparks when logs collapse in fire. The crowd sucked my mother away with them, leaving me alone with the embers, my brother wailing in my arms.

When Da got home, I told him what Mum had said. In my haste, I jumbled the facts, but he left at once, white-faced and shaking with fury. 'Ungrateful scum, these villagers take what they need and bite the hand that heals them.'

20

My aunt Judith, a chunky woman with loving arms, soon arrived to look after Michael and me, her face as pale as Da's.

'*Trial by water*, they call it,' she said. 'But you're not to worry, Rose, for your mum's innocent. Any babe can have a bad arm. They'll learn soon enough what fools they've been. And that's the last of Joan helping Wiltshire villagers, shilling or no shilling.'

Aunt Judith explained that they would row Mum into the middle of the river with a rope around her waist and throw her overboard into the depths. I gasped. I knew Mum feared the dark grasp of the water.

'If she floats, they name her guilty.' Aunt Judith's voice trembled then, and I started to shake.

To keep my mind off my fears and keep Michael happy, I drew pictures for him upon the hearthstones – scary shapes that turned into familiar creatures after all: sparrows and kittens and butterflies. Drawing calmed me, comforted me, gave me a place to change my nightmares into hopes. Michael laughed and pointed to the cat, gurgling, 'Muggie!' – baby talk for 'Mugwort', our yellow kitten, golden as a clump of mugwort flowers.

I shivered on my hay mattress that night, bringing Michael beside me when he whimpered, and promising him, with a confidence I didn't feel, that all would be well. Lying in darkness, remembering Mum's instruction, somehow I kept fear – and tears – at bay. But once I finally slipped into sleep, the cry of *Witch!* haunted my dreams.

CHAPTER TWO

Mary, 1575

They shared everything: books, dreams; hopes, disappointments; adventures.

Wherever they lived – from Ludlow Castle on the Welsh border to Penshurst Place in Kent – the Sidney sisters plotted their future together. Their mother, Lady Mary Dudley Sidney, described to her daughters both the delights and dangers at the court of Queen Elizabeth – the colourful social whirl, but also the constant palace intrigues among the courtiers, back-stabbing and jockeying for favour.

And there were accidental, unanticipated dangers as well. Lady Mary's own face was disfigured by the pox she caught while attending the Queen when Mary was only a baby. A healer herself, she nursed the Queen back to health, but had no remedy for the terrible scars that marred her cheeks after she recovered from her own bout with the disease. The cosmetic creams and powders that she prepared from her own recipes inspired her daughters to 'play alchemist', mixing 'curative' potions as gifts for their mother, to no avail. She regularly used a mask or veil at court to hide her disfigurement.

'Not every ailment has a cure,' their mother warned.

Still, to Mary and Ambrosia the world seemed full of possibilities, each challenge a puzzle to solve together. The first Sidney daughter, Margaret, had died before Mary was born and Elizabeth, the only sister they had known, died when Mary was six years old and Ambrosia only three. The two remaining sisters invariably formed a threesome for games with their middle brother, Robert, while their adored older brother, Philip, was away at school in Shrewsbury, and their younger brother, Tommy, was still in the skirts of a baby. But they spent more hours with each other than with anyone else. Mary and Ambrosia studied under the same tutor, played and embroidered together, and shared secrets only with each other.

Until the year Mary turned fourteen.

Ambrosia's illness struck with no warning. Even when she was forbidden to leave their bedroom, wrapped in warm woollen shawls against the chill air that seeped through the windows punctuating the thick stone walls of Ludlow Castle, their parents insisted there was no need to worry. The family physician would identify and treat this ailment. Even when Ambrosia was confined to her bed, coughing and shuddering, Mary chose to believe her parents.

Putting on a bright face so as not to worry her sister, Mary treated Ambrosia's illness like a passing winter snowfall that would surely vanish come spring.

The most beautiful morning of the newly budding season dawned almost too bright to be believed, the March sky promising a cerulean blue. After slitting their window open a crack to taste the air, cool as spring water, Mary closed the casement, returned to the bed they shared, and kissed her sister's damp forehead. Ambrosia's eyes flew open and she fixed her gaze on her sister.

'Today is the day?' But it wasn't really a question, and her pale lips curved in a smile when Mary nodded, smoothing her sister's straight, dark hair, such a contrast with Mary's own unruly red curls.

Less than three years apart in age, the sisters had always devised each day's adventures together, well or ill. Even now, when Ambrosia could no longer rise from her bed. Especially today.

'Where?' Ambrosia's voice was faint but insistent.

'At the top of the Great Tower of the Gatehouse Keep, where he watches from dawn.'

He was Jake, the bailiff's son, sixteen and newly promoted to the Ludlow Castle guardsmen. Mary and Ambrosia had known him since childhood, sharing games of marbles and hopscotch during the months the family lived at the castle, while their father oversaw the border counties as President of the Council of the Marches of Wales. Now, Mary had decided to taste her first kiss, and had chosen Jake to bestow it. He didn't know this yet.

24

'When I arrive at court next season, once Mother finally deems me ready, I'll be readier than she knows.' Her chuckle sounded bright, bravado masking her qualms about joining Her Majesty's circle. Her little sister couldn't guess she was nervous if she wouldn't admit it to herself. And Ambrosia needed something to lift her spirits, now more than ever. They both did.

Ambrosia's violent coughing interrupted their murmurs, until Mary held a cup of water to her lips. 'Promise me you'll come right back and tell me all!' Mary leant close to catch the breathy whisper as Ambrosia sank back upon her pillow and closed her grey-green eyes.

'Promise *me* you'll wait patiently and listen to all of it,' Mary demanded softly. 'I'm not going through with this unless I have an audience who matters.' She was rewarded with the glimmer of a smile.

As Mary rose to go, Ambrosia was seized with another paroxysm of coughing. 'I'll stay. Jake can wait.' Mary's offer carried genuine relief. But Ambrosia shook her head.

'You must live the story . . . before you can tell it,' she murmured.

'I'll be back sooner than you think.' Suddenly, Mary just wanted to get it over with.

Clutching her skirts in her fists, she walked quickly across the courtyard from the household quarters to the Great Tower that topped the Gatehouse Keep of the fortified castle. She climbed the twisting steps quickly at first, then more slowly as her calves started to ache, marvelling that Jake mounted these steps every day. Rounding the last curve, she could hear the wind. Then she was blinking against the bright sun, catching her breath. The novice guardsman turned, surprised to see her, and smiled.

'Come see the beauty of Wales, me lady,' he urged, spreading his arms and wheeling in a half-circle to face the western horizon. The Shropshire countryside rolled westward into the Welsh hills in a vast panorama, alive with spring green. Jake's voice was warm with the Welsh lilt Mary had come to love once she had learnt to make sense of it. It was the sound of his voice that had decided her choice, more than his floppy dark hair or startlingly blue eyes.

Suddenly, looking into those eyes, Mary felt unsure. To give herself a moment, she gripped the cold stone parapet and peered over the edge, her coppery hair flying out behind her in the brisk wind. The landscape seemed more like a tapestry from the Great Hall than a real place, threaded with thin silvery streams and dotted with trees. No people that she could see, but then it was just past dawn.

'Stop calling me *lady*, Jake. We've known each other for years.' Mary tried to laugh, but shivered instead. 'I didn't expect the wind.'

She felt a rush of vertigo – from looking over the lofty parapet, or from fear of looking at Jake? Swallowing once, she used the giddiness as a spur to action. Turning to him, Mary reached up, pulled Jake's face to hers, and planted her lips on his.

Startled, he began to pull away, but Mary's grip was insistent and his mouth fixed upon hers like a bird dropping into a nest. When he closed his eyes, Mary kept hers wide open. She had promised Ambrosia to remember everything and report back. Her lips opened reflexively, and she tasted his tongue, darting towards hers. Abruptly, she released him, smiling stiffly to conceal the confusion that now flooded her. Her cheeks blazed.

'Thank you kindly,' she murmured, already considering how to describe for Ambrosia the oddly mundane sensation of two pairs of lips meeting.

'You owe me no thanks, me lady,' Jake's face, too, was flushed, his expression quizzical, then anxious. 'Are you all right?'

'I'm fine.' With a final glance over the Welsh hills, now bathed in morning light, Mary turned and started down the curving stairway.

That was when she noticed the wind carrying a disturbing sound. It was the high keening of maidservants.

CHAPTER THREE

Rose, 1573–74

Mum returned home the next day, soaked in filthy river water but alive. When I ran into her arms, she knelt and hugged me, hard, and finally my tears burst forth, streaming down my cheeks and mixing with the water still dripping from her hair. Even Da wept dry sobs, while Michael bawled in Aunt Judith's arms. But after Mum had bathed and dressed herself in dry clothes, we sat down to the midday meal Aunt Judith had prepared, as if all was well. The sharp cheese, the warm buttery griddle cakes and the tangy-sweet apple slices were comforting. I savoured the flavour.

My parents sent me to bed early with Michael, but I could hear snatches of their speech.

My mother, her words like a prayer: 'Healing is my gift.'

My father's raised voice: '*Witch* is a name that lingers . . . You must never practise healing again, Joan, or . . . seal your fate and break this family for ever.'

My mother again, too low for me to hear her words, but insistent, like the distant calling of geese across the autumn sky. Then my father's voice like thunder, rumbling ominous warnings.

When I brought Michael down for breakfast the next morning, the calm mother who had told me not to be afraid was gone. Now Mum couldn't stop trembling. But not from cold. Nor from fear. My mother was the bravest woman I knew. It was anger that flared just behind her eyes. I could feel its heat.

At my insistence, she reluctantly told me what had passed. She had been locked overnight in a farmer's cellar, then taken down to the river at dawn in a procession headed by leaders of the angry mob. Two men, one of them the father of the child with the withered arm, rowed her out to the middle of the stream and threw her in. When she sank, she was drawn back to the surface by the rope they had bound her with and pronounced innocent.

'I want you safe,' she murmured now, stroking my wispy hair gently, although her voice was tight. 'And I want you free of taint. The lady in the great house will teach you what I can't.' Her voice was low, but I could hear the flames burning her hopes to ash. And she wouldn't look at Da.

A fortnight later, I was sent to Wilton House – ten miles and a world away from Amesbury – to serve the Lady Catherine Herbert.

By the time we reached the outer gates that crisp autumn afternoon, the cart that carried me from my home village had jolted over too many holes to count. The westering sun cast netted shadows over everything that passed beneath the towering trees that bordered the long drive. At the end of the avenue, Wilton loomed high and wide, no ordinary house but a great stone building that seemed to straddle the horizon. The cart finally stopped beneath a vast stone arch. My body ached as I clambered down and reached out my arms to catch the lumpy sack of belongings tossed my way by the burly carter my father had hired to deliver me. Catching his sympathetic smile, my eyes stung and I rubbed them hastily. As I shouldered my sack I felt its contents shift – the substance of my old life, now broken up and gathered piecemeal into a cloth bag.

An imposing man was waiting for me, standing as erect as a soldier, dressed in blue and red livery trimmed with gold braid. He didn't bother to introduce himself, just sniffed and led me from the entryway through a maze of corridors and down a flight of stairs to the servants' hall.

'Here's the new girl,' he snapped as we entered the kitchen, a stone-walled room with two huge, roaring fireplaces. Then he turned on his heel and was gone.

A short, vigorous woman with plump cheeks athwart a prominent nose hurried across the room and took my bag from me. 'That's Master Wilkins, the steward. He's more bark than bite. Sit down, lass, and have some supper. Cook Corbett has left a plate for you.' As I seated myself at one end of the long table running down the centre of the room, she continued briskly, 'I'm the housekeeper, Mistress Roberts, and I'll have you settled in a trice. You'll sleep in my room tonight. Cicely, she's one of the chambermaids, will show you round the house tomorrow. She'll introduce you to the folks who keep this grand place running. Once you know your way about, you'll be ready to meet the mistress.'

I was too nervous to eat much, but managed a few mouthfuls of bread and cheese before Mistress Roberts brought me to a flock mattress tucked into a corner of her chamber, warmed by a cosy fire. Crawling under the blanket, I curled into a ball around my fears, but dropped asleep at once.

I awoke the next morning to an unfamiliar silence. At home the cocks' crowing always roused me. Suddenly I missed those roosters more than I could have imagined. How could people sleep in such deafening silence? Mistress Roberts greeted me briskly and handed me a russet smock and kirtle, 'to be getting on with'. A knocking at the door interrupted her description of the proper garments I'd soon be supplied with. 'That'll be Cicely!'

She opened the door to a broad, sturdy girl a few years older than me, with a snub nose and eyes as blue as cornflower petals, startling under strong dark brows. Her face broke into an enormous smile when she saw me. 'Thou'rt smaller than I thought, but no matter – ye'll grow on Cook Corbett's fare for sure. Come with me now, and we'll get thee started on breakfast afore I show thee round, for thou hardly ate last night.' Her warm voice was coloured with an unfamiliar lilt. At my puzzled look, she explained that marked her as *a Yorkshire lass*. 'Don't worry if tha miss owt I say at first. Ye'll catch on soon enough.'

I wondered how Cicely knew what I'd eaten, until I arrived at the kitchen on her heels. Cook Corbett, a tall, bony woman of few words but deft fingers, clearly knew who ate what and made sure that nothing was wasted from her stores. Wiping her hands on an impressively stained apron, she plumped me down before a plate piled high with golden fritters – apple slices dipped in batter and fried in butter. Suddenly, I was ravenous.

That day, as my ears slowly grew accustomed to Cicely's Yorkshire burr, she led me on a tour of Wilton House, introducing me to so many servants that I felt I had moved into another village, not just a house. 'Two hundred, we are,' she told me proudly. 'Bigger than any other great house hereabouts.' As we passed through the grand entry hall, I bobbed a curtsey before Master Wilkins, the steward, whose keen gaze still terrified me. We greeted the housekeeper more than once that day – she seemed to be everywhere. 'Mistress Roberts may seem a bit starchy, but she's the kindest housekeeper ye're likely to meet in a lifetime of service,' Cicely observed, moving me on as quickly and efficiently as, I soon learnt, she did everything.

We made our way through the warren of Wilton chambers. 'Follow the doors,' she explained. 'In one side, out the other, then all tha need learn is the order of the rooms, and ye'll not be so flummoxed. I arrived only last year meself and had to learn right quick. Me mum knows Mistress Roberts, as she grew up not far from here, afore she married me da and moved north. So she sent me from Yorkshire all the way here, to earn me wages in service. Treat Wilton as a game, and ye'll learn thy way in no time.'

I hoped she spoke true. I tried to fix the rooms in my mind by the views from their windows – the long drive and alley of trees on the east side, to the west formal gardens with ornamental flower beds and sculpted hedges, a kitchen garden of vegetables and herbs off the north wing, wide lawns rolling down to the River Nadder to the south – but despaired at ever being able to move from one corner of the house to another without getting lost.

Crossing in front of the stables that afternoon, on our way to pick some herbs from the kitchen garden for Cook Corbett, we ran into a sturdy young man whose hearty greeting lit Cicely's face with delight. 'Me brother, Peter,' she explained. 'Best lad in the household!' His body, like his sister's, was more compact than tall, with a core strength that suggested industrious labour. He nodded a bashful welcome, his eyes a darker shade of blue than his sister's, but his smile just as bright.

'No need to meet all the footmen and grooms, of course,' Cicely explained earnestly as we passed through an oak-panelled room lined with imposing portraits. 'Except for Toby Saunders, Sir Henry's new valet,' she added, as a young man in the now-familiar blue and red livery came into view. 'Toby joined us only two months ago, after training in the household of milord's brother, Sir Edward, and I must say he looks after milord very well.' A blush rose in his pasty cheeks and his hands fiddled awkwardly with his cuffs. 'And this here's Rose,' she told him with a smile, 'just arrived in service.' The young man barely nodded at me as his eyes slid away to fix on the chambermaid. Not that I minded. But those eyes troubled me – dark and unblinking in their focus on Cicely – and the smile

33

on his face, so tight it seemed one tap would break it apart.

Cicely continued her bubbling account of the various tasks of the household staff we encountered as we walked briskly along the passageways that connected the lofty Great Hall, a velvet-curtained library walled with floor-to-ceiling bookcases, too many bedchambers to count, and the solar, whose south-facing windows flooded the cosy, wood-panelled chamber with afternoon sunlight. Finally I covered my ears with my hands and groaned. 'I'm happy for the introductions, I'm sure, but I'll never remember all of this!'

Cicely squeezed my shoulders reassuringly. 'More fool me! 'Tis only thy first day – of course tha needn't keep it all in thy head. Sit down with me in the kitchen, Rose.'

It was a relief to sit at the worn oak table with Cicely and Mistress Roberts, as Cook Corbett set a plate of biscuits before us, crisp with such buttery sweetness that I closed my eyes happily. When I opened them, I saw that I was fixed in the unfriendly scowl of the scullery maid scrubbing the pots. 'That's Sarah,' Cicely explained when we left the kitchen, 'Sarah the Sour, we call her, cause – well, ye'll see.'

Before I knew it, Cicely was bidding me goodnight at the end of what felt like the longest, and busiest, day in my life. My last thought before sleep was that I was lucky to have Cicely for my first friend at Wilton. My first friend ever.

The next morning, Steward Wilkins took over from Cicely. Without offering a greeting, he led me from Mistress Roberts' chamber, my cloth bag of possessions clutched in my hand. Already I missed Cicely's reassuring presence. If only I could have more time. But he was pushing open the door to the library.

Seated beside a tall, arched window was an elegant lady with dark hair, pale cheeks and sad eyes. She stood when the steward announced me, and her shiny green skirts rustled like the whispering leaves of the black poplar tree outside our cottage. I could see what looked like pearls stitched to the toes of her fancy slippers. I kept my eyes on the floor.

'Welcome to Wilton, Rose.' Lady Catherine's voice was kind. The stones that had been lurching about in my stomach started to settle.

'Yes, milady,' I replied as Mum had instructed me, not daring to meet her eyes.

'I was happy to take you when your mother sent word that you needed a place,' she explained. 'Joan and I joined paths as healers many years ago. I was only newly the mistress of Wilton House, and I needed another hand in treating some of the labourers when a course of pestilential fever swept the village. I know your mother's skills.'

At this my mouth dropped open and I looked up at her face without meaning to, then quickly lowered my gaze. *My mother's skills*? That meant she must have heard the charge of witchcraft. Even worse, what if she *hadn't* heard? Would she be angry at Mum for sending me once she found out? I started to shake, and my homespun bag slipped from my hand, spilling its contents across the richly patterned carpet. Flushing, I sank to my knees and began to scoop them up, the keepsakes I'd brought from home – an old rattle of Michael's, new mittens knitted by my mother, the tiny bell I used to fasten to my kitten's collar and a few sheets of paper. Lady

Catherine interrupted my frenzy with a hand on my shoulder.

'Don't be afraid,' she said. The reminder of Mum's words and voice was too much, and tears started to slide down my cheeks. As if she weren't facing the most laughable excuse for a serving maid that she had ever seen, Lady Catherine extended an open palm.

'Might you show me those papers, Rose?' I heard courtesy edged with curiosity.

'They're nothing, milady,' I apologised, my voice trembling. 'Just my scribbles from my mother's garden.' When the weather was fair, Mum encouraged me to use the back of my father's old account papers to sketch her prized herbs: delicately forked leaves of common wormwood, used to treat ailments of the stomach; cheery skirted petals of chamomile flowers, for wakefulness and muscle aches; beaded clusters of bayberries, dried to brew in an infusion or crushed to seal an open wound. So I drew what I saw using sharpened charcoal, allowing plants to unfurl and blossom in delicate lines, while my mother instructed me on their uses. My favourites were fuzzy balls of pennyroyal blossoms mounting their stems and frothy sprays of fennel curving downward.

As she leafed through them, Lady Catherine caught her breath. 'These are *good*, Rose. No wonder your mother sent you to me!' I beamed and felt the shame over my clumsiness lifting. Maybe what the villagers thought of my mother didn't bother her.

'We'll go over your work tasks on the morrow, Rose,' Lady Catherine promised. 'I know you're still getting acquainted with the people and the house. There will be plenty of time for you to learn your duties. But having seen what you just showed me, I want to start with something else.'

She crossed to her writing table and held out a large, heavy book.

'I cannot read, milady!' I blurted, hunching my shoulders in dismay.

'Open it, Rose,' was all she said, putting it in my hands. And so I did. Beneath large dark letters appeared the graceful curves of a plant.

'Wormwood!' I whispered, my pulse quickening. I turned the page, and then another, on each one an image of the flowers, leaves and roots of a different plant. Some I'd never seen before, but – 'Garlic?' I murmured, my voice getting stronger. 'Chickweed! Amaranth!' The names rolled off my tongue and Lady Catherine patted my back.

'This book is *A New Herball* by William Turner. It identifies the medicinal uses of common plants, each one illustrated to prevent confusion.' Her voice quickened with delight. 'You think you cannot read, but once I teach you your letters, you'll find that you already know the plants named by these words.'

'Thank you, milady.' To be allowed to draw – and learn to read! My heart was racing.

'One more thing, Rose.' She patted the stool beside her chair, inviting me to sit. 'I know what happened in the village. Too many false accusations spring from ignorance and fear – more every year. I'm deeply sorry your mother had to suffer for her learning.' I twisted uneasily on the stool, but she squeezed my hand. 'In my household, you needn't ever worry that your gifts will bring you under suspicion – or into danger.'

I released the breath I hadn't known I was holding.

'Meanwhile, I shall be delighted to teach you to read and write. In return I'll ask you to illustrate my own notes on herbal remedies. I can give you quill pens and paper, chalk for colour. As for household responsibilities, you can spend time with different servants, learning their duties and getting a sense of how the household works' – she paused, taken by a sudden thought – 'starting with my own maid, Mabel.'

My eyes felt like they would pop out of their sockets. I had much to learn, but I vowed to myself I'd learn everything I could and be the best servant she had ever had. Lady Catherine explained that I would eat the food of the household and wear the clothing provided me, but not receive wages until I was given a formal position. 'I hope to keep you with me for many years,' she added, 'and intend that we shall both profit from your time at Wilton House.'

The next morning, I was roused by sharp-nosed, brown-eyed Mabel. She had attended to Lady Catherine's clothes and belongings for seven years now, she told me. She had been tasked with taking me in hand as I became acquainted with the doings of the great house. For now, I was to assist her in looking after Lady Catherine.

I readied myself quickly, washing my face from a small pail of water, then scrubbing a coarse linen cloth over my limbs. The russet smock and kirtle Mistress Roberts had given me were too big, but I reassured myself with Cicely's promise that I'd grow. Then Mabel walked me upstairs to my lady's bedchamber, showed me the small truckle bed along the wall that I would share with her, then pulled back the long curtains and awakened her mistress.

Mornings, I soon learnt, were the busiest times. After Lady Catherine washed her face and cleaned her teeth with a cloth scented with cloves, Mabel rubbed her entire body with linen cloths. The dressing process involved more pieces of clothing than I had ever seen. First on was a freshly laundered linen smock and silken hose, followed by embroidered petticoats, resting on an underskirt of wire called a farthingale that gave an upside-down tulip shape to the gown itself. Mabel then attached the farthingale to a bodice, laced at the back, followed by satin skirts and a pair of matching sleeves.

'Sometimes milady lets me choose the sleeves,' she added unexpectedly, and Lady Catherine smiled. While Mabel fastened these layers together, I cleaned my lady's slippers, polishing the pearls edging the embroidered silk, tidied the pots of creams and powders that she used on her face and tucked fresh lavender into her bedding. Mabel dressed her hair, drawing an ivory comb through her rich brown locks, before binding it up with silk ribbons. Finally, she attached the stiffly starched ruff that topped the gown and fanned out behind Lady Catherine's head in the shape, it seemed to me, of a fully blossoming flower.

Over the following days, Lady Catherine kept me close. I trailed after her as she went about her daily tasks of managing the estate, responding to workers' petitions and prescribing cures for ailments with remedies she had concocted. Knowing how much labour it took my mother to distil a small amount of essential oil from fresh herbs over boiling water in the kitchen, I wondered how my lady produced all the cordials and elixirs that she prescribed for the staff and the many villagers who sought her aid.

At the end of my first week, as she had promised, my mistress summoned me to the library to begin teaching me my letters, using the illustrated *New Herball* as a primer. I worried that learning to read and write might take me so long that she'd tire of the task, but soon discovered that she had been right – my knowledge of herbs would help me, not just to learn, but to *want* to learn.

On afternoons when the weather was fine, Lady Catherine gave me a sketchbook and sent me into the garden to draw. I filled page after page with rough sketches in charcoal or chalk and perfected them with greater detail using the quill pens and ink pots my lady had supplied. She taught me how to sharpen the nib of a quill with a small knife, shaving off the edge against a hard surface. 'Look closely, and draw slowly,' she encouraged me. As I drew, finely cross-hatched leaves appeared in ink alongside softly smudged petals in chalk. Herbs that I had drawn first in my mother's garden took on details I hadn't noticed before. Unfamiliar plants unfurled more gradually, revealing their special markings without my planning or intent. Line by line, the natural world budded, bloomed and withered on the pages of my sketchbook, as if drawing brought its own seasons.

'You capture the essence of these herbs,' remarked Lady Catherine, stroking my miniature sketches of the fluted openings of the betony blossoms with admiration, almost as if my drawings were precious. 'Your work reminds me of the healing process itself. Just as tinctures of betony alleviate aches of the head, so resting my eyes on your drawings of betony achieves the same end.'

Once completed, I handed my drawings to my lady to include in her collection of herbal remedies. Each day, as well, I watched her during our hours together, then let my pen capture what I saw, drawing by the window in the last hours of daylight or at dawn before the start of my duties, while my lady slept. But these sketches were not true to life. When I drew my lady's face, my pen slipped over the paper swiftly, capturing her features alive with health rather than illness. Someone seeing these sketches might have thought them portraits of a younger Lady Catherine, not yet worn by care and wasted by illness. When I tried to include the lines of weariness and pain that etched her face, I found myself drawing herbal blooms along the margins of the paper instead, twining leaves and blossoms that framed my lady's face with life. On one page, I filled the space around her head with whimsical whorls of betony flowers, brushed softly with rosy chalk, while in another I adorned her hair with red clover blossoms.

These drawings I did not share with her. I hid the sheets in the bottom of the trunk my lady had given me for my few belongings.

I could tell from the start that Lady Catherine wasn't well. I had learnt from Mum to recognise the signs of sickness, and my lady's were unmistakable – shortness of breath, lack of appetite, dizzy spells, yellow cheeks, trembling fingers. But I didn't know what the signs meant.

One bright morning near the end of my first month at Wilton, I sat with Lady Catherine beside the River Nadder that meandered past the estate near its confluence with the River Wylye. Suddenly she raised her hand to her forehead and pressed as if to push away pain. 'Do you know what ails you, milady?' I ventured. At her sharp glance, I shook my head regretfully. 'I haven't the gifts of my mother, but I know what's not right.'

'Ah, Rose,' she sighed. She looked out towards the river for a long moment. Then, 'I wanted to believe my spirits were failing from the failure of my womb.' She regarded me thoughtfully. 'Although you're young yet, surely you know of women's cycles. My monthly flowers continue, but still I have no child to give my husband. Eleven years is too long, but for all my studies of herbal and other remedies, I cannot heal myself.' She passed one thin hand before her face. 'Now my courses come and go unevenly, and I fear that whatever ails the rest of my body has overtaken my womb as well.' Her eyes glistened. I wanted to throw my arms around her, but knew I had already overstepped my station. Instead, I picked up *A New Herball* and started to sound out the words I was learning. It was slow going, and I stumbled over more words than not. She stopped me halfway through the page. 'Please, Rose,' she said, 'show me your drawing of hyssop flowers.'

I sorted through the sketches from that week and plucked the one she wanted from the pile. To my surprise, she folded it in half and wrote a name atop the fold, before setting it aside. Then she bade me continue my reading, though it was almost time for her to join Sir Henry for the midday meal.

When her eyes closed in weariness, I fell silent, set down the book and picked up my pen and paper. Where words failed me, drawing remained my most trustworthy practice. If I could have drawn Lady Catherine into health, I wouldn't have stopped until she was well. Already, I loved this mistress I hadn't wanted to serve. And even had I known the dangers of loving too well too soon, I couldn't have changed what came next.

Chapter Four

Mary, 1575

Her chest heaving from her dash down the tower stairs and across the keep, Mary pushed past the maidservants moaning in the hallway and burst into the chamber she shared with her sister. Ambrosia lay motionless on the bed, her eyes closed, her cheeks as white as the sheet drawn up below her chin. Standing beside the bed, Mary's mother met her eyes, then bowed her head.

'She's gone, dearling.'

'No!' How could Ambrosia be gone? 'She told me she'd wait for me to come back – she promised! I need to tell her the story.' The ache in her side bound her lungs like a bodice of chain mail, making it painful to draw breath. 'You told me she would get better!'

Her mother's silent acceptance of responsibility for

that fiction scorched Mary with her own complicity, never admitting the possibility of another truth.

'You lied to me, Mother.'

Tears ran down Mary Dudley Sidney's cheeks.

'No – I hoped.'

Her mother wrapped both arms around her so tightly that Mary could feel her trembling. 'We wanted the two of you to share the joy of each other's presence without fear for the future.' What future? There had never been a future awaiting her sister.

'If I had known, I could have—' Mary broke off, choking on her own words. Could have what? She hadn't been willing to admit her own deepest fears to herself, let alone to her sister. How different was that from her parents' reluctance to speak what they dreaded to acknowledge?

At the very least, she could have put off that visit to the guard tower, instead of losing the last precious morning of Ambrosia's life. Never kissed Jake at all. Her stomach roiled at the memory of that foolish kiss. An idiot, that's what she was. Who didn't deserve the moments she had cast away.

She couldn't blame her mother for that. Sinking to her knees beside her sister's body, she let black guilt engulf her.

'Your father wishes to speak with you.' Her mother's voice was calm, but with an undercurrent of urgency that struck Mary like the off-kilter dissonance of a lute string out of tune. What could be urgent any longer?

Two weeks after Ambrosia's death, a semblance of daily life had returned to Ludlow Castle. But to Mary this forced semblance was almost worse than death itself. Worse, certainly, than the death she longed for every day – her own.

'Go to him, my dear.'

Mary found her father in the Great Chamber, gazing out a mullioned window into the castle's inner courtyard, darkened by an approaching storm. He turned and led her to a chair beside the stone fireplace where a log crackled against the spring chill.

'Her Majesty has sent for you.'

Henry Sidney paused, perhaps to allow his daughter to respond, but Mary was stunned into silence. *Her Majesty?* Her father's expression, patient and steady, was the one that accompanied his most challenging chess lessons, intended to hone her skills in the strategic thinking required to control the board. *A pawn on the seventh is worth two on the fifth.*

Suddenly, she felt dread. Her father pulled a folded parchment from his doublet and gave it to her. She saw the Queen's script, dark and firm.

The formal opening, *Right trusty and well-beloved*, had been crossed out, replaced by a simpler and more personal salutation:

Good Sidney – We comprehend your grief as parents whose daughter has been taken by Almighty God, and we would have you know we take part of your grief upon us. But God has yet left you the comfort of one daughter of very good hope, whom if you think good to remove from those parts of unpleasant air, and send her to us before midsummer, be assured that we will have a special care of her.

Mary handed the Queen's letter back, still without speaking a word.

'Her Majesty's invitation is a great honour and a kindness.' Henry Sidney looked intently at his daughter. Mary took a deep breath and exhaled sharply, but couldn't breathe out the panic. Instead, she focused her attention on the rain that was now pelting the windows that framed stormy arches of sky.

'I have no desire to go to court, Father, great honour or not.' Beneath her stiffly spoken words swelled a silent scream. 'All I want is to remain at home and grieve in private – with no audience – to give my sister the honour *she* is due.' The imagined glories of court life that she had turned into stories to share with her sister now seemed no more than dreams. As for her future – she was but a solitary pawn on the chessboard of the court.

Ambrosia had been buried with full ceremonial honours in the parish church of St Laurence in Ludlow, its tower overlooking the bustling market town like a serene stone sentinel. For two weeks, Mary had left the grounds of the castle daily to visit her sister's tomb. Kneeling on the smooth stones behind the altar, she stared up at the gilded family arms above the tomb's inscription – bright gold letters marching across a dark blue background:

Here lieth the body of Ambrosia Sidney, 4th daughter of the right honourable Sir Henry Sidney and of the Lady Mary his wife

Each time, her eyes locked on that first cold phrase and filled with tears. Each day, bowing her head to pray for Ambrosia's soul in heaven, she added the prayer that she might join her sister soon. For if God had taken Ambrosia, surely He could take her as well. She only wished He would do so quickly.

But her father was shaking his head, more silver in his pointed beard than she had noticed before. 'Mary, my child, we're all grieving. But the Queen speaks true – you're our *one daughter of very good hope*.' He straightened his shoulders. 'Your mother could not bear such another blow, having lost three daughters now. Our family will go to court together in the summer, and you shall remain with the court once we depart.' His tone was final, brooking no protest. A pawn indeed.

Mary flung her arm across her face and shook her head so sharply that her neck cracked. Then she scrambled to her feet and fled the chamber to her own quarters, bolting the door to the bedchamber she had shared for so many years with Ambrosia.

An hour later, Mary still couldn't bring herself to respond to the entreaties of her mother, spoken softly yet clearly through the door. She was ashamed that her selfish grief had pulled her mother from her own mourning to attend to this *daughter of good hope*. What hope? The pouring rain outside the windows drowned Mary's whispered responses, intended solely for herself.

Only when she heard Philip's deep, calm voice did Mary finally slide back the iron bolt. Comforted by the dear familiarity of his face – the slightly quizzical gaze beneath perpetually arched brows and a tall forehead surmounted by a ginger thatch of hair – Mary dived into his embrace. Ever patient with her moods, Philip had always been able to console his closest sister by listening, above all, and not hesitating to share his own hopes and disappointments.

Countering his years of absence at the Shrewsbury School and then Oxford, when he was at home Philip regularly made time to talk with Mary about the pursuits that engaged his passions, from poetry to politics. Seven years apart in age but sharing a love of reading inherited from their parents, they had devoured many of the same books, from *Aesop's Fables* to popular Continental romances. Philip liked to ask his sister how she would change the stories if she were their author, and readily offered his own story ideas in turn.

In the best of earlier times, they had shared a dream of future collaboration as writers, although Philip had recently been too much abroad for that dream yet to be realised. Now twenty and the Member of Parliament for Shrewsbury, Philip had been travelling to Europe to meet with other politicians and was creating quite a name for himself as a diplomat. But in this worst of times, he was once again her big brother and protector.

In the safety of her brother's arms, Mary let her sobs escape. 'I cannot bear to attend the Queen and mingle with the ladies-in-waiting without Ambrosia, when we made plans to enjoy the court together – and now she never will.'

Philip held her close and didn't try to speak until her sobs turned into muted whimpers. 'I understand,' he said softly. 'I miss her too.'

Taking Mary by the hand, he led her across the bridging passage from the Great Chamber Block to the upper gallery of the family chapel of St Mary Magdalene. They descended to the ground floor in silence and entered the circular nave. As was their custom since childhood, they paced the entire circumference, passing its fourteen arches before kneeling beneath one of the simple round-headed windows to pray. Mary welcomed the pain of the hard stones beneath her knees. Close to her brother and away from Ambrosia's elaborately beautiful tomb in St Laurence's Church, she found she could breathe again. Still, she prayed to join her sister.

Later they walked around the outer bailey of the castle, sharing another circle while the rain-drenched grass squelched beneath their feet and they inhaled a breeze punctuated with scents of crabapple blossoms and flowering cherry.

'My good friend Walter Raleigh has promised to look out for you at court, where he has great hopes of success,' Philip assured her, squeezing her hand. 'We started at Oxford together and have pledged to defend each other's interests for life. You can trust him as a brother.'

Philip's promise was Mary's touchstone in the days that followed, filled with fittings for new gowns and instruction in conduct becoming a lady at court. A 'lady' of thirteen, obliged to leave behind the games of childhood and play the game she had been raised to master.

'I understand, Mother – I know what I may and may not do and say.' Mary brushed aside the jewelled brooches her mother had laid out from her own collection, impatient with the preparations. 'None of this matters any more.'

Mary Dudley Sidney scooped the brooches into a small muslin sack. Her voice was as steady as her eyes, pinning her daughter in place. 'You're right, my dear. None of this matters by comparison to the loss we've suffered. But you're also wrong.

This matters more than ever, because your new path starts here.'

When Mary shook her head, her mother smoothed her tangled red curls and tucked them behind her ears. 'You're beautiful, Mary, and your beauty opens doors. But it also brings dangers you cannot possibly foresee.'

Touching her own cheek, scarred in the Queen's service, she explained. 'Once I lost my own beauty, people no longer cared to look at me. They would speak before me as if I were invisible, because they had ceased to see me. But when you arrive at court, ladies will compare their beauty to yours and measure how they can surpass you. They may be called *ladies*, but they can be vicious. And meanwhile, gentlemen will compose speeches and poems to ensnare your attention, as if hooking a fish to satisfy their appetites.'

Mary was shocked. She had never heard her mother speak quite this harshly of court circles before.

'And as for the Queen – the cynosure of all eyes holds the loneliest position of all. You may not receive her favour at your first attendance on Her Majesty, but if you speak truly, she may well welcome such a rarity from one not striving to share in her power. Unlike the rest of the court, whose eyes are too easily captured by spectacle, the Queen sees beyond the trappings of power because she must be able to recognise truth.' Her mother was folding the embroidered veils and stacking the jewelled masks of silk and velvet that she wore at court to hide her pockmarked face, their ribbons draping her fingers.

'When Her Majesty saw my face fouled by these scars that had transmuted my beauty into deformity, she did not pity me or offer sympathy. Instead, she offered truth. She shared lines from a poem she had written: '*All fair earthly things, soon ripe, will soon be rot, and all that pleasant springs, soon withered, soon forgot.*'

Mary's attention was captured by the oppositions in the Queen's verse. This was a voice that used rhyme not just for sound, but for sense. Mary Dudley Sidney set down her masks and veils and turned the face she had termed *foul* towards her daughter.

'All I can give you are my jewels and my counsel, which you may use as you see fit. All I wish for you is your health and well-being, which I have no ability to safeguard. Walk the path ahead with caution.' She brought her arms around her daughter then and pulled her to her breast, so close that Mary could feel her mother's heart beating beneath her cheek.

'And carry your sister in your heart, as I carry you.'

Mary arrived in London with her parents and Philip in July, just in time to discover that the court moved with the Queen. Embarking on one of her celebrated progresses, Her Majesty brought the court to Kenilworth Castle in Warwickshire, the lavishly appointed seat of Mary's uncle. Robert Dudley, Earl of Leicester, had prepared a month of festivities fit for the Queen who favoured him above all others.

As the procession of courtiers attending the Queen approached the outer gate at dusk, Mary glimpsed trumpeters on the ramparts, sounding a royal welcome from impossibly long horns of silver that extended over twice the length of their arms. Crossing the tiltyard towards the lake, the Queen was greeted by a sinuously garbed Lady of the Lake on a floating island, lit by torches that flared against the gathering darkness.

'Uncle Robert always did excel at giving a show,' Philip murmured. 'Never a dull moment for the Queen. You wouldn't believe the expense! He's had the whole place refurbished for her . . .' But Mary had stopped listening. The pillars of light blurred.

'She would have loved this.'

'Yes, she would.' Philip gently brushed away her tears. 'She would have wanted you to love it also. Why don't you write about it as if you could tell her the tale?'

A sharp rattle of gunshots split the air and Mary clutched his arm. 'The final salute,' explained her brother, 'before Her Majesty is led to her chambers.'

That night, Mary sat down by candlelight and pulled out a sheet of paper. But she set it aside without writing a word. It wasn't the spectacle that she wanted to describe for her sister. It was the Queen herself.

The next morning, Sir Henry Sidney and his wife introduced their last surviving daughter to Her Majesty. Dressed in her finest gown, creamy satin with amber sleeves and ribbons, Mary entered the Presence Chamber for the long approach to the Queen. She had difficulty breathing, not just from her tightly bound corset but from fearful anticipation. By the time she reached the throne and sank in a deep curtsey, Mary's forehead was beaded with sweat. In the flesh, the Queen was even more imposing than her portraits, Mary thought, drinking in every detail.

'Greetings, Sidney. So this is your daughter of good hope! Quite as striking as I had expected.' Mary caught the glance of appreciation that passed between the sovereign and her mother, acknowledging Mary Dudley's loss of beauty in service to her person. Now her mother had a daughter to take her place at court. 'We shall show our favour towards you in the care we take of her.' And with that, Mary's first audience with the Queen was over. Her father bowed low and led his wife and daughter from the chamber, past the curious eyes of the surrounding courtiers. Heedless of the glances, Mary's mind was occupied with what she wanted, impossibly, to tell Ambrosia.

That night she pulled out the sheet of paper that she had set aside.

Dearest sister –
Her Majesty was grand, certainly, just as we imagined when we anticipated this moment. What I didn't expect was that she would be so real at the same time, not at all like the queens in the old tales we loved to read. She was not larger than life, but more intensely alive than any tale.

Her Majesty was attired in a white satin gown with ebony slits, embroidered in gold thread, her sleeves of diaphanous white silk covered in gold flowers and her neck beneath its golden ruff encircled with a collar of rubies dripping with shiny seed pearls.

But what truly commanded awe, dear sister, was not her clothing, but her gaze – level and piercing at once beneath finely arched brows. And her narrow jaw with its strong chin. The face of a leader. Not beautiful, precisely, but powerful, certainly. A real ruler.

Also real, and embarrassing, was the sweat bathing my face, which I only hope she didn't notice!

Uncle Robert has arranged plenty of spectacles to entertain the Queen. Fireworks by daylight this afternoon, after Her Majesty visited the parish church. And then a masque performance, dazzling, but you would have said it dragged on too long.

I'm writing to you now because Philip believes that written words can unlock secrets deep within. But I have no secrets from you.

Only you can understand how much it hurts. Do you?

Your loving sister always

The following day, having fulfilled their duty to the Queen, Mary's parents departed for Penshurst Place, their Kent estate, entrusting Mary to the protection of her brother Philip and her uncle Robert, the Queen's host. 'Be guided by your uncle and your brother,' her mother counselled. 'You may trust those they bring you to meet – and not many others.' Behind her composed words, her mother's eyes shone with unshed tears.

Lady Mary turned to her firstborn son. 'She's the only daughter I have left. Take care of her.'

That afternoon, walking with Philip across the little arched bridge spanning a glittering stream that snaked through the Kenilworth gardens, Mary was accosted by a pimple-faced courtier who darted past her and then turned, dropping down on one knee, his effort at elegance marred by the wince when his knee struck the wooden planks. Undeterred, he pulled from his doublet a wilting nosegay of primroses and violets and thrust it towards her. 'My lady – for you!' Curious, Mary took the posy and discovered a verse attached by a ribbon. Then he was off again. She saw him drop to his knees before another lady on one of the garden paths, wincing again, and producing another posy.

Philip laughed aloud. 'It's a tradition on the Queen's progress that the ladies of the court receive verses and flowers, and so gallants compete for attention.'

'Flowers fade and verses wither. I'd toss that posy into the stream, along with the words.' A new voice, warm with amusement, but something else as well. A challenge? An invitation to a different path?

Mary turned to see a striking young man her brother's age standing on the path at the end of the bridge. Philip beckoned him closer. 'Mary, this is my friend Walter!'

As he bent to kiss her hand, Mary took him in. Fine-featured, dark-browed and, Mary noted, fond of bright hues. Clothed in a crimson satin doublet streaked with silver over a black silk shirt, paired with crimson velvet hose, Walter Raleigh cut a far more dashing figure than the awkward posy-bearer. The elegant lines of his cheekbones and jaw might have been sculpted by one of those artists specialising in classical gods. But it was his lively gaze that captured her attention. Those dark eyes offered a promise of questions and retorts, of secrets as yet unspoken, stories as yet untold.

Which god might Walter play in a drama? Mary wondered, as he bowed with a flourish. Apollo, perhaps – god of music and poetry.

'*A honey tongue, a heart of gall, is fancy's spring, but sorrow's fall.*'

'Have you been working on that long?' Philip thumped his friend affectionately on the back. 'You might want to sweeten your verses if you hope for favour – whether from the Queen or any other listener!'

'That is my point, Philip – speaking truth in poesy is all too rare.' Mary heard the amicable challenge clearly this time and embraced the chance to meet it.

'Indeed, sir, speaking truth in any sphere is all too rare – even in these amiable surroundings.'

Walter's eyes widened. 'Your sister has already uncovered the secret of court life!'

Her brother beamed.

That night, brother and sister sat together at a writing desk. Philip was toying fitfully with his quill. 'I've become enchanted with a lady,' he confessed, his glance bright. 'Her name is Penelope. She is my north star, my light in darkness – and she is beyond my reach.' He sighed. 'What do you think of this? *Biting my truant pen, beating myself for spite, 'Fool,' said my Muse to me* . . . Then what?'

'Give that Muse something to say that's worth listening to.' Then, jumping up, the words rushing into her head and illuminating her own feelings: '*Look in thy heart and write.*'

'*Yes*, Mary. Thank you!' She glowed at her brother's affirmation, the sparks between their minds suddenly brighter than all the Queen's fireworks.

'Together we can achieve more than apart,' he mused, scrawling her suggestion onto the paper, already much scribbled over and crossed out. 'I may have no chance at her hand, but I intend to give it my best shot.'

This was the brother she knew – always seeking a new path, the more untrodden the better.

They wrote together every night. In this shared endeavour, Mary found space to live again, comforted by knowing that Ambrosia, could she only speak to her now, would urge her to compose as much as she could. With Philip, Mary practised leaping first and rethinking later, trying out multiple phrases. She learnt to locate and ruthlessly discard imperfect lines. Composing verse in private kept her mind fully engaged, while making it even more onerous to simulate courteous interest in public when young gallants vied for her attention with extravagant and badly written verses that only garnered her disdain. As Walter had observed, *flowers fade and verses wither*, particularly when they're just for show.

What she kept to herself was the bruising memory of that ill-considered first kiss at Ludlow. She hadn't spoken again to Jake after that morning, not even to say goodbye – but it was herself she blamed, not him. Now, whenever she caught a would-be suitor's eyes on her lips, Mary turned aside, self-disgust silting her memory. And before long, she acquired a title. '*The Unattainable*,' she heard Lettice Devereux, Countess of Essex, whisper mockingly to another lady one afternoon, nodding in Mary's direction before arranging her brightly coloured silk skirts to attract the attention of Mary's uncle Robert, who was passing by. Mary observed all too clearly that the whispering ladies-in-waiting collected bevies of admirers as a competitive sport. The prospect of striking up a friendship with any of these insipid women revolted her almost as much as the thought of responding kindly to the court dandies who sought her attention.

The stay at Kenilworth felt oddly unreal, like living on a stage, always playing a part – at thirteen, enacting the role of a grown woman among the lady courtiers. Mary mixed only reluctantly with the other women, but she couldn't help being fascinated by the intermix of blatant and subtle bids for power. Not unlike her father's chessboard after all. She might not enjoy court politics, but she told herself that she could master its strategies. Until, one day, the secure boundaries of her newly constituted position at court were redrawn.

'I need to travel to the Continent, Mary,' Philip told her, two weeks into the Queen's sojourn at Kenilworth. 'Her Majesty has asked me to communicate with diplomats abroad regarding the resurgent Dutch revolt against the King of Spain. I may be away for as long as a fortnight, so I'm entrusting you to Walter's care.'

But who will I write with? wondered Mary in sudden despair. Her brother seemed to hear her thoughts. 'You must continue to write on your own and save your verse to show me upon my return.' Philip had always known how to read her, better than anyone except Ambrosia.

After Philip's departure, Mary sequestered herself in her chamber, shunning her uncle's ever more spectacular displays for the Queen, who seemed to be growing weary of his incessant attentions. That was where Walter found her on the second afternoon of Philip's absence. Although she admitted him to her chamber, Mary felt uneasy. To her surprise, Walter reached across the space between them and touched her shoulder. In the weeks since their first meeting, she had come to understand that Walter, despite his flowery speech, was not falsely flamboyant like the court dandies who so often crossed her path, but sincere. His touch was gentle.

'You still grieve for your sister, do you not? I see you take small pleasure in the entertainments that accompany the court.'

Mary's eyes welled up at his kindness. 'How can I enjoy the court with my sister gone?' she responded, her voice dark. 'These spectacles fizzle to ash and don't come close to filling the endless hours of missing Ambrosia.'

'You must allow me to introduce you to the art of alchemy,' Walter said, taking her hand. 'There, creation begins with ash.' Persisting despite her sceptical frown, he added, 'During our years at Oxford, your brother and I spent many hours in the still-room, sharing a passion for alchemical exploration. I have found that the practice enlivens my own hours, when I tire of the endless plots and counterplots to advance the interests of the courtiers before the Queen that otherwise compose – and decompose – my days.'

Walter reached into his doublet and pulled out a small velvet pouch. 'I have been waiting for the right moment,' he ventured, his dark eyes warm. When he emptied the pouch into Mary's hand, a small gold ring slid out. She saw a slender snake biting its own tail, its ruby eyes bright and its scales finely detailed.

'An ouroboros,' said Walter. 'The alchemical symbol for completion and regeneration.'

Mary released the breath she had caught when the little snake landed in her palm. Regeneration was impossible, completion beyond reach. Her life was fractured by Ambrosia's death. What consolation could a mere symbol offer?

'I received this ring from an ancient practitioner of alchemy I met on my travels in France, when I was first exploring that art. I have been waiting to find a receptive spirit to complete the connection offered by his gift.' His expression was serious, his eyes intent on her own. 'Alchemy is more than a matter of physical transmutation, Mary.' He was holding her hand, and she could feel the warmth of his fingers. When he rubbed his thumb across her knuckles, an unexpected tingle ran up her arm. 'Indeed, my friend John Dee converses with angels.'

Conversing with angels? She wasn't sure she had heard him aright. Was Walter trying to comfort her with fairy tales? Did he think she was still a child? She pulled her hand away, her pride hurt.

Then he leant forward and kissed her on the cheek. Startled, she turned her head to meet his eyes and instead found herself meeting his lips with her own. Her eyes closed.

This wasn't a kiss for a child. Tasting his mouth, her doubts dissolved. This kiss was as different from that meeting of lips with Jake as wine from water. Instead of feeling awkwardly separate from her body, she was suddenly more aware of inhabiting it than ever before, the sensations so absorbing that the room surrounding them disappeared. Only this kiss remained, this single elongated moment. This time, it was her tongue that invited, her mouth that demanded more.

Then his palms were framing her face, and the kiss was over.

'I would ask you to forgive me for taking such a liberty with my friend's sister – except that I'm not sorry.' Walter's voice was warm and intoxicating, heady as spiced mead. 'I've been drawn to your dazzling spirit and quicksilver voice since Philip first introduced us. And I could not resist the chance to complete the connection.'

Fingering the ouroboros ring, Mary found herself, unusually, at a loss for words. She wondered what Walter intended with his gift. *A receptive spirit to complete the connection*? All she knew of alchemy was its apparently fruitless obsession with transmuting base metals into gold. And yet, the feel of his kiss on her lips – *more than physical transmutation* didn't begin to cover it.

CHAPTER FIVE

Rose, 1574–75

The library door flew open and Sir Henry entered, his ungainly valet in tow. Though milord was more than ten years older than his wife, he seemed much younger, with a vigorous gait and erect bearing that belied his years. He stopped short and gasped when he saw my lady, her eyes closed, her head resting against the cushions of her chair. Moved by his alarm, I rose from my stool in the corner and whispered, 'I didn't think I should disturb her rest, milord.'

'Of course not,' he said, noticing me for the first time and frowning down his long nose. Gesturing me out into the hallway, he murmured, 'When Catherine didn't appear at dinner, I feared—' He broke off abruptly, mayhap realising there was no call to explain himself to a maid. His voice was irritable and anxious at the same time. Then he seemed to gather himself together. 'Toby, go and ask Cook Corbett to prepare a cold plate for Lady Catherine.' With a jerky bow to his lord, the valet departed. He was so tightly wound that I imagined his attendance on Sir Henry must only add to his lordship's anxieties. But now the earl was speaking to me.

'Thank you, Rose.'

'My l-lord,' I stammered, remembering, finally, to drop him a curtsey. My cheeks flushed with shame. He could have me dismissed for lack of respect.

'Never mind,' he said. Then, abruptly, 'You'll be coming with us to France next week.'

France? In all my ten years, I'd never even been out of Wiltshire.

'The Queen is sending us in search of doctors who might restore Catherine's health. As you know, Mabel is about to leave our household to serve Catherine's niece Elizabeth as her lady's maid. And over the past year, my wife has come to rely on your presence. It seems you bring her comfort.'

As soon as I set foot on the ship moored at the dock in Dover, I was assaulted by sour odours of decaying fish and briny sailcloth. I screwed my face into a twist and was rewarded by hearing my lady chuckle for the first time in days.

'Ah, Rose – I'm glad to have planned for this.' Setting aside her woollen cloak, she opened a cloth bag fastened to her bodice and pulled out two handkerchiefs, handing one to me and raising the other to her nose. I buried my face in its folds and inhaled the sharp, clean scent of rosemary.

'Breathing herbs keeps my head clear and settles my stomach,' she confided. Nonetheless, when the ship lurched out of port into rough seas, I sat at my lady's feet in her cabin and emptied my stomach several times over into a chamber pot. As did my lady. 'We're in the same boat, Rose,' she whispered with a weak smile.

A carriage was awaiting our arrival in the port of Calais, as well as a cart to carry our belongings and the other household servants who had accompanied us to France. Sir Henry lifted my lady inside the carriage, then dropped me beside her with an easy swing of his arms, before mounting a horse to ride alongside. The jolting ride was almost comforting in its regularity, after the unpredictable swaying of the ship. Lady Catherine took my hand. 'All right now, Rose?' Always focused on others before herself. I forced an answering smile, hardly more convincing than hers, and gathered together some fruit and cheese from a basket to urge her to eat.

'Nothing for me – my head aches too much – but watching you eat will help me to settle,' she assured me. The tart, juicy crunch of the apple tasted like a new start. But soon enough, lulled by the horses' hooves, my eyes closed and the familiar dream of losing my mother to the cry of *Witch!* took me under. I awoke with a whimper in the comforting arms of Lady Catherine.

The journey was long, obliging us to spend two nights in roadside inns. At long last, as the coach mounted a rise, Lady Catherine gave a cry and gestured. 'Look, Rose – Paris!' The great city spread out before us, the double towers and singular spire of a majestic cathedral rising above the haze.

Lord Pembroke had my lady carried in a litter into a grand mansion overlooking a grimy avenue. I longed for home. The air outside the windows seemed stained – smoky and thick. Street clamour penetrated every room. Accustomed as I was to the clean breezes of peaceful Wiltshire, I didn't like Paris at all.

A parade of foreign physicians came and went – old men in dusty velvet robes and skullcaps who smelt of dirty coins and ashes left in the grate. They only tired Lady Catherine. Speaking a language that sounded to me like a series of hiccoughs and sneezes, the doctors, waving their arms in argument, couldn't agree on anything. My lady mustered a laugh when I complained that their words scratched my ears.

'Although my husband trusts physicians, my own work on alchemical cures, along with much reading, has taught me that women alchemists tend to know more about our bodies and ailments than do men,' she explained to me one afternoon. 'Madame La Grande will visit us tomorrow.'

The woman who arrived the next morning was as different from the quarrelling physicians as water from sand. Her skin was creamy and smooth, her brows finely arched. She wore a headdress of russet velvet studded with tiny pearls atop her raven hair, while a gleaming chain of pearls graced her bust and bodice, descending across a collarpiece of flocked lace. A faint scent of musk and sandalwood recalled the fragrance of the silks my father purchased from traders who journeyed to Asia. I was used to being ignored by the visitors, but this woman looked at me with interest and smiled to see me noting all the details of her appearance. My lady's conversation with her lasted much longer than with the doctors. My mistress seemed to trust her, and once she brushed away a tear with one thin hand. Instead of speech that spitted and sparked like the other

French visitors, Madame La Grande's words flowed like the clear stream of the River Nadder beside Wilton House. With a graceful flourish, the woman withdrew a golden flask from the leather bag at her shoulder and handed it to my lady. I could see that the bulbous base was engraved with strange symbols, and I shuddered. *Magic?*

When my lady uncapped the flask, an aroma of blackberries, aniseed and mint scented the air, mixed with a tangle of other fragrances that it took me some time, closing my eyes, to identify: violets certainly, maybe roses as well; cinnamon and honey. When I opened my eyes, Madame La Grande was pouring from the flask into a tiny silver cup. Darkly red, closer to purple, the liquid slid slowly, thickly, into the cup. My lady lifted the cup to her lips and sipped once, twice, then smiled and drained the draught. '*L'eau cordiale*,' she breathed. Now the woman was beckoning me close. She spoke in a melodiously accented voice that I drank in eagerly, without understanding her words.

'*Dans les temps anciens, il y avait une femme sage nommée Cléopâtre l'Alchimiste.*'

My lady supplied the meaning. 'In ancient times there lived a wise woman named Cleopatra the Alchemist. She wrote down the most important alchemical symbols in her search for health.'

Madame La Grande raised the golden flask and invited me to trace the engraved symbols with a tentative finger. A circle with what looked like two fronds curling from its stem was *gold*. A tiny trio of spears or arrows, *silver*. A cross topped by a circle with horns, *mercury*. And finally, the engraving that made me shudder, a snake biting its tail: *ouroboros*.

'The serpent eating its tail symbolises infinity.' Lady Catherine squeezed my hand so I wouldn't be afraid. But Madame la Grande hadn't finished. Her next words were addressed to both of us.

'Cleopatra taught that an alchemist is like – a loving mother who cares for her child and feeds it.' Translating these words, my lady's voice was wistful. The room fell silent.

'*Merci, Madame.*' Lady Catherine handed the alchemist a silk pouch, heavy with coins. She received, in turn, a folded piece of parchment.

'Alchemy is an ancient art of distilling remedies that I have studied to bring healing to others, even while failing to cure myself,' my lady explained to me that afternoon, resting easier upon the pillows in her chair than I had seen her in many days. 'Madame La Grande offered me a cordial that might treat maladies of the matrix – the womb,' she explained. 'If I could bear a child, this other illness would be as naught to me, dear Rose,' she whispered. It seemed to me that she would not be well enough to bear a child unless her *other illness* was healed first, but I kept my thoughts to myself.

At the end of our first week back home at Wilton, I was awakened before dawn by soft moans from my lady's bed. I found her forehead burning to the touch. Sir Henry summoned the household doctor, who prescribed steaming poultices and, even more terrible, slippery leeches that he attached to her arm. Watching my lady's drawn face and heavy-lidded eyes, I didn't need my mother to tell me that my lady was failing. Lord Pembroke spoke not a word, but remained by my lady's bed after the doctor left the room, sitting as stiffly as if carved from stone.

My lady slept for much of the next day. Her cheeks had some colour when she insisted that I accompany her to her study that afternoon. We walked slowly, my lady supporting herself with her hand on my shoulder. I held myself steady, to help her. But even that short walk exhausted her, and as soon as we entered the room she sank into the chair behind her desk and rested her forehead in her hands. Then she took a deep breath.

'When I am well, I will bring you to my still-room to show you the box of black walnut where I store all my recipes. The box is unlocked with this key.' She showed me a small gold key, its head marked with a character I now recognised, thanks to Madame La Grande – the alchemical sign for gold. Sorting through her growing sheaf of recipes, my lady added sheets of my drawings from the days before our trip to France, sliding them carefully between her close-written pages of notes. 'You can assist me in keeping these in order when I add these new sheets to those I have saved already.' Smiling at me through her fatigue, she added, 'You have been a great help. We may yet compile a book of herbals of our own! Mayhap some of your sketches will help English healers who know the herbs of our region by sight.'

English healers. I held her words close to me that night as I listened to her laboured breathing even in sleep.

The next morning, I decided I had to speak to Sir Henry. His distinguished eyebrows shot up when I slipped into the library unannounced. Edgy Toby, lurking in the shadows behind my lord's chair, stepped forward to block my intrusion, but my lord stopped him.

'Milady needs help.' I met the earl's eyes with a confidence I didn't feel. 'My mother is a healer.' The terrible name I didn't speak. My mother had a gift more powerful than the foreign doctors with their garbled speech and useless knowledge.

Sir Henry needed no other prompt.

Busy whispers scurried through the household like spiders, the web of gossip spreading. *Named a witch . . . Dunked in the river . . . Who knows what she'll do?* How the servants knew the dark rumours about my mother was no mystery – talk of Mum's trial by water was a favourite pastime throughout Wiltshire. It infected the market town where my father sold his goods and where many of the servants' families lived.

'Never mind her faffing,' Cicely murmured when Sarah the scullery maid made a sign with her fingers crossed to avert evil as she passed me the next afternoon. 'Sarah's so simple she'd be scared of her own shadow if Cook Corbett told her shadows were cursed. Worse, she always wants others to feel worse than her.'

I tried to laugh it off, but bit my lip instead. 'Why aren't you scared of me?'

Cicely shrugged. ''Tis not me first time facing other folks' fear.'

When I stopped still, Cicely set down the basket of clean linens she was carrying to my lady's chamber and leant towards me. I breathed in the reassuring aroma of newly laundered cloths.

'Me granddam was hanged as a witch.' Her voice was dark, coloured with her own pain. 'A false accusation, of course, but Dilton Marsh was a fearful place that long ago, and the villagers wouldn't wait for a trial. They dragged her away and hanged her on a tree, afore the vicar could stop them. I wasn't born 'til the next year, so all I know is what me mum told me. Peter was only two, and grew up with the story burned into him by the taunts of other boys. I had me own share from the girls.'

My own mum could have hanged, I thought, innocent or not. When I started to shudder, Cicely pulled me to her ample bosom.

'I'm not meaning to shock thee, Rose. Just tellin' thee why I'm not afeard of the name of witch, which proves nothing – nothing at all.' Encircled by Cicely's soft warmth, my shivering eased.

When my mother arrived in Sir Henry's carriage that evening, I rushed into her arms with a cry of relief, and my secret burst from me: 'I fear she's dying!' This was the first time I'd admitted my fears, even to myself. 'I know what Da told you, but there's no one else.' Pushing past Master Wilkins' grimace of disapproval, I pulled her through the warren of chambers that led to Lady Catherine. At the door I stopped, wondering if I had made a terrible mistake. But it was too late.

The steward had caught up to us and was already pushing the door ajar with a scowl.

'Joan Commin, my lady,' he growled.

Lady Catherine was resting against the pillows of her four-poster bed like a queen. Her wan features bloomed in a smile at the sight of my mother at my side.

'Thank you for coming to see me, Joan. I'm sorry it has taken this occasion to bring us together again after' – she paused, searching for the right words – 'that trouble in the village. Had Lord Pembroke not insisted that we travel to France, I should have called for you to visit Wilton much earlier.'

She smiled at me, standing at attention at my mother's side. 'Your gifted daughter has been the joy of my days.'

'I knew I could trust Rose to your care,' my mother replied. She released my hand and walked to the bed, where she took my lady's wrist in her fingers and closed her eyes, counting beats. 'Now you must trust yourself to mine.'

I left them and sat outside my lady's chamber to block spying eyes and ears. When other servants skulked into view, as I had expected, I gritted my teeth and waved them away. Cicely sat with me when she could take time from her tasks, and I was comforted by her warm, reassuring presence, her refusal to brook any gossip about my mum. The glare from her blue eyes could scotch a whispered conversation faster than swatting a bluebottle fly. I listened to the murmur of voices from the chamber, punctuated by a soft laugh from my lady or a soothing flow of counsel from my mother.

Finally my mother opened the door and beckoned me inside. 'Lady Catherine wants you to hear the treatments she and I have agreed upon, so that you can help her once I'm gone. First, a tisane brewed from galangal root.'

'Imported from China,' Lady Catherine interjected, 'with power to strengthen the heart, promote digestion and stimulate appetite – which your mother requires,' she added wryly, 'before she will allow me to employ Madame La Grande's remedy for the matrix.'

'Steep a spoonful of ground galangal root in a cup of boiling water for ten minutes,' my mother instructed. 'Lady Catherine must drink it every evening and morning.' Then she drew a small phial out of the cloth sack bound to her waist.

Unlike the golden flask of cordial water my lady had brought back with her from Paris – the image of the snake biting its tail still made me shudder – my mother's was a plain vessel of faintly greenish glass stoppered with a rough cork. I recognised it as one of only three glass phials that she owned, purchased when Da had supported her work on herbal remedies. She had refilled those phials many times with the various cures she took with her on her visits to the homes of those who were ailing. Now the phial held a clear liquid flecked with darker green particles.

'I distilled this hyssop oil in my kitchen,' my mother explained to my lady, 'when you sent me Rose's drawing.' *My drawing*? Dimly, I remembered my lady requesting that sketch before we left for Paris. 'I thought you might be seeking its benefits for the womb.'

'You were entirely correct, of course,' my lady replied. 'But my body was so muddled by fevers and tremors that I scarcely knew what I hoped.'

'Adding three drops of this oil with fresh rosemary to a steam bath will relieve your cramps, and rubbing it into your middle may strengthen the effects of the cordial for the matrix and restore your courses,' advised my mother. 'But you must regain your strength first. If you send me one of Rose's drawings of anything else that you discover you need, I will supply it if I can.'

Lady Catherine nodded her thanks. Then, she sighed, darkness shadowing her eyes. 'It may be too late for me now, Joan. But I must try.'

Their eyes met in shared understanding.

'Your presence has been a boon to me today, Joan,' said my lady. 'And even more than any remedy, your Rose has restored my spirits again and again.' Evening sunlight warmed the chamber as Lady Catherine beckoned my mother closer to her bedside and I stepped back. I didn't catch the rest of their murmured conversation, but I saw my lady press my mother's hands.

'Make her rest,' my mother told me as she departed. But my heart dropped when she shook her head at the hope in my eyes. 'I'm sorry, my dear. I cannot predict the course of her illness.' She sighed, and I understood that, for all her knowledge of herbs, my mother had long ago accepted their limitations. I almost wished that Mum knew magic after all.

'You were right to ask Sir Henry to call for me, Rose,' she added, catching the glimmer of tears in my eyes. 'Lady Catherine deserves some ease. When no clear cure is at hand, the truth can bring more comfort than false hope. And offering comfort through herbs is a gift I hadn't thought to be able to bring again – ever.' Both of us understood the cost she was still paying for her success in rescuing that twisted babe from his mother's womb. 'So you've given *me* a gift, dear daughter, by allowing me to bring ease.'

I stayed close by my lady in the weeks that followed, reading to her, brewing herbal infusions, and rubbing fragrant hyssop oil into her belly daily. She seemed less careworn and more peaceful, but she failed to regain her strength. I now spent more time drawing in her chamber than sketching in the garden. I was slowly learning to read, and she had me form a large illustrated letter to begin the name of each plant that was my subject. Within and around each letter I drew the leaves of the herbal, with blossoms peeking out of the openings. I grew bolder as my illustrations became clearer and more vivid. I found space for flights of fancy in the margins, sketching images to embody the spirit I imagined for each plant. In the first such picture, fanning fingers of mugwort were parted by a delicate sprite gesturing soothingly from the cleft of the *M*, suggesting the plant's power to invite sleep and peaceful dreams.

One morning, with bated breath, I showed it to my lady.

She laughed with surprise and pleasure. 'You've a second sight, Rose. When I see your drawings, I do believe spirits might well inhabit the natural world, beyond what most of us can see.' Then, after a long pause, 'Your art is more powerful in conjuring the natural world than the spells of any witch.'

Seeing me flinch at the name, she shook her head. 'Don't fear the word, Rose. In truth, many practices called *magic* work for good rather than ill. And magic relies on belief, which often arises through sight. Your sketches do more than render surface appearance – they bring your images to life. What might we call that if not magic?'

As autumn faded into icy winter, my lady shivered in the draughts that curled through her bedchamber, sliding under the heavy curtains that shrouded her bed. I read to her by candlelight from *A New Herball*, stumbling over many words but taking care to study the pictures first.

One evening, as fragrant logs crackled in the fire and sparks took flight up the chimney like mischievous spirits, she called me to her. I curled myself at the foot of her bed.

'I want to tell you about *Rosa Mundi*, the Rose of the World.'

Seeing my surprise, she nodded. 'Yes, this is a story both for you and of you, my Rose. Studying alchemy, I have come to appreciate the rose as the Queen of Flowers, a source of essential oils that complete the binding of many other substances. Some recipes call for the quickening fragrance of rose water, others for the warming power of its oil.' When her voice itself quickened, for just a moment I glimpsed the eager alchemist and healer she must have been before this illness laid her low.

'Rose quartz is considered the *heart stone*. I have a remarkable specimen that you will see when I show you the cabinet in my still-room. In the meantime, I'd like you to keep this rose quartz gemstone as a token of our bond.' She pressed a translucent pink pebble into my palm and patted my cheek. 'Alchemy is an art of union as well as dissolution, in which the rose, unfolding its petals from a closed bud, represents new beginnings as well as completion.'

Caught up in enthusiasm for her tale, she ran out of breath coughing. I settled her more comfortably against her pillows, fragrant with the lavender I had slipped into her bedding to invite sleep. When I tucked a loose strand of her dark hair behind her ear, her pale lips curved in a smile of thanks.

'The *Rosa Mundi* signifies the culmination of alchemical perfection that brings contrasting forces into union,' she explained. 'Your art embodies not simply my remedies' elements, but their essence. More than accurate, your pictures are *true*.' She shifted on her pillow as a stab of pain briefly clouded the brightness in her eyes. Then, she continued. 'They should not go uncredited. So I have a special request of you.'

In the next weeks, following my lady's bidding, on each of my finished sketches I added a signature – *Rosamund*.

My mother returned frequently to Wilton, sometimes bringing fresh herbals, sometimes dried flowers to scent the chamber, once a bluebird's feather. She stayed to converse with my lady, often for hours. They both understood that the aid she brought was neither simply medical nor magical, no matter what others believed. And my father could hardly gainsay Lord Pembroke's request that Mum attend to Lady Catherine's health.

Lord Henry visited my lady every morning, sitting quietly beside her bed if she remained asleep and kissing her cheek as soon as she awakened. He told her tales of the court, and she showed him pages of her collection of remedies with my sketches leaved between them. He praised my drawings for their details, but raised his brows at the fancies adorning the illustrated letters and the margins. My lady only smiled. 'Rose's drawings restore my spirits.'

One afternoon, when the sky framed by the tall windows was bright with spring sunshine, Lady Catherine beckoned me close.

'I believe that each of us has a purpose in this life, although it may take a lifetime for us to accept that purpose.' Her voice was weak, but clear. 'I thought my purpose was motherhood. I was wrong. My path led me through many lessons of alchemy, although I never found the cures I was seeking.' Unexpectedly, she smiled, and it was not the smile of someone who was dying, but of someone who was fully alive. 'But I found you. So perhaps I wasn't wrong after all.'

She placed her palm against my cheek. 'I've left something for you with your mother. It signifies wholeness and renewal. Passed from me to you, it holds my promise – that your gifted sight as an artist can reveal what others may not see, even as your drawings have completed my collection of remedies.' Seeing my confusion and sadness, she added, 'Wholeness may arise from fragments pieced together aright.'

When a sharp sob broke from my chest, Lady Catherine gathered me into her arms. 'Having you at my side, my child, has been more wholeness than I expected to know in this life.'

Lady Catherine Herbert passed from this world on the twenty-first of May, one month short of the summer solstice.

That day, I completed my lady's practice of sliding my herbal drawings between her neatly ordered notes. I also retrieved the secret sketches I had made of my lady's face from the bottom of my trunk and chose my best drawing of Lady Catherine, her hair adorned with red clover blossoms, her features shining with life. I added it to the bottom of the sheaf of notes. Not accurate perhaps, I told myself, but *true*. I placed the sheets beside the first volume of *A New Herball* on her desk, wishing I could have put it with her collection of recipes in the still-room, as she had intended. The lonely stack echoed my own position. Lost in loss, I no longer belonged to the household.

Lady Catherine was buried in the churchyard of the Salisbury Cathedral on a morning whose sunshine belied the funeral's dark solemnity. The Wilton House servants followed the procession of family into the graveyard. We were led by Sir Henry, who clasped an enormous bunch of fresh rosemary –

for remembrance, I whispered to myself – and cast it upon the coffin as it was lowered into the ground. Clutching Cicely's hand, I looked past the cathedral spire piercing the pale blue sky, smudged with clouds and scrawled with birds in flight, and lifted a silent prayer. *May wholeness arise*. But it was no good. Now there were only fragments.

That summer, Henry Herbert left Wilton a widower, to attend upon the Queen. And I went home to my family in Amesbury. To a life that no longer fit.

CHAPTER SIX

Mary, 1575

The memory of the kiss heated Mary each time she touched her fingers to her lips or rubbed her ouroboros ring. The very next day, Walter greeted her easily, his smile warm but dispassionate. Mary was confused. Did he regret that impulsive kiss? Or was he simply hiding his feelings like the practised courtier he was becoming?

His words, too, were impersonal, as they walked in the Kenilworth gardens. 'I'd like you to meet someone. Sir Henry Herbert has long been an ally of your family. He is newly arrived at Kenilworth to attend the Queen, after a personal loss.' Was this, then, the next step in her family's plan for her ascent at court? The next move on the chessboard? She puzzled over Walter's role. Was he a pawn or a knight? And what was she to him? As they crossed the bridge, music and applause wafted across the grounds from yet another entertainment for the Queen.

'Your uncle has asked me to introduce the two of you.' Ah, her uncle Robert, Earl of Leicester, master of Kenilworth, a lord who must be heeded. Walter's voice was light, although less animated than usual, and for the first time in their acquaintance he didn't meet Mary's eyes. 'Henry has heard of your learning and looks forward to conversing with you – at a different level than he encounters from many of the ladies here at court.' That familiar, sardonic glimmer, hinting at complicity of understanding, but again he didn't hold her gaze. Apparently choosing to take her silence for acquiescence, Walter set Mary's fingers upon his silk sleeve and drew her towards the knot garden.

'Walter?' Her voice came out higher and more tremulous than she had planned. Mary wanted – no, needed – to reaffirm their connection. But he maintained his pace. Mary's face flushed with chagrin. So – she was only a child to him after all. Had that kiss been an accident? Or was he, a man of the world, simply toying with her because he could? She withdrew her hand from his sleeve as if burned. They arrived at the heart of the knot garden, where a single courtier walked apart from the others, on one of the garden's meticulously trimmed paths.

'Allow me to present Henry Herbert, Earl of Pembroke,' Walter said, bowing. 'Lady Mary Sidney, sister to the remarkable Philip Sidney.' With that, Walter offered a perfunctory excuse and departed. Only a pawn then, thought Mary, fulfilling his obligation to the Earl of Leicester. *Pawn to queen's knight*. Her father's voice. Hadn't Walter himself warned her not to trust the romancing of male courtiers?

Shrugging Walter from her thoughts, she straightened her spine and took a good look at the courtier standing before her. The gentleman was old, was Mary's first thought, and worn. No dandy here and, thank goodness, no would-be suitor. His lined face was kind, and his smile gentle, a welcome contrast to the simpering youths who so wearied her with their attentions. It might be pleasant to converse with a man not courting her, for a change. Or pretending to court her. Suddenly her eyes stung.

'My lady,' Sir Henry said. Apparently lacking more words, he kissed her hand and measured her with quiet regard. She took in his black garments and wondered who he was mourning. Instructed by her mother explicitly to dress for court circles, the only signs of mourning Mary was allowed were the black velvet ribbon encircling her throat and the small bracelet of ebony beads about her wrist. 'I hear from your uncle that you have been reading Boethius's *Consolation of Philosophy*,' he continued after an uncomfortable pause. 'Walter told me of your recent loss. You have my sympathies. I fear no consolation is possible.' The darkness in his voice was unmistakable, his lips drawn thin beneath his moustache.

'I read Boethius not to raise my spirits, but to challenge my mind,' Mary explained awkwardly. 'Dwelling on things of the mind offers the only source of light I can find.' Another silence.

'I lost my wife this year.' Sir Henry's words were spoken so softly that she almost didn't catch them. 'She died childless, to our mutual sorrow.' The unexpected confession seemed to escape the widower without forethought. Spontaneously she took his hand, squeezing his fingers in an instinctive offer of comfort, before realising that was not appropriate behaviour for a lady. She dropped his hand, her face and throat flushing with the red splotches that invariably marked her embarrassment.

'Thank you,' he said. And his voice was so despondent that Mary's own long-suppressed grief surged to the surface, streaking her face with silent tears. When Sir Henry handed her a handkerchief embroidered with the Pembroke family crest, she wiped her wet eyes without thinking, as if he were her father offering comfort.

Mary found herself pondering her sombre exchange with Sir Henry as she distractedly watched the afternoon's entertainments, which included a mock rustic wedding with morris dancing, performed by the folk from neighbouring farmsteads. The impressive spectacle of the evening meal, featuring a roasted peacock that had been re-covered in its own skin and rainbow plumage before being served to the Queen, only turned Mary's stomach. Walter joined her as the banquet closed with spiced wine in stunning goblets of golden sugar. 'Forgive my peripatetic appearances – and disappearances.' He spoke with self-mockery, where Mary had hoped to hear genuine apology. 'Sir Henry told me that he looks forward to conversing with you again. He is a widower of some months only and has no companion to share the things of the mind.'

'*A receptive spirit to complete the connection?*' She didn't attempt to soften the whiplash of her hurt. But Walter only nodded.

'Unlike me, Henry's worthy of you.' This time he did hold her eyes. 'Forgive me, Mary. Impulse cannot justify my behaviour last night.' Only men could give in to such *impulse* without consequence, she thought sourly. But at least he had enough honour to admit the misstep without trying to justify it. If the kiss had no significance for him, she must let go of any naive hope that he sought a romance.

Then, incredibly, Walter's lively glimmer of a smile reappeared. 'But make no mistake – our connection is real.'

Indeed, Mary assured herself, she would make no more such mistakes.

There was no second encounter with the sympathetic widower, as her uncle's grand Kenilworth production ended in failure. Crushing the Earl of Leicester's hopes and everyone else's speculations, the Queen bid a surprisingly brusque farewell. *Queen takes knight.* Mary couldn't help but feel relief. She was weary of festive celebrations and importunate young gallants, as well as Walter's confusing attentions. When the Queen's entourage returned to London, Mary journeyed home at last to Penshurst Place, her family's ancestral estate in the Kent countryside, with a sense of resignation as well as release. The ache of Ambrosia's absence remained unchanged, no matter where she stayed.

The weight of remembrance and mourning started to lift only when Philip returned to Penshurst from the Continent in October. His wiry energy quickened the very air as he recounted crossing paths with authors and politicians as an ambassador for the Queen. Young Robert listened so earnestly to his brother's tales that Philip laughed. 'Not yet twelve, and already fitted for life abroad!' Six-year-old Tommy cavorted with excitement, demanding his eldest brother's attention, while their parents discussed strategies with their firstborn for his advancement at court. Mary waited patiently, knowing that Philip would make time for her once the other family members were satisfied. With her, she knew, he had space to dream aloud.

'I have plans to write both serious and fabulous matter,' he told her once they were alone, giving her hand a squeeze as they shared the window seat of the library after dinner. 'And I embrace the project you proposed for us – translating the Psalms into English in new poetic forms. As we discovered at Kenilworth, where I most wrestle with words, you wrest new meaning from them!' Mary glowed at her brother's praise. Honing a phrase to embody a thought was her pleasure. Metaphors were her passion, her liberation from the literal constraints that framed her existence, from her sister's death to her future path at court – a path that she knew must include, someday, a marriage that advanced the family's fortunes. As the sole remaining daughter of the illustrious Sidney family, a dynasty accustomed to great esteem at court as in the world, Mary grasped the obligations – and lack of choice – associated with her pedigree. Only language was under her control.

Writing verse came almost as easily to Mary as singing. As breathing. The best times with Ambrosia had been when her sister danced to Mary's lute-playing, skipping and scampering in circles to popular airs, to which Mary set invented lines of verse. She loved braiding words into lyrical lines – lilting cadences neatly tied off with rhymes. Ever since Ambrosia's fifth birthday, when Mary had first invented a song for her sister, she had made it her aim to conjure worlds from words for Ambrosia's delight.

Breakfast the next morning in the solar, in celebration of Philip's homecoming, featured the cook's specialty, Philip's favourite – a heaped platter of tiny pancakes, sprinkled liberally with powdered sugar and accompanied by pots of blackberry jam. Philip's presence completed the remaining family circle, and everyone enjoyed the moment. Tommy smeared jam on his face, showing off to his big brother, and Robert, acting the grown-up, poked Tommy in the ribs and handed him a linen napkin. At that moment, Mary's father cleared his throat with the familiar rumble that signalled a weighty announcement.

'Last night we welcomed Philip home from the Continent. I'm proud that he will continue his path of advancement at court.' Mary noted the beaming smile her parents directed at her older brother. This must be why he pushed so hard to prove himself, not because he needed to, but because he was resolved to outshine all expectations. So accomplished, her brother, still only twenty, and so proud, her parents – both of whom, she realised suddenly, were looking in her direction.

'Mary, your own path opens before you as well.' Her father's voice was proud, but her mother's brows tightened, signalling anxiety. 'You carried yourself so beautifully during your debut at court this past summer that several noblemen have written to express their interest in a match with you.'

A match. Mary recalled those vapid Kenilworth gallants whose weak verse had repulsed her. The delectable little pancakes settled at the bottom of her stomach like pebbles.

Sensing her distress, her mother rose and walked around the table to rest her hands on Mary's shoulders. 'Did you find a connection with any of the courtiers?' Her gentle squeeze urged Mary to respond.

'Only one – but not as a suitor,' she answered, thinking of Sir Henry Herbert. She had no intention of mentioning that giddy moment with Walter, least of all to her brother. No good could come from confiding his ebullient friend's misstep and jeopardising their long-standing bond. It was her parents she needed to answer to now.

She bowed her head, pressed her chin sharply against her chest for courage, then raised it and looked her father in the eye. 'I don't choose to be matched, Father – not yet.' Claiming choice to be her prerogative had always worked before. Her father admired spirit and independence, even in a girl. Inside the family, relying upon her quick wits and innate confidence to grant her access to choices not otherwise offered, Mary was used to getting her way.

But not this time. Stroking his ginger moustache the way he did when pondering any problem, her father shook his head slowly. 'Good matches don't come along every day, or even every year. I wish for you the best match that may be found. And your uncle Robert has proposed the possibility of an excellent match.' Her father's gaze was kind but firm. 'In all conscience, I must pursue what seems to be the best possibility for securing your fortunes into your future.' Just as Mary was opening her mouth to argue the meaning of *fortunes*, he closed the door. 'I have invited this suitor to dine with us tomorrow.'

Tomorrow? She was done with the role of compliant daughter. Mary pushed her chair back from the table so suddenly that it hit the floor with a clatter. Tommy's eyes widened in alarm.

'So I have no choice in the matter? Ready or not?' Mary enunciated each syllable clearly, biting off her words.

'None of us is able to exert personal choice in this inevitability, my dear.' But her mother's warning dissolved beneath the pounding beat of blood in Mary's temples.

She turned on her heel and fled the solar, chin high, holding back her tears until she reached her chamber. No longer a child, newly turned fourteen, she knew better than to treat her father with such disrespect when, in truth, he had her best interests at heart. But reason was no comfort.

Later, when she hadn't appeared for the midday meal, Philip found her sheltering inside the long yew hedge that separated the central pond from the rose garden, where she and Ambrosia used to hide from their brothers on long summer evenings. Her face was scratched with twigs and stained with tears. He crawled in beside her, reaching out to untangle her long curls from the branches. She was trembling – with furious misery as much as the October chill. He draped his cloak around her shoulders and took her hand.

'Marriage needn't signify the end of your prospects, dear one. There is space at court for a brilliant lady to distinguish herself – and with your wit, I imagine you will soon do precisely that.' But his attempted words of comfort only burned.

Mary snatched her fingers away. 'You may marry who you please, but I may not. What do you know of despair?'

'All too much, in truth.' Her brother's voice was unexpectedly sombre. 'It seems certain that I may not marry my own beloved Penelope.' Abashed, Mary saw the lines of disappointment marking Philip's jaw.

'Her father, the Earl of Essex, favoured the match, but since her father died she is the ward of her cousin, Henry Hastings, who does not look favourably upon my suit. So I shall likely be matched, just as you, with someone Father deems suitable for our rank and fortunes, regardless of my wishes.'

Mary's fury cooled as rapidly as it had flamed. She thought of Philip's newly emerging sonnets, in which the love of the fancifully named Astrophil for his Stella disguised Philip's own starry passion for Penelope. To marry someone while loving another must be an even worse fate than to marry someone while loving no one. How little she knew of life, after all.

She straightened her shoulders and pushed snarled strands of hair away from her face. Together, they walked along the yew path as light drained from the late afternoon sky and the moon's calm globe marked the horizon. Philip's presence steadied Mary. His practical acceptance of the realities of matchmaking at court, combined with his far-reaching ideals, supported Mary's resolve to forge her own path, one way or another. Migrating swallows swept the sky above the path, landing along the tops of the yews, their chittering cries punctuated by clicks and squeaks. Who knew what sad secrets they told each other?

'No matter who we marry, writing together we can inhabit, at least for a time, a different world.' The promise came from Mary, for both of them. And voicing this, she felt herself leave her childhood behind. Philip's face registered his awareness of a new mutuality between them. For this moment, that was all they had.

When Philip went back to the house, Mary remained in the garden, yielding herself to the darkness. She trailed her fingers in the inky pond, silvered by the moon, until its entire surface shimmered with reflected light. On returning, she apologised to her father for her outburst and consented to meet the suitor he had invited to Penshurst. But she refused to hear any more about him, even his name.

'I'd rather not contemplate this future before it faces me in person,' she explained.

'I shall not force you to marry someone you cannot abide,' Henry Sidney reassured his daughter. 'I ask only that you allow sufficient time for the courtship to move beyond first impressions. Over a season, you may come to appreciate qualities that aren't visible at first.' His words sounded so reasonable. And yet they clamped closed her unuttered hopes and longings with a terrible inevitability.

The next day, adorned in a green silk gown trimmed with ivory lace, chosen by her mother to set off her long red hair, Mary tried to quiet her dread by transforming the looming prospect into another letter for Ambrosia.

I've no idea who they've chosen, except that it isn't Jake who is coming to call! Which is just as well, because I was going to tell you that morning that kissing a mere lad isn't very special after all. A messy matter of meeting lips and tongues, if you must know. Not at all like kissing a man – which is another story entirely. More on that later.

Father seems to be aiming at a meeting of fortunes. For my own good, I understand. But surely there must be more to marriage than that? I think I'd rather have a meeting of minds. Or at least the chance to know my own mind.

She set down her pen. Fisting her fingers with frustration beneath her lace-draped sleeves, Mary descended to join her parents and meet her suitor. She had no sooner settled herself into one of the solar's elegant high-backed chairs than the butler entered. In sonorous tones, he announced, 'Lord Pembroke, my lord!'

Mary caught her breath. She couldn't believe her ears. Henry Herbert, the recent widower? The one courtier she had believed free of any designs on her hand? The one she had regarded with friendship? Then, watching his entrance – a strong stride, but a head of dark curls already streaked with silver – the one old enough to be her father?

Sir Henry entered the room with steady steps, bowing in response to her parents' welcome. Taking Mary's hand, he bowed again and met her eyes with a warm smile. She watched him as he engaged in pleasant conversation with her parents. At least the man seemed kind. Certainly not shallow and insipid, like most of those youths at court. But what kind of man was he, beneath his dignified good manners? Pushing those thoughts aside, she reminded herself what her father had promised: *I shall not force you to marry someone you cannot abide.*

Fading sunlight streamed through the arched windows, illuminating the long oak table at the end of the Great Hall, punctuated with bowls of red roses, her mother's favourite selection to scent the air. Her father seated himself at the head of the table and beckoned Mary to her seat across from Sir Henry, who was flanked by her brother. Immediately, the visitor started an animated conversation – with Philip. The first course arrived: a bowl of summer pottage, savoury meatballs bobbing beside currants and almonds in an orange broth flavoured with saffron, ginger and cloves. Tearing off a piece of white manchet loaf to dip in the broth and savouring the union of sweet and peppery flavours on her tongue, Mary felt her shoulders relax a bit. She was ready with her own smile when Henry addressed her.

'I have recalled our conversation in the knot garden at Kenilworth many times, Mary. Your brother tells me that you collaborate with him on his writing and are already an accomplished poet.' His voice was deep, his glance serious and, it seemed, genuinely intrigued.

'An aspiring poet would be more accurate, my lord,' Mary replied.

'Surely you must call me by my name, if I address you by yours?' His eyes twinkled. 'And what of the prose romance that Philip is embarking upon – shall you join him in that endeavour as well?'

'Truly, Mary has become my most trusted reader *and* collaborator,' Philip interjected. 'I write for her eyes because she reads with knowledge and writes without pretension.'

Mary blushed, and Sir Henry nodded appreciatively. Then, turning back to Philip, 'And just what is it that you are writing *for her eyes*?'

Her brother waxed eloquent, as always. 'It's a new kind of romance – an *English* romance, if you will, unlike those magical tales from Italy and Spain. To be sure, my *Arcadia* is amply supplied with kings and shepherds, lovers and villains, shipwrecks and mistaken identity, but it doesn't depend on monsters and sorcerers for adventure. My tales take place in the natural world, one in which readers may find mirrors of themselves. Why turn a plot on sorcery when love and envy are sufficient to drive men mad?'

Or women, for that matter, Mary thought.

Henry raised his brows, but declined to take up the topic of going mad for love. A prudent suitor, at least.

Before going to bed, Mary lit a candle and finished her letter to her sister.

> *I so wish you were here to tell me what you think of him. I believe you'd mention his kindness and courtesy. I appreciate his love for the wife whose loss he mourned this summer, while I mourned losing you. But I can't imagine loving him as a wife. And could he possibly love me, or only my position as a Sidney – and my dowry?*
>
> *I suppose this marriage might be interesting, at least, rather than dull. But is that enough? Without you to confide in, it seems a dismal prospect indeed.*

Her pillow that night was wet with tears.

CHAPTER SEVEN

Rose, 1575–76

I arrived home in a summer downpour, delivered by the same burly carter who had taken me to Wilton those two long years ago. Sodden with rain and grief, I rapped on the oak door, my childhood impossibly distant. The door burst open, tugged by a sturdy little boy with a thatch of straw-coloured hair who ran away before I could call him by name. And then my mother was before me, pulling me into her arms, and suddenly I was a child again, greeted by the warmth of the hearthfire and the familiar fragrances of sourdough oat bread and pease pottage. I felt like weeping and laughing at the same time.

'Welcome home, dear one.' My mother's voice, rich with love, filled my thirsty ears and quenched a longing that had never left me during my time at Wilton House. All the learning and all the kindnesses of Lady Catherine hadn't eased the ache of my mother's absence. As this homecoming couldn't erase my grief at my lady's death.

'Don't send me away again, Mum,' I whispered into her ear, and she held me closer, tighter, her own cheeks wet. Finally releasing her embrace, she dried my face with her apron and looked me up and down. She touched the linen smock topping my kirtle of Pembroke blue. 'These fine clothes must be set aside now that you're home. I'll take in some of my own smocks and kirtles for your everyday wear.'

'Rosie, Rosie, will you play All Hid with me?' Four-year-old Michael had conquered his shyness and was tugging eagerly on my skirt.

'Your brother has been practising places to hide ever since I told him you'd be coming home,' Mum explained. I poked my brother with a gentle finger, amazed to see a tumbling boy rather than a snuggling babe.

The next moment Da pushed open the door and stepped inside, scattering raindrops over us as he removed his cloak and took in my return with a broad smile. 'Come here, lass!' His hearty greeting and bear hug dissolved my anxiety that he would hardly remember me. 'You're quite a lady now, aren't you?'

'Not yet, Da, but I aim to be,' I replied boldly, surprising even myself. My parents exchanged a quick glance. Then I grasped Michael, bid him close his eyes and turned him thrice around. 'Don't seek until Mum counts to ten,' I warned. I tiptoed into the kitchen in the rear of the house and tucked myself behind the door to the storeroom. The scents of Mum's dried herbs, swinging tidily from the rafters, mingled with the fragrance of scented candles. I noticed several small puddles of wax marking the floor. Before I could ponder why they were there – had my mother been working in the storeroom at night? – my brother pounced upon me in triumph.

'Found you, Rosie!' As he hugged my waist, around my ankles twined – 'Mugwort!' Delighted to find my kitten grown into a cat, and that she remembered me, I scooped the golden tabby into my arms and buried my damp cheeks in her striped fur. Packing to leave Wilton, I had tucked Mugwort's bell into my skirt for this very moment. I fastened it to her collar and knew I was home.

The rest of the evening was a blur of food and stories. Mum served the pottage along with lamb stewed with mint and thyme, prepared especially for my homecoming. Our supper finished with a fancy dish of pears poached in wine – wine! – and a plate of my favourite sharp Cheddar cheese. Then I cleared the table while Mum put Michael to bed and Da settled himself before the fire with a willow branch to whittle.

I waited for Mum to rejoin us before I spoke aloud the question that had been circling my mind since I boarded the cart bound away from Wilton. My duties at the great house had kept me from returning to Amesbury. Apart from accompanying Lady Catherine to Paris, I hadn't been away from Wilton House for almost two years. Now I was home again – perhaps for good.

'What comes next for me?' I made my voice quiet and clear, trying to sound more curious than anxious. Mum glanced over at Da – a darting query.

'Well, you're eleven now,' Da observed slowly. 'You've learnt your letters and I could use your help with the accounts – particularly now that the lad I was training has taken it into his head to return to farming.' He gave a dry chuckle. 'Some have it in the blood, eh, Joan? I was lucky you'd consider wedding a merchant rather than a farmer like your own father!' Mum gave a small smile that didn't reach her eyes. Or mine. Still, she remained silent.

'Your mum has been a great help at market, as I've increased my selection of fabrics, and sales have picked up.' His voice was too hearty. And not a word about the herbals that Mum used to prepare for sale alongside the cloths. So the damage caused by the accusation of witchcraft hadn't healed. Not yet.

'Rose, you must be tired after your journey.' Mum's voice was gentle. 'Your da made you a box bed that I've fitted with a newly stuffed flock mattress, so you should rest well tonight, my dear.' I bid my parents goodnight and found my way by candlelight to the small room off the kitchen that I shared with Michael, who was sleeping soundly in his own truckle bed. But even my soft new mattress couldn't bring sleep quickly enough to erase my unease at Da's forced good humour or the darker thread stitched through Mum's happiness at my return.

The garden behind our house had more than doubled in size during my absence, as if Mum had turned her energies to growing what she could no longer sell. Vegetables still occupied the centre of the garden, from peas and lentils to carrots and cucumbers, while one small plot overflowed with bright red clusters of juicy strawberries. But the herbs! – parsley, ginger, sage, rosemary, angelica and rue, suffusing the garden with their fragrances. And some that even I couldn't name, for all my study of Turner's *Herball*. When I knelt in the earth to push aside leaves and uncover hidden plants, I glimpsed the blue starflower blooms of borage, nestling beside bright golden buttons of tansy and mugwort. The garden was a festival of colour. My fingers itched for coloured chalk, ink and paper.

Catching a footfall behind me on the path, I turned to look up at my mother, brimming with pride in what she had achieved.

'There's more herbs here than your father sees any call for,' Mum admitted, seeing my astonished delight. 'I planted new species when I started going to visit Lady Catherine, hoping for the impossible.' A silence fell, opening the pit of loss I'd been gazing into all this past month, unable to look away.

'She gave me something for you.' My mother reached for my hand and drew me up to stand beside her. My heart began thudding, hard, in my chest, and I shivered. From the pocket of her smock Mum pulled a slender leather thong with a round black shape dangling from it. 'She told me to give it to you in the garden, where your own gift first bloomed.' Mum placed the thong around my neck.

I touched the cool black shape with the tip of one finger.

'What is it?' Suddenly my chest filled with bubbling wonder.

'I know not, my child – your lady told me you would understand.'

Fingering the pendant, I realised that the blackness was a residue, like a coat of ash but more stubborn, cloaking a secret. When I rubbed it with the hem of my cloak, the grey linsey-woolsey came away stained black, and I cried out in dismay. But my mother pointed at the shape, a dull curve of silver now visible in the sunlight.

'Polish it with a good linen cloth. Then we shall see.'

Sturdy scrubbing removed most of the tarnish, though some still clung to the textured crevices. The piece was covered with a pattern of tiny overlapping triangles, with an opening at the top just large enough for the slim leather cord to pass through. Rubbing away at the bumpy midpoint of the round, I suddenly glimpsed a miniature serpent's head and almost dropped the piece. I recalled the engraving that circled the base of the golden flask that Madame la Grande had given my lady. *Ouroboros – a serpent biting its own tail*

'A garden snake?' wondered my mother, eyeing the shape cautiously. 'She did tell me to give it to you in the garden. But I've never seen a snake eating its tail.' She touched the shape. 'What does it mean?'

I could hear her voice in my head. *It signifies wholeness and renewal. Passed from me to you, it holds my promise – that your gifted sight as an artist can reveal what others may not see.*

'Milady believed in the possibility of . . . renewal.' I spoke slowly, sharing the core of the message that I had been pondering since her death. I knew my lady would tell me not to fear the path ahead.

'I believe that to be truth, Rose.' Mum sat beside me on the low stone wall that bordered the garden. 'I know your father wants you to work with him in the business, managing his accounts as his reputation as a clothier grows. But I see a different future for you.' Her voice was steady. 'When Lady Catherine passed her gift for you into my care, she told me she hoped you would find a place for your art to grow.'

'But – to draw, I'd need to buy my own supplies, now that milady is gone.'

My mother simply nodded. She beckoned me into the house and crossed the bake-room to the pantry where I'd hidden from Michael the previous evening. Her head brushed the dangling bundles of herbs, releasing scents of marjoram, thyme and mint. 'I've been selling some jams and preserves when I work the stall for your father at the market.' She selected a clay pot tucked within a collection of assorted pots of jam and emptied it into my palm. A cascade of shillings and sixpenny pieces spilled out. 'That isn't all.' She removed a knotted linen cloth from her bodice and untied it with care. Nestled within the cloth was a coin – a gold angel, worth ten shillings. I took it up and rubbed my thumb over the image of the archangel Michael slaying the dragon. On the other side was the shape of an English galley with a rose set below the topmast.

'For you, Rose,' she concluded. 'To buy your own paper and pens and ink. At least to start with.'

'But Mum – what will Da say?'

My mother closed her fingers around the angel. 'This didn't come from selling jams.' She turned her gaze to the shelf that had once been lined with phials and tubs of herbal remedies and now bore only a few for family use. 'I was sought out at the market last year by a gentleman needing a remedy. His wife was with child and had lost so many babes already that they feared she would never carry this one to term. He offered me money, and I brought him the last bottle from my store of remedies.'

I clutched her shoulders. 'But Da said—'

'I know what your father said. But the life of a babe was at stake. I wasn't going to turn away.' Her voice conveyed the same steady confidence she had as a healer in my childhood, before the accusation that had shattered our lives. The confidence that, even when healing failed, she could yet bring some ease.

'Nine months later, he came to find me at the market again, to introduce his wife and bonny new babe. I never told your father. After that, I started to get requests from those who care more about the future than the past. So I mix remedies in small batches now. And I grow the herbs you see.'

I blew out my breath in wonder. My mother hadn't let the name of *witch* stop her after all.

'I set these earnings aside, Rose – for you, not for your father. I want you to use your gift.' I heard again the dark thread that was in her voice when I arrived home, and now recognised it for what it was. Not resignation, but determination.

All summer and into autumn, I worked alongside my mother, weeding her garden, harvesting vegetables, drying herbs and preparing meals. In the evenings, as winter closed round the cottage, my father sat me down beside him to learn the accounts. I struggled to follow his example as he recorded each week's expenses and earnings in neat lines and columns. I was surprised to learn the difference between a certain fabric's cost and how much he could sell it for in the market. Satin was the finest, at three shillings a yard, but his busiest sales came from cheaper stuff – frieze, russet and canvas, which he stocked in larger quantities and popular shades. Slender bolts of brightly coloured silk for fancier dress supplemented the bulk sales, along with ribbons and braids for trim.

'You've a fine hand for script, but no mind for figures,' he told me after I muddled the sums for the sixth time in a single evening. 'Let's hope you improve over time.' But when I idly penned the image of a borage starflower from my mother's garden into one corner of an account sheet, he lost all patience. 'You're a child no longer, Rose. There's no time for these scribbles when there's real work to be done.' He glared at Mum. 'You shouldn't encourage the girl's fancies.'

'I'll keep to the accounts from now on, Da,' I said quickly. 'But it was my lady encouraged me, not Mum. She taught me my letters and asked me to draw for her every day.' I choked back a sob, remembering how Lady Catherine had handled my sketches as if they were precious.

'Well, you're not at the great house no more. I've a business to maintain that keeps a roof over our heads and bread on the table.' Da's voice was gruff. 'Your place now is to do what *I* teach you.'

I gritted my teeth, but Mum shook her head, signalling me to hold my tongue as she had learnt to do to keep the peace in this household. No good could come from angering my father. But my stomach churned.

All that winter, though I spoke respectfully to my father, the dark thread I'd seen in my mother now belonged to me as well. And in stolen moments, I continued to draw.

'I've a mind to bring these to market, Rose,' Mum said softly one early spring afternoon, when I showed her the sheaf of new sketches I'd made in our garden. 'Folk might pay money to see these pretty pictures on their walls.' To some of the drawings I had added fanciful images – healing spirits rising from the roots of herbs and peeping out from behind flowers. 'These I'd set aside for now, lass,' Mum cautioned. 'Your father mustn't see these, for he'd not understand.' So I stashed those drawings out of sight under a pile of old accounts on a low dusty shelf in the storeroom – another thread connecting me to my lady severed.

On Midsummer morning, I left our cottage in the pre-dawn darkness and headed for the Stones. The timeworn circle the villagers called Stonehenge had captivated me from my first ride there on Da's shoulders. My path took me from the outskirts of the village through fields and across grassy ridges, past the humped shapes of earthen mounds known as the Barrows. As the sky lightened, I broke into a trot to reach the Stones before the sun. Clambering across the ditch that circled the site and then up the bank, I scraped my legs and dropped to my knees, breathless.

The gigantic standing stones marched away from me on either side of a circle, their weathered faces streaked with darkness and light together. Framing the horizon, their natural magic unlocked by the passage of light – sun in summer and moon in winter – they promised the existence of forces not to be named, a world grander and far more ancient than our village. The Stones were my first subjects, shapes that I drew from memory with a stick in the earth of my mother's garden or traced in the ashes on the hearth, until Mum persuaded Da to give me charcoal sticks and paper on my sixth birthday. This sunrise, I had lived the same number of years since that birthday.

Whenever I felt too confined by the cottage, I had always escaped to the Stones. I had become used to sharing them with the resident rooks, who built nests in the crevices at heights beyond the reach of earthbound predators. On this morning, a clamour of rooks swarmed the windy skies over the Stones, wheeling and worrying overhead. One, black as midnight, landed beside my foot and cocked his head at me. His wings were dusted with splotches of grey, like ash, but his head was sleek and shining, his long pale beak a blade. I fingered the small silver snake on the thong around my neck. 'I've no food for you, sir.' I spoke apologetically. In my haste to reach the Stones before sunrise, I had neglected to place breadcrusts in my pocket as I always used to do. My companion pecked for a few moments at my feet. Then, with a loud cry, he swept upwards towards his fellows still scattered across the clouds.

Directly across the Circle from me, the solstice sun rose through strands of mist. Brushing the side of the slanting stone everyone called the Heel Stone, the sun poured its amber blaze full upon my kneeling figure. I closed my eyes, lifted my arms, and offered up the prayer that I had been holding since my lady's final words to me.

May wholeness arise.

Then I picked up my charcoal and began to draw.

My bond with Da was steadily fraying, unravelling like ill-made cloth. After he caught an adding-up error that could have cost him several pounds, he gave up on having me work with his accounts. I knew he wished I was working for wages and had spoken to some of his fellow merchants to offer his daughter's reading and writing skills for hire. But money was tight these days, and no one was eager to spend for such a luxury.

I wondered how long I'd be fated to live as a shadow of my mother, with skills that couldn't contribute to the household. One late September evening while I entertained Michael, drawing on the hearthstones to illustrate a tale I was telling him, I heard Mum and Da speaking softly. All evening he had been frowning at his sheets of figures, sighing and shaking his head. Seeing the worry on Mum's face, I kept one ear cocked.

'When I tried selling more fine fabrics this year, I knew it was a risk,' Da was saying. 'The gamble hasn't paid off. Folks aren't buying costly cloth in these hard times.'

He leafed through a pile of papers he'd recovered from the storeroom. 'If I compare this season's sales with them from the past few years—' He stopped suddenly, and my heart froze. Then he pushed his chair back from the desk with such force it clattered to the floor. 'What's this?' he barked, glaring down at me.

He waved a sheaf of papers in the air – my spirit sketches. How could I have been so foolish as to think they'd be safe stashed among his old records?

'I told you not to waste your time with these scribbles!' His voice gained volume. 'With your time in service, plus knowing how to read and write, I thought to find a good position for you with a merchant family – but no one wanted you.'

I flinched at his disappointment.

'Since you're not able to contribute to this household, it's time we found you something else. The Ashby farm on the other side of the village has been looking for help feeding their animals while the wife is abed with her new baby. I'll talk to them in the morning. Maybe you can board with them, since you're so little use to us here.' *Board with them*? Live in a stranger's family again?

Mum placed a steadying hand on Da's arm. 'Rose helps me with the garden, Martin, and with Michael.' But Da wasn't finished. 'And where'd you get the money to buy these clean sheets to draw on and ink to draw with?' Startled by Da's anger, little Michael began to cry, and I saw the alarm on Mum's face. If Da found out she had been selling her remedies after he had told her to stop, who knows what he'd do. And for her to give the money from her secret sales to support my art when times were tight – he'd never forgive her. I spoke before she could.

'My lady gave me some pence before she died and told me to keep drawing,' I said, the half-lie slipping quickly off my tongue. But, scanning the images again, Da's anger only grew.

'These unnatural pictures could bring another charge of witchcraft upon this family!' Before Mum could stop him, he had flung the entire pile into the hearth fire. It caught the new fuel and flared up. Michael stopped wailing and stared in fascination. Now it was I who wept, watching my drawings turn to ash – and with them, my aspirations.

But after my lady's death, and my return to the old life, what did my hopes matter?

CHAPTER EIGHT

Mary, 1576

'Sing to me, Mary.' Philip handed his sister her lute. 'Putting one of our Psalms to music will help us hear how well it works.'

Of course! Her face alight, Mary wondered why adding the dimension of music to their translations hadn't occurred to her. After all, what were the Psalms if not songs of praise? Adapting one of their verses would be a simple matter for Mary, who had loved singing since childhood and had taken to the lute almost as easily as the pen.

From the start, brother and sister had shared the aim of exploring alternatives to the predictable rhymes and jog-trot metre of the traditional English Psalter. To that end, Mary had pestered her father until he finally agreed to allow her to study Hebrew with her tutor, as Philip had already studied it at Oxford. If daily study of the Psalms were to be part of her education, then she wanted to make them her own, paraphrasing them into English verse that soared instead of plodding.

Cloistered daily with Philip, Mary dedicated herself to their project, rendering the Book of Psalms in graceful English verse with both metrical and metaphorical variety. The work, she found, was heart-thumpingly exhilarating, and served to divert her from the troublesome prospect of marriage. While Philip took up the early Psalms, Mary chose to start near the end. In Psalm 139 she found a celebration of God's creation that assured her of both His care for her beloved Ambrosia's immortal soul and the sisters' undying connection: *Each inmost piece in me is thine.*

Now, Mary's voice carried this promise aloft as her fingers supported the melody with the neighbouring harmony of the lute. Working with Philip was pure joy. Unlike the aftermath of that connection with Walter, which had left only disappointment in its wake.

So when she unexpectedly encountered her brother's friend as she walked one afternoon with Philip in the gardens of Hampton Court, Mary's first reaction was chagrin. The Sidney family was attending upon the Queen, and Mary had been looking forward to this distraction from uncomfortable thoughts. She greeted Walter's appearance with a cool toss of her head, hoping to convey that their summer kiss had meant no more to her than it apparently had to him. *To complete the connection,* he had told her. What rot. But at least she had kept it to herself, so he hadn't lost her brother as a friend. He owed her for that.

Walter smiled in glad surprise and, bowing low, kissed her hand. Despite her better judgement, a thrill quickened her pulse. Nodding a greeting to her brother, Walter offered Mary his arm. As they walked along a flower-bordered path, the river breezes lifted Mary's long curls off her shoulders, but all she could feel was the tingle of Walter's kiss upon her hand. Overhead, the rising cries of lapwings punctuated their steps.

'I trust you have not forgotten my offer to introduce you to the study of alchemy,' Walter said.

Indeed she had not – he had made it just before kissing her in her chamber at Kenilworth. 'Do you consider alchemy to belong to the "natural" or the "supernatural" world?' Mary asked in response. She was eager to focus on matters of the mind – less perilous than conjunctions of the body – but also genuinely curious.

'I believe that the practice of alchemy might cross, or perhaps blur, that line,' Walter replied. Mary raised her eyebrows sceptically. 'Indeed, Philip and I embarked on the practice of alchemy together in order to probe the transformative possibilities of the material world.' Walter's fervour was as infectious as ever, but this time Mary refused to be swept away by mysterious generalisations.

'What of Doctor Dee, who, according to you, speaks with angels? Do you expect me to believe that the practice of alchemy includes *angels*?'

'Doctor John Dee is the most learned alchemist in court circles and advisor to Her Majesty,' Walter retorted. 'For him, the natural and supernatural worlds are one and the same. He believes that alchemy can both spiritually and materially transform the world. I have heard him say that angels walk among us.'

Unconvinced, Mary turned to her brother. 'And what of you, who want to write a romance without supernatural devices?'

'Tenacious, your sister,' murmured Walter.

'Who can tell the truth of it?' her brother admitted. 'I'd certainly like to believe in powers beyond the mechanics of the still-room. And although my romance doesn't depend on visible magic, part of me longs always to believe in greater powers than I can see.' Then, grasping her hand, 'The best writing, like successful alchemy, is about wholeness. Each stage encompasses all the ingredients of the previous stages, transformed.'

Clearly sensing that Mary's doubts duelled with a growing fascination, Walter pressed further. 'I have had the pleasure of setting up a still-room at Leicester House, where your uncle has been kind enough to host me for much of this year. If you visit me there' – his pause was pregnant with such possibility that even Philip took note, a questioning frown creasing his brow. Clearing his throat, Walter continued in a more casual tone – 'I promise to show you the practice of alchemy at first-hand – so that you can begin your own investigation into natural and supernatural worlds.'

Mary rose to the challenge, bearing the remnants of her scepticism as a trusty shield.

'Tomorrow, then?'

She caught the glance that passed between the two men – Walter surprised and clearly pleased, Philip wary.

Then, with a chuckle, Philip turned to Walter. 'If you intend to maintain your friendship with my uncle, I advise you not to blow up the still, the way you did at Christ Church!'

'That was the fault of an overly eager assistant on the bellows, not any ill practice on my part,' protested Walter. Turning to Mary, he added, 'Dress lightly, for there shall be *ignis* aplenty – fire and heat.'

The imposing bulk of Leicester House, the newly completed London home of Robert Dudley, Earl of Leicester, towered over its older neighbours, affording an elevated view of the Strand as well as the Thames. Walter appeared at the entrance as soon as Mary's carriage came to a stop in the courtyard. Had he been watching for her arrival from one of the many mullioned windows?

'The earl spends much of his time at court, but we may see him later on,' Walter observed as he handed Mary down from the carriage. Mary was glad of that possibility, for she had not seen her uncle since her sojourn at Kenilworth – and very little of him then, as he had been engrossed in the ill-fated courtship of the Queen, for whom he had ordered the sumptuous entertainments. Walter wasted no time but led her up three flights of stairs to the still-room.

When he opened the door, Mary stopped short. Strange aromas of metal and burnt spices scented the air. Lit from without by a row of windows, the chamber was cluttered on every flat surface with glass flasks and flagons of all shapes and sizes. Pride of place was claimed by an oddly shaped furnace at the centre of the room, capped with a tower exuding heat and surrounded by basins, some filled with water and others with sand. Mary took a moment to absorb the profusion of objects and odours. Her ears filled with the steady wheeze of a bellows operated by a lad with a kerchief around his temples, accompanied by bursts of heat that soon drew sweat upon her own brow. Fortunately she had followed Walter's advice about dressing lightly.

'My athanor, the Tower Furnace.' Walter gestured proudly. 'The water and sand baths offer methods of heating substances more gradually than fire.'

A shadow moved in the darkest reaches of the chamber. 'Allow me to introduce my half-brother and partner in experimentation, Adrian Gilbert.' A short, squat man emerged from the darkness, clothed loosely in a robe of ash-grey silk, his face flushed with heat. His thinning brown hair and flyaway eyebrows presided over cheeks pouched with flesh, his darting eyes surveying Mary with a nervous energy that called to mind a squirrel searching for a desirable nut. Certainly Mary wouldn't have taken this stout bundle for any relation to the long, elegant Walter.

Walter handed her a silk robe and knotted the cord of another one about his own waist. 'These over-garments will shield us from the soot,' he explained. And indeed, the air was permeated with fine black particles. Walter continued the introduction. 'Adrian – I've brought Philip Sidney's sister, Mary, to survey our still and observe some of our alchemical process. Should she embrace this practice, her intellect promises a swift advance.' Adrian gave a sceptical chuckle – at such confidence expressed in a novice or, perhaps, a woman?

Mary set her annoyance aside. 'I'm pleased to meet you, Master Gilbert.'

Suddenly obsequious, he pressed his plump lips to her fingers. 'The pleasure is all mine, Lady Mary.'

'There are many different paths to the Philosopher's Stone,

and I am resolved to find one of them,' Walter asserted with assurance. 'My goal is to transmute base metals into gold, as alchemists have done successfully in past times.'

Mary found his confidence unexpectedly endearing. 'To be honest, I'm more interested in medicine than in gold,' she ventured. 'After studying my mother's books of medicinal remedies, I know I want to learn not just how to dose illness with prepared remedies, but how to produce them myself.' This field was one she desired to master, all the more now that she was preparing to assume the role of healer that she knew was expected of the mistresses of great households.

'Gold may arrive in many forms,' Walter rejoined. 'Paracelsus, the father of alchemy, teaches that medicine is the true gold. Rather than simply relying upon nature's remedies, man can create more powerful substances through distillation and coagulation, refining ingredients through experimentation.'

Walter's enthusiasm sparked with almost tangible heat as he continued. 'I have been experimenting with what I consider to be a more readily attainable goal – the concoction of my very own Great Cordial, combining animal, vegetable and mineral components in the most harmonious balance.'

This fired Mary's own zeal, given her interest in producing remedies. Each station in the crowded still-room seemed suddenly to embody possibility.

'To begin,' Walter continued, 'I have ground the horn of a hart in middle age, along with a bezoar stone from the stomach of a goat, thus drawing upon the natural spirit and heat of these vigorous animals, which I baked with musk and joined with a viper's antidote to its own venom.'

A viper's venom? Mary couldn't disguise her shudder, which invited Walter to squeeze her shoulder reassuringly.

Striding towards a pear-shaped vessel attached at one end to a still-pot sitting atop the furnace, from whose beaked cap liquid was dripping into the receiving vessel, Walter had more to say. 'In the meantime, I have been dissolving pearls in a menstruum – a solvent of distilled wine.'

Walter's discourse was interrupted by a sudden shout. Adrian was holding a long-necked glass vessel afizz with dark fluid, froth mounting up the neck until it foamed over the top. He set the vessel abruptly on a table before the foam could slide over his fingers.

'Take care with that matrass, man – it's the last one we have,' Walter snapped.

'Didn't want my hand eaten away by acid, did I?' his partner snapped back.

Dazed by the unfamiliar fumes and alarmed by the urgency in the men's voices, Mary put a hand against the table to steady herself, overcome by dizziness. The next moment, Walter was lowering her into a chair. He shook his head. 'I must apologise for my own explosion here. Your brother was right to warn you about my enthusiasm in the still-room, which tends to bubble over – as you have just witnessed.'

'Once started, I suppose it is difficult to stop,' Mary agreed, smiling faintly.

'You may wish to hire Adrian as your assistant,' Walter suggested as they descended the stairs. 'You'll find his aid invaluable in setting up your own still-room. And despite his seeming carelessness, he is well-versed in alchemical procedures and knows how to avert *most* of the dangers.' His arm offered steadying support as her dizziness subsided.

'The shifting distractions of the court will pale before the rewarding challenges of this practice,' Walter promised. 'I know that your quick mind will devour the many writings to be had on this subject, starting with Paracelsus.' His smile conveyed an instinctive understanding of her search for a path of her own, while his gift of the ouroboros ring encircled her finger reassuringly.

As they reached the landing above the final flight of stairs to the ground floor, Walter suddenly paused and drew her into an alcove. Less assured than the first time, he took Mary's fingers in his and pulled her close. Her mouth opened instinctively. Impossibly deep, this kiss drove all thought from Mary's mind. Responding, she was all body. All tongue. She was only aware of the heat – the *ignis* – drawing their bodies together.

Until the noise just below, of doors opening and servants bustling as her uncle arrived home, recalled her to where she was. Who she was.

Walter groaned as they stepped apart. 'Mary,' he murmured. But she placed her fingers on his lips, interrupting – what? Another confession of regret? Nothing she wanted to hear. She wanted to hold this kiss close.

'The ouroboros requires neither explanation nor excuse,' she affirmed. The ruby eyes of the little snake winked from her finger. She would carry this unexpected bond into a future she had not chosen. Mary dropped her fingers and descended the stairs without looking back.

In the entrance hall stood her uncle, the Earl of Leicester, a striking gentleman with a long moustache that framed his lips and beard, and, on his arm, a handsome lady just past the bloom of youth. Lettice Devereux. The recently widowed dowager countess was decked out in an ebony satin overskirt and pearly grey bodice adorned with silver laces and points – a parody of mourning. Lettice's arched brows conveyed reciprocal surprise at Mary's regard.

Robert Dudley welcomed his niece warmly. 'Leicester House is ever open to family – and I have come to regard Walter as such over his residence here this year.'

Moments later, seated in the solar with Lettice while her uncle remained behind to speak with Walter, Mary took a too-eager gulp from a glass of wine to cool her dry mouth and parched throat, and coughed.

Lettice raised her finely drawn eyebrows. 'The still-room heated me,' Mary explained weakly.

'I fail to see the attraction of the still-room for ladies,' Lettice drawled. It was difficult to conceive how this mistress of appearances had begotten such a daughter as Penelope, Philip's beloved. Lettice's disdainful eyes lingered on Mary's soot-rimmed skirts. 'I would have supposed you might be preparing your trousseau – in celebration of your engagement.'

'My – engagement?' Catching Walter's dark gaze as he appeared in the doorway, Mary stumbled over the word. Surely the seemingly inevitable outcome of Sir Henry's suit was not already public? Walter stopped in mid-stride, turned, and left the room.

'Robert told me that he has been negotiating your dowry on behalf of your father.' Lettice's sly smile intimated a more-than-casual connection with Mary's uncle. 'Allow me to offer you a gift of some counsel, my child. As the soon-to-be third wife of Lord Pembroke, you may want to consider the fates of his first two wives.' Pressing a cool hand atop Mary's own, Lettice delivered her words in a steady stream that contained icy undercurrents. 'First, having to annul his marriage to Lady Katherine Grey – politics is such a cruel game! – and then to have his second Catherine die, so young and, alas, childless.'

Her narrow face crinkled in a show of concern. 'You must know, child, that Sir Henry cherished his second wife above all others, so it won't be easy for you to step into her place. Unless you're able to supply him with an heir, as she could not – which, of course, is the earl's motive in pursuing yet another marriage so soon.' This last was accompanied by a malicious glance that left Mary feeling soiled.

The woman was not quite finished. She wagged a jewelled forefinger in Mary's face. 'But, my dear, you must never underestimate a man's capacity for jealousy,' she added, inexplicably, and then, 'Certainly I wish for you a better fate than his other wives.' With a satisfied smirk, Lettice Devereux rose to her feet and swept out of the solar.

Walter was waiting to escort Mary to her carriage. No space for parting speech, but his searching expression spoke volumes. And *ignis* aplenty remained.

Chapter Nine

Rose, 1576

The next morning, as I swept the ashes of my drawings from the fireplace along with the other burnt-out embers, there came a knocking at the door. I was greeted by a wide grin on a familiar face atop broader shoulders than I remembered.

'Peter!' My glad surprise suddenly turned to concern. 'Is all well at Wilton? How is Cicely?' My questions were met by a bow and then a wink.

'Me sister sends her greetings!' Then he spread his arms to make sure I noticed his rise in station. He sported a blue and red livery coat with pride. 'Me days as a stable-hand are behind me now – I'm a footman!'

I took the paper he held out to me and broke the seal, embossed with the Pembroke arms. With some difficulty I pieced out the bold characters, being more used to reading printed pages or my lady's even hand.

Rose – I write to you because I have need to engage a lady's maid for my new wife. I hope you will accept this position. If so, I ask you to return to Wilton as soon as you receive this so that we may discuss your new duties.

HH, Pembroke

Our daily routine dissolved in a frenzy of activity. Mum invited Peter to stay for supper, adding bacon to the pottage in his honour. Michael was overjoyed to have someone to wrestle with. When Peter got down on his hands and knees to give Michael a ride, my brother grasped Peter's dark curls with such glee that I winced and reached to lift him off again. But Peter chuckled, a deep, bubbling sound as comfortable as a warm stew. ''Tis no bother – better sport to *be* a horse than tending them!'

Da seemed surprised that my services were required elsewhere. Even valued, I thought with a crooked grin. Peter had already arranged for the carter to take me to Wilton at the end of the week. A future not determined by my father opened before me after all.

'But surely Wilton's new mistress hasn't yet arrived? Must Rose leave so soon?' Where my father was relieved to have a solution to the problem that was me, my mother's words were a lament. Thus the dark thread shifted from the fabric of my days back to hers. Passing it back and forth, the burden was shared, but I knew she bore it harder.

On my last day at home, Da presented me with a small wooden chest. It was fashioned from plain oak, but on its lid was carved a starflower. 'For your drawings,' he explained awkwardly. 'You might as well have someplace to keep them safe. Mayhap Lord Pembroke will have more call to appreciate them than I.' I understood this admission was the closest he could come to an apology.

Mum came to my bed to bid me goodnight. No tears, though her eyes were bright.

'This might be the wish of your lady after all.' She spoke gently, but squeezed my fingers tight. 'Having you home completed the circle I thought I broke by sending you away. Now I see that mayhap it served a larger purpose. My thoughts and prayers are with you each day.'

Her voice was sharp with loss.

Wilton House stood serenely at the end of the drive. I entered with an empty box and a hopeful heart. Steward Wilkins seemed, if not happy to see me, at least satisfied that I couldn't stay away. Sir Henry was awaiting my arrival in the library, sitting in the big chair behind the desk, his hand resting atop my lady's sheaf of remedies, now bound neatly with black string.

'Thank you for coming, Rose.' His voice was still kind, its tone strong and even, but his face more lined with care. The loss of Lady Catherine was carved there, plain for any to see.

'She loved you.' He spoke simply. 'And trusted you to the end.' That last word came hard to him, and was hard to hear. I dropped my eyes to the carpet, patterned in flowers – the closest my lady could come to her garden in that final year.

'I loved her too, milord.' When I looked up at him, he nodded silently.

'I need you, now, to serve the lady I shall marry next year, who will be the new mistress of Wilton House. You have been well trained and, despite your age, I believe you will be well suited to the task. You shall receive wages of ten shillings per quarter, in addition to room and board.'

I gasped. Ten shillings a quarter! That meant two pounds a year to send home to Mum.

He cleared his throat and rose from the chair, pacing to the window that looked out over the courtyard. 'There's more, and this is what I want to discuss with you,' he said, turning to me. His narrow lips, pressed tightly together, suggested judgements made but not voiced. 'I need you to observe carefully – something that my wife assured me was one of the skills that enabled your sketches. But what I need from you now are not drawings of plants, but of people.'

I frowned. What was the purpose of his command? His words came slowly, ponderously. 'I need you to watch my new wife, Lady Mary, particularly when you accompany her to court. She is young and beautiful and witty, and will have many admirers. I wish to know who they are. Because you won't know most of them yourself, I want you to draw what you see.'

My chest tightened. So I was to spy for him. Hardly a task my new mistress would thank me for. But she was no one to me yet, and he was already my lord.

'I will require your promise to hold all that you learn in confidence, for my eyes and ears alone. For this service, you will receive an additional ten shillings per quarter.' This time

I couldn't even suck in enough breath to gasp. He tapped the sheaf of Lady Catherine's remedies. 'Remember – she trusted you, and now, so do I. Such a task will not be easy, and I charge you with it only after much contemplation.'

He turned from the window, and on his face I saw hope and doubt entwined. 'Lady Catherine is gone now. What she brought to this household, and to me, cannot be recovered.' His voice cracked, and my heart went out to him. 'I must protect what comes next.'

I had no idea what he meant. But his orders were clear, and I had no choice but to obey if I wanted to keep my new position.

'Your first task will be to clean Lady Catherine's still-room in preparation for its new mistress. No one has entered that room since she – since she died.' He seemed barely able to force that word from his lips, that terribly permanent fact that had changed all of our lives.

'Once you mount to the top floor of the house, this key will open the door.' Lord Pembroke extended his palm. On it rested a ring of three keys, the largest, of brass, tied with a scarlet ribbon. 'Of the others, this silver one unlocks her cabinet of treasures, and this one' – he held up a small golden key – 'is for the box of black walnut where she stored her recipes for cures.' He slid the keys into a muslin pouch and placed it into my hand. Then he handed me the packet of her remedies, layered with my drawings, that I had left on her desk. 'You may add these to that box – I have been unable to visit the still-room.' He swallowed, then added, 'She would have wanted them kept together.' My heart skipped a beat. He was entrusting me with my lady's legacy. And my own future.

I dropped a curtsey. 'My lord, I will serve you as truly as I served my lady.' I left the library, the keys tucked into the muslin sack fastened to my bodice and the packet of remedies in my arms. My pace was steady, but my mind was spinning. My only thought was to reach the sanctuary of my lady's still-room. I had pledged to serve my lord, and I would do so. But first I needed to find my way back to my lady.

'Rose, thou'rt a sight for sore eyes!' Cicely's encircling arms were warm and reassuring. I dearly wanted to sit beside her in the warm kitchen and catch all the news I'd missed. But I couldn't delay completing the task I'd just been given.

'Peter can show thee the way,' Cicely assured me. 'When Lady Catherine was well, he'd carry up the chests of spices she ordered from overseas and stack boxes as she had need. He knows that room – full of strange smells, he said! When ye're finished, come back down and we'll have a good, long chat.'

Peter appeared as if only awaiting his sister's direction. He led me through the linked rooms to the north-east corner of the house, to the staircase leading to the attic. I had hoped that passing through the familiar chambers again would comfort me with reminders of my lady's presence, but instead they pierced me with her absence. Rooms can't hold spirits. The memories were like nettles, stinging to the touch. By the time we mounted the stairs and reached the door to the attic, I had ceased listening to Peter's jovial efforts at conversation. Shaking my head when he asked if I needed his help, I waited until he descended the stairs. Then I turned the brass key in the lock. With a rhythmic clacking of metal, the latch released. The heavy door creaked plaintively on unused hinges.

Inside was a ruined treasure house.

Light from the large square windows was dimmed by gathering clouds and accompanied by a sharp clatter of raindrops against the leaded panes. Relieved that Peter had left me a lantern to light my task, I made my way gingerly into the long chamber, which seemed to run half the length of the house. Every surface was covered with a layer of dust, and a flicker of lightning caught an answering gleam across the floor, marking a trail of shards of glass. Shelves along the wall were lined with books and a fantastical array of glass vessels, one of which must have ended up in those fragments on the floor. Chests were lined in ranks beneath a long worktable. Near one end of the room stood a strange tower of bricks with a peaked roof, like a miniature castle. I took it to be the furnace where my lady had told me she would heat liquids and distil essential oils. But the furnace was cold and the worktables empty, save for the dust. A chill shivered my spine. I was the first person to enter this room since my lady herself. I set the lantern down with a long sigh. She wasn't here, either.

Taking up a broom leaning by the door, I began to sweep the floor. The storm thickened, rain drumming the roof, interrupted by clamorous bursts of thunder. It wasn't until I reached the window at the far end of the chamber that I noticed a clay flowerpot placed on the sill to capture the light. The plant was long dead now, but I would have recognised those distinctive columns of needles in any condition. My lady's plant. *Rosemary*.

When I poked the dried needles, they broke away beneath my touch, releasing their faint but singular essence. I gathered the needles into small handfuls and placed them in the pocket of my smock with budding purpose. After the room was swept, I pulled a linen dust-cloth from my bodice and began to attend to the shelves. At least I could dust the books without fear of damaging them. As I reached one end of the shelf, I realised with a spark of excitement that I was looking at the spine of another volume of William Turner's *New Herball*. And beside it, another. Two more volumes!

The shelves of glass containers would need to wait until I had better light, or I'd only produce more broken glass to sweep up. At the thought, I realised that the rain was becoming fainter, the light stronger, the storm passing away. With relief, I straightened, and that was when I saw the finely inlaid cabinet against the wall facing the shelves. *Her cabinet of treasures.*

I approached it, eager to discover what my lady kept here, ensconced in this high sanctuary like a rook's nest atop the Stones. I pulled on the twin door handles, but the cabinet was locked. Then I remembered the key ring and pulled it from the cloth sack tied to my waist. I placed the silver key into the lock and twisted it carefully. At a click, the door swung open. A shaft of early evening sunlight illuminated an array of stones and mineral pieces on a long shelf. The glittering angles of a large, rough-edged pink stone that looked like crystallised sugar held pride of place at the centre of the shelf. This must be the rose quartz my lady had told me about. A treasure indeed. I brushed its edges with my fingertips in wonder. The large stone was encircled by a ring of small polished stones of the same quartz – like the rose pebble my lady had given me. With that gift, I realised, she had invited me into her still-room.

On the lowest shelf of the cabinet I glimpsed the black walnut box Sir Henry had wanted me to find. Bringing it to the table, I saw that it was inscribed on every side with alchemical symbols. I could hear my heart beating in my temples. Closing my eyes to steady myself, I gripped the smallest key, of gold, and placed it in the keyhole.

Inside the box was a pile of papers slimmer than the thick sheaf Sir Henry had handed to me. The rest of my lady's remedies. Then I noticed, tucked beside them, a folded paper sealed with crimson wax. I lifted the paper from the box. The seal was impressed with an image – a snake biting its tail. From beneath my smock I pulled my own snake, the ouroboros pendant that I wore always around my neck, the other gift from my lady. I set it against the wax seal and felt the match with a thrill that transfixed me. My lady had given me her own seal – her promise of regeneration.

So eager was I to hear her voice that I almost started to break the seal and open the letter, when I noticed the writing above the fold in my lady's distinctive hand.

This letter was not addressed to me, but *To the next Cleopatra*.

Reluctantly I slipped the letter back inside the box, where my lady had left it. But I wasn't satisfied. I wanted the box, when my new lady opened it, to contain not simply my lady's words, but her essence. I untied the black string around the sheaf of papers I'd brought here, slipped the final page from the bottom and placed it on the top. The drawing of my lady's face. Then I retied the packet as neatly as before, placed it in the box atop the other pages and sprinkled a handful of rosemary needles over it, like the finishing touch in a recipe.

I closed and locked the box and set it back on the bottom shelf of the cabinet. My task here was finished. But before I left the room, I scooped volumes Two and Three of *A New Herball* into my arms, to take downstairs to the library. She would have wanted me to read them aloud, and now I could.

Retracing my steps to the still-room door, I pulled handfuls of rosemary needles from my pocket and scattered them across the floor, scenting the air with my lady's presence.

Wholeness may arise from fragments pieced together aright. My lady was here after all.

CHAPTER TEN

Mary, 1577

She had read and then refolded the letter so often that the paper was creased and soft. It was a mass of scribbled lines and mixed messages. Difficult to read. Impossible to save. So she committed the words to memory before finally setting the paper alight, on the eve of her wedding. Only a trace of ash remained on the windowsill of the solar, easily brushed away.

My lady – my dear –
I offer my best wishes on your betrothal to Sir Henry Herbert.
The fact of it, for no reason I can explain to myself, was like running headlong into a stone wall. Certainly I knew why your uncle Robert had asked me to introduce you to Sir Henry at Kenilworth. So the outcome was hardly a surprise.

But I cannot drive you from my mind, Mary.

Let me be clear, with no other way forward. It's not simply your lips that have set me aflame. It's your quicksilver speech, once uttered slipping beyond chance of capture or retort.

Your mind – sparking my own.

What do I wish for you? A successful marriage, of course. But more than that, the chance to apply yourself to alchemy as assiduously as to poetry. No telling what you might discover.

And I shall be only one among many who are watching.

Ever yours, Walter

The wedding reminded Mary of her first kiss in the tower at Ludlow – looming larger in anticipation than in fact, oddly mechanical in the moment and leaving little happiness or satisfaction. Following the ceremony, held at Penshurst Place on a crisp April morning, the celebration continued throughout the day and long into the night. The bride and groom were sumptuously feasted and lavishly toasted while musicians played in the minstrels' gallery overlooking the Great Hall. As the final hours and minutes of Mary's girlhood slipped away like a receding tide, she faced into the future she had accepted, but not chosen. Her role as a wife now stretched out endlessly before her.

Henry Herbert's delight at the sight of his bride – 'Beauty beyond compare,' he murmured in her ear – she took as tribute more to her mother's talent as a costumer than to herself. 'Success resides in the details,' her mother assured her. White satin skirts embroidered with gold thread were paired with gold-embroidered sleeves and a bodice stitched with pearls. She took no particular pleasure in the knowledge that her fiery hair, upswept beneath a golden circlet studded with rubies, drew all eyes to her face, powdered white as befitted a countess. She appreciated the powder not for its supposed portrayal of ideal beauty, but as an effective tool to hide her embarrassing tendency, when swept by emotion, to blush crimson from her chest and neck to her cheeks and forehead. The circlet, a gift from her betrothed, pressed uncomfortably against her brow.

Before the ceremony itself, her mother had drawn her aside in the Pages' Room. Mary Dudley Sidney had dispensed with her embroidered masks for this occasion, not wanting to separate herself from her daughter, scarred face or not. Penshurst was not the court but their home, and their guests were relatives and allies, not rivals or adversaries. In the weeks leading up to the wedding, she had schooled Mary with advice about marriage in general and managing an estate more specifically. Now, she caressed her daughter's cheek and unfolded a paper in her hand.

'Ambrosia spoke words for you, Mary, on that final morning, and asked that I save them for your wedding day. I wrote them down so I'd not miss one.'

As her mother began to read, a sob burst from Mary's chest.

Sweet Sister – I know this day will come, and I want my words to hold you. Believe I'm with you, even if I'm not there. All I want you to remember is to keep living your stories – for both of us.

Both their faces wet with tears, mother and daughter held each other as tightly as they had once held Ambrosia.

* * *

While the wedding was a ritual to be endured, binding her to an uncertain future, Mary's departure from Penshurst the next day felt truly like an ending. Leaving her childhood home, the dear, familiar setting for so much of her life, was an irrecoverable loss. She tried her best to view this departure as a scene change in a play, from one domestic backdrop to another, less important than the storyline itself. But leaving Penshurst Place for Wilton House felt more like going into exile than journeying to a new home that she could claim as hers. It was all she could do not to weep like a child when she hugged her parents and brothers farewell.

The first hours of the long journey to her husband's home were spent in a silence almost unbroken by her companion. From time to time, as the carriage jostled over the muddy roads, Henry enquired about her comfort, but offered no further conversation. Was she married to a dullard after all? Perhaps his brightest moments as a suitor had only masked a dim husband? What if the best she could hope for from marriage was tedium? Her mind raced in furious, pointless circles. She tried telling herself that she did not really know him yet, so there was no purpose in speculation. But her fears weren't allayed by her conviction that she knew Walter Raleigh better by far, after their precious handful of meetings, than she might ever know Henry Herbert. Catching her breath, she blocked the torrent of memories. That way only heartbreak lay.

Mary was relieved when they stopped for the night at a large half-timbered inn in Guildford called The Lion. After a plain supper of bread and cheese, chased down by what the red-faced innkeeper assured them was 'some of the best ale in Surrey', they parted to sleep in separate chambers, as they had the previous night at Penshurst. Henry kissed her cheek as politely as an uncle. Lowering her travel-weary body onto the bed, she tried not to imagine the marital event that was sure to follow their arrival at Wilton. Night owls hooted outside the window, breaking her rest. By dawn, her eyes gritty from lack of sleep, she had resolved to break yesterday's silence.

After an hour jostling along the bumpy road, Mary cleared her throat. 'I wish to gather a library at Wilton equal to the collection at Penshurst, so that I may read widely as I continue to work with Philip on our translation of the Psalms – and on other projects as well.'

If Henry was taken aback, he was too courteous to convey anything other than pleasure in his new wife's interest in learning. And Mary's request seemed to loosen his tongue, for he had a suggestion of his own.

'My late wife, Catherine, was known for her skills with herbals and the alchemical production of medicines. I would be very pleased if you take up that practice as well. I've had her still-room readied for your use. I know your brother Philip has assiduously pursued alchemical learning, and I hope that his advice might guide you along this path in time.'

Averting her eyes to look out the carriage window at the rolling hills and fields bordered by long hedges, Mary gritted her teeth. Was this to be the pattern, then? Was Henry's beloved Catherine to be offered up repeatedly as the model for her to follow? She could hear Lettice Devereux's counterfeit concern – *It won't be easy for you to step into her place.* She almost regretted the conjunction of her husband's directions with her rising interest in alchemy, because he'd assume that in pursuing the study of alchemy she was carrying out his will. And she wasn't, she told herself. This was her own will. *Would it do any harm to let him be happy?* She sighed as Ambrosia's voice entered her head.

She compelled her voice to enthusiasm. 'I'm pleased to say that both Philip and Walter Raleigh have already encouraged me to study alchemy. I had my first taste of a still-room when I visited the space my uncle Robert has set aside for Walter's practice at Leicester House. If you agree, I'd like to engage Adrian Gilbert, Walter's half-brother and sometime assistant, to help me in the still-room at Wilton House.' *Stop looking for an opportunity to speak Walter's name, to savour its taste on your tongue*, she told herself sternly.

'I believe the study of practical alchemy to be an essential part of your new responsibilities at Wilton,' was Henry's only response.

'I remember your grief after Catherine passed away, for it was then that we first met,' Mary ventured after a pause. 'I know that I cannot replace her in your heart, any more than my sister Ambrosia's loss can ever be remedied.' When Henry remained silent, she took a breath and pressed on. 'I will do my best to fulfil all the duties that accompany my role as mistress of Wilton. At the same time, I hope that you and I may find a way to communicate about more than daily duties – and in time even to speak of matters of the heart as well as the mind.' Her own heart was pounding. In too far to go back now. 'I have been taught to appreciate language,' she explained, 'and while I understand all too well that words cannot express everything, often I find my way forward through words. I wanted to speak that truth to you from the start.'

Now she fell silent. Had she said too much? Words always spilled from her mouth in the service of her ideas as readily as the bubbling spring she and Ambrosia used to visit outside the walls of Ludlow Castle. Hadn't her mother warned her, at the start of this marriage to an older husband, to moderate her enthusiasms? *He might need some time to appreciate fully how extraordinary you are.* Her father had said much the same, explaining that her mother had so swept him away with her eloquence and verve that it had taken a while to regain his footing.

No regrets, not once, her father had assured her. *Your husband is more seasoned than I was, and may not be unsettled by the passion of your pursuits. But it may be wise to give him time to come to know you.* As if she were a frisky puppy savaging a slipper, Mary had thought impatiently. Given the dowry she was bringing him, he should be able to accommodate some of her passions as well as his own – if he had any.

Henry interrupted her thoughts by taking her hand in his own. 'Thank you for mentioning Catherine. I'm not looking to replace her, Mary – that has never been my goal. Given time, I believe we can have a good life together.'

They spent the rest of the journey more easily conversing about a range of matters, as they had been accustomed to do during Henry's courtship visits to Penshurst. But still, Mary reflected, only a scene change. The storyline remained uncertain.

The carriage approached an imposing entrance arch of white stone surmounted by a bell tower. The facade of Wilton House was grand enough, but it was the human scale of the enterprise that Mary found intimidating. Henry had told her that his staff included almost two hundred servants – four times the number in her own father's household. Humphrey Wilkins, the steward, resplendent in the Pembroke blue and red livery with gold braid, handed her down from the carriage, pulling his cap from his balding pate with courtesy if not precisely enthusiasm. Lined up below the archway were the household's head servants, overseers of Wilton's multiple domestic functions: the housekeeper, butler and head cook, the chaplain, the bailiff of the estate and Lord Pembroke's secretary, comptroller and treasurer. Her new lady's maid, Henry explained, would await her summons. Mary's heart sank. How long would it take her to learn so many new names and faces? The steward, Mary understood, managed the daily business of the household staff, but she knew from her own mother's dedication that it was the responsibility of the lady of the house to understand the details as well.

Mary recognised that this was her first test. All the servants had known and loved Lady Catherine. As they bowed or curtsied one by one, they seemed to regard her warily, measuring her manner and appearance against an ideal that she could scarcely hope to meet. Most of them were quite a bit older than she was, and Mary wondered if they were speculating how long it would take their lord to find his young bride wanting.

After her belongings had been arranged in her bedchamber, she sent for her new lady's maid. When the girl appeared, Mary was first startled, then dismayed. Too young to be a 'gentlewoman', as a great lady's personal attendant was properly termed, Rose was truly just a maid – no more than a child, hardly suited for such a position. Was Mary herself esteemed so lightly by her husband that he didn't think fit to appoint a more experienced servant for the post?

'What is your age, Rose?'

'I'm thirteen, milady,' the girl replied, looking up at her. Her voice was soft, but her gaze was surprisingly direct. Her face, haloed by wispy hair the colour of dust, was entirely unremarkable – save for those eyes, which were the deep, dark green of midsummer leaves, reminding Mary of the cat she and Ambrosia had had in Ludlow Castle. They named the cat Athena and had mourned her disappearance during one of their long absences from Ludlow.

Then she took in what Rose had said. The girl was the age Ambrosia would have been, had her sister lived to this day. Had Henry chosen Rose for that reason? If so, he knew nothing of her heart. Instinctively, she turned away, pushed by the ache of Ambrosia's absence. She had no desire to be this girl's mistress. This simple country girl bore no relation to her lively, loving sister, and never would. Her voice tight with the strain of her unfamiliar position, Mary's first act as Rose's mistress was a peremptory command.

'You may return tomorrow, when we shall discuss your duties.' Almost as soon as the girl curtsied and turned away in silence, Mary regretted her curt dismissal. But it was too late to take it back. The sudden dryness in her mouth as she watched the girl walk away was not indifference, as her tone had surely conveyed, but her own sense of inadequacy. Like a new serving maid herself, Mary feared she might be tried and found wanting.

* * *

'My maid seems very young,' she remarked to Henry when he entered her chamber later that evening. 'I wonder if she is fit for the position, particularly the responsibilities associated with life at court. I had hoped to be attended by someone who might know, better than I, what a countess requires.' To her annoyance, she couldn't quite keep the anxiety from her voice.

Henry nodded, and Mary guessed he had expected this response. 'Rose's mother assisted Catherine with her study of herbals, and so she sent her daughter to serve here. She was capably trained by Catherine's former lady's maid. She's a bright girl and a quick study. My wife was very fond of her, taught her to read and write, and valued her greatly in the final year of her life. I believe she will prove a good maidservant to you, if you give her some time.'

But Mary had no time – she must carry herself in public as the Countess of Pembroke immediately. Her eyes narrowed. Everyone was already watching her, and her husband was telling her to accept a child as her maidservant when she herself was barely grown! Indignation clogged her throat.

Henry continued. 'I took the liberty of engaging Rose in your service before your arrival in order to ease your transition to Wilton, for she already knows the household and our habits. As for the court – where I am unfortunately obliged to spend a good deal of time – those routines are easily learnt.'

Mary was neither comforted nor convinced.

Henry embraced her lightly, then, and she stiffened in anticipation of her wedding-night duty. Seeming to sense this, he explained, to her surprise and relief, that they would continue to sleep in separate chambers, and that he was content to wait until some time had passed before lying together as husband and wife. 'Such matters shouldn't be rushed. I propose instead that we read aloud to each other nightly from some work that we both appreciate.'

Mary's spirits lifted slightly. Reading aloud was a pleasure she and Philip still shared, so she would be happy to occupy her evenings at Wilton with such activity. After Henry bid her goodnight, Mary noticed the empty truckle bed along the wall that must usually be occupied by Rose. She wondered where the girl was spending the night, after being abruptly dismissed. But that was not really her concern. At least not yet.

It's you I miss, she told Ambrosia before sleep. *Now more than ever.*

CHAPTER ELEVEN

Rose, 1577

My first night in the service of the new Countess of Pembroke was spent in Cicely's bed.

Peering from an upper-storey window, I had watched Lady Mary descend from the carriage with Sir Henry, to be introduced to the household's head servants by Master Wilkins. She was beautiful, no question, with a fair, oval face atop a strong chin. Her hair was the colour of red zinnia petals, flowing over the shoulders of her gold-embroidered gown – an explosion of colour that assaulted my senses after the muted shades of Lady Catherine's gowns in lavender and plum. She gave a gracious nod to each servant's bow or curtsey, but to my eyes she seemed stiff and distracted. When she sent for me an hour later, I brushed my new maidservant's kirtle and moved as quickly to her chamber as if I hadn't been dreading this summons from the moment Lord Henry had engaged my services for his new wife.

My new mistress asked my age as if she could scarce believe I was out of the nursery. Stung, I stood straighter and lifted my head. She regarded me with a cool, grey gaze as hard as the rocks that lined the River Nadder. Her disdain and disinterest were clear. When she dismissed me, almost as soon as I had arrived in her presence, I walked without stopping until I reached Cicely's room. Then I burst into tears.

'Don't tell me she has let thee go, Rose?' Cicely enquired anxiously. Relieved to learn that I had been commanded to return the next morning, she patted my shoulder and told me not to worry. 'Come spend the night with me, love. Ye'll be ready for the morrow bright and cheery!'

Cicely didn't seem worried at the curt dismissal. 'She knows nowt, yet, of the duties of her station, tha may be certain of that. Not yet sixteen is what I heard – me own age! – and married afore she's had any chance to test her wings. Just a fledgling. I feel sorry for her, surely I do. She has much to learn.'

I dried my tears, but the bitter sting of rejection remained.

Cicely brought me into her own bed that night, stroking my hair until I drifted towards sleep. Enveloped by her fragrant warmth, cuddled within her arms, I felt my limbs loosening, my muscles unknotting, for the first time since my return to Wilton the previous week. I had been distracted by loss, mourning my lady while tidying her chambers for a new mistress I did not want to serve. Now this mistress had proven herself even worse than I feared. But I had accepted Sir Henry's charge and must strive to be successful in my new lady's service or fail my lord – which would mean returning to a home where I no longer belonged.

Still, I was not alone here. I had Cicely. Every day as we worked together in our lady's bedchamber – I attending to the mistress's clothes and creams while Cicely cleaned and tidied the chamber – we developed a habit of sharing our hopes and wishes. With her, I was beginning to feel at home.

I soon discovered that I had to compete for Cicely's attention. Not with Peter, who was happy to spend our free time as a threesome. Other male servants in the household hovered near Cicely's wide, blue eyes and generous bosom like flies drawn to honey. Sweet, shy Brian, one of the stable boys, had a ruddy face, a ready laugh and, I noted, saucer eyes whenever Cicely was near, but she gave him no encouragement, if she even noticed. To my surprise, it was black-eyed Toby, Sir Henry's valet, who was able to capture her attention – Toby, who seemed uncomfortable in his own skin and hardly looked his fellow servants in the eye, so fixed on Cicely that the rest of us might have been invisible. When I asked her why she bothered to thank him so kindly for the bouquets of roadside wildflowers that he often thrust at her, she chuckled and told me I'd be happy, someday, to have flowers from a boy who didn't expect favours in return.

In the days that followed, my new mistress came to tolerate my attendance. She seemed surprised, even pleased, that I knew how to fasten a farthingale and raise a ruff worthy of a countess. But her manner remained cool, and though I now slept in her chamber, the absence of kindness and care left me longing for Lady Catherine more each day. The greater my unhappiness, though, the greater my attention to each detail of service, while I schooled my face to reveal none of my real feelings. Good training for a spy.

The worst moment arrived towards the end of my first month in her service.

'Sir Henry speaks highly of you,' my new lady observed that morning as I was lacing her bodice. 'He said that you have the keys to Lady Catherine's still-room. I'd like you to take me there after the midday meal today.' And with that, the last private tie to my first lady was snapped.

Outside the door to the still-room, I handed Lady Mary the sack of keys. When she turned the big brass key in the lock and the bolt shot back, I flinched. As she entered the room, her skirts swept through the rosemary needles scattered across the floor. 'These must be cleared away,' she said firmly. 'I want this room kept clean and tidy, no matter how much work takes place here. I'll expect you to maintain the same order in this space as you and Cicely do so well in my bedchamber.'

The compliment was so unexpected that it was all I could do to muster an answering curtsey.

'I plan to engage the services of an experienced alchemical assistant,' she continued, 'but tidiness is not his strong suit. So your services here will be valuable to me.' Her face was almost kind, now, her eyes shining with unmistakable enthusiasm – not for my *valuable services*, I could tell, but the prospect of starting her alchemical work. Still swept by the absence of my lady, I didn't respond.

Lady Mary examined the shelves of glass vessels, then the books and the chests of spices and dried herbs neatly arrayed beneath the worktables. Finally she turned to the inlaid cabinet. Frozen in place, I watched her pause before the cabinet, ponder the keys resting in her palm and insert the silver key into the lock.

When the cabinet door swung open, she caught her breath.

'What a lovely specimen of quartz!' I closed my eyes, briefly hearing my lady's voice. *Rose quartz is considered the heart stone.*

'And quite an impressive collection of cordials.' She was not addressing me, but musing to herself.

I opened my eyes again to see Lady Mary reaching for the black walnut box as if she knew it was waiting for her. She set it easily beside her on the long worktable. As she rested her hand on its lid, engraved with alchemical symbols, I suddenly noticed what I hadn't before. On her finger, a ring, in the shape of a serpent biting its tail: the ouroboros. I stifled a gasp and touched the pendant nestled out of sight against my breastbone.

'Sir Henry told me about Catherine's remedies,' she said as she closed and relocked the cabinet. When she addressed me, her tone was brisk. Speaking to a servant. 'You may take this to the library.'

Then she swept from the room with that erect carriage that reminded me of a queen. I followed obediently, carrying the box – and suddenly realising what she would find in it.

Lady Mary spent many hours each day with Master Wilkins, learning the household accounts. I guessed she was a quick study, as his chilly regard slowly warmed to her. For my part, during the afternoon hours that Lady Catherine had instructed me in my letters or asked me to read to her, my new mistress shut herself alone into the library, organising the books that arrived by the chestful each week. Peter was often called upon to carry these heavy chests into the library and help to shelve the books, and would later marvel with Cicely and me. 'How she can read so many books is beyond me!' he exclaimed, winking at me. I liked Peter for his easy laugh and carefree manner. The other servants had become accustomed to my return to the household, but they were still not as friendly to me as Cicely and Peter. When he began inviting me to walk with him during our free time, I accompanied him, mostly to give myself something to do besides complain to Cicely about the challenges and disappointments of my service to Lady Mary. It was important to return kindness where it was offered.

'What about thy drawings?' Cicely asked one afternoon while she was beating the curtains in the bedchamber free of dust and I was rearranging the pots and brushes on my lady's cosmetics table. I had confided in her how unhappy it made me to pass on to Lady Mary all that had once belonged to Lady Catherine. 'Why don't ye put pen to paper again, as Lady Catherine was always encouraging thee to do? Tha told me drawing makes thee happy.'

'There's nothing much I wish to put on paper,' I explained, but the excuse sounded unconvincing even to me. 'Truth be told,' I confessed, 'it's myself I'm discontented with.' I ran my fingers through my dusty brown hair. 'Look at me! – a country lass with no beauty and no charm. How can I be expected to travel to court with my mistress and brush shoulders with other fine ladies' maids?'

'Nonsense!' Cicely snorted. 'Those other maids are no better than the Wilton servants, and likely inferior. I guess they'll envy thee for serving a countess. There can't be too many of those, even at court.'

Her spirit demanded a response. She had that effect on everyone. My eyes were drawn to Cicely's assured movements with the broom in the dust-flecked afternoon sunlight, her shoulders flexing so energetically that her lustrous mane started to escape its pins. Her lively face, alight with pleasure, offered an enticing subject.

'Let me sketch *you*!'

I drew her towards a chair and arranged her gently in a ladylike pose illumined by the window. Tucking her escaping strands of hair back into the tidy knot at the nape of her neck, she twisted to glance at the door. 'But – what if Lady Mary returns to her chamber?'

'Her library will hold her attention for the rest of the afternoon.' I spoke with greater certainty than I felt, now that the urge to draw had repossessed me. I had no remaining patience for anticipating my new mistress's wants and needs. My first lady would want me to use my gift. Cicely rose and touched my chin, tilting my face towards her own. Her fingers were gentle, but her expression was practical.

'Peter helps her in that library every day, it seems. Let's try this tomorrow, when he can warn us afore she finishes her work. We must take care not to vex her.'

I shrugged carelessly, but nodded. I could hardly deny Cicely's common sense. She mustn't risk her own position either. She could set aside time to pose for me when she finished cleaning the chamber with her usual efficiency before Mistress Roberts would expect her to move to the next room. But if she was caught simply sitting when she was supposed to be working, the consequences might be as serious for her as for me.

* * *

That evening, when Sir Henry came to the chamber to read aloud with Lady Mary, I listened carefully to their conversation from my truckle bed. They never paid me any mind after they thought me asleep, no more than one of milord's spaniels dozing on a cushion. But I was coming to realise that paying attention to my new mistress's passions might be the key to pursuing my own.

'Is your library growing to your satisfaction, my dear?' Sir Henry's voice was hopeful.

'I have almost completed my record of both the existing books and the new ones that have arrived, so that we may easily locate any volume in the collection. Thank you, Henry, for supporting this endeavour.' It seemed books could always be counted on to excite Lady Mary's enthusiasm. At least Sir Henry understood this was one way to connect with his new wife. But I reminded myself that if she had almost completed her work in the library, I couldn't count on the same expanse of time to myself in the afternoons. It would be important to rely on Peter's watchful eyes.

'Let me read to you from the newest arrival, which I have longed to share with you – Marguerite de Navarre's *L'Heptaméron*!'

Sir Henry and his lady often read aloud to each other for more than an hour each evening, in language so fanciful that it seemed scarcely to be the same English as the *New Herball* that my lady had taught me to read for myself. Instead of words that described natural life, the passages sounded more like musical notes lacking melodies – obscure meanings without a tune. But this book wasn't in English at all, but French! The oddly sputtering sound of the language brought back memories of attending my first lady in Paris. Because I could understand none of the words, I soon fell asleep with eager thoughts of my return to drawing.

The next afternoon, while Cicely attended with extra vigour to the cleaning of the chamber, I opened the starflower box given to me by my father and pulled out the quill and inkpot Mum had purchased. I seated my friend beside the window so the afternoon sunlight angled onto her face. Then I perched on a chair and dipped my pen into ink for the first time since returning to Wilton. My hand gained assurance as I drew the arc of Cicely's forehead and soft cheeks, the gleaming knot of hair resting on the nape of her neck. Pleasure flowed from the tip of the quill, rendering the lines of Cicely's features and then the slope of her shoulders, the curve of her arms that had so often brought me comfort, down to the hands clasped loosely in her lap. I had lost all sense of the passage of time when the spell was broken by a soft knock on the door.

I opened the door to find Peter smiling down at me expectantly. I shook my head. I could tell he wished to be invited in to watch the progress of the sketch, but I was adamant. This was between myself and Cicely.

'Well,' he said, stepping back, 'our lady will be returning to her chamber within the hour.'

'He means well, he does,' Cicely assured me as I took my seat. We still had a little time to work. 'And one day, mayhap ye'll think on him in a new way.' She laughed at my evident surprise. 'Can ye not tell he likes thee, girl?' I had never thought of him that way. Since my first days of service, all my affection and trust had resided with Cicely, not her brother.

What drew me to him was all the ways he reminded me of her.

Romance must have been on her mind, for a few minutes later there crept into her face an expression I hadn't seen before. She looked almost gleeful, like one of the nymphs whose statues surrounded the fountain in the courtyard, brimming with delight. 'Aye, it happens that way.' When I raised my eyebrows, she actually blushed, and I saw the glow overtaking her cheeks. Hastily I pulled out a piece of red chalk and smoothed it gently against my rendition of her face.

''Tis Toby,' she admitted.

I dropped the chalk as my heart sank. 'Sir Henry's valet? Are you serious?' Lean and stealthy, with the fleeting focus of a wild fox. 'Whatever do you see in him?'

'He's been courting me awhile. At first I paid him no mind, but he wouldn't stop.' As she spoke of him, telling how he had captured her favour with those bunches of wildflowers, she suddenly seemed older – and apart. All at once, I saw her outside the frame of those shared confidences I so treasured.

'Do you like *him* in that *new way*?' I couldn't fathom the attraction. Spirited Cicely and slippery Toby? Apparently so. His attentions had edged out the other suitors, including Brian, the groom with the liveliest eyes and merriest laugh.

'Toby don't put on airs. Also, I can make him smile.' My friend must have caught my scepticism, for she stood now and smoothed her kirtle. 'Never mind me idle talk,' she murmured. 'We must be gone.'

Deflated, I slid my sketch into the starflower box without a word. By the time Lady Mary returned to our chamber, I had moved the two chairs back into their usual places and was awaiting her arrival with a suitably impassive face.

On the day I received my first quarter's wages of ten shillings from Master Wilkins, Sir Henry called me into his presence. He gave me the same amount again.

'Your additional wages for the first quarter.'

I was alarmed. 'But I've naught to tell, my lord,' I protested. 'No drawings to show.'

'We shall be visiting the court this winter, and that is when I shall expect more news,' he explained. Then he added, 'Or no news at all.'

Chapter Twelve

Mary, 1577

The best writing, like successful alchemy, is about wholeness, Philip had told her. Missing Ambrosia with the dull ache that still darkened each morning's awakening, Mary knew herself to be deficient. Insufficient. But she was prepared to embark on any experiment that might satisfy her yearning for completion.

The moment she had glimpsed the symbols of alchemy covering the black walnut box in Lady Catherine's cabinet, excitement had coursed through her body, fizzing like the chemical reaction she had observed in Walter's still-room. But she had forced herself to set the box aside for Rose to take to the library. She understood, all too well, that she needed to act the part of lady of the great house with her new maidservant.

In their first weeks together, Rose had seemed notably unresponsive to praise, unwilling to warm to her new mistress.

Mary still couldn't fathom why her husband seemed so taken with her. She would need to pay careful mind to this girl, whose competence with Mary's wardrobe couldn't be gainsaid, and yet whose reticence made it difficult to establish the type of friendly rapport that she had observed between her own mother and her maids. The girl seemed almost to harbour a secret grudge.

Mary considered dismissing her from service. That would be one way to eliminate this unsettling reminder of her predecessor's influence over the staff.

More like Lettice than you to choose dismissal as a solution. Find a way to connect with the girl. Ambrosia's quiet voice in her head.

Indeed, Mary sensed that, on a practical level, Rose's quiet capability might be the perfect complement to Adrian's more flamboyant style in the still-room. But there was more to do as mistress of Wilton before she could think of practising alchemy.

Every morning she studied the management of the Pembroke household and holdings under the tutelage of Steward Wilkins. Growing up, Mary had readily mastered any subject she was set, from classics and languages to history and music. She was determined that learning to be mistress of Wilton would be no exception.

Every afternoon, now that the library was in order, she worked on the Psalms, fashioning literal translations from the Hebrew into English poetry and revising drafts into polished verses, equally absorbed in both sides of the task of composition. Philip's words about alchemy returned to her as she worked. *Each stage encompasses all the ingredients of the previous stages, transformed.*

Her brother wrote to her frequently from court, where his star was rapidly rising. He sent pages from his *Arcadia* for her to read and mark with her thoughts until they could once more work together. 'These characters need your eye!' he wrote in a hasty scrawl that accompanied one packet. Warmed by the collaborative process, she eagerly jotted her notes in the margins.

With so much to occupy her attention, Mary relegated reviving the still-room to the back of her mind. But every evening she spent reading the volumes of Paracelsus Walter had given her, familiarising herself with the aims and precepts of alchemical production. She also studied the books of remedies she had received from her mother, prescribing courses of treatment as well as preventatives for various ailments, along with appropriate dosages of tinctures and cordials.

Autumn had chilled the air and brightened the leaves on the trees bordering the Wilton gardens before she finally penned a letter requesting the services of Adrian Gilbert as her alchemical assistant. After sending off the missive, she placed the black walnut box before her, almost formally, on her desk in the library. She had waited long enough. Fingering the small gold key, topped by its alchemical symbol, Mary unlocked the box and lifted the lid, breathing in a fragrance of dried rosemary needles.

A face met her gaze. The drawing, atop a sheaf of papers neatly bound in black string, could only be her husband's late wife, whose features looked down upon her every day from the full-length portrait on the library wall. But this was a younger Lady Catherine, her hair punctuated with tiny red blossoms, her eyes bright with life. So knowing, those eyes, and so kind. How could she compete with this presence who could never age or disappoint anyone now?

Mary looked in vain for a signature. She could ask Henry, of course, but she didn't want to remind him unnecessarily of Catherine by showing him the drawing, although he had surely seen it before. Untying the string, she flipped through the packet and discovered that many of the remedies, written out in a flowing hand that she assumed to be Catherine's, were matched with pen-and-ink drawings of the herbs they listed. Yet if Catherine had been the artist who sketched the herbs, who had drawn Catherine?

Looking again at the portrait, Mary noticed what she had not seen at first – tiny alchemical symbols lurking in the shadows of the delicate lace collar that fronted Catherine's garment, seemingly a night-chemise. Clearly the shadow symbols were an invention of the artist's fancy, since no lace could hold such characters. But who would Lady Catherine have permitted to see her in any state except fully gowned, even in illness?

Mary turned back to the first page of the sheaf of remedies. *Receipts gathered by Catherine Talbot Herbert, lady alchemist, with drawings by Rose Commin, artist.*

Rose Commin! Her maidservant – no common rose, but an artist of some skill. But surely the portraitist must have been someone else, for the hand conveyed a level of insight into the subject no mere girl could have possessed. Nonetheless, the sketches of herbs were remarkably accomplished. Why had Henry not mentioned this?

She returned to her examination of the contents of the box. Tucked beside the sheaf of remedies was a folded sheet of paper, sealed with red wax – in the shape of an ouroboros. Mary touched her own gold ouroboros ring. An odd coincidence. She picked up the letter. It was addressed, in the same flowing hand, *To the next Cleopatra*.

Why? What did that antique Egyptian queen have to do with Lady Catherine? Or with her, for that matter?

Then she remembered that Philip had mentioned one of the earliest practitioners of alchemy – a third-century woman called Cleopatra the Alchemist. 'So there is ancient precedent for lady alchemists, dear sister!' She could hear his voice again, feel his fervour flash like sparks from Walter's athanor. But why would a letter addressed *To the next Cleopatra*, whoever she was, be resting in this box?

The only way to find out was to open the letter. Surely taking over Catherine's practice of alchemy meant that in inheriting her predecessor's space, she also inherited the responsibility to oversee and comprehend the contents of the box of recipes that included this letter. Excitement fizzed again, just as on her first visit to the attic still-room. She felt almost like a girl once more, puzzling out a conundrum set by Philip for her and Ambrosia to solve. And with that memory, her heart was seized again by *the knot that anguish ties*, as she herself had put it in one of her Psalm translations.

Just as she broke the seal, there was a knock at the door. When she spoke her permission to enter, it was Rose who appeared. Mary slipped the letter back in the box and closed it before Rose could approach the table. 'Pardon, my lady. It's time for me to dress you for dinner.'

Of course. Where had the time gone? 'Thank you, Rose. Give me a moment.'

The maid curtsied and departed, her face revealing nothing. What would it take to set this girl alight? Had Mary herself been too distant? Perhaps she had been too demanding in these first months at Wilton, caught up in learning her responsibilities as mistress of the household. And yet – surely it was neither necessary nor appropriate for her to be on friendly terms with a maidservant.

But when had she ever been concerned with the appropriate? Then, with a sharp intake of breath, she was struck by the obvious. It was the coincidence of age between Rose and Ambrosia that had put her off from the start, when the girl's presence had served only to recall the ache of her sister's absence. Why was this girl alive and her sister dead?

But it wasn't fair to take against Rose because she no longer had Ambrosia. As Rose combed out her hair before dinner, Mary met her servant's eyes in the mirror with, she hoped, no pretence at authority. To her surprise, Rose returned her gaze.

That night, Henry joined Mary in her bed for the fourth time that month. 'My mother eagerly anticipates an heir,' he had explained on the first occasion. 'I know this is new to you, and I shall be as gentle as I can.' That initial coupling had been painful – an unpleasant matter of insertion and withdrawal – but quickly over. She couldn't help wondering if it might have felt different with another man – if Philip's good friend had stepped forward as his sister's suitor instead. But the second son of a third marriage had no family standing to command her father's interest. And as to her own interest, by the time Walter had sent that unsettling letter she was already betrothed. No point in speculating about unattainable pleasures now – no *ignis* here.

Observing her discomfort that first time, Henry had introduced a pot of ointment on the second occasion, prepared by Catherine for such needs. Mary hadn't expected to profit from the products of alchemy so soon, but in this matter she was grateful for her predecessor's expertise.

Henry's visits never took long, leaving Mary alone in her bed. Tonight, she allowed herself to imagine what it might have been like to have Walter beside her. His touch, however brief, had shimmered her being. Fingers dipping into her cleft, Mary recalled the glistening surface of the Penshurst pond at night, silvered by moonlight.

The next morning, Henry's mood was buoyant. Over breakfast, he repeated a jest Mary had heard before – that his late father, the first Earl of Pembroke, would have declared, 'The sooner you can pop out a babbie, the better.' Henry's imitation of his father's broad Welsh accent reminded her of Jake, and that first kiss atop Ludlow Castle, overlooking the border of Wales. But she was not amused by her husband's remark, even less so when Henry observed that his father had seen fit to comment on all aspects of his son's life.

'He warned me to keep an eye on my wife at court, for he predicted her beauty would draw men close, which might endanger her virtue.'

When Mary raised an eyebrow, Henry hastened to assure her that he saw marriage differently than his father. 'He spoke his mind with no regard for courtesy. There's a reason he was

156

known as Black Will – not simply for his hot temper, but for his tendency to offend.'

'I'm not sorry, then, that I missed the opportunity to meet him,' Mary observed tartly. In a gentler tone she added, 'I would have liked to meet your mother. I'm sorry she died before seeing you to manhood.'

When Henry's face softened, Mary ventured to broach the question that had troubled her since she had opened the walnut box the previous day. 'Why didn't you tell me that Rose supplied drawings for Catherine's remedies?'

Henry's eyebrows lifted. 'So you've seen them? I'm glad of that. I couldn't bring myself to look at them again after she died,' he confessed. 'I never valued those herbal drawings as greatly as Catherine did. I found some of them too fanciful. Rather than mentioning a skill I thought you'd have little use for, I wanted to emphasise Rose's loyalty to her first mistress as a valuable quality commending her to you.'

Too fanciful? Mary recalled the alchemical symbols hidden in the lacy shadows at Catherine's throat. Perhaps Rose had made that drawing after all. There was indeed more to that girl than met the eye. But she responded, 'I fear that her loyalty to Catherine may stand in the way of her service to me. She follows my direction obediently, but less than enthusiastically.'

'Give her time,' Henry urged again. 'I believe she can serve you well.'

If not her skill as an artist, what was it that Henry valued in the girl? Not for the first time, Mary resented the long shadow Catherine still cast over their marriage.

* * *

In December, Mary and Henry travelled to Baynard's Castle, the Herbert family's London home, to attend the Queen's Yuletide festivities. The imposing former palace overlooked the Thames, just a stone's throw from St Paul's Cathedral.

Knowing that Catherine had been much beloved by the Queen, who truly mourned her loss, Mary couldn't help dreading the visit. Her Majesty had been gracious enough when Mary had first been presented at Kenilworth, calling her a *daughter of very good hope*. She was not her parents' daughter now, though, but the young bride of a trusted counsellor to the Queen. What if the monarch responded to her as she herself had responded to Rose, convinced that the one who was alive in her presence could never replace the cherished other who was gone?

Henry's imperious stepmother, the Dowager Countess of Pembroke, had come to Wilton with the purpose of instructing her daughter-in-law on every detail of the forthcoming visit. Mary's first Christmas as the Countess of Pembroke was a glorious opportunity, her mother-in-law had assured her, to take her rightful place in court at Richmond Palace, the Queen's favoured winter dwelling, on the banks of the Thames upriver from Baynard's Castle.

'While you and I, Henry, may bring to her Royal Highness a sum of gold, as in past years,' Lady Anne had declared, fingering a jewelled brooch, 'Mary's first gift might be an embroidered doublet, fashioned by the seamstress to match one of the Queen's gowns of state. Her Majesty may look favourably upon a new lady in her retinue with an eye for fashion.' Catching her husband's acquiescent nod to his mother, Mary hadn't voiced her scepticism. Her experience at Kenilworth, where her uncle's spectacular display for the Queen had seriously depleted his coffers and gained him nothing, had taught her that court protocol required strategic gifts from courtiers. But perhaps a more original gift would prove more interesting to Her Majesty – something worthy of the *very good hope* the Queen had seen in her.

Mary found the social hive of the court both tedious and taxing. The fortnight of attendance at Richmond Palace proved more challenging than her first experience of court life at Kenilworth. No longer pestered by suitors, she now found herself the object of competitive glances directed at the new Countess of Pembroke by the other ladies. Lettice Devereux, on the other hand, was positively convivial, regularly seeking Mary's company as if they were friends. Was this because Lettice sought any occasion to bring herself to the attention of Mary's Uncle Robert, the Earl of Leicester?

The pleasantest part, also the hardest, was seeing Walter again. With Henry mostly in the company of senior members of the Privy Council, Mary was free to spend time with Walter, who, although a bachelor, was considered a safe companion thanks to his friendship with both the Sidney and Herbert families.

The memory of his kiss still lingered on her lips, but now Walter seemed the soul of courteous friendship, as if they had never shared more than a smile. Some days they walked in the Richmond gardens, Rose trailing behind them with her mistress's gloves and her own sketchbook. Walter's observations were invariably grandiloquent, but provocative.

'War begets quiet, quiet idleness, idleness disorder, disorder ruin,' Walter declaimed. 'But ruin in turn begets order, order virtue, virtue glory and good fortune.'

'So destruction initiates renewal,' Mary observed. 'Rather like the ouroboros.'

'Precisely!' The thrill of sparking minds, but no more than that.

Even more challenging than seeing Walter again was the seeming indifference of the Queen. Her Majesty acknowledged Sir Henry's presentation of his young wife civilly enough, and expressed her approval of his *satisfactory match*. But her imperious nod lacked the warmth or interest she showed to the other female courtiers. Henry's insistence that the Queen did indeed value Mary's presence as his wife did little to reassure her. She remembered the Queen's letter to her father upon her sister's death, assuring Mary's parents that *we will have a special care of her*. Where was that promise now? Dissolved, apparently, in unfavourable comparison to her husband's late wife, who the Queen had truly loved.

She accepted, reluctantly, that she couldn't outshine the memory of Catherine Herbert, neither with the Queen nor even, it appeared, her own maidservant. Yet, faced with what seemed to be a regal distance too great to bridge with the gift of an embroidered doublet, she was doubly determined to present a more worthy offering to Her Majesty. To her next audience with the Queen, she brought own voice.

When Elizabeth gestured her forward, Mary gathered her courage and took a breath. 'With Your Grace's permission, I'd like to offer a verse of the Psalmist.' The Queen raised an eyebrow, then nodded. With a glance, Mary summoned Rose, who was standing on the margins of the gathering of nobles in the Presence Chamber. The girl brought forward the instrument case and handed Mary her lute.

Across the constant murmur of voices, Mary opened her mouth and began to sing. The text was her own versification of Psalm 73, exploring the nature of goodness, which closed with the words of a soaring spirit singing of God:

> *O what is he will teach me climb the skies?*
> *No good on earth doth my desires detain,*
> *But cleave to God, my hopes in him to place,*
> *To sing his works while breath shall give me space.*

As she began, the burble of conversation in the Presence Chamber began to ebb. By the time she finished, complete silence surrounded her.

Queen Elizabeth had given Mary sharp-eyed attention as she sang. Now with the flicker of a smile, she spoke. 'I have heard that you and your brother are constructing livelier versions of the Psalms than provided by our common Psalter. I presume that you wrote these verses yourself?' At Mary's cautious nod, the Queen continued, 'Your words show me the spirit as a bird, which no other version offers. And your voice, singing God's works *while breath shall give you space*, renders the existence of the spirit in a material world. I like that, child. Very much. Too often we divorce spirit from matter, instead of recognising their interdependence.'

Murmurs of wonder at the monarch's approval eddied around them. Drawing Mary near, the Queen added, 'We shall exchange poems someday. Those of us who trust our voice to verse must listen to each other.'

Next she beckoned to the Earl of Pembroke. 'Your songbird has a voice worth listening to, Henry. I shall expect to see and hear her more often.'

That evening in Baynard's Castle, Mary expected, if not praise, then surely appreciation for her success. But Henry was furious.

'Never approach Her Majesty again without consulting me first,' he hissed. 'The court is a viper's pit, where any who steps forward may be shunned by others, no matter if it be in disregard of the Queen's favour or in response to it.' He paced the chamber, his face flushed with anger. 'You cannot imagine what opposing forces I must negotiate at court. I prefer working behind the scenes, not drawing all eyes to my affairs.'

Catching the hurt on Mary's face, Sir Henry paused and softened his tone. 'Your youth might explain your desire for attention, but I expect greater discretion from my wife. It is not your place to make decisions.'

Stunned at first, then frustrated, then infuriated, Mary didn't attempt a response. Pulling herself erect, she turned on her heel and swept from the chamber. The Queen had praised her Psalm, had valued her verse. But her husband had seen only a youthful *desire for attention*, as if her choice to sing had been simply a bid for fame and not a unique gift for the solitary Queen.

Shutting herself into the library, Mary buried her face in her hands, muffling the sobs she couldn't quell. Her first visit to court as the Countess of Pembroke had proved a disaster in every imaginable way. Blows to her pride. Hopes unmasked as delusions. And no one to turn to for comfort.

As her sobs subsided, she picked up a quill and sought the only comfort available to her.

She began to write.

CHAPTER THIRTEEN

Rose, 1577–78

I should have been excited at the prospect of accompanying Lady Mary to London to attend the Queen at Richmond Palace. How many country lasses wouldn't jump at the fairy-tale chance to spend Christmas at the royal court? But I was not eager to leave the comfort and familiarity of Wilton. And I could see that my mistress, too, had misgivings.

I quickly discovered that life as a servant at court was as trying as I had feared. Not yet fourteen, I was the youngest of the ladies' maids, and all the others treated me as a child of no consequence, even though I served a countess. As Cicely had guessed, the standing of the Countess of Pembroke, no matter how young, was higher than many of the other ladies, whose husbands ranked lower than earls – to think that I'd ever know such things! – but that only made their attendants try harder to show themselves better than me. I knew I was there to serve not only my mistress but my lord as well. I did not forget Sir Henry's commission to observe my lady's interaction with other courtiers and report back to him. My sketches were rendered in stitched-together fragments of borrowed time, and I took pride in using only a few lines to capture the essence of my subjects. Slyness figured in the arc of an eyebrow, greed in the pursed grimace of a mouth, elegance in the curve of a gentleman's bow or a lady's curtsey. Just impressions, really, for there were none who spent enough time with my mistress that I needed to remember what they said.

Indeed, hardly any of the courtiers who consorted with my lady were men. The circle of ladies at court was so busy and elaborate that few men penetrated the dense web of women's activities, which mostly involved gossip. I made a few sketches of my lady with her brother Philip and his friend Walter Raleigh. I couldn't help noticing that my lady's face came alight more readily when she was with Master Raleigh, but I knew my lord would not be interested in drawings of Lady Mary with her brother and their old friend. So when they walked in the Richmond Palace gardens, I focused my sketches on the beauty of the marvellous flower beds.

What I most observed was how much Lady Mary kept to herself, apparently not concerned to compete with the other ladies for attention. Sir Henry was at court as well, of course, but I saw that his own duties kept him so busy that he rarely spent time with his wife at the palace. That was when I glimpsed for myself how lonely she must be – a solitary spirit in the midst of the bustle of court business. She seemed to tolerate court affairs rather than embrace them. I wondered if she hated being at court as much as I did, and wished, as I did, to be invisible.

That is, until the afternoon she stepped forward and commanded all eyes and ears.

She directed me that morning to place her lute in its case and carry it with me when we travelled to Richmond from Baynard's. That day, she chose a gown of dark green – 'like the colour of your eyes, Rose!' – with a pale green bodice and deep purple sleeves, reminding me of flowering betony. As I dressed her, layer by layer, and pinned up her hair with jewelled clasps above a crisp white ruff, I couldn't help remembering that dressing Lady Catherine also called to mind a delicate flower coming into bloom. Even in illness and disappointment, her spirit couldn't be damped down. It suddenly struck me that Lady Mary, though younger and healthier, and burdened with different disappointments, was equally resolute. She was married to an older husband who apparently distrusted her beauty, separated from her own family in order to produce a family for the earl, probably not quite happy with her fate, but clearly determined to forge a path for herself.

'You look well, my lady,' I told her, and met her eyes in the mirror with a spontaneous smile – for the first time. She smiled back at me in surprise. Perhaps we surprised each other.

When we entered the Presence Chamber, I circled the edge of the room, keeping an eye on my mistress as she moved through the press of great ladies and gentlemen. I saw her approach Her Majesty with a question and receive a nod. Then she turned her head on that long, swan-like neck, as if she knew exactly where I was to be found. As soon as our eyes met, I found myself drawn to her side, unhindered by the crowd, no longer invisible but necessary. I knelt beside her, opened the instrument case and handed her the lute.

Lady Mary plucked the strings, then opened her mouth in song: '*O what is he will teach me climb the skies?*' – her voice so pure that unexpected tears sprang to my eyes – '*To sing his works while breath shall give me space.*'

The Queen's voice broke the breathless silence that followed. 'Your words show me the spirit as a bird.'

What a triumph! Rising to my feet with pride, I imagined a bird's-eye view of the Presence Chamber, surveying the awed and earth-bound courtiers. As I followed my mistress from the room, a leaf bobbing behind a swan, I looked around in vain for Sir Henry, certain that now he would appreciate his extraordinary wife.

But he did not. Instead, back at Baynard's, my lord punctured my lady's achievement.

His voice was all the harsher for being low. 'The court is a viper's pit!' I could hear his anger through the closed door to the chamber. 'I expect greater discretion from my wife.' Silence from my lady, then the door opened as she strode from the room. An exit worthy of a queen. Except that I could see, for the first time, she was more captive than queen.

Cicely was with child. Almost four months gone before she even told anyone.

Toby proposed marriage straightaway, but I believed Cicely deserved better. And I told her so. Which led to our first quarrel.

'Better than life as a servant's wife? Rose, thou'rt too young to understand that we must stay in the places appointed to us in this life.'

'What places do you mean?' My voice came out sharper than I had intended. But at thirteen, I didn't like being treated as a child – especially by someone not much older than myself.

Cicely frowned. 'I mean the places we're born to. Both me parents are in service. Peter thought to escape that by joining one of those sailing expeditions to the new world, but it only drove him back to service.'

'Why should our lives be determined by our parents' trades?' I thought of my grandfather the sheep farmer, shovelling manure from the pens, caring for creatures whose fleeces might clothe the finest in the land. My father the cloth merchant, fingering fabrics and frowning over his accounts, fearful of earning less than he spent. And what was my mother's *appointed place*? Healer or witch?

'You deserve better than that cozening varlet who got you with child,' I insisted.

But Cicely shook her head. 'He didn't cozen me, Rose. After tha left Wilton when Lady Catherine died, I lacked companionship, and Toby needed the same. He sought me out so many times, and I was flattered. No one else had ever needed me that much. Truth is, I managed to put him off long enough that he went a bit mad, handled me rough and then bawled over it – bawled! I'd never seen a man's tears afore. When I gave him the forgiveness he was begging for, it was as if I'd given him the moon, he was that happy. He swore he'd never lay a finger on me again. And when he came to me bed that night, mad with longing, I knew I could make him the happiest man in the world.'

Cicely fairly glowed. 'That day tha drew me portrait, I felt like a lady, Rose. Same age as our lady, I am, and luckier, I told meself. For I have a young suitor instead of an old husband.' Cicely took my hot cheeks between her palms, as if her touch could convince me. I wished her hands could stay just so.

'Dreaming of a lady's pleasure, I let Toby go further than I thought to, and soon I couldn't stop him – nor meself, either.' Then, with a blush, 'I found that a quiet man can flare brighter than a charmer.'

Her story confused me. I couldn't tell if it had been an accident or a choice. I certainly wasn't convinced that Toby was her heart's desire. But she persisted, though I couldn't help wondering if only by persuading me could she assure herself of this path.

'Me parents consider me lucky to have found a lad in service under the same roof. Even Peter believes that, wanting what's best for me.'

It was the resigned hope shading her voice that broke my heart. If she truly wanted to marry Toby, I should hear about *her* happiness, not just Toby's. Feel happiness myself. And I didn't.

No good could come from arguing further. Cicely had no more choices. And she had more than her own place to consider now. She would have the care of a child to occupy her. That, and the care of a husband. And with that I realised – she would always belong to others before me.

'It's no sin to be eager in love,' I overheard Mistress Roberts telling Sarah, the scullery maid, as I left Cicely's room and passed by the kitchen. 'They'll be married soon enough and that's what matters. So keep your snippy views to yourself, miss!' Sarah was always seeking occasion to speak ill of others – like the gossip about Mum's spells that she had tried to spread. I never liked Mistress Roberts better than that day.

One frigid midnight, as wind lashed the trees outside the window, I awoke with the sudden knowledge that Cicely was in trouble. Creeping from my truckle bed, I slipped down the stairs to the servants' quarters. I found Cicely curled into herself in her box bed, shaking and moaning. She had been overtaken by cramps that evening, after most of the household was asleep.

'She won't let me call for help,' Mistress Roberts whispered.

I had none of Mum's remedies at hand and no clue how to stop the dark oozings between Cicely's legs. Worst of all, I had no means to relieve her agony. It tortured me to hear her cry out with each fresh stab of pain, as if her insides were being twisted into impossible shapes, wringing out the new life she harboured deep within. Close to dawn, she gripped my hands fiercely and uttered a shriek as a small, dark mass slid from her body, followed by a sudden flow of bright new blood.

Terrified, I asked Mistress Roberts for permission to awaken Lady Mary, but Cicely shook her head, her face streaked with tears and sweat.

'Nowt to be done – the babe's gone now. No call to mither her ladyship. I must abide the loss on me own. 'Twas me own fault.'

How could it have been her fault? And where was her husband-to-be, who should be comforting her? But when I wanted to hunt him down, she told me to leave be.

I knew only to clean her with hot water and fresh linen cloths, and to help Mistress Roberts shift her onto a clean rush mat. I brewed a strong infusion of chamomile and sage that Mum had given me to lessen the pain of my own monthly courses, sweetening the tisane with honey to give her strength. Then I wrapped her warmly in her own quilt and stayed by her side until she finally drifted into sleep. What use were my fanciful drawings of herbal spirits? I asked myself bitterly. No use at all, to my dearest friend. I wept myself to sleep on the floor beside her mat.

I roused to find Lady Mary beside me, a partlet thrown over her night shift, her hair spilling unbound over her shoulders. I jumped to my feet, alarmed and embarrassed, but she laid a cool hand on my arm.

'I was concerned when I awoke to find you gone, but Mistress Roberts has explained what happened. Thank you for being here, Rose.'

'Rose cared for me, milady.' Cicely's voice was weak, her gratitude only piercing me more sharply with my own failure to help her as she needed.

'You must summon me at once when any in the household falls ill,' Lady Mary instructed Mistress Roberts. 'While I don't yet have Lady Catherine's skills, I do have her remedies, as well as books of recipes, which I have been studying closely and can apply as needed.'

Mistress Roberts bowed her head before my lady's calm

confidence. All through the household, from the steward down to the chambermaids, Lady Mary was slowly but surely earning the regard of each person who crossed her path.

As soon as I finished attending to my lady and dressing her, I hurried back to Cicely's side. 'You needn't marry Toby now!' But my voice was too jubilant, my relief too apparent. Cicely's face froze as if the icy season outside had penetrated our bond.

'Ye know nowt, Rose.' Her voice wasn't angry so much as resigned. Speaking from a place far away. 'Ye can't know how it feels to have a life inside – an' even worse, to lose a babe.' She turned away from me and wouldn't speak, even when I returned later in the day with a sketch of her face from happier times. What a fool I'd been. So happy that the marriage was no longer necessary that I'd not counted the cost of Cicely's loss. And thus lost my own dearest companion by my own fault.

I gave the sketch to Peter to save for her if she ever forgave me.

'I'm sorry Cicely lost her babe,' Lady Mary told me that afternoon in the library. 'I sense that you blame yourself, because you were there. I don't believe I could have prevented that outcome any more than you, Rose. Loss cannot always be evaded. But learning can bring greater success at treating what goes wrong, and sometimes preventing it. And I mean for us to learn together.'

How could we possibly learn together? A countess and a maid? Seeing my scepticism, my lady only nodded. Then she opened the black walnut box, which I had brought from the still-room, and I caught my breath. Both of us looked down upon my drawing of Lady Catherine, sitting atop the sheaf of remedies. I flinched at my stupidity. Wanting to celebrate my lady's spirit, I had instead exposed our bond to another's gaze. Now I waited for her rebuke.

She spread out several of my more fanciful drawings of herbs on the library table, where, surrounding the enlarged first letter of the plant's name, I had sketched my vision of spirits conveying that herb's capacity for healing.

'Did Lady Catherine request these interpretive representations of the natural world?'

I could not read her tone of voice. At a loss, I attempted a hesitant explanation.

'I first learnt the uses of each herb from my mother – she is an accomplished herbalist in our village – and next from *A New Herball*, which I used to read aloud to my – to Lady Catherine.' My old mistress's face stared up at us from the stack of drawings.

Lady Mary said nothing. That wasn't what she wanted to know. I would have been better off simply saying 'No' and holding my tongue.

'What of the spirits?' she asked quietly.

Taking a breath, I began again. 'Lady Catherine asked me to draw images of the herbs to accompany her collection of remedies – the way William Turner's book includes illustrations.'

'There's nothing like this in Turner's volumes,' she replied, holding up my sketch of the chamomile blossom, accompanied by a tiny figure stretching at ease in the curve of the letter *C* and another figure extending a helping hand to raise the reclining figure. Nothing to be gained by hedging or denying. I swallowed hard.

'I imagine spirits for each herb that illustrate its healing properties. Thinking of the herb, the figure takes shape beneath my pen. *Chamomile in subtleness is like the rose. It is good against weariness, assuages aches, and unbends and looses what is stretched out.*' To my surprise, I found myself speaking words I had memorised from *A New Herball*, hearing my own voice reading aloud to Lady Catherine.

'Ah – so your drawing interprets the benefits?'

'One of the benefits, milady.' I didn't want her to think I had no understanding of the variety of uses for each herb. 'Lady Catherine told me to draw whatever connections struck me. She said we could choose the best sketch to include with each remedy later on. She believed we would be working together on this for a long time—' At that, my voice broke. I couldn't help it. But Lady Mary didn't seem to notice.

'And the drawing of Lady Catherine herself – what did she think about this?'

'She never saw that one, milady. She never knew I drew her face.' By now my own face was wet with tears. 'I saved my drawings, and after she was gone, I put one with the remedies, to honour her spirit.'

Lady Mary was silent for a long time. But it wasn't the uncomfortable silence of someone who doesn't know what to say next. It was the listening silence of one who hears the unsaid. When she replied, she looked not at me, but down at Lady Catherine.

'When I first saw this, I thought it could not have come from the hand of an artist as young as yourself. But after looking closely at the other drawings in the collection, I've come to appreciate your gift for producing images where the imagined coexists with the visible.' Now she looked up at me and smiled. 'I look forward to seeing your skill as an artist continue to evolve. Perhaps, in time, you will share more of your drawings with me. I'm interested in connections between the material and spiritual worlds. Your sketches render the possibilities in fresh and surprising terms.' She tapped a fingertip on the sketch of Lady Catherine. 'I'd like to have this one framed and hung in the still-room. *To honour her spirit*, to use your own words, Rose.'

In her mouth, my own words sounded eloquent. That was when I understood what I had, finally, to do. Tugging on the leather thong about my neck, I pulled out my first lady's token from beneath my smock and closed my fingers around it. Then I held it out towards my mistress and opened my hand. Lady Mary leant forward to see the pendant resting in my palm.

'An ouroboros,' she breathed out, the word only a whisper. Her gaze met mine and comprehension flared. 'Lady Catherine's seal.'

As I tucked it back out of sight, she nodded. Then, to my surprise, she touched my shoulder.

'I admit that I didn't welcome your presence when I first arrived at Wilton, Rose. I'm sorry for that now.' Her frank speech shocked me. Not simply because she was speaking what she felt, but because she had decided that a servant – me! – deserved an apology.

'It's difficult for me to say this. Still, I believe in using words not just for facts, but for truths that need to be acknowledged, however uncomfortable.' Her grey eyes no longer reminded me of river rocks but of the Stones, mysterious and arresting. 'My sister Ambrosia, who died almost three years ago, was the same age as you.' She took a deep breath and continued. 'What can I tell you but the truth? Seeing you, and knowing I'd never see her here, knotted my anguish all over again.'

Still, I had no words to offer. She wasn't the only one who had lost someone she loved. I remembered my first lady's kind eyes and voice. I saw Cicely's tear-streaked face and her sorrowful glare.

'I've had to find another way of regarding you – for yourself, without comparing you to my sister.' Lady Mary held my gaze without wavering, and I knew what must follow even before she spoke. 'All I ask in return is that you find a way of regarding me for myself, without comparison to your previous mistress.'

Another long silence fell. This countess had glimpsed what I'd thought to keep hidden. She had measured my loss through hers. Her request for something *in return* was a challenge. And a revelation. Perhaps Lady Catherine was right. *Wholeness may arise from fragments pieced together aright.*

I nodded. And in so doing, I accepted Mary Sidney Herbert as my lady.

INTERLUDE: THE STARS

Joan Commin

The stars govern our fates. Simon's voice runs through her head. Long gone now, that stargazer, but not a day passes when she can't summon his words at will. *We cannot control our own destinies any more than flowers choose when to bloom or when to wither. All we can do is pay attention to the stars.*

Now, wrestling with what to tell her daughter, Joan looks to the stars, and the lessons from her husband's apprentice, to decide which parts of her story she dares to share.

As a watery ray of moonlight slides through the mottled pane of glass, Joan slips quietly from her bed, careful not to rouse her sleeping husband. She pads across the smooth dirt floor of the cottage, her toes curling against the dried rushes that she'll sweep up in the morning before scattering new ones to preserve the fragrance of the home. Diligent housework secures time to spend on her craft when her husband is at market with his clothwares. But sometimes she must work through the depths of the night. She's out the cottage door and into the garden now while her family sleeps.

Harvest hyssop by the light of the waning moon. Simon's voice again. But four years ago Lady Catherine needed a remedy right away, so Joan didn't wait, gathering the herbs under a new moon. And Lady Catherine died. Even though Joan lit candles at each of the cardinal points, spoke the healing incantations. She defied the warnings of her husband, and to no avail. The blackness of that failure covers her dreams like ash.

But no setback – or label of *witch* – can erase her resolve to practise the healing arts. Still she labours, healing at least some of those who seek her help. In her garden, powerful herbs bloom alongside innocent flowers, masking her work more effectively than any hidden corner plot.

She is again seeking hyssop, this time for herself. Not to relieve the body, but to purify the darkness that stains her soul.

Joan's mother taught her the skills of herbal medicine – so well that the merchant Martin Commin had sought her hand.

'I sell folk what they *need* – cloth for garments at prices they can afford,' he told her father, and often proudly recalled the words of his suit, though they only served to confirm for Joan the purely practical nature of the match. 'Joan has what they *want* – herbals for ailments, cures for complaints. I can sell those remedies for a tidy profit. Together, we can grow a business that will support a family.' Martin was full of plans when he wooed her, and at sixteen, Joan was willing to abide by her father's choice of a husband, even one ten years her senior, because, well, no one else had come calling for her. After a childhood spent watching her father toil over his sheep while observing her mother's magic with plants, it made her happy to work with herbs for her livelihood. She pleased her husband by agreeing to his request that she also take on the training of his sixteen-year-old apprentice, Simon.

'He's a quick learner is Simon. He's worked for me ever since his father died. We can use the extra pair of hands in planting and harvesting your herbs while I attend to the cloths.' Martin was a planner, not a dreamer. Each choice either added to or subtracted from the sums in his account books. Instructing Simon to work with Joan, like the marriage itself, was a business decision.

Joan remembers her first sight of the lad, his untidy curls the colour of the earth in her garden, his eyes the deep green of fresh bay leaves. He watched her, unblinking, when Martin introduced them, then gave a slight bow that somehow managed to convey great confidence. Who does he think he is? she asked herself, a smile of amusement playing on her lips. Unexpectedly, he smiled back.

Simon Forman was his name – from Quidhampton, near Salisbury, he told her. He went on without needing any invitation to relate the entire story of his early life. What struck Joan from the start was Simon's passion for learning. Son of an embittered bankrupt and a mother who regularly beat him, he escaped into his studies at the local grammar school, then at the free school in Salisbury. When Simon was twelve his father died, his schooling ended, and he was apprenticed to Martin.

'I know something of the healing properties of plants, but

Master Commin says book-learning isn't enough.' Joan was suddenly aware of her own inability to read, which hadn't seemed a hindrance until that moment. Simon told her that he studied the stars and believed they governed everything from humans to plants. 'The cycles in the astral world and the natural world correspond,' he explained. She had no idea what he meant at first, but over those early weeks, they came to appreciate each other's passions.

Joan thinks, now, that she should have known better than to listen to a stargazer. But she was just married and eager to satisfy her new husband. Customers who came to his stall in the Salisbury market for fabric stayed to peruse the herbals, and increasingly the other way round. Sales for both wares improved every season. The more closely Simon worked with Joan, the more the business grew. Life seemed brighter, for a while.

Joan moves to the plot of hyssop, her footsteps sure in the shadows. Kneeling, she brushes her fingers up each hairy stem until they reach the clustering blooms. Quickly, she pinches a few of them off and places them in her basket. Inhaling the sweet, woody fragrance of the herb, she lifts her face to the waning moon and offers a prayer for purity and forgiveness.

As Joan retraces her steps to the cottage, the high, mournful notes of a nightingale, punctuated by its chattering refrain, spray the darkness. Then she's inside, and alone once more.

Even when we cannot see them, the stars light our path, Simon had assured her. But can she still find her way?

PART TWO: 1578–1603

ALBEDO *(solutio/ablutio)*: the pure, white stage, representing cleansing, washing, purification.

CHAPTER FOURTEEN

Mary, 1578–79

The coachman turned his team into a wide lane fronting the Thames and drew up outside a sturdy brick mansion. The wind off the river chilled Mary through her thick wool cloak as she descended from the carriage. She was here at the invitation of the illustrious Doctor Dee – astrologer, alchemist, seer, advisor to the Queen and a controversial figure in a court divided between doubters and disciples. Curiosity and trepidation warred within her.

Her husband's anger at Mary's presumption in singing for the Queen had shaken her confidence, and the fact that she had not been summoned in response to the chambermaid's miscarriage sharpened her awareness that her own knowledge was insufficient. It might be a while before she could truly be the mistress that Wilton required, but she was determined to investigate every opportunity. And resolved not to seek Henry's permission to make this journey.

Walter had introduced Mary to John Dee the previous month, during the Yuletide festivities at Richmond Palace. The magus was tall and slender, with fine white hair, haunting amber eyes and a white beard twisting down from his chin, garbed in a long gown with hanging sleeves. Mary suppressed a smile, as he put her in mind of Merlin, wizard of the Round Table.

'Your mother has been a generous patron,' Doctor Dee said, kissing her hand. 'And your brother, of course, is a student of mine. A bright lad, though perhaps better suited to the pen than the alembic – as his misadventures in the still-room with our friend here can attest.'

Walter laughed, a bit too heartily, and changed the subject. 'Like Philip, Mary has a great interest in alchemy, as well as the confluence of the natural and supernatural.'

'Splendid!' exclaimed the doctor, and immediately invited Mary to visit him at his home and laboratory in Mortlake, a few miles upriver from London. Mary declined Walter's offer to accompany her. This investigation she would conduct on her own. On a cold, clear January day, when Henry was once again closeted with the Privy Council at Whitehall, she sent for her coach.

Now, Mary looked up at the house, from whose peaked roof smoke curled up into the sky – insubstantial and enticing, suggestive of secrets that might escape the confines of solid walls. She thought of Rose's drawings of invisible spirits attending each herb in nature. Might there indeed be truths not visible to her own eye?

The door was opened by a buxom young woman with flushed red cheeks, hands resting serenely on a swelling belly. Without a word, she led the visitor up several flights to a room beneath the peaked roof, protected by two sets of doors. These she unlocked in turn, ushered Mary in and departed.

The room was suffused with pale winter sunlight. Sturdy shelves lined the walls, overflowing with books of various sizes and a bewildering array of objects, from coloured gemstones to golden scales, crystal flasks to porcelain pots. More books were piled on the desk, the floor and the window seat, almost as if multiplying of their own volition, Mary thought. On a stand in front of one window was a great crystalline sphere, shielded from the light by a thick curtain. Beside it rested an obsidian mirror, its surface an opaque blackness. Gazing into it, wearing the same flowing robe she had met him in, stood John Dee.

He turned as Mary entered. 'My wife, Jane,' he said in brief explanation as the young woman closed the door behind her. A wife perhaps thirty years younger than her husband, Mary thought – like herself, and pregnant, her own destiny as well.

'I see you wear an ouroboros on your finger,' he stated, approaching and taking her hand. 'Regeneration in a single round.' Locking long fingers around his smoky beard, he continued, his voice coloured with the Welsh lilt she associated with her years at Ludlow Castle. 'I sense that you're a voyager.'

'I seek to gain more facility in the production of medicines in the still-room,' she began. But that offered only a truncated explanation of her interest in meeting with this man. What she sought to probe was the elusive boundary between the natural and the supernatural, the material and the spiritual. Of course she had her doubts, fuelled by the rumours of sorcery associated with his name at court. But rumours are not facts, and she pushed forward as resolutely as making her way through a hedge maze. Follow each turn to the heart of the labyrinth.

'Do you really converse with angels?'

The man's eyes widened slightly in surprise. She hadn't intended to question the doctor so bluntly, but her doubts were coming to a head.

'Indeed I do,' he replied calmly, a small smile curling his lip. 'It's all a matter of concentrating the angelic light – which is the purpose of my showstone.' He beckoned her to the window and drew aside the curtain. The crystal sphere captured a shaft of sunlight and cast a gleaming rainbow upon the floor. *Angelic light?*

'That looks like natural light to me.' Another blunt challenge, to which the magus only nodded.

'Only scryers can see the visions produced by the angelic light that rides the sun's rays.'

Mary was not convinced. 'And how does all this connect to alchemy?'

'The goal of alchemy is a state of spiritual perfection, represented on the material level by a transmutation of base metals into gold or, if we look to Paracelsus, by a transmutation of minerals into medicines – all of which aim to achieve the power of the Philosopher's Stone, which can perfect all that comes into contact with it.'

Mary remembered her sceptical response to Walter's similar claim, that alchemy was *more than a matter of physical transmutation*. But perhaps there was truth in it after all. The doctor held her gaze.

'At a core level of existence, the material manifests the spiritual. For those who have eyes to see, angels walk among us every day.'

Suddenly, she was driven by an urgency deeper than intellectual knowledge, no longer able to contain her longing.

'Shall I ever again speak with my sister?' she blurted and fell silent, a blush flooding her face.

'I cannot speak for other spirits,' the magus answered quietly. 'But I can tell you that eternal truths are attainable. Your work on the Psalms surely indicates as much.' So he knew of this, too. Indeed, the Psalms brought Ambrosia close, reassuring Mary that her sister's spirit could hear her words.

'Such learning is not without risk,' he continued. 'Remember, in charting your voyage, not to lose sight of your coexistence with the spirit world.' His tapered fingers brushed Mary's forehead in what seemed almost a benediction. 'I wish you well in your journey.' And with that, Mary's interview with the astrologer was over.

Before moving to the door, Mary gazed into the obsidian mirror, its face a well of utter blackness. The afternoon sunlight striking its surface was swallowed by darkness. But beside it, the crystalline globe gleamed with light.

For those who have eyes to see . . . eternal truths are attainable. Just who was this man – sublime mystic or slightly mad? Or both? All that winter the magus's tantalising promise circled around the opening words of Lady Catherine's letter *To the next Cleopatra*:

Wholeness may arise from fragments pieced together aright.

The lessons of alchemy – comforting but useless. In her everyday world, *wholeness* was an ephemera.

Since Henry's harsh reprimand after she had sung for the Queen, their exchanges had remained stiff and cool. Philip had responded to her letter of outrage with practical sympathy.

I am most happy that the Queen appreciated your Psalm, my sister. And I regret that Henry responded otherwise. But your husband has a long history with Her Majesty, and it would be wise for you to defer to his experience. Don't let one storm disrupt your path together.

Mary recognised that she could be impetuous when excited and volatile when provoked, but she was certainly capable of strategic planning. After her striking debut at Richmond, she had become the object of both admiring eyes and spiteful tongues. She had since taken care not to be overly visible in the circle of ladies surrounding the Queen, contenting herself with private conversations with Lady Margaret, Countess of Cumberland, who alone among the ladies-in-waiting shared Mary's probing interest in alchemy. Mary knew that pursuing her twin passions for literary and scientific production required the support of her husband.

Still, she put off raising the subject for fear of a prickly response that might dash both those hopes. Then, one summer night, as a soft breeze played over the Wilton gardens and their evening reading had sweetened Henry's mood, Mary sat beside her husband on a stone bench beside the privet hedge and took his hand.

'Thanks to your encouragement, I plan to take up Catherine's mantle of alchemical production,' she began. 'On the advice of Philip and Walter Raleigh, I have been reading as many alchemical texts as I can.' She refrained from mentioning the controversial Doctor Dee.

'Raleigh seems to be taking a disproportionate interest in your pursuits,' Henry interjected. 'You hardly need his advice when you have your brother to consult. You need to watch your step with courtiers who find occasion to draw too close.'

Mary stiffened at the unexpected response. Unbidden, the warmth of Walter's kiss at Leicester House, the passion in the letter she had burnt, flooded her memory. Apparently Lettice Devereux had spoken truly in warning her to *never underestimate a man's capacity for jealousy*. But whatever Henry's power to regulate her behaviour, he could not contain her thoughts, or her desires.

Mary changed the subject, taking up another topic she had been intending to broach. Piecing the fragments together would have to wait.

'When a chambermaid at Wilton recently lost a baby to miscarriage, I keenly felt the absence of the family physician who, I understand, left your service shortly after Catherine's death. I would like to secure the services of a first-rate practitioner of Paracelsian medicine to join our household at Wilton.'

Henry's rigid stance softened. This suggestion, apparently, he was happy to embrace.

'Indeed, Mary, I had been considering that as well, but it slipped my mind. And I may know just the man. Doctor Thomas Moffett was educated at Cambridge and Basel and is newly returned to England as a practitioner of the Paracelsian system of treating disease with drugs. He would be an excellent choice. I'm very pleased that you've reminded me of the need. Tomorrow I will seek him out at court.'

Unexpectedly, Henry drew her into his arms and held her close to him for several breaths. Releasing her, he said, 'I have much to learn, myself, as the husband of such a gifted woman as you, Mary. I've often thought of what you said to me on our first day as husband and wife, about speaking together of matters of the heart as well as the mind. I admit I have failed in that, my dear, aware that my facility with words can't keep pace with yours.' He broke off with a sigh.

His next words came more slowly. 'Indeed, perhaps my response to your success in singing your Psalm to the Queen at Richmond was not as wholly about politics as I had convinced myself, but was also a matter of, well, envy. With a few lines of verse, you reached the Queen's heart as I haven't come close to doing in years of service at her court.' He reached out, then, and stroked her cheek tenderly. 'I'd like to see you flourish at your own pace, unhindered by – let me name them as such – my own uncertainties.'

Mary breathed an inward sigh of relief. For over a year she herself had been dogged by uncertainties as she worked diligently to master the household's manifold responsibilities and activities. Now, with the prospect of collaborating as closely in marriage with her husband as in literature with her brother, she felt ready to move forward more confidently.

Within a year, that confidence would be shaken.

From her mother, Mary had learnt that political survival depended not just on ambition but on level-headed planning for contingencies. That lesson was driven home in the sweltering summer of 1579, when first Henry, then Philip, incurred the Queen's wrath in the wake of ill-considered actions.

Henry had been summoned to Hampton Court, where the Privy Council was considering the implications, both diplomatic and religious, of the most recent marriage proposal to Her Majesty. The suitor was François, Duc d'Alençon, a French nobleman twenty-two years her junior whose attentions had, no doubt, flattered the ageing monarch. But the controversy over that issue was briefly overtaken by the public airing of a long-simmering scandal.

While Mary and Henry were at court, a secret closely kept from Elizabeth for many months finally reached the Queen's ear. Mary's uncle, Robert Dudley, Earl of Leicester, had married Lettice Devereux the previous autumn in a secret ceremony witnessed by only six family members and close friends. Henry had been one of the witnesses.

'Her Majesty feels betrayed,' Henry confided to Mary, 'as much by the secrecy as the marriage itself. Lettice has been banished from court and Robert, too, may never regain her favour.'

Mary could well understand the Queen's ire. Hadn't her uncle assiduously courted Elizabeth for years, abandoning his suit only after the fruitless royal entertainment at Kenilworth? And hadn't Lettice shamelessly pursued him even before the death of her husband, the Earl of Essex? Of course Her Majesty was incensed, implicated by association in the scandal that was now on every courtier's tongue. And Henry, too, was implicated by his tacit support of the marriage.

Mary could appreciate her husband's sense of loyalty. What she couldn't understand was the nature of Robert's bond with Lettice. Angler or catch? If angler, was Lettice the bait in a now-failed bid to hook the Queen, or the prized catch for whom he'd relinquish his own desire for a royal match? Or was Lettice the angler and Robert the catch? Whether enacting a tale of political advancement or true love, her uncle had never been faulted for pursuing his own ambitions. And yet his paramour had been counted the villain for pursuing the Queen's favourite. Too often, Mary reflected, a woman's path to power seemed to depend upon men. No wonder the Queen tired of, or toyed with, the ambitious pawns who surrounded her.

'When Robert asked me to support him in this move I was torn,' Henry admitted. 'But I was swayed by our long-time friendship and, to be honest, our new-found family connection, forged by my marriage to you. Now I fear the Queen will view my loyalty to your uncle as disloyalty to her.'

'I don't doubt Her Majesty will nurse her anger for a while,' Mary responded. 'But I'm sure she will recognise your duty to a friend – and kinsman – and forgive. Besides, the Queen depends too much on your good counsel. She won't let this episode disturb that bond.'

'I appreciate your support – and your clear-eyed analysis,' Henry said, taking her hand. He heaved a sigh, lines of weariness and age scoring his face. In this realm, she realised, her husband required more than tacit support from his wife. And henceforth, she vowed, he would receive it.

Soon afterwards, the Queen's fury fell upon another member of Mary's family – her brother. Always a risk-taker, Philip had taken the bold but foolhardy step of presuming to advise Her Majesty on the subject of the Duc d'Alençon's marriage proposal. In a letter, he sternly warned his sovereign of the dangers in marrying *a Frenchman and a Papist*, reminding her that Protestants *are your chief if not your sole strength*.

The Queen's response was instant and unforgiving. Philip was banished from her court and would remain so until such time as she saw fit to readmit him to her presence.

Mary lamented that Philip tended to burn bridges before seeking counsel. More of a daredevil than canny Walter Raleigh, Mary's brother had something to learn, she reflected, from his charming and equally ambitious friend.

For her own part, Mary was relieved to discover that Queen Elizabeth welcomed her without reference to the men in her family. On the contrary. One afternoon at court, Her Majesty called Mary to her side in the withdrawing room adjacent to the Presence Chamber and pressed a folded sheet of paper into her hand.

'I shared this verse with your mother once. Perhaps it will have meaning for you.'

Mary unfolded the paper. On it was a poem written in the Queen's own hand – the same hand she had seen when Elizabeth wrote to her father after Ambrosia's death, inviting Mary to court. But this was not the comforting voice of that sovereign. This voice lamented the impossibility of receiving comfort:

I grieve and dare not show my discontent;
I love and yet am forced to seem to hate;
I am and not; I freeze, and yet am burned,
Since from myself another self I turned.

That *other self* might easily be the Duc d'Alençon or the Earl of Leicester, thought Mary, refolding the paper and handing it back to the Queen. Or even one of Her Majesty's gentlewomen, some of whom, such as Mary's own mother, knew her more deeply than any man might hope to. If turning others from herself was the Queen's burden, the queenship must be lonely indeed. But no. That *other self* might be the Queen herself, obliged by her station to play a role that must deny the fullness of her spirit.

And why had she chosen to share this verse with Mary? Perhaps she'd heard of Henry's displeasure at his wife's unsanctioned boldness in singing before Her Majesty and sensed the strictures of Mary's own role. Clearly, a response was required.

'What I hear is solitude's necessity for survival.' Her Majesty gave a small, slow nod and placed a jewelled hand on Mary's own. 'Good. You have grasped half of my riddle-in-verse.' And with that, Mary's audience was at an end. *I am and not.* The Queen remained an enigma.

Just before departing from London, Mary received a letter from her brother, seeking permission to retire to Wilton House while in disfavour with the Queen. Mary was beginning to grasp, at first-hand, the truth of her mother's warnings about politics and her husband's harsh characterisation of court circles. In this game there were more losers than winners – including, thought Mary, the Queen herself, whose authority remained tied to the judgements of men.

When Philip arrived at Wilton to begin his exile, Henry offered him the use of nearby Ivychurch, a former abbey now leased by the Pembroke family, which Henry had converted into a dwelling house. The mottled stone walls, their mortar whimsically studded with seashells and traced with rambling roses and ivy, were counterpointed by the ponderous pillars standing guard over the ruins of the old cloisters. Surrounded by green meadows and giving a spectacular hillside view of the distant spires of Salisbury Cathedral, Ivychurch was at once a sacred space and a haven immersed in nature. There, brother and sister could read and write and speak together at length, far from the bustle of the household. Facing each other across adjacent writing desks, as they had done when working together on the Psalms, throughout the summer they shared ideas, sought one another's opinions, and offered challenges.

One grey, rain-soaked morning, as water streamed down the mullioned windows of the study, Philip put down the pen he had been chewing on. 'Sister, let me ask you something.' Mary placed her own pen in its brass well and looked up.

'I'd like your opinion of the characters in my *Arcadia* – as a woman.' At her questioning glance, he explained, 'Most romances have women readers. I want to write at once for a wide readership and for the most discerning of readers. That's why I write for your eyes.'

Mary's look was sceptical and amused. 'Who can write for all and for one at the same time? I can tell you that I read not *as a woman*, but as myself. In your romance, power resides in the hands of men. So it's the heroes who draw my attention, not the ladies.' She spoke earnestly, appreciating that she could think through her own reactions in expressing them aloud to him.

Philip pulled his notebook from his doublet to transcribe her thoughts. Mary was heartened – with Philip, there was never a limit to where the story might lead.

Later in the day, as the last storm clouds drifted down the valley, the siblings circled the ruins of the old cloisters, much as they had done in the precincts of Ludlow Castle, lost in their own thoughts.

Then Mary spoke. 'Philip, the contrast between your male and female characters that we talked about this morning raised a question for me. Why should men always take the lead in tales of romance and adventure? And that very question has given me an idea. I'd like to take on a story with a woman at the centre – perhaps a queen.' Philip's glance invited explanation. 'Not an imaginary queen in a fantastical world, but a real woman, facing the challenges of rule as well as the heartaches borne by all women.'

'If you're interested in writing about an actual queen,' Philip cautioned, 'I'd suggest choosing one from another country or even another era – a figure from the world stage who in no way resembles our own monarch. You must avoid a characterisation that implies any criticism of Her Majesty.'

Mary gave him a long look. 'Did you consider that danger in offering Her Majesty your counsel criticising her willingness to consider the marriage proposal of the Duc d'Alençon?'

Philip bowed his head, conceding the point, then gave her a wink. 'And yet, for all that she sent me away, Her Majesty turned down that proposal.'

'Have you considered that perhaps she never intended to marry him, but only wanted to rattle her overbearing male counsellors?' Mary took her brother by the wrist and gave his arm a little shake. 'How else is the Queen to maintain her authority, if not by challenging the assumptions of the men who surround her?'

Philip smiled ruefully. 'Well, Her Majesty has certainly put me in my place. So I intend to make the best of my enforced sojourn by continuing my tale of *Arcadia*. And thanks to you, I *will* reconsider the roles that women play in it.' The light in his eyes, and the eager shoving back of his curls from his face, reminded Mary of the times her brother would set a conundrum for her to solve. And the challenge in his response to her notion to write about a queen set her thinking.

A figure from the world stage. Mary grasped the thought eagerly. Why not a play? And in the next moment, the solution presented itself.

The English theatre did not offer much space for women in leading roles, not least because of the injunction against women appearing on the public stage. But the new vogue in France for 'humanist tragedy' had produced works on classical themes in which women often figured prominently. A volume containing Robert Garnier's *Marc Antoine* had recently been added to the Wilton library. And although the play was named for the male hero, its driving spirit was a woman.

Cleopatra.

As portrayed by classical authors such as Horace and Plutarch, the Egyptian queen was a marvel and a monster – a mistress of enchantment with the power to enslave the heroic Antony, her passion matched only by her ambition. Garnier's queen, by contrast, was no conniving temptress, nor a moral warning to other women, but a tragic heroine whose struggles could give Mary space to explore the questions of female power that she had been wrestling with since her arrival at court. What's more, in fashioning an English drama from the French example, she could conceive a queen who was also a wife and a mother, a lover and, not least, a hero.

Indeed, Mary realised, translation offered a venue, at once approved and subversive, for women authors to put their words into print. Under cover of linguistic paraphrase, original voices could be created, with the source text providing a starting point, a bridge rather than a cage. Moreover, as she and Philip had found with the Psalms, translation offered a way to create a work anew for English readers who might find no other passage into it.

Each 'day of the mind' spent with Philip at Ivychurch, walking the fields and writing in the study, was exhilarating. And when she returned to Wilton in the evenings, her creative energy invigorated her husband. They enjoyed more intimacy that summer than in their two years of marriage, as the coolness between them following Mary's Psalm offering for the Queen slowly melted away.

As summer waned, Mary found herself emptying her guts into a basin every morning. Her husband's open delight in her pregnancy matched her own secret joy in the conception of her first play. She fingered her ouroboros ring each morning. Could this be the *wholeness* Catherine had evoked in her letter?

CHAPTER FIFTEEN

Rose, 1579–80

Cicely married Toby on a blustery autumn day in a small ceremony in the Wilton chapel. I was still uneasy about the match, but she seemed happier than ever with him as they observed 'a proper term of courtship', as she put it with a twinkle in those cornflower-blue eyes.

Because her parents were in Yorkshire, Master Wilkins stood in for her father, even offering a little smile as he gave the bride away. As Cicely's bridesmaid, I held her chosen bouquet of flowers – a lovely cluster of pink and purple hydrangeas that filled me with dread. We had argued about the flowers, as well as almost everything else leading up to the wedding.

'Yes, they're beautiful, but they're poisonous, Cicely. Choose any other flower, I beg you.'

'Backend brides haven't many choices,' Cicely insisted. I knew that *backend* was simply a Yorkshire term for autumn, but I couldn't help hearing the word as a judgement on the marriage itself, forced from circumstances that were no longer true.

'They're not to be tasted, love, just summat to be seen.' Cicely stroked my arm, but I was not to be comforted. It wasn't really the flowers that concerned me, but her future. Of course no guests would eat the hydrangeas, which wouldn't be more deadly than apple seeds in any case. They offered just one more excuse to oppose the wedding.

'Why must you marry Toby when you're no longer pregnant?' The first time I asked her that had been too soon after she had lost the babe. It had taken time to regain our closeness after that misstep, and it wasn't until a week before the wedding that I ventured to pose the question once more. Anything to free her from what I was sure was a mistake. Her eyes overflowed at that and I bit my tongue.

'He means well, Rose, truly he does. He told me when we were 'trothed, he understood marrying me was what he wanted more than anything else. And he's stayed true. I cannot fault him for owt.'

'But you can start over now, Cicely,' I urged. 'Why not wait until you know if you truly love him?'

'I love that he loved the babe we made. I've no call to give backword on him now. He deserves better.'

You deserve better, I thought, but did not say. And so I carried her flowers and cheered with the other servants to celebrate their match, and shared in the wedding feast that

Cook Corbett had concocted – funded, I later discovered, from Mistress Roberts's own savings. But the sausages and sweetmeats were mud on my tongue.

Once Cicely and Toby commenced their married life, in a larger room in the servants' quarters, she and I had less opportunity for daily sharing. We still saw each other when we worked together in my lady's chamber, but Lady Mary kept me at her side for longer hours each day, helping her to organise the papers in the box of remedies.

Meanwhile, my lady's belly grew rounder by the week, though she didn't seem to pay much mind to her state, apart from its discomforts. Her attention was on Adrian Gilbert's slow resurrection of the still-room. Against his loud objection – ''Tis too much labour, my lady!' – she tartly instructed him to fit a window into what she called her athanor, the tall furnace that stood at the far end of the room. 'I plan to observe the effects of the fire and witness the colour changes that accompany each stage of transmutation.' I smiled to myself as Master Gilbert's reluctance melted into obedience under the heat of my lady's will.

Once she was too large to mount the stairs with ease, Lady Mary sent me to observe Master Gilbert's work in the still-room. 'While I'm confined, you are to keep an eye on Adrian and report to me the results of his experiments in the athanor. Paint what you see, so that I can witness it as well.'

Nothing would have pleased me more. I had seen some miraculous changes through the newly installed furnace window, as the raw materials blossomed into a rainbow of colour. But my lady was clearly blind to the problem posed by her command. I summoned my courage.

'My lady, I've never used paints or brushes, only pen and ink, shaded with chalk.' Growing up in the village I had gained access to pen and ink only because Da kept accounts of his sales. I'd been encouraged to put my gift into practice by drawing herbals for Lady Catherine. But I had never received training as an artist, never learnt how to mix pigments or apply paint to canvas.

A crimson flush spread over my lady's neck and cheeks as she recognised the gulf separating what we each took for granted. A lady would naturally learn the use of colour from her drawing lessons, but not a maidservant. As usual, Lady Mary identified a solution as soon as she glimpsed the problem.

'Henry has commissioned a talented young painter, Marcus Gheeraerts, to make a portrait of our family group after this baby arrives. He is much admired at court. When he comes to Wilton, I shall ask him to train you in the use of pigments.'

My eyes grew wide, and my lady's warmed with pleasure. After seeing the colour changes of alchemy, I'd begun to notice those colours in everything else. Flowers in the garden, threads in the tapestries, embroidery on my lady's gowns. And I wanted to capture all of it. But, 'Thank you, my lady,' was all I managed to say.

Yet for all of Lady Mary's passion for the changes within the athanor, I wondered at her seeming indifference to the changes happening in her own body. Were it not for the watchful care of the newest member of our household, the dapper and energetic Doctor Moffett, she would undoubtedly have supervised the work in the still-room herself. But the doctor was able to persuade her to limit her activities to reading and writing with her brother Philip.

Sir Henry took joy in his wife's robust health, and I marked the lightening of the darkness that had shadowed him during Lady Catherine's final illness. Once Lady Mary's condition prevented her from accompanying him on his visits to court, he called me aside and assured me that my charge to 'observe carefully' would continue, as would my additional wages. He had appreciated the drawings I made at Richmond – though he scowled over the sketches of my lady walking in the gardens with Walter Raleigh.

The closer I drew to Lady Mary, the more uncomfortable I felt in my role as spy. But I was grateful for the extra shillings, which had greatly improved my family's circumstances back in Amesbury. Da always had some new scheme for expanding the scope of his sales. As often as not, they didn't come cheap, so my wages sent home came in handy. At Mum's urging, I set some aside for myself every quarter.

As my lady's pregnancy entered its final weeks, Doctor Moffett advised Sir Henry to engage a midwife. And so my mother was summoned once again to Wilton. Mum wasn't trained in midwifery, but she had delivered enough babies to qualify as an expert. Had she not sent me to Lady Catherine, she would have trained me to assist her in childbirth as well as garden care, but my years away from Amesbury meant I'd never had a chance to see her deliver a baby, let alone help her in the task. Sir Henry trusted her to attend his new wife because of the comfort she had brought to Lady Catherine. Yet even his high esteem couldn't quash the dark whispers scuttling like rats in the corners of the household.

Sarah was the cruellest. The spite that Mistress Roberts had kept her from venting against the pregnant Cicely she now directed at me. 'How comes your mum can pass as a healer, when she couldn't keep Lady Catherine alive?' she taunted. 'Surely it's a marvel Sir Henry allows her to attend our new lady's birthing, after harming that other babe.'

Without thinking, I launched myself at her sneering face, landing a punch dead centre in that poisonous mouth and splitting both her lip and my knuckles. It was Peter who dragged me from her, holding me close and warning Sarah, 'Keep thy foul mouth closed in future, unless ye want Mistress Roberts to send thee packing for theft.' I knew Cicely had caught Sarah filching one of Lady Mary's lace handkerchiefs from the laundry. Soft-hearted as always, she had promised not to report her as long as it didn't happen again.

'Never fret, sweet Rose,' Peter told me later, pleased at having cowed Sarah with her secret. 'That slattern shall never more slander thee and thy mum.' My eyes had remained dry and burning under Sarah's jeers, but now they filled with tears. I was weeping for Mum, for ever vulnerable to causeless cries of *witch*. Weeping for the loss of Cicely, my first protector, now bound for ever to tenacious Toby. That puzzle worried me more than any of Sarah's jibes. But Cicely would hear no ill of her husband when I had wondered aloud about his temper, which seemed to flare so easily.

Now, Peter dried my tears and did his best to comfort me in his plain-spoken way.

'Thou'rt a wonder, Rose.'

'A wonder?' I was still sniffling, my mind reeling from the fight.

'Tha used to flummox me – at times tha seemed both bold and bashful, afeard to show thyself for fear of mock.' His blue eyes, the same cornflower shade as his sister's, shone with affection. 'Now I think thou'rt afeard of nowt.'

At that, my own eyes overflowed anew. Peter's comfortable laugh rolled forth as he tried again to distract me from sorrows he couldn't begin to grasp. 'I was chuffed when I saw thy bonny drawing of me sister. And I've summat else to ask thee to draw – Pepper and Clove!'

Sir Henry doted on his spaniels, named for two of Lady Catherine's favourite spices, and Peter was charged with their care and exercise. His eyes lit with enthusiasm. 'Come with me now, while I walk them.'

Knowing he wanted only to comfort me, I said yes. Peter made me smile as he showed off Pepper eagerly retrieving his cap when commanded to fetch, delivering it only slightly damp. Pepper's placid sister was happy to sit for me while I sketched her form in red chalk before rewarding her with a bit of bran bread.

'She likes thee, she does,' Peter assured me. 'Dogs know who's kind. Clove won't go near Sarah.'

His simple goodness warmed me. But as soon as we returned to the house, Mum saw my red eyes.

I didn't want to repeat Sarah's words, for fear of hurting Mum, but she sat me down until it all came out. She offered not comfort but a bigger picture. 'Your father is right. The name of *witch* sticks in some minds for ever. But there's another side to that. More good people want healing than fear witches, and all I can do – all *you* can do – is pay no mind to the whispers. It's more important what you do than what some folks say you do.' She patted my arm. 'In this household, there's naught to fear. You served one good lady, and another one now, who deserves your best skills. Lady Mary's pains have already started, but this being her first, it may be many hours. Rest tonight, Rose. I will want you at my side tomorrow. I'm going to teach you how to draw down a baby.'

I gulped. I was to be present for the terrifying marvel that Lady Catherine had died wanting, and which Lady Mary had so little care for.

'Ah, Joan,' my lady cried out to Mum when her pains took her hard the next afternoon. 'Is there any way to get this babe out more quickly? If I could only push now, without stopping, and be done with this, I'd do it.'

'Breathe through the pains, my lady, and try *not* to push. You're not yet ready, I fear.' Mum directed me to prepare an infusion of raspberry leaf with ginger for my lady. Settling her against her pillows and sliding deft hands between her legs, Mum rubbed the opening with primrose oil to ripen the passage. Once she deemed my mistress ready, Mum showed me how to knead and stroke the belly to work with the contractions rather than against them. At first, I flinched from my lady's cries of distress, remembering the dark gush that had come with Cicely's shrieks of pain. But Mum taught me to breathe with my lady's cries and follow the rhythm of the pains, as she reached inside with nimble fingers to guide the baby's head.

Finally, 'Ready yourself for the babe!' Mum placed my hands in position to receive the enormous head that was somehow emerging between my lady's legs, until, with a long, guttural wail, Lady Mary pushed her babe out into my waiting hands. Mum cut the cord, striped with blood, which linked the baby's body to its mother's. As my lady gave a final cry, I swaddled the infant in linen, while Mum coaxed out the glistening afterbirth, still fastened to the cord. The silvery veins spreading out from the milky cord across the crimson surface of the afterbirth reminded me of the fanning branches of a tree – a tree of life. And in my arms wailed my lady's first child, a boy – my Lord Pembroke's long-awaited son and heir.

'His name shall be William, for his Herbert grandfather and his Sidney great-grandfather,' Sir Henry exclaimed proudly when Mum brought him the wailing babe. Then she turned him over to Bronwen, a hearty wet nurse with the most enormous breasts I had ever seen, who Sir Henry had brought to Wilton from Wales in readiness for the birth. When I asked Mum later why Lady Mary couldn't feed her babe herself, like she had nursed Michael, she shrugged.

'Fine ladies don't nurse their own children. They believe that's better done by a commoner – like getting milk from a cow.' Her voice was flat, but not unkind. 'They pay for it by falling pregnant with one babe after another, since nursing will delay pregnancy. Commoners can't afford too many babes, but highborn folk can't afford *not* to have as many as possible, hoping at least one heir will survive. Think how happy Sir Henry is with a son.' She paused, while we listened to the snuffles of the nursing babe. 'But it's Lady Mary who had to go through the labour.'

My lady kissed her new son, once. Then she sank into a restless sleep, troubled by moans. 'Write this down, Rose,' Mum advised, reciting her recipe for a tisane brewed with two parts chamomile, two parts hibiscus, one part rose petals and one part lavender flowers to renew my lady's strength. 'Who knows, you may deliver one of her babes yourself one day.' I had no wish for such a role. Most particularly I didn't relish the uncertainty of the outcome, having already seen that miscarriage to weigh against this live birth.

But I was fascinated by the spectacle. And that night by candlelight, using pen and ink shaded with red and white chalk, I drew the image this birth had impressed upon my brain like a seal in hot wax – the creamy cord twined with scarlet threads of life, rooted to the ruby-hued afterbirth, silvery veins brushed with vermilion branching out across its surface, connecting the babe to the mother's body like a living tree. From the end of the cord peeped a lively spirit, to show the life that had been inside the cord all along – the first such spirit I had drawn since Lady Catherine's death. This drawing I put directly into my oaken box, sharing it with no one. I guessed that showing birth as a space *where the imagined coexists with the visible*, to use Lady Mary's words, might be regarded as witchcraft indeed.

Lady Catherine had put it another way: *Your sketches do more than render surface appearance – they bring your subjects to life. What might we call that if not magic?* Fingering my bandaged knuckles, cut upon Sarah's sharp teeth, I decided I should keep this magic secret.

* * *

Lady Mary called me to her the next morning, even before Bronwen brought the new babe to her arms. On this, the second day of her first child's life, her grey eyes were bright and dark at once, like the Heel Stone bathed in the dawn.

'You must go to the still-room today and observe what Adrian is doing. Look through the window in the athanor and draw what you see. Even without colour, I want to understand the effects of fire.' There was an urgency to her request that puzzled me. Why worry about the still-room now, when she had a new baby to occupy her attention?

Bronwen arrived, bearing baby William. Boasting a large head with no hair and eyes the indigo hue of the dye that coloured Da's fanciest bolts of cloth, he looked into his mother's face, as if memorising her features. My lady patted his plump cheeks gingerly, kissed him once on the forehead and handed him back. I felt sorry for this child. Lady Catherine would scarcely have agreed to let her babe from her arms, even for the wet nurse, I thought. But then I reminded myself that it was Sir Henry who had decided a wet nurse was best for the infant. And after all, I could only imagine what Lady Catherine's response would have been to the child she had never had. But like trying to chalk over a flawed drawing to replace it with a new image, my effort to reform my assumptions failed. It was turning out harder than I had expected to keep my promise to regard Lady Mary for herself.

Instead, I did what I could, which was to climb the stairs to the still-room, sketchbook in hand. As soon as I pushed open the heavy door, I was assaulted by waves of heat and a fog of foul odours – burning metal, sour vinegar, singed herbs. Wiping his protruding forehead, stout Master Gilbert bustled about, shouting at Brian, the stable boy, to maintain the bellows – unnecessarily, it seemed to me, for the lad was pumping for all he was worth, sweat running into his eyes. I guessed he must have volunteered to work in the still-room as a way to rise out of the stables. I wondered if he might be rethinking his ambitions.

So much for the order I had brought to the empty still-room. The place was now in complete disarray. A chaotic assortment of glass and copper vessels lay spread across the worktables, several half-filled with various coloured substances, shining like jewels scattered among ruins. When I approached the tower furnace, the heat and the odours intensified, and Master Gilbert hastened to my side. 'Keep your distance, miss,' he growled.

'My lady wants me to view the process of distillation—' I began stubbornly.

'Through the athanor window, I know,' he interrupted. 'What she hopes to learn from your observations I can't imagine. But this is her space to command, so look as much as you will, child – or as long as you can take the heat.' Offering me a slippery smile that didn't quite include his eyes, the alchemist placed a grimy hand on my arm that left smudges behind when I moved briskly away from his touch and approached the stinking furnace.

'I am distilling a compound of marcasite, vitriol, common tartar, gold and sal ammoniac in an alembic that rests in a sand bath over the fire,' he explained grudgingly. 'You can see the distillate collected already.' I squeezed past Brian's vigorous bellows to peer cautiously into the window. A tower of globular vessels was stacked precariously within the furnace, the head of one vessel extending into the bottom of the next. The stack rose past the viewing window and above the open brick top of the furnace itself. I saw an ashy black substance in the bottom vessel, which was resting in sand, then grey ash in the next vessel up. To my amazement, a substance white as snow was coating the vessel above that, visible above the open roof of the furnace, on top of which were perched two more empty vessels.

'Over the remainder of this week,' explained Master Gilbert, 'if the procedure goes as planned, you shall see golden yellow and finally ruby red in the topmost aludel, producing perfect sulphur sublimate with many curative properties.' Such alchemy of colour was worth recording indeed! Clearly I would need more than ink and chalk if I was to truly capture the process on paper for my lady. But I relished the challenge. Rendering what I saw and didn't yet understand had always been one of the attractions of drawing, particularly when my sketches made visible new details I hadn't noticed before they appeared on the page.

Master Gilbert guided me towards the cooler end of the still-room, pressing me forward with insistent fingers. 'The heat can be too much for one as young as yourself,' he murmured solicitously, in a tone as greasy as his fingers. Mistaking for fear my grimace of discomfort at his touch, he added, 'The process is only safe to observe with careful supervision.'

At that moment, the air was split by a terrific noise, a surge of heat, and a scream. An empty vessel shot up into the air above the furnace, bursting into pieces, while the tower of remaining aludels tipped over and shattered, spilling onto the floor and sending glassy fragments coated with ash of different shades through the room. Master Gilbert shielded me from the flying glass with his body, but Brian was not as lucky. Facing the furnace to work the bellows, he was caught in the shower of burning glass and collapsed to the floor, shrieking as he landed upon heated shards that set his clothes smoking and pierced his flesh. Moving surprisingly quickly for such a stout man, the alchemist rushed towards the boy and scooped him into his arms, carrying him back towards me, barking an order to hand him a blanket. With quick, sure fingers, he removed splinters of smoking glass from Brian's face and body, burning his own hands, and wrapped him closely in the blanket I snatched from the shelf of linens near the door.

'We must smother the heat first. Then we'll treat the burns. Never fear, lad, I have you safe now. This isn't my first explosion.' His voice was surprisingly calm. Instructing me to wet linens with the water jug and place them around Brian's head and face, he returned to the athanor to examine the disaster.

'Excessive heat,' he muttered. 'The aludel exploded. The procedure is ruined.' The chain of destruction had wrecked the other vessels in the athanor and generated a plume of black smoke where the ash mingled with the heated sand. Satisfying himself that the immediate danger was over, Master Gilbert sent me to fetch some servants to carry Brian downstairs where he could be treated.

Peter saw me as I reached the ground floor, covered with bits of ash and shuddering by now with shock. He caught me in a reassuring embrace, then led three other manservants in a race back up to the attic to collect Brian. Sir Henry directed them to place Brian in one of the guest bedchambers, to be treated by Doctor Moffett alongside Master Gilbert, who had multiple burns on his hands and back. I assured my lord that I had no injury and only needed to clean myself and put on a fresh kirtle before I could attend my lady and the babe. But he pulled me aside.

'Your mistress mustn't learn of this accident yet, while she is still recovering from her labours in childbed. Do not discuss this matter with her until she has had some weeks to recover.'

Some weeks? I could not imagine keeping this matter from her at all.

But at this moment, I desperately craved fresh air to clear my lungs of the burning smoke. Once Brian was settled, I gratefully agreed when Peter invited me to accompany him while he walked Pepper and Clove. For a while we followed a garden path behind the romping dogs without speaking. After the chaos in the still-room, I was glad of the silence. But I noticed in Peter's manner an unease that hadn't been there before. At length, he spoke.

'Rose, when tha told us about the explosion, I wanted to pummel that fool alchemist who put thee in harm's way! And I can no longer keep silent – about what tha means to me.' He picked up the pace, as if he meant to plough through whatever blocked his way, then suddenly stopped and faced me. 'Wilt tha marry me, Rose?'

I stopped still in the path, trembling in the cool spring air. Peter's words were pebbles dropped into the well of my silence.

'Not now, but when the time seems right?' Peter brought the dogs to heel and looked into my eyes. 'Cicely said to wait 'til I had summat to offer. This morn, Mister Cobb, the coachman, asked if I'd return to the stables as chief groom, for I've always been good with horses. And I said yes. So me wages will rise now.'

I couldn't stop shivering. When he draped his own cloak awkwardly but gently around my shoulders, I inhaled the comfortingly familiar tang of his sweat. But – a proposal of marriage? Truly, nothing about the idea attracted me. The last thing I wanted was to bind myself to some man for life. Sixteen now, I was a year older than Lady Mary was when she wedded. Unlike her, I could never marry an earl. But also unlike her, I could choose to say no. I couldn't say what I wanted, but it wasn't this. Still, Peter deserved an answer.

'You're like a brother to me, Peter. I don't want to marry, and certainly not yet. I appreciate your offer, but you'd be happier, I'm sure, with someone else.' Peter shook his head, his eyes sad. I turned back on the path. I needed to return to the house to clean myself and work out what to do – not about Peter, but Lady Mary.

How could I possibly give a satisfactory report to my lady, who awaited my observations from the still-room, if I concealed what had just occurred there? And yet if I told her the truth, my lord might terminate my service for such blatant disregard of his orders.

I washed myself clean of ash, changed my clothes and combed out my wispy hair, hoping the odours from the explosion wouldn't still cling to me when I went to my lady. When I peered around the door to the chamber, I was relieved to find my mistress sleeping, Mum rose from the bedside and beckoned me into my lady's closet, the side-chamber where Lady Mary did much of her writing. The closet was a more confined space than the library, containing little more than a desk, supplied with paper and ink, but I guessed that she preferred to work without a full-length portrait of Lady Catherine looking over her shoulder.

'Are you hurt, Rose?' Mum ran her fingers gently over my face and neck, checking for burns. With her sewing scissors, she snipped the singed bits from my hair and smoothed it back along my shoulders. 'It must have been terrifying.'

If Mum thought the still-room was dangerous, she might not want me to continue there. I knew that if I was to become indispensable to my mistress, the still-room was at the heart of it. And only there could I see the remainder of the changing colours that I had imagined already in my mind's eye. So I described the explosion as briefly as I could, and how Master Gilbert had sheltered me – but without mentioning the unwelcome intimacy of his voice and hands. Then, my problem.

'Sir Henry instructed me not to mention the still-room accident until my lady has regained her strength. But I know she'll ask me what I observed today, and I can't imagine how to hide it from her.'

My mother smiled.

'Her ladyship is young. She should be walking about by week's end. I'll be surprised if she needs the two-week confinement most great ladies enjoy.'

Seeing the question in my eyes, she continued, thoughtfully, 'It's never a good idea to step between a husband and a wife. You might mention to her ladyship that there is much to tell her, but explain that Sir Henry asked you to wait, being concerned for her health.'

As it turned out, the matter of the still-room didn't even come up. And contrary to Mum's confident prediction, Lady Mary needed more, not less, than the usual period of confinement. She seemed overtaken by sorrow, as if she had suffered a loss instead of a successful delivery, her spirits harmed more than her body. She appeared to welcome Bronwen's visit with William on that first day after the birth, but on the third day, she ordered the wet nurse not to bring him, and soon sent no directions at all. She curled into herself in her darkened bedchamber and refused to do more than taste and then turn away the tempting meals sent up by Cook Corbett. Some food returned to the kitchen untasted. Only Mum, watching over her at the bedside, could persuade Lady Mary to drink the herbal tisanes and juleps that we brewed.

I didn't understand it. How could my new mistress reject what my old mistress had so desperately longed for? My headstrong and confident lady had been replaced by a shadow, a listless body with no concerns or desires. I would have welcomed a reprimand, when I brought her yet another dish that she didn't care to eat, but she only turned her head away silently, as she did when Bronwen placed William beside her in the bed. I preferred the Lady Mary who issued orders like a queen.

When Sir Henry brought his wife news of the congratulations of the court and the celebrations of the parish at the birth of their first son, she only nodded, as if he was speaking a language as foreign to her as French was to me – merely a succession of meaningless syllables.

Doctor Moffett told Sir Henry that he could find no physical ailment to explain Lady Mary's state. Mum seemed less baffled than the physician and advised Sir Henry to be patient. But by the end of the second week, with no change, I could see my lady's darkness beginning to overtake him as well.

The intensity of my concern at Lady Mary's condition surprised me. I had come to care for my lady more than I realised. And who was I to cast judgement against her? After all, I could not even imagine myself a mother – nor, for that matter, a wife.

CHAPTER SIXTEEN

Mary, 1584

Four pregnancies in four years. The lot of a countess. Although she had now survived three births and a miscarriage, the darkness that had enveloped her following William's birth, as treacherous and impenetrable as river fog, still shadowed her.

Only after the darkness passed could Mary take stock. The density of the gloom that smothered her after William's birth had felt like a windowless prison, walling her off from life and her child, insensible to the passage of time in her darkened bedchamber. Lines from the Queen's poem circled mercilessly in her head. *I am and not; I freeze, and yet am burned, since from myself another self I turned.*

Thankfully, Joan recognised the dark tide that swept Mary away. She prepared a concoction of St John's wort for Mary to drink twice a day. And instead of urging her to resist her feelings, Joan spoke of her own experience with that darkness.

'When you cannot fight it, you may yet find a way through it. My sister, Judith, bless her, helped me to keep going in the first weeks after Rose's birth. I've never felt such despair before or since, my lady. Not with my second child, Michael. Not even' – Joan's voice broke, her face dark – 'with the charge of witchcraft,' she managed. Mary lay pale and inert beneath the silk comforter on her bed, taking in more of her companion's confession than she was able to acknowledge.

Joan continued, 'It hurts most when the heart is bruised already, whether with loss or fear for the future. When the birth of the babe alone is not enough to supply joy, the mother should be supported, not blamed.' A tear slid down her cheek. 'Sometimes the darkness is inside.'

Mary felt the fog beginning to feather and dissolve only when she allowed herself to hear William's eager sucking at Bronwen's breast. Such vigour was itself life. Then, one day, when Joan placed the baby in his mother's arms after his feeding, she didn't turn away but bent her forehead to his and inhaled the sweet milkiness of his breath, as if breathing in new life from her own child. Slowly, day by day, Mary's blood began to warm, her mind to clear. Having vowed in the darkness to put the entire wrenching experience of childbirth behind her, she felt a wary surprise at the blooming of such an intense craving for the baby who had caused her so much agony.

Before returning to Amesbury, Joan prescribed a regimen of herbal remedies, including an infusion of dried sage in boiling water and an amber tisane brewed from yarrow blossoms. 'Sooner than you think, you'll have your body back, my lady,' the healer assured her. But it wasn't her body that Mary wanted back the most, it was her mind. All the more for her relief that the darkness had burned away, she wished to pursue a thought to its conclusion or pen a line of verse without her attention fracturing into numberless motes of dust suspended in sunlight.

One morning, for the first time in – what was it, weeks? Months? – Mary called Rose to her bedside. Finally, she felt ready to resume her life. When Rose told her, haltingly and fearfully, of the explosion in the still-room, Mary's first thought, after confirming that all involved were safe and well, had been to wonder how the room's very existence could have disappeared so completely from her awareness.

As the spring days lengthened into summer, she found herself not only taking pleasure in her infant son but looking forward to other pursuits as well. The daylight itself seemed rare and precious, slanting across the handwritten pages of verse on her desk and warming the stack of remedies that called her to the still-room.

That had been four years ago now. Nearly each year since William's birth had brought another pregnancy. First a daughter, named Catherine by Henry. Swallowing her resentment at the choice of his dead wife's name, Mary called her simply Kate. The child drew Mary close simply by the fact of her existence, her vitality countering the dulling aftermath of the birth-pains and the diminished appetite for life that inevitably followed them.

Seeing through her child's eyes, Mary took comfort from wonder. Together, they dabbled fingertips in ripples of light and shadow spreading over the floor of the nursery when Kate woke from her afternoon naps. Even William, a demanding, headstrong little boy, softened in his sister's presence, patting Kate's cheek so tenderly that his mother's eyes welled with tears.

I feel this daughter connected to your spirit, my sister, she told Ambrosia. *And I pledge to you that I shall love her and guard her against all ills as I wish I could have guarded you.*

The following year, Mary lost a baby to miscarriage, in a pregnancy so easy in its early stages that she had been confident that this time she would master the process. So she was quite unprepared for the blood, and the cramps, and the unformed figure of the foetus slipping out of her womb. She was unprepared, as well, for the piercing grief of this loss – a child she had been so determined to birth into light rather than darkness.

When her second daughter was born, two years after Kate, Mary selected the name herself. Baby Anne honoured a bevy of godmothers, including Henry's own sister. By the end of Anne's first week of life, the ribbons of fog that darkened Mary's consciousness and spirit after each pregnancy had already begun to dissipate. Still, she was troubled by the quicksilver escape of thoughts from her mind, vanishing like slippery beads of mercury spilled upon the worktable.

She chafed against the limitations of her body, unable to easily mount the steps to the still-room for fully three months after the birth. Reminded of Joan's observation that *a woman can't birth babies as easily as a cat can deliver a litter of kittens*, she wished she could have all of her babies in one litter instead of labouring anew each time.

Now, in the summer of 1584, at the age of twenty-two, Mary was pregnant again. This fifth pregnancy was proving the most difficult. From the start, she was unable to keep any food down, her body feeling like a city captured by a tyrant determined to bring its sovereign to her knees. And it was on her knees that she spent most of her mornings, sick to her stomach and sick at heart, for she could feel the darkness encroaching already upon her awareness, and she was afraid.

But she would not give in to it, for her younger brother Robert was planning a wedding. He was to be married next month to the Welsh beauty Barbara Gamage, cousin to Walter Raleigh.

'It's her voice that I love the most,' Robert confided to his sister. 'That Welsh lilt that brings back our childhood in Ludlow.' Just as the musical rhythm of Jake's speech had been part of Mary's decision to choose him for her first kiss atop the tower of Ludlow Castle. How young she had been, how sophisticated she had thought herself, and how wholly lost after Ambrosia's death that day. Perhaps, she told herself now, one of the Sidney siblings might finally find happiness.

Robert and Barbara were married in the parish church, followed by a celebration in the gardens of Penshurst Place, where autumn crocuses and dahlias supplied a stately chorale of colour and fragrance. Ever generous to his younger brother, Philip expressed only pleasure at the wedding, but Mary could sense beneath his smile the lingering pang of loss associated with his own marriage, arranged, like Mary's, by their father. His beloved Penelope Devereux, the subject of his passionate sonnets to 'Stella', had been married against her will to a rich nobleman, the Earl of Warwick. What's more, Penelope's mother, Lettice, had produced a son by the Earl of Leicester, thus disinheriting

Philip, who had been his uncle Robert's primary heir. Another coup for the scheming Lettice, Mary reflected.

On her return to Wilton from the wedding celebration, Mary determined to visit her still-room, where she hadn't ventured since William's birth four years and three more pregnancies ago. She laboured up the stairs, aided by Rose's steady arm. She had come to rely not just on Rose's physical assistance but also her calming presence during the bodily disruptions of each pregnancy.

At the entrance, Mary paused, breathing in the scent of fresh wood.

'Master Adrian installed new shelves for the equipment after Brian cleaned the mess from the explosion,' Rose explained.

'Except that it's still a mess.' Mary's voice was sharp. The new shelves were filled with a random clutter of alchemical vessels, large and small, competing for space. Under Adrian, disorder reigned.

'Don't worry, milady, I can set it to rights.' Mary saw Rose press her palm against her breastbone, drawing strength from her hidden talisman.

On impulse, Mary drew a volume from the bookshelf by the door. Flipping through the pages, she found the image she sought. A double ouroboros – two serpents, one wingless and the other winged, the head of one biting the tail of the other, symbolising the union of opposites necessary to create the Philosopher's Stone. She wondered how an artist would make sense of this.

The girl studied the drawing carefully. Unexpectedly, she looked up at Mary with a smile.

'It makes more sense to me, my lady, than the single ouroboros. It connects two creatures in a never-ending bond.'

Renewal through connection rather than isolation.

In the evenings these days, Mary retreated to her closet with Garnier. Transmuting his *Marc Antoine* into her own words was, she mused, her first act of literary alchemy – not simply a translation but a transformation. She refocused Garnier's story to emphasise what had first captured her attention: the heroic strength of the tragic queen. Thus immersed, Mary was able to override her pregnant body's demands for inactivity and drive back the darkness that leisure only encouraged.

Attending to her work in order to escape the encroachments of this difficult pregnancy, she paid only scant attention to what was going on around her, missing signs she might otherwise have heeded.

Her mother's joy, Kate wasn't one to complain. At three years, a fountain of high spirits and unquenchable curiosity, she was equally content to play by herself with a cloth doll fashioned adroitly from scraps by Rose and Cicely, or with her brother. Her fever wasn't discovered until four-year-old William marched into Mary's bedchamber to announce earnestly, proud of his new word, that he had cured his sister with his own 'cordjal', but that she had 'frowed up'. Hastily summoned to the child's room, Doctor Moffett reported that little Kate had vomited her brother's harmless concoction of milk and honey. But she was burning with fever. As Kate tossed in her tiny bed, Mary knelt at her side, consumed with love and fear for this child whose wonder at the world had restored her own.

Doctor Moffett placed a reassuring hand on her shoulder. 'I have a remedy that may bring some ease to your daughter and support her body to cast out the seeds of illness. Meanwhile you must rest yourself, my lady, so as not to bring harm to your advanced pregnancy.'

She clung to the doctor's confidence, allowing him to draw her into a chair, but refused to retreat to her own chamber. Her head pounded. And not just her head. Her womb had started to pulse with cramps that she recognised all too well.

'Send for your mother, Rose,' Mary gasped to her maidservant. 'This baby is arriving too early!' She tried to remember what she had read in Catherine's collection of remedies about slowing down early labour. Tincture of valerian, perhaps? No time now to search Catherine's cabinet of tinctures. But trusting Rose's reliance on her mother's remedies, she downed her raspberry leaf and ginger tisane.

By nightfall, Joan had not arrived, and Kate's restlessness had subsided into an even more terrifying inertia. Sobbing, Mary knocked the next cup aside. But even as she clutched Rose's hand in apology, her waters broke, flooding out of her cramping womb with a vengeance. Briefly, she tasted relief – she might yet pass through this delivery in time to watch over Kate. Then Rose held up a cloth soaked not just with birth waters but with bright blood. Doctor Moffett's attention was focused solely on Kate, who was now shaking in the grip of a fever-induced seizure. Rose took a deep breath and knelt between Mary's legs.

She felt gingerly for the head, then looked up at her mistress. 'It's crowning already, my lady.' Too early. Birth now must inevitably tear the tight ring of flesh that Rose hadn't had time to prepare with primrose oil. But there was no way back.

Rose breathed with her mistress, rubbing her abdomen through several more contractions. Mary's moans sharpened into one long scream when the head finally broke through. Moments later, her pulsing womb expelled the baby into Rose's waiting hands. The tiny wail of the new babe was lost beneath Mary's own crescendo of accelerating moans as she yielded to new waves of pressure bearing down upon her and crushing the breath from her lungs. This time, the longed-for delivery from agony didn't arrive in a clear release but was prolonged across a ribboning series of painful ruptures.

Before the darkness took her she saw, in Rose's arms, the swaddled babe, and on the doctor's face, a terrible compassion.

CHAPTER SEVENTEEN

Rose, 1584–85

Learning to render the visible world in colour was like creation itself – beginning in chaos. Master Gheeraerts had never trained a girl before, but he agreed to take me on.

At first it seemed his visit was for naught, since he'd arrived at Wilton to create a portrait of family life only to discover a house in mourning. Little Kate was dead, Lady Mary had almost died, and tiny baby Philip, born too soon, was barely clinging to life. Hardly the family group he had anticipated for his subject.

The painter had been expected four years ago, after William's birth, when Lady Mary first suggested that he could instruct me in colours. But my lady's first bout with the darkness, and then four more pregnancies in quick succession, had continually delayed the portrait sitting. Now, determined to hold onto the hope that Lady Mary would make a full recovery, my lord resolved to summon Master Gheeraerts to Wilton and house him there until the portrait was achieved. He also insisted that I must study with the painter.

'Your mistress would wish it so,' he told me sternly. Every afternoon since his youngest son's birth he had spent at my lady's side, sometimes reading aloud, sometimes simply sitting and holding her hand. 'She is already receiving the best possible care from your mother and the doctor, so you're not needed here for now. If you can show her what you've learnt as her body begins to heal, I believe your gift for art, and my wife's faith in it, will help her to recover her spirits.'

We both knew my lady's battles against the darkness after childbirth. *The mother must be supported, not blamed*, Mum had said, in order to recover not just in body but in spirit. Now that Lady Mary had delivered one child and lost another within a single day, she would need even more care.

'I cannot lose Mary as I lost Catherine,' Sir Henry whispered, almost to himself. Nor could I. So, with some misgivings but buoyed by my lord's confidence, I began my study of the art of painting while my lady lay in her chamber, white as death after the blood loss from the damaged afterbirth. By day I learnt to grind pigments and mix powders alongside Master Gheeraerts' apprentice. At night I slept with Mum in the housekeeper's chambers. Before entering sleep I was haunted by the memory of that curdled afterbirth, which the doctor had finally been forced to cut free of her womb – no stunning tree of life, this time, but a glistening mass of flesh the shade of blackcurrants, steeped in my lady's lifeblood.

On that terrible night, my mother had arrived just after the death of little Kate, in time to hear my bitter confession to the doctor. 'I failed her.'

'Doing the best you can is never failure, Rose.' Mum's voice was firm, coming even before Doctor Moffett spoke his agreement.

'Suffering the shock of her daughter's decline, the Countess went into labour before her time, when the womb was not ready to release the child. Without your swift assistance, the baby might have remained trapped inside. Thanks to you, the infant is alive.'

But my lady's other child had not survived. Her Kate.

Each morning before joining Master Gheeraerts in his makeshift studio, in an outbuilding adjoining the stables, I visited my lady's bedchamber. I hoped my mistress would at least notice me, but she seemed scarcely aware of her surroundings. I returned to the painter more determined than ever to learn the art of colour – for her as much as myself. It was endless. In truth, both my lady's recovery and my apprenticeship seemed at times to be making no progress.

Helpless to comfort my lady, I turned to the only skill I had. I loved to draw children, whose faces changed with each rendition, and I had filled loose sheets with charcoal sketches of the siblings at different ages and stages. Now I collected my drawings of little Kate. From these souvenirs and my own memories, I resolved to create a portrait of the living child.

After the burial of little Kate, daily life in the household had moved on in muted fashion. Cicely was recovering smoothly from the delivery of her own second child, named Stanley after Toby's father, as robust a babe as Philip was frail. Kate's nursemaid had been dismissed before the funeral, and now one was needed to watch over Anne while Bronwen nursed Philip. Mum recommended Cicely – the obvious choice. She had the biggest heart of all of us, and the most energy to spare. And as I had found since my earliest days at Wilton, her deepest instinct was to care for anyone in need. Sir Henry readily agreed, and Cicely adopted her new responsibilities with relish. She proved particularly good at entertaining Anne with fables and fairy tales while she nursed her own babe. Mum even persuaded Sir Henry to allow Cicely's three-year-old daughter Angelica to join her with the Pembroke children in the afternoons.

My announcement one morning that our mistress had greeted me with a weak smile brought an engulfing embrace from Cicely. Her cheerful insistence on taking Anne and Philip for regular visits with their mother had helped to slowly but surely lighten our mistress's darkness. And in the days that followed, as Lady Mary's health and spirit steadily rallied, I discovered, to my amazement, that both my mother and myself had been transformed from distrusted meddlers in enchantment into heroic attendants of life. After all, little Kate had died under the physician's care, while we were credited for saving Lady Mary's and Philip's lives. Though this was no truer than the dark whispers holding Mum accountable for Lady Catherine's death or the birth of the deformed babe, the household now firmly believed in both of us as true healers.

Cicely's cheeriness had been my touchstone during this dark time for my lady. Which is why the shadow on her face scared me, one winter evening when I stopped by to visit Angelica and Stanley. I considered myself their honorary auntie and often came by when Cicely fed them supper and prepared them for bed. That night, as I approached their chamber, Toby pushed by me without a word of greeting. As he passed I caught a whiff of ale.

'Had yourselves a quarrel, then?' I asked Cicely lightly, knowing she could sail forward with an even keel through the waves that Toby often stirred up. To my surprise, instead of shrugging it off, she beckoned me closer. She lowered her voice so that it wouldn't reach the ears of Angelica, who was entertaining baby Stanley with a new rattle.

'I don't know what's got into him, Rose! Brian came by to drop off the rattle Peter carved for the baby, since me brother had to work late this afternoon. I was just thanking him, when Toby burst in and shoved Brian to the ground. He bellowed some blether about Brian sniffing round for my favour, which brought the poor lad almost to tears – he'd done nothing of the sort! I told Toby that, but he insisted I was fuggling him blind. He made me so angry I wanted to throw him out – and after Brian left, I told him so. Toby shoved me so fast I didn't see it coming and I hit me head.' She winced as she fingered a swelling bump.

Now it was me who wanted Toby gone. For good.

'Lock the door against him, Cicely. Don't let him back into your chamber. The steward will have him dismissed for this, and good riddance I say.'

But she was already shaking her head. 'He cradled me in his arms after, kissed me and said he was sorry, asked me to give him another chance, just one more chance. He told me he wasn't himself – Master Wilkins told him this afternoon Sir Henry might look for a new valet if he didn't take more care with our lord's things.' Her face was woeful now. 'I'm afeard he's drinking too much because he's worried. If I shut him out, he'll only come back more mardy than afore. If I stay calm, mayhap he'll be less mithered.'

'You can't quiet him every time, Cicely.' My fears about the knife-edge of Toby's moods only multiplied. But Cicely wouldn't listen to reason, determined to fix this on her own. She made me promise to say nothing to Lady Mary, who was still emerging from her own world of grief.

So I threw myself more doggedly into my lessons with the painter.

Master Gheeraerts was a slim, long-faced Netherlander of about my lady's age, his high forehead balanced by a jutting beard. He rarely smiled, but his brusque manner was in no way unkind, and he treated me no differently than he did the boy apprentice who came with him from London.

Before my first meeting with him, I had sorted through my drawings, gathering those that depicted visible rather than imagined subjects. He nodded curtly at my herbal illustrations for Lady Catherine, my studies of her face and my sketches of the Pembroke children. To my surprise, it was the hastily rendered line drawings I had made at court for Sir Henry that produced murmurs of approval. The painter praised my attention to how posture revealed character – vanity visible in a courtier's angled stance with hand resting on hip, curiosity captured in the tilt of a lady's head.

Each morning after I visited Lady Mary, I ground pigments – black from burnt almond shells, ultramarine blue from lapis lazuli stones. Unbroken lumps of vermilion and yellow orpiment needed to be ground repeatedly on a slab with clear water, sometimes mixed with powdered glass, while the coppery green of verdigris required working up with vinegar. The painter's apprentice, a lad with clever eyes and quick fingers named Jeremy, taught me to mix the brilliantly coloured powders with linseed oil to make the paints. After relying on chalk and charcoal for so long, I was awed by the array of hues that could emerge from layering paints in these basic shades.

'A master portraitist may render faces and bodies, clothing and surroundings, light and shadow, so true to the surface that you might think you can touch their subjects,' Master Gheeraerts told me in his gruff Flemish accent. 'Ah, but the greatest success occurs when, for just a moment, you see the figure *breathe*.' He inhaled grandly. 'The *life* of such a likeness depends on the visual harmony of the whole.'

I didn't understand his lesson, at least not at first, but I heard his dedication. Watching him work on charcoal sketches of Sir Henry or young William in preparation for the family portrait to come, I saw how he echoed the shadows of worry marking the hollows of Sir Henry's cheeks in the shadowed drapery of the curtains behind his head. And how William's long-lashed eyes shared the bright intensity of the spaniels cavorting at the foot of the stool where he sat, suggesting the lively spirit of the boy even in stillness.

Painting in oils, though, was another matter entirely. Before long, to my dismay, Master Gheeraerts set me to copying Hans Eworth's full-length portrait of my lord's father, mounted on the wall of the Wilton gallery. 'You must learn the life in the art of others,' he explained.

My first attempt was a disaster. The combined effect of the earl's black cap, doublet and hose was merely dark, not dashing. Even worse, I had neglected to paint the silvery background draperies first. Painting those in, around the existing figure, muddled all the lines. Jeremy found me slouched on my stool beside my failure.

'He's learnin' ya to see colours not as background and foreground, but as a single painting, like,' he observed in his jaunty London lilt.

I was indignant. 'So he *wanted* me to fail?'

He shrugged. 'He knows ya'll be readiest to study what he teaches all his 'prentices if ya falls flat at first. It's his way, girl – he's treatin' ya like one of us.'

So I persisted, and slowly the mysteries of colour began to flow from my brush. My second attempt at the copy received a nod of approval from the painter. As I began work on my portrait of Kate, Jeremy helped me choose the palette and Master Gheeraerts guided me in the moulding and shading of the child's face. But it was I who decided to include, along the borders, drawings of her from infancy to three years old, before she fell ill. In this way, I hoped to distil the spirit captured in my hasty sketches over the years, her lively eyes inviting the viewer to return her irrepressible smile.

When Sir Henry came across my work on the portrait during a visit to the studio one day, his sombre face was animated by a spark of unexpected happiness at this tribute to his child. Then his eyes filled with tears.

'When you are finished, bring me the picture to be framed, Rose. I'd like you to present it to your mistress yourself.' I blushed with surprise and pleasure. We had become partners in restoring Lady Mary's vitality.

At length, my lady was well enough to sit for the family portrait, and I was permitted to watch Master Gheeraerts at work. In his composition, he united the members of the family through details of hands and eyes. Sir Henry, his eyes no longer shadowed, rested one hand on Lady Mary's shoulder seated at his side, the other hand on young William's shoulder, standing before him. The infant Philip, gowned in lacy white, was cradled in the curve of my mistress's arm, while her other hand supported baby Anne, sitting on a velvet cushion the same rosy hue as her cheeks. The group embrace was knitted even more closely by where they were looking – not out at the viewer, as in traditional portraits. My lady's eyes were fixed on William and Anne, while my lord's rested on my lady and baby Philip. At their feet sat the spaniels, looking up adoringly at their master and mistress. Just as the painter had said, life arose from the visual harmony of the whole.

While the painter worked, so did I, sketching the family group during their sitting for the portrait. In my drawings, the children were in motion, not yet fixed by the painter. Anne, starting to squirm off her cushion, was righted by her mother, who handed Philip to his father. William was already pulling away from his parents, his gaze fixed outside the family in the direction he wished to go. The only way my sketch corresponded to the painter's version was in Sir Henry's eyes, fixed on his wife.

Before Master Gheeraerts had completed the painting, another death occurred. Now it was my family's turn. This time, as I travelled home to Amesbury, I was approaching loss rather than leaving it.

Mum held me close when I arrived. Michael, now a gangly lad of fourteen, hung back awkwardly until I grasped him from behind in a tight embrace that he couldn't escape. Truth be told, Michael seemed sadder than Mum. He talked about the times Da had brought him to the market stall and encouraged him to speak with other merchants, to consider what trade he'd like to take on when he was older.

Da had never offered me such encouragement, of course, for I was a girl. When I met Mum's eyes, I could tell she knew what I was thinking. 'So, have you decided?' I asked my brother, if only to interrupt his recitation of all our father had done for him.

'I'm going to be a sheep farmer!' he exclaimed, his eyes shining. He laughed at my look of amazement. 'None of the trades at market excited me, but one day Da took me to visit Grandda's old sheep farm. It's now owned by the Lovells – you remember they had the next farm over from Grandda. They've converted their own land to pasture and doubled the herd of sheep. They need farmhands. They let me help a bit with the shearing, and I decided that's what I want – to be a sheep farmer like Grandda.' My brother's enthusiasm was infectious, momentarily lifting the pall.

It was a trade with good prospects, for wool production had become one of the most profitable occupations in our part of the country. 'My little brother – up to his knees in sheep muck,' I teased. 'Who would've thought?'

Mum and I stayed up late that night, sitting by the hearth with steaming mugs of sweet perry. 'What happens now?' I asked the question slowly, not able to envision a future that didn't include Da. For all our differences, I had never known him without a plan.

Mum paused, then took my hands in hers. 'Martin's business was not doing well, Rose. He was thinking of giving it up and selling off the stock to pay his debts when he died last week so suddenly. The doctor said it was a seizure to his heart – there was nothing to be done.'

'How poorly is *not doing well*?' I demanded. 'How many debts did he have?'

'Too many to pay off with what remains of the business. It was a constant struggle to make ends meet.' I could picture Da frowning over his account books. 'He had ventured into the silk trade recently, hoping to expand and open a regular shop of his own in Salisbury. Pursuing that dream, he bought more costly fabrics than he could readily sell. Now his debts are mine, and I have no means to repay them.' Mum's voice was hard, the dark thread that was always present when she spoke with my father now composing the entire fabric of her circumstances. But for all that, she wasn't giving up.

'Michael will be fine – he's moving in with the Lovells next week. They'll give him room and board in return for his labour and a wage when the business prospers further.'

'But what about you, Mum?'

She remained silent for a long while. I watched the flames dancing on a log. 'Your aunt has invited me to live with her family, but I still have the debts to pay off. If there was some way I could support myself selling herbal remedies, I would, but even if I could cover my costs, my remedies won't serve to repay the debts.'

I squeezed her hands, my mind busy with possibilities. 'I've money set aside that I can give to tide you over,' I exclaimed, but Mum was shaking her head.

'Never mind, Rose. I'll find a way.' Then she took a deep breath. 'I have something to tell you, my dear, now that Martin is gone. I hope you'll forgive me for not sharing this earlier – I didn't want to disrupt our family's life together.' Mum was twisting the edge of her apron between two fingers. A trickle of dread ran down my spine.

I thought of the distance I had observed between my parents. The current of darkness that seemed to run beneath Mum's giving in to Da's order not to practise herbal medicine after the witchcraft incident. I wondered if Da had sought solace elsewhere for the space between them. He hadn't seemed the sort of man to pursue other women. Still, I wondered. 'Did Da . . . have a mistress?'

Mum gasped, then chuckled. 'Just the opposite, in fact.' A curious smile curled her lip. It struck me that, for all the financial woes she was shouldering, she seemed not so much bereaved by my father's death as liberated. I was completely in the dark. Mum pressed her fingers to her eyes. When she removed them I saw both hope and fear.

'Martin isn't your father, Rose.'

Still, I didn't understand. What she was saying wasn't possible!

Mum clasped her hands together in her lap, as if to give herself courage. 'When Martin married me, I was sixteen. He had an apprentice named Simon. When I came to Amesbury as a wife, Martin set Simon to work with me on the herbals side of the business, seeing that we shared an interest in plants.'

I had heard this much of her story long ago. But as she continued, her cheeks flushing with colour, I realised this was the opening to a different tale entirely.

'Every day, as we worked on remedies together, we talked, and we found a delight that had been missing from both of our lives. Simon loved the stars. He studied astrology for timing the planting, gathering and preparation of different herbs. He gave me a star chart that showed connections between the constellations and the seasons. His passion for the astral world connected with my own for the natural world.'

Suddenly, I was afraid to hear more. I opened my mouth, but Mum took my hand, her face resolute.

'I fell in love, Rose – or what I believed to be love. And Martin was so focused on building up his trade, he didn't even notice.' Her jaw tightened. 'One afternoon when Martin was at his stall in Salisbury, Simon and I . . . did more than talk together.'

Now I was the one to gasp.

'I told him we couldn't do it again – but that one time was enough.' Without haste, as if the worst part was now over, Mum told me the rest. 'At first, even I wasn't certain what the truth was. You could just as well have been conceived in the

240

marriage bed as the barn. But when I saw your green eyes, I knew. I feared Martin might suspect the truth, but he was so happy to have a child that I do believe he never noticed the colour of your eyes.' She squeezed my fingers. 'I know you had your differences, but Martin loved you, Rose. He was trying to raise you according to his beliefs, as best he could.'

I bowed my head, knowing Mum would paint the best possible picture of the others in the story, as was her way.

'As for Simon, he was so caught up in his astrology that it didn't occur to him to wonder if the child might be his. When he wasn't working with me or your father, he studied and dreamt of setting up his own practice as an astrologer-physician in London. He told me he wasn't cut out for village life, where folks more likely feared his skills than admired them. Eventually, he asked to be released from his apprenticeship to Martin. I supported his request. Martin was not happy about it, but he let him go. I was relieved that he'd be gone before Martin could guess what had passed between us.'

Our mugs were cold. But Mum wasn't finished.

'Simon was always caught up in pursuing the next dream. I understood, even then, that for all his brilliance, I couldn't count on him. He was like a comet streaking fire across the heavens – dazzling, but not here to stay.'

A long silence opened between us. And with it, a chasm.

'Did he love you?' I had to ask. Maybe I hoped for a story of devotion foiled by fate, a father who had adored my mother and left us only because he had no choice. But Mum shook her head.

'Simon loved the stars more than me. And I loved him for

his passion for the stars, so much bigger than the world I'd been raised in, filled with smelly sheep and back-breaking work. Even garden herbs became more exciting once I knew they were ruled by the stars – which herbs matched which constellations, and how to increase their powers by planting and harvesting under different quarters of the moon.'

Suddenly, Mum smiled. 'By the time he left, I realised what I'd thought was love was really fascination.' I was not smiling, but she was too caught up in her memories to notice. 'Simon was afire with a passion for discovery, for exploring possibilities not visible to the common eye, and he lit me with that fire. You were born of that passion, Rose – and I've seen that passion from the start, in your gift. Even more than your green eyes, that's what shows me you are your father's daughter.'

Mum rose. Moving stiffly as if finally released from bondage, she poured us each another mug of perry.

'He taught for a year in Salisbury, studying medicine on his own, still dreaming of setting up in London, but still not going. Mayhap he wanted to be near me. I don't know – and I didn't care. I saw him from time to time – once when I was with you, in the market. You were six, I suppose. I was large with Michael then. He boasted of his plans to practise astrological medicine in London – quite the showman. I admired his ambition but wondered why I had ever thought I loved him.'

Mum laughed softly and shrugged. 'I had grown up, I suppose. I found that the search for remedies in my own back garden was even more exciting than the stars. And that my true love . . . was you.'

I watched the crimson coals in the grate fade slowly to black.

At length, she went on. 'That day in the market, Martin saw us talking together and drove him off. He hadn't ever forgiven Simon for breaking his apprenticeship. Then, three years later—' She paused, as if remembering something, then shook her head and began again. 'Three years later, my part in the birth of the infant with the withered arm shut down my healings, and my hopes. That's why I sent you to Lady Catherine. I wanted you to have a wider world than my own, even if it meant losing you.'

My eyes stung. The wound of being sent away had never really healed, and it didn't help knowing my mother had given me up out of too much care, not too little. And now a new wound had opened.

After the funeral for the man I still thought of as Da, I took myself off to the Stones. I brought my sketchbook. I wanted their shelter and the company of the rooks circling and cawing overhead. Surrounded by the Stones' familiar mystery, I tried to think through the newly unfamiliar shape of my world, my identity. Part of me was relieved to learn that Da wasn't my father, because he hadn't understood my hopes any better than I had understood his ambitions. Part of me was sad that he was gone, mostly because of how much Michael would miss him. Part of me was angry that he'd left Mum with no security for her future. But part of me, a large part, was afraid of what I'd just learnt from Mum. I was – I struggled to even form the word in my mind – illegitimate. I had a father I'd never met, who didn't know I existed. I wondered if I really was like that father, as Mum had said. I tried to imagine meeting him. And I worried, because there was much in Mum's story that caused me not to trust him.

My drawing that day was not of the Stones, or even of the visible world – or at least not the commonly visible. From memory, I drew my favourite herb from Mum's garden – borage, whose distinctive five-pointed star petals were carved on the oaken box that was my lasting gift from Da. Now that I had access to pigments, I could paint those wooden petals violet blue, bringing the colours of the garden to my box. But in this moment, working only with charcoal, I drew the starflowers not for colour but for the harmony their shapes brought to my burdened heart. In the scale of my drawing, the starflowers were as large as the Stones, while behind and above them, in the heavens, shone the constellations of the night sky. A view of starflowers from the perspective of a beetle. Once the pinprick shapes of the constellations emerged beneath my hand, the stars appeared not as the background to my drawing but as a heavenly reflection of the starflowers upon the earth. I glimpsed an intersection between two worlds – my mother's and my newly discovered father's – flowers and stars, earth and heavens.

But who was I? My mother's confession had smudged my sense of myself like charcoal, the edges blurred. And that wasn't all. Discovering a different father, I lost the mother I had always known.

CHAPTER EIGHTEEN

Mary, 1586

No more pregnancies. Doctor Moffett had been firm. After this last difficult birth, her womb simply couldn't bear another baby to term.

Mary saw his pronouncement as a just judgement by God upon her own maternal inadequacies. Ambrosia's death had taught her the lesson that life means loss and that God's will is inscrutable, and often harsh. Kate's passing only confirmed it. Now, two years after that night of agonising birth and unjust death, she had made her peace with God.

For Henry, though, there was no peace. 'How many deaths before God says enough?' His anger and despair rang clear as a church bell as they walked together one cool moonlit night by the River Nadder that skirted the Wilton estate. 'I could not forgive God for Catherine's passing. And I will never forgive

Him for taking Kate – nor for the ravages of your womb.' Guttural with confession, his voice rose from a pit of loss too deep for reason to fathom.

'What if it isn't a matter of forgiveness? Or even of comprehension?' Mary's voice was sharp. Living daily with her own anguish, she had scraped and sifted through the ashes of her mourning to arrive at hard truths. 'What if fate – or let us call it God's will – is beyond human capacity to understand or forgive? What if each Psalm reaffirms not faith so much as the will to create? *To sing his works while breath shall give me space.*' She grasped her husband's cold hands. Inside her, a flame burned. 'That's what I believe, Henry. Even if I can find no greater purpose in these losses, I can yet create.'

Watching the moonlight play upon the ripples in the river, Mary's thoughts returned to her most recent losses. Both her parents had died that summer, within three months of each other. Mary grieved her father's death but accepted its inevitability. She unflinchingly carried out his final request, that his heart be buried at Ludlow in Ambrosia's tomb – an acknowledgement, she realised, that Ambrosia had owned all their hearts. She had decidedly mixed feelings about the fact that upon Henry Sidney's death, Henry Herbert had succeeded to the Presidency of the Council of the Marches in Wales – and with it, the lease of Ludlow Castle. Mary would now be mistress of the household that held so many scenes of happiness and heartbreak.

'My mother's death was harder,' Mary said, suddenly realising she was speaking aloud. Now she continued, taking her husband's arm. 'Although her duties to the Queen often distracted her during our childhoods, she understood and supported my aspirations. I miss her – her calm voice, her wise counsel—' She broke off, a sob catching in her throat.

'Come,' Henry said, 'the wind is picking up. Let's return.'

He led her back along the riverbank towards the house. As they passed through the gardens, Mary reflected that only her brother Philip remained. He was abroad in the Netherlands, on a perilous mission in the Queen's service. Every day, Mary feared for his safety and longed for his company, her dearest soul and partner of the mind.

Mary was not alone in mourning. Last year her maidservant had lost a father as well. When Rose returned to Wilton, Mary drew from her the revelation of her father's debts, now burdening her mother. The Countess immediately invited Joan to join the Wilton household. Joan's herbal expertise, she assured Rose, would be of great use in the production of medicines and would allow her to gradually pay off the debts.

Mary was grateful for Joan's calming presence to balance Adrian's commotion in her still-room. She noticed a new distance between mother and daughter, but accepted that there was more to their lives than she had a right to know. She began to train Rose in the chemistry of alchemy, so that Joan's knowledge of herbals could work in concert with her daughter's growing comprehension of the use of minerals as well as plants. And Mary increasingly valued Rose's keen eye in keeping a visual record of their work. The more closely they worked together, the deeper her appreciation for the potential her predecessor had recognised.

While Mary recorded every detail of her experiments, intent upon understanding the causes and consequences of any misstep, Adrian adjusted his practices seemingly as much by instinct as experience. Under Adrian's supervision, the athanor, finally and without further mishap, produced crystals of sulphur sublimate, a valued medicine for the relief of pain. Over several months, the initial distillation of black ash had metamorphosed into a snowy residue, followed by the golden coagulation that produced the ruby stage of the elixir – a process at once tedious and thrilling. Rarely discouraged by failure, Adrian was driven above all by the hope of so many alchemists, that he would one day attain the Philosopher's Stone.

'What *is* the Philosopher's Stone?' Rose asked one morning, as she and Mary worked together in the still-room, chopping dried hyssop flowers and leaves into bits for an oil.

'Well, it's not really a stone,' Mary began. 'Some alchemists consider it to be the elixir of life, others a mystical symbol of all perfection. For an alchemist like Master Gilbert, the Philosopher's Stone represents both the transformation of base metals into gold and, as he puts it, *mastery of the secrets of nature.*'

As if the secrets of nature could ever be mastered, she thought. Men's drive for mastery was as ancient as alchemy itself. Attuned to Mary's tone of voice, Rose grinned.

'For myself,' Mary continued, warming to her subject, 'I seek what Paracelsus teaches is the true gold – the curative power of chemical medicines, which conjoin distillations from herbs with metals and minerals.' She gestured to Rose's portrait of Lady Catherine, now framed and hanging on the still-room wall above the writing desk. 'Your first mistress practised more herbal than mineral distillation, but even her remedies call for such materials as antimony, mercury, sulphur and lead, which can be poisonous if not properly distilled and transmuted.' She nodded towards the cabinet of treasures. Understanding the risk was part of the process, and Rose's growing understanding of the multiple possibilities deserved encouragement.

'Grinding pigments and layering paints to arrive at the right hue, you are practising your own stages of alchemy,' Mary observed. This time, the maid did not blush at the compliment, but bowed her head in agreement. Another collaborator, Mary realised.

After a year's exile from court, Philip had not only been restored to the Queen's favour, but soon knighted. He was now a cavalry officer on Her Majesty's service in the Netherlands, under the command of his uncle, the Earl of Leicester.

He was also married.

As he had predicted to Mary, their father had arranged an 'advantageous' match. The chosen bride was the daughter of the family's closest Protestant ally, Sir Francis Walsingham. Queen Elizabeth's Principal Secretary – and spymaster – had pledged a dowry that included the repayment of over one thousand pounds of Philip's debts. Marriage as a matter for negotiation rather than love. And yet, Mary reflected, Philip's brilliant love sonnets remained, voicing a passion that might live beyond both his and Mary's marriages to others they did not love. They conveyed the *truth in poesy* that Walter had once observed was all too rare, the truth that had prompted the creative collaboration between brother and sister. That collaboration had supplied a more satisfying union, in its own way, than either of their arranged marriages.

'Why must it be you to lead these troops?' Mary had protested when Philip received his commission. 'Surely other generals have more experience on the battlefield, and less to lose,' she added. 'You leave your wife with a new baby.' She did not say, *You leave me without your voice, which supports and calls forth my own.* After the death of Kate and her own near-death in delivering baby Philip, her brother's namesake, she was determined to hold onto those dearest to her within her family – most of all, her brother.

'It is a great honour to be commanded thus by the Queen, and further proof of Her Majesty's favour,' her brother replied. But as far as Mary was concerned, Philip's position with the Queen was sufficiently assured. He had nothing more to prove as a soldier, and much greater feats ahead as an author.

'You've embarked upon a full-scale revision of the *Arcadia* that demands your attention. That work is truly new, Philip, reshaping the very idea of prose romance – brave women heroes as well as men, allied to vanquish the spirit of villainy. Others can lead the charge in the Netherlands. It's dangerous and, to my mind, foolhardy.'

Mary was all too aware of the Queen's reluctance to commit large numbers of soldiers to the struggle in that country, despite the dedication of her most senior courtiers to advancing the Protestant cause on the Continent and freeing the Netherlands from Spanish control. The force she had assigned to Philip's command was relatively small, with an indefinite promise of more troops if the struggle advanced.

But Philip could not be moved. 'Acting on the world stage,

I shall make you proud, Mary. It is a noble conflict. Our spirit can surpass a larger force.'

His eyes alight with the familiar fervour of creation, he promised to draw more stories from the battlefield itself. 'I'll be home sooner than you think. Meanwhile, I leave my manuscript in your care, with the revised fragments that I've already produced. I shall return with the missing pieces.'

The months of absence Philip had expected had now stretched into a year, interspersed with brief bulletins from the front.

> *Although the Dutch resent Leicester's policy of caution, they*
> *seem to love me because I believe in their potential to resist*
> *the Spaniards. I've been made the governor of Flushing, and*
> *people here speak of me as a future governor general!*

Mary was not greatly comforted by his enthusiasm, and longed only for her brother's return. She felt silenced by his absence, unable to concentrate on their Psalms or her Cleopatra. How she wished to be volleying words back and forth with him again.

Philip's young wife Frances, married at sixteen, had come to stay at Wilton while Philip was away, bringing one-year-old Elizabeth, named after the sovereign. From Frances, Mary learnt that Philip was struggling to maintain the morale of his troops, who deserved reinforcements and better pay. He had written to his wife's father. Surely the Queen's principal adviser could prevail upon Her Majesty to provide more troops and funds. Nonetheless, Frances reported, Philip was confident that their cause would prevail as long as they did not falter in spirit. Ever the optimist, Mary thought.

When first their father and then their mother died that summer, Philip had been at the front, unable to attend their deathbeds or even their funerals. Now, as the flowers in the Wilton gardens began to fade, word came that English and Dutch troops had besieged the strategic town of Zutphen, seeking to wrest it from Spanish control. Philip was among the Earl of Leicester's commanders who laid the siege.

One night in late September, Mary was awakened by urgent knocking at her chamber door. It was Henry, his eyes wild. 'News from the front,' he exclaimed hoarsely.

'Philip!' she breathed, drawing her gown around her. 'Is he—?'

'Not dead. Sorely wounded.' Henry's voice shook slightly. 'Your brother led three charges through enemy lines while heading a military action to prevent the Spaniards from sending supplies into the garrison at Zutphen. But his forces were outnumbered.' So the Queen hadn't sent more troops. Mary felt a stab of bitterness at this ruler who placed policy before people. How far must her brother suffer in service to the Queen? But Henry was still speaking.

'Philip had removed his thigh armour for greater mobility. His leg was shattered by a bullet above the knee.' Mary swayed, and Henry caught her in his arms.

Word came the next day that the surgeons were optimistic about Philip's chances of full recovery. But Frances wanted to be with him. Accompanied by Mary's brother Robert, she travelled to the Netherlands, leaving baby Bess with Mary at Wilton.

'Is Uncle Philip a hero now?' asked six-year-old William, watching his mother hold his baby cousin close to her as they sat in the solar.

'He was already a hero, William.' She couldn't explain to the boy that she didn't believe his uncle should ever have been sent into battle with insufficient forces. That she was starting to hate the Protestant cause that had brought her family so much woe. That she would rather have Philip alive, writing at her side, than beloved of the Queen. So she said nothing more. Better to remain silent and pray he will return.

They say he'll recover, she reminded herself. *So he* must *recover. And when he returns, he'll want to resume our work.*

The door opened and Rose entered, carrying a letter. Henry stood framed in the doorway, rooted in place. Even before unfolding the flimsy sheet, she knew.

Philip was dead. Gangrene.

Mary no longer wished to understand God's mysteries. After wresting away two siblings, heart-mates who had been her inspiration and audience, He had become utterly incomprehensible.

How could she ever have believed that God valued her creations, when He clearly didn't value His own? From here on, she vowed, she would create for others, but she would work alone.

Solitude – the price of self-sovereignty.

CHAPTER NINETEEN

Rose, 1587

My lady and I had lost our fathers within a twelvemonth.
But I lost my father twice – first to death, then to the
news that he wasn't my father at all. Da had disapproved
of my aspiration to capture the world on paper, to explore
connections between the seen and the unseen, creating with
my pen even as Mum used herbals to create remedies. I had
defined myself in opposition to Da's disapproval – and it had
been liberating. Like striking a blade against flint to draw
sparks for a fire, opposing his will set my own desire ablaze.
Now, knowing that Da was not my father, my conviction
that I could forge my own path by pursuing a gift that
belonged to me alone dissolved like the primary material in
one of the alembic vessels in Lady Mary's still-room. For
if I was to believe that I was, in Mum's words, my father's

daughter, not knowing my father meant that my path had no starting point.

'I want to find him,' I told Mum when she arrived to join the household. 'I want him to know that I exist, to know who I am.' And I needed to find out who I was.

I didn't try to conceal the anger and sense of betrayal that fuelled this quest. It was her fault, after all, that I had lost my bearings. Mum didn't pretend not to know who I was talking about.

'When I saw him in the market that day, Rose, Simon told me he planned to set up as an astrologer-physician in London, in Billingsgate. That's all I know.'

For a country maid with no knowledge of London, it wasn't much to go on. But it was a start.

I expected my mistress to be engulfed in another black fog by the death of her brother, following hard upon those of her father and mother. Instead, to my surprise, my lady responded to this loss as a fighter, not a prisoner. Instead of relinquishing her work tasks, she took on more. She began spending time daily in the still-room. But I discovered that her activity masked a deeper darkness within – not a fog, but a cavern, closed to outsiders. When an entire week passed without my lady once meeting my eyes, I took matters into my own hands. One morning after I had dressed her hair, as she made to rise from her chair, I leant the framed portrait against the mirror.

Shock flashed across her face. Kate smiled out at us, her head framed by copper curls, her cheeks rosy with health. I had managed to capture the indigo shade of her eyes, lit by her unquenchable smile. Surrounding the central image were the pen-and-ink sketches capturing Kate at various times in her short childhood – pulling herself to stand and looking over her shoulder for approval, clapping her plump hands together in delight at the sight of a butterfly, cradling her cloth doll ever-so-gently in her arms, laughing out loud at the antics of her big brother, who could entertain his sister as no one else.

'Kate *alive*,' my lady whispered, meeting my eyes for the first time. Then she gripped my fingers so tightly that I almost cried out. 'I was terrified I'd lose my memories of Kate, that she would fade. But your portrait has restored her.' She began to shake. Suddenly, her body was shuddering with short sobs. Trying to help, had I only reopened her grief? Helpless to speak the right words, I did the only thing I could. I took my lady into my arms, holding her the way Cicely held me when I needed comfort. She wept for a long time.

Finally, wiping the tears from her cheeks, she straightened. 'I thought Kate's death was my fault. That I didn't deserve to keep living. But when Philip died, his loss awakened me to an awareness that my life can yet have a purpose – to keep his voice alive. The way your portrait keeps Kate alive. Thank you for that reminder, Rose.'

In stark contrast to the small family service for Kate in the Wilton chapel, a large state funeral was planned for Sir Philip Sidney in London. It had been delayed by several months while Sir Francis Walsingham arranged an appropriately lavish commemoration honouring his son-in-law – courtier, statesman, poet, and now, fallen hero. My mistress, though, would not be accompanying Sir Henry to London.

'The funeral is intended to celebrate my brother's heroism and allow the public to honour him as a soldier and statesman.' Her grey eyes, the shade of water iced over in winter, were bleak. Her voice grew sharper as she looked off towards a future I couldn't see. 'I shall instead honour his life as a writer whose influence will continue to shape the world when everyone now living is dead.' Her closing word was a thunderclap. Affirmation and resistance together. Her flame-red hair framed a face pale as the whitest of lilies, her eyes dark with loss. But her voice was firm, her resolve clear. She had emerged from her cavern.

That night I sharpened my quill by candlelight and pulled out my sketchbook. I drew my mistress, standing proudly erect and defiant of death's power to dictate the terms of her life. Considering how the painter used context to bring the viewer inside his subject, I framed my lady's figure, not with draperies but with a vast window. Outside the window, lightning split the sky and raindrops rushed down the windowpane.

With my mistress remaining at Wilton instead of travelling to London for the funeral, I lost the most obvious means of journeying to find my father. I also hoped to study further with Master Gheeraerts, who had returned to London after completing the Herbert family portrait and even now was preparing to paint a portrait of the Queen herself. So I devised a plan. One evening, readying my lady for bed, I requested permission to travel with those members of the household who would be accompanying Sir Henry to London, where he would remain for a fortnight after the funeral, so that I could resume my training with the painter.

'I'd like to further my studies in colour and composition – to better contribute to your records for the still-room.' I spoke softly but firmly, the pigments in my mind's eye colouring my array of hopes like the arresting spread of a peacock's tail. With Mum assisting her in the still-room, Lady Mary could more easily spare my services during this absence. And her personal care could be accomplished by one of the younger chambermaids she had encouraged me to begin training.

The other reason driving my request I kept to myself. Until I found my father, I didn't want anyone to know about him. Only to myself could I admit that the two reasons for my journey to London were linked.

My lady looked at me closely, and I wondered if she suspected I wasn't telling her everything. But she simply nodded, adding, 'Whatever you learn, trust your eye.'

One of the grandest funerals in living memory, they all said afterwards. I watched the procession from an upper window in Baynard's Castle along with the other maidservants, craning to identify members of our household in the hundreds of mourners streaming towards St Paul's Cathedral. Sir Philip's brothers led the procession and Sir Henry rode behind the hearse, which was draped in black velvet and studded with coats of arms. Peter, Brian and other menservants followed, holding aloft the Pembroke colours. In the sketch I made from memory later that day, the hearse looked like a star fallen to earth, trailed by a river of darkness.

After the funeral, while Sir Henry was occupied at court, I worked in Master Gheeraerts' London studio alongside his stable of apprentices. In the mornings I ground pigments and mixed powders with linseed oil for the master's palette, and spent the afternoons applying painstaking layers of colour atop my charcoal sketches. Being the only girl in the studio, I was stared at, but my friendship with Jeremy protected me from the other apprentices' unwelcome attentions. And Master Gheeraerts himself was unfailingly kind, for such a busy artist, making the time to stop by my easel to offer instruction and advice. He also showed me the preparatory sketches for his portrait of Queen Elizabeth. I was fascinated by his charcoal renditions of the painting's design. Standing upon the great globe of the world, her feet resting on a map of England, the haughty Queen was framed on one side by thunderous storm clouds split by lightning and on the other side by the sun breaking through, as if her presence could command not just the fate of England but the very elements.

Composition, I was beginning to understand, was all.

One morning at the end of my first week in London, I set out for Billingsgate. Brian, who made friends more easily than anyone, had learnt his way around London from the stable boys in the other great houses near Baynard's Castle, so he knew the warren of streets extending north of the Thames like the lines in his own palm. He offered to accompany me if I could wait until after he had attended to the horses, but I didn't want either Brian or Peter to know what I sought, so I thanked him and said I could follow his directions on my own.

Easier said than done. So many shops and stalls lined Upper Thames Street that my head was spinning with the sheer abundance of goods for sale – everything from ribbons and spices to raw meat and fish. The Amesbury market suddenly seemed like a thinly rendered charcoal sketch compared to the colourful oil portrait of London's crowded thoroughfares. Life in multiple hues, from grimy gutters to colourful carriages, their wheels splashing mud from those gutters. So many scents, from sour piss to fresh-baked pastries, that I found myself covering my nose one moment to keep the stenches from turning my stomach, then suddenly breathing in the mix of fragrances drifting from the window of a perfumer where I paused to catch my breath – lavender, anise, almond oil and, yes, rose water.

I hurried on through the hurly-burly, excited and awed but mindful of Brian's parting words. 'Keep an eye out for those street urchins – they'll snatch the cloak right off your back!' By the time I reached London Bridge, almost an hour after setting out, I was exhausted by the hubbub. That was when the glowering clouds that had been leaking a chilly drizzle all morning finally burst and released a flood of pelting sleet and rain.

Pulling my hood closer around my head, I tried to dash for shelter on the bridge, but found it so closely packed with shops and customers that I was frightened of losing my bearings and forgetting Brian's careful directions. I reached St Magnus the Martyr Church, one of the landmarks he'd promised me, just as a thunderclap exploded over my head, and I passed hastily into the nave to escape. I shrugged off my sodden cloak and slipped into a pew, praying I might find my father before the storm washed me away. But with as sudden a turn as it had burst overhead, the watery gusts of the tempest gave way to wavery sunlight that illuminated the stained-glass windows of the church, spilling transparent pigments of sapphire, ruby and emerald across the floor in a palette of light. For a moment, looking up from the coloured flagstones to the coloured panes of glass, I was lost in fixing these jewelled colours into my memory.

My body's shuddering cold recalled me to my mission. I emerged from the sanctuary and passed along Pudding Lane, its steep narrow length overhung with casements now opening to catch the sun. Every shopfront I passed was identified by a painted sign with a picture identifying the trade within – fishmongers and jewellers, stationers and scriveners. I marvelled at the busy community of craftsmen and wondered if women artisans operated shops as well. Had we lived in London, Da could have set up a shop to sell his wares to an endless stream of customers with money to spend. Surely this was why Simon Forman had chosen to settle here, because London offered a bigger market for his astrological and medical skills than Salisbury.

At length, a pungent stink told me I had reached the precincts of Billingsgate, where freshly caught fish were offloaded at the Thameside dock for sale in the open-air market. I had no idea how to find my father in the district's sprawling streets and alleys. My only recourse was to knock on doors and enquire if anyone had heard of Simon Forman. I first tried my luck with a cobbler who told me he had never heard of the man but, eyeing my simple slippers, wondered, 'Would you like to buy this fine pair of furred buskins?' I dearly wished I had the money, because my feet were icy and numb from the sleet-storm.

I was stumbling with fatigue and hunger by the time I knocked on a door that was opened by a wizened woman, her head wreathed in smoke, sucking on a pipe. My mouth dropped open – a woman using tobacco! – before I remembered to ask my question. 'Oh yes, miss,' she rasped. 'Doctor Forman, he has a room in the Stone House, just round the corner in Philpot Lane.' As I thanked her and turned away, she plucked at my cloak. 'Mind you, he's a charlatan, he is – pretends he has charms for women's ailments, both the body and the heart. Step careful with that one!'

Around a turn in Philpot Lane I came upon an imposing building that looked out of place among the huddle of small shops and houses. A board on the gate read *The Stone House*. A series of doors lined the broad porch, each with its own sign. *Stephen Napier, Apothecary*, read one. Beside the next door, painted in a slapdash hand and hanging crooked, was *Simon Forman, Astrologer-Physician*.

Wringing the corners of my still-dripping cloak over the stone path, I hesitated, suddenly doubting my resolve to meet this father who didn't know I existed. When a chilly burst of wind pushed me towards the sign, I let the weather shape my fate. I gripped the heavy brass knocker and let it fall three times against the plum-coloured door.

But now I was trembling from anxiety as well as cold. I had no plan beyond arriving on my father's doorstep, and no idea what to say. The sound of quick footsteps, then the door swung open. Green eyes, as sharp and dark as bay laurel leaves, met my own, beneath sandy brows and dark, thinning hair the shade of newly turned earth in my mother's garden. His face was sombre, almost gaunt-cheeked, framed by a dark bushy beard above a white linen collar, its edges stained with sweat. His tawny robe suggested, if not wealth, at least some means, for I recognised the fabric as one of those among Da's more costly bolts of cloth.

'Do you seek a cure for an ailment?' His voice was higher and sharper than I had expected – quick and confident, but not particularly inviting.

'I've come to paint you a better sign.' It wasn't until I heard the words slipping out of my mouth, bolder than I felt, that I realised they contained a plan. Buoyed by his confounded expression, I pressed on. 'Outside the door – your sign isn't well-painted, sir. If you offer services that many seek, then your sign should reflect that quality.'

He stared at me, hard. 'And what would you ask in return?' Still sharp, his voice was genuinely curious now, coloured with amusement at this wet, bedraggled female on his doorstep.

'Perhaps you can tell me that yourself,' I replied, gaining confidence and beginning to enjoy this game – a game where I set the rules. I wasn't about to tell him what I really wanted. 'If you can indeed read the stars to learn what's to come, you might have known I'd arrive on your doorstep today.'

His earthy eyebrows shot up towards his receding hairline.

'Who are you?'

'Look into my eyes, sir, and tell me what you see there – not my fortune, but yours.'

Confusion mixed with curiosity on his features. As if recalling his manners, or perhaps to buy time, he motioned me across the threshold and shut the door. He removed my sodden

263

cloak and draped it over a chair beside the glowing fireplace. Then he wrapped a warm wool blanket around my shivering shoulders and led me to a window. Looking into my face, he scanned my features and his brows contracted briefly.

'You remind me of someone,' he muttered. 'Your eyes, green as a cat's . . .'

'Yes?' My voice quickened with excitement. But he frowned and gestured towards the door. 'I don't have time to waste on riddles. Go your way, young lady.'

I was not about to let go. So I decided to bait the hook.

'I'd like you to cast my horoscope.' He looked at me quizzically. 'I was born on the fifteenth day of March, 1564.'

'Ah – the Ides of March.' He seemed to be thinking, calculating the mathematics of that date. 'And your birthplace?' Now it was my turn to be taken aback. I had never had my horoscope cast and hadn't realised he needed that piece of information, which would surely give everything away. But I was in too deep to pull out now.

'Amesbury.' At that name, those green eyes first widened, then narrowed, scouring my features again.

'And your name?'

I paused, then leapt. 'Rosamund.' I wondered if he would recognise the alchemical significance of the name, a transmutation of my natural name that connected me to my lady and her powers.

'You may wait here – *Rosamund*,' he told me, inflecting the name with a sceptical emphasis. 'I shall cast your star chart in the next room. Then we can discuss our bargain.'

'And I will make a sketch of my proposed design,' I

replied, growing bolder. 'Do you have paper and a quill?'

Again, that frown, as if he was still trying to place my face. Without a word, he went to a desk, pulled a sheet of paper from the top drawer, set out a quill and inkpot, waved me to a small side table at the window and left the room.

I looked about me for the first time, and saw a room in a state that I could only call ordered chaos, reminding me of Master Gilbert's working disorder in the still-room. Pots of herbs near the windows surrounded a larger pot from which rose a small tree bearing yellow fruit. Shelves were stacked with an uneven assortment of books and papers, and crowded as well with bottles and phials, pots and flasks. A large star chart was fastened to one wall, calling to mind my conversations with Peter about constellations. Along the dusty windowsills were arrayed small figures in both male and female shapes – completely naked! Below one window rested a slatted wooden crate that emitted a sound. It proved to be coming from a fat green snake that reared its head when it saw me and flicked its forked tongue.

Startled, I pressed my hand against the ouroboros pendant beneath my smock. I could hear Lady Catherine's reassuring voice in my head. *Many practices called magic work for good rather than ill.* Then Lady Mary's voice. *Trust your eye.*

So I sat at the table, carefully avoiding the hissing crate, dipped my quill into the ink, and began to draw. In large letters, the name *Simon Forman*. The 'S' was a snake balanced on its tail, the 'F' a tree, its arms branching with leaves. Beside the name, an unstoppered apothecary bottle, out of which, like smoke, poured the constellations of the night sky, spreading across the top border then descending to encircle the title beneath the name: *Astrologer-Physician*. I was so engrossed in the composition that I didn't even notice when he re-entered the room.

'You're the daughter of Joan Commin.' Not a question, but a statement. His scrutiny pinned me in place. He held up a chart and pointed to his finely scripted calculations with a surprisingly slender index finger. I realised it was trembling slightly. 'Pisces ascendant, the Sun in Pisces, Jupiter in Sagittarius and the Moon in Virgo. You're unpredictable but adaptable. Possibly even unstoppable.' He fell silent, and on his face I saw the question he had started with. Why was I here?

'Joan Commin is my mother, sir, you're right about that. I'm her firstborn.'

He nodded with satisfaction. 'It was her determination I read in your face when you arrived.' But his voice was no longer assured – as if he couldn't take the final step. So I took it for him.

'Mum's first child was fathered by you.' Suddenly my voice was raw, streaked with abandonment.

First a glimmer of anger at my presumption. Then, comprehension, with a flash of wonder.

'You're – my daughter.' The hand holding the star chart fluttered upwards, then sank to his side.

'An accident, I presume,' I confirmed, bitterly.

'I can tell you there are no accidents under the stars.' His voice sounded pompous, not as wise as he surely intended. Then questions spilled forth, a stream breaching a barrier. 'Did

Joan send you? Does Martin know?' Seeing my closed face, he checked himself.

'My da died last month. I came to seek you on my own. I wished to discover what part you played in forming me.' I spoke coldly, unwilling to give him any reassurances. 'Mum told me that I inherited from you the gift of seeing possibilities not visible to the common eye.' I could give him that, at least.

After a long moment, he straightened his linen collar and cleared his throat. 'One of my gifts is the practice of celestial magic – governed by the stars.'

My jaw dropped. Mum had told me nothing of this sort. 'You're a magician?'

His eyes darkened. 'If by *magician* you mean the hucksters who lurk on street corners selling spells – no. I practise magic, I don't sell it to be practised by the uninitiated.'

Then, for the first time, he looked at my drawing of his name and title, drew a breath, and nodded.

'In return for the sign you offer, I will fashion an astral ring that will support you in your aspirations and harness the power of the stars that rule your fortunes.' His eyes flashed with a pleasure I recognised – the challenge of creation. 'I shall complete your ring according to the appropriate magical hours.' Seeing my puzzled frown, he condescended to explain. 'While natural hours are measured by the clock, magical hours must be calculated according to the ecliptic line of the eighth heaven.'

I said nothing. He might as well have been speaking French, like Madame La Grande, for all I understood. He moved to the door and opened it.

'Come back in a week. I shall have the pigments ready for you.'

I nodded and collected my cloak, now dried by the fire. 'Goodbye, Master Forman,' I said, coolly.

It wasn't until I was outside, where a milky sun was drying the puddles in Philpot Lane, that my knees buckled. I leant against a pillar of the porch to get my bearings.

If this was a game, I had played it well. But to what end?

Who was this father I had so eagerly sought out? – this *astrologer-physician-magician*? A seer? A charlatan? Or a madman?

CHAPTER TWENTY

Mary, 1587

On the day of Philip's funeral, Mary was alone. When Henry had departed Wilton to attend the lavish ceremony, she was relieved. As a woman, she was barred in any case from participating in the funeral, and she couldn't bear the prospect of watching from a window as her brother's casket travelled with aching majesty past Baynard's Castle on its way to St Paul's Cathedral. And now, she had a promise to keep.

In the months before the funeral, Mary had felt nothing. Worse than nothing. She felt dead herself. Her grief over Philip's death had at first been so enormous that it smothered everything, until all she was aware of was the futility of drawing breath each day in a world that no longer included those she loved best. Her sister. Her firstborn daughter. Her parents. And now, her brother.

Mary's was a private grief. She craved solitude, not the world's condolences, not even her husband's. Solitude seemed a fitting container for the deathly numbness that she experienced after Philip's death.

Then, Rose had shattered her carefully preserved shell, presenting her with that vibrant portrait of Kate. Deep within her, a hope had awakened – if Rose could celebrate Kate's life with paint, perhaps Mary could celebrate her brother's life with words. She had vowed to try.

As the funeral procession was winding its way to St Paul's, Mary was at Ivychurch, where she and Philip had spent so many happily productive hours writing and sharing their work. Looking south-east over woods and pastures to the Salisbury Cathedral's tranquil spire rising from a profusion of green towards the silvery clouds, Mary could almost hear her brother's voice, rehearsing plot lines for his romance or refining a metaphor in one of his sonnets.

Combing through loose pages of his revisions for *Arcadia*, Mary was gratified to discover that Philip had taken to heart her challenge to enhance women's roles in the narrative. In one passage, she found a woman entering into battle as a knight, unbounded by the constraints of her sex. Another character disguised himself to fight, and woo, as an Amazon. Now, engaged once more with her brother's prose romance, Mary felt more joy than pain.

When Rose returned from London with Henry's entourage, Mary immediately sensed that something had changed in the girl. As Rose readied her mistress for bed that evening, her eyes conveyed an awareness of loss that Mary had felt from no one else, for all the eloquent tributes to her brother that had come across her desk from friends and would-be friends. Rose understood that loss couldn't be repaired with words, nor the chasm of grief filled with sermons or elegies. Mary found the silence they shared peaceful. How she had ever judged Rose unremarkable was astounding. She clung to the comfort of Rose's quiet presence like a rope cast into a whirlpool, keeping her head above water.

And yet, her maidservant seemed troubled herself. She examined Rose's face in the mirror, observing the new lines of care around those startlingly green eyes, noting the way the fading sunlight lit her wispy hair like a halo.

'Is all well, Rose? How is your mother?'

Rose's face registered surprise, then she sighed.

'It's not Mum – it's *me*. I don't have your gift for words, my lady, so I can't rightly say what's muddling me. I'm trying to find my best way forward.'

Without Rose, Mary knew, she herself might still be mired in the solitude of her grief. How could she reach out in turn? Rose was certainly not muddled when it came to capturing truth in pictures.

'I'm still trying to find my own way forward, Rose,' Mary admitted. 'For me, as you know, that usually means through words. So I've started working on creating a play – about a queen of Egypt.'

Rose stared, and Mary smiled.

'Yes, I know, that might seem far-fetched. But working with words comforts me. For you, it's pictures.' Then, an idea. 'Perhaps you'd like to draw what you see when you hear me read it aloud. Not so far removed from your drawings to illustrate Lady Catherine's remedies.'

Rose's face brightened. This, Mary thought, might help both of them move forward.

Mary regularly revisited Lady Catherine's letter to *the next Cleopatra*, hoping to fathom its lessons. She had read and reread the letter, trying to untangle its veiled references to Cleopatra the Alchemist – *a wise woman who lived in ancient times, who taught that an alchemist is like a loving mother who cares for her child and feeds it* – which were interspersed with Catherine's desire to pass on her craft to a successor and grief over her failure to produce a child.

The notion that *an alchemist is like a loving mother* left her cold. Alchemy offered an *escape* from maternity. What could her childless predecessor know about mothers and children? But it was the enigmatic opening that both puzzled Mary and captured her imagination.

Wholeness may arise from fragments pieced together aright.

It went on –

Only when you discover how to unite what is opposed – spirit and matter, male and female – will you approach the essence of the hermaphrodite within your own being. Identify the process itself as your aim and you will know the truth of Cleopatra.

What intrigued her about Catherine's counsel was the figure of the *hermaphrodite*, conceived not as monstrosity or abnormality, but as an ideal to be embraced. Mary found herself drawn to the prospect of actively uniting the opposing forces that threatened to overpower her.

Whatever its full meaning, this was a voice to be attended to, and Mary hoped that by studying the collected remedies she could learn to know her predecessor better. In another world, she imagined, they might even have been friends.

She wrote to Ambrosia:

Slowly, step by step, I'm learning a new way to carry myself. Sharing more of my thoughts with the husband I did not choose, appreciating the connections between spirit and matter in the drawings of my maidservant, also unchosen.

Perhaps it wasn't a question of choice, she thought, twisting the golden ouroboros on her finger, but of a willingness to bite the tail, to complete the connection between contrary parts of oneself.

In each day's work, dear sister, I find myself more willing to entertain conundrums I would have hitherto dismissed: in the Psalms, the interdependence of doubt and faith; in the still-room, the distillation of potentially poisonous substances into a healing remedy.

Over the long months that Philip had been abroad, Mary had worked on organising and cataloguing the remedies, especially those for women's ailments, that she had inherited from Catherine and, latterly, developed for herself. The catalogue proved indispensable when Mary received a letter from her sister-in-law Barbara, her brother Robert's wife of two years, lamenting her inability to conceive a child. Mary herself had always conceived so quickly that she hadn't had cause to seek such knowledge on her own behalf. Now she closeted herself in the still-room, seeking the remedy that had eluded Catherine. As she studied, she reached out to trusted women healers, consulting Joan Commin about herbs and writing to her good friend Lady Margaret Clifford, who had explored this particular problem. It became clear that if successful conception was to be achieved, it must be addressed with both husband and wife.

Mary experimented with recipes that might address Barbara's excessive courses and cramps, as well as those that could support Robert's fertility. For Barbara, she concocted a triple tincture of motherwort, the herb named for its goal – motherhood. She filled a retort with the feathery pinks and mottled greens of coarsely chopped motherwort blossoms and leaves, and covered the mixture with aqua vitae she had previously distilled. The refining process yielded a minty liquor that Barbara was instructed to take as soon as her monthly courses concluded and continue until they started again, or she conceived.

For Robert, Mary distilled several flasks of oil from the costly cinnamon bark that Catherine had purchased from Dutch traders coming from Ceylon. The still-room became so aromatic that Mary and Rose found reasons to spend extra time together in the laboratory, savouring the sweetly spicy air, an invigorating change from the chemical fumes of Adrian's mineral sublimations.

The birth of her niece and goddaughter, another Mary Sidney, at Baynard's Castle in October, just over a year after Philip's death, restored Mary to a state of joy that she had not expected to experience again. Liberated not only from the physical pains of labour, but the darker burden of its aftermath, Mary marvelled at the experience viewed from the light. Rose deftly assisted Joan, who attended Barbara's labour as calmly and reassuringly as if midwifery were no more demanding than overseeing herbal distillations in the still-room – as if each birth were not a matter of life and death. The new baby emerged bathed in blood, eyelids squeezed shut. Only after little Mall, as her father had already dubbed her, was swaddled and handed to her godmother, did her dark eyes open and her rosy lips part in a lusty wail.

Mary found herself instantly, implausibly, in love.

CHAPTER TWENTY-ONE

Rose, 1587

Facing my birth father in Billingsgate only sharpened my sense of grievance. My mother's confession had ripped the canvas of our family portrait – or rather, my own vision of it. The family I had always envisioned never really existed. The worst of it was, the rupture split the image of myself in that portrait down the middle. I wanted to question Mum further – to confront her, really, about what the astrologer had told me. But my days were so busy, and my mind so confused, that I found myself delaying the conversation I both craved and dreaded.

I removed the astral ring from my finger and stored it in my oaken box, and told Mum only that I had found Simon Forman and the encounter had been as illuminating as my studies with the painter. I was relieved when she asked no questions. I wasn't ready to talk about what I'd found out, and perhaps she wasn't ready to tell me more. I was convinced there was more to hear – but I feared the knowledge.

I had completed my bargain with Master Forman on the day before Sir Henry's retinue was to return to Wilton. I set off that morning, not for Whitehall, where I'd been studying with Master Gheeraerts, but in the opposite direction, for Philpot Lane. This time I was no longer awed by the vibrant bustle of the city, but wound my way deftly through the foot traffic on Upper Thames Street. I took care to keep a tight grasp on the sack into which I'd placed three brushes borrowed from Jeremy – a blunt miniver, a pointed round and, my favourite, a filbert, whose oval shape could be used both for sweeping strokes and fine lines. These weren't typical sign-painting brushes, but I wanted to produce an image I could be proud to claim.

The slapdash sign was still hanging out front, though it had been straightened from its careless slant. I banged the knocker firmly and listened expectantly for approaching footsteps. No sound. After banging again with no response, I made my way around the side of the Stone House and peered into the window of his consulting room, where I had drawn my vision of the sign. No astrologer.

Moving to the next window, I stretched up as far as I could on the tips of my slippers, and was just able to peep into the back room. I caught sight of a circle drawn on the floor with chalk, marked by candles at four points. Simon Forman was kneeling at a short-legged table in the centre of the chalk circle, an engraver's tool in one hand. He was peering through spectacles at the object he was working on – a ring.

My grip on the windowsill was beginning to slip. I banged on the window with the flat of my palm, and he started, dropping his tool and hastening to the window. Seeing me outside, he gestured impatiently to the front of the house.

As I arrived at the plum-coloured door, it burst open. 'You interrupted my completion of the engravings on your ring,' he bellowed, pulling me into the house. 'You might have spoilt the entire process!'

'A week has passed, Master Forman,' I replied, refusing to be cowed. 'I have come to paint your sign.'

He let go of my arm and raised his brows, regarding my smock stained with pigments and dabs of paint.

'I've been studying with Master Gheeraerts the painter,' I explained curtly. 'Tomorrow I leave London, so this is the last day that I can fulfil my side of our bargain.'

Suddenly, surprisingly, the astrologer smiled at me, not in amusement but with evident pride. 'My daughter studying with a court painter,' he murmured. 'Not even in my dreams – and I can tell you I have many – have I seen such a sight.'

He produced a smoothly planed piece of oak and a tray of pigments – azurite, verdigris, lime white and burnt black – as well as a dish of egg yolk for tempering the colours and a phial of linseed oil for mixing the paint. Then he left me to my work and returned to his own in the next room. Immersed in our separate tasks, we didn't exchange another word for three hours. In that time, I outlined the design upon the wood in charcoal, fixed it with ink, and then applied the colours, one layer at a time.

The snake starting his name curved upright in a brilliant

emerald shade that would catch any eye, followed by the rest of the letters in black, while the brown oak of the 'F' sprouted green leaves the colour of our eyes. The apothecary bottle I painted in violet, with the constellations, rendered in lime white, streaming out of the bottle like magical smoke. His professional title, of *Astrologer-Physician*, ran across the bottom of the sign in azurite blue. When I finished, I regarded my work with an unfamiliar combination of frustration and pride. Each waver where the line wasn't perfectly smooth was a flaw I had no time to fix, but the harmony of the entire image was unmistakable.

He gazed at the sign so long that my confidence started to waver. Then, a whisper. 'Extraordinary.'

My eyes filled. Here, at least, was a father who appreciated my gift. With a sigh of satisfaction, he handed me a small velvet pouch. 'Rosamund, in return for your visionary work I present you with your astral ring.'

From the pouch, I drew a silver ring set with a polished rosy stone, engraved with curving lines and symbols.

'Rose quartz,' he told me. 'Not your birthstone, but the perfect stone for your ring, given your name – Rosamund.' The astrologer traced the symbols with his own finger and explained the significance of each sign: Pisces ruled by Jupiter, the Moon in Virgo and the rising arrow of Sagittarius, which would bring me luck, growth and wisdom. Inside the ring, he had engraved the name *Rosamund* and the initials *SF*.

Unexpectedly moved by the care he had taken, I bowed my head in thanks. 'My birth name is Rose.' I felt I owed him an explanation. 'My first lady, who was an alchemist, gave me the name Rosamund.'

He nodded in immediate comprehension. '*Rosa Mundi*.' Then he took my hand and slid the ring onto my finger. 'For your future, Rose.'

I had thought he bore no relation to me, despite our blood kinship, but now I understood that he did. Engraving the same stone for my ring as my gift from Lady Catherine, he had made visible a connection I couldn't ignore.

But I needed more.

'I want to hear your story.'

The astrologer gestured to a stack of notebooks on the topmost shelf. 'I've been recording my story without an audience for so many years now that I hardly know where to begin.'

'Did you know that my mother was accused of witchcraft?' My words burst out without thinking.

He nodded sadly. 'It's a shared story. To this day I regret that I couldn't protect Joan from the ignorance and fear of those we tried to help.'

We? Mum hadn't mentioned his presence in that story. I wondered what else she hadn't told me.

During that long afternoon, sitting before the fire while Master Forman's snake rustled softly in its crate, I heard a tale more fantastical than any in my lady's romances. My mother and my birth father were bound together by more than me.

'It's true that, together, Joan and I employed celestial magic as well as herbal remedies in our efforts to assist the birth process. But because I owned books of medicine as well as books of magic, I was protected by my book-learning – and by being a man.' Seeing my quizzical look, he explained, 'Women healers are far more vulnerable than men to the charge of witchcraft

– and to the trial by water. For most of them, your mother included, their learning doesn't come from books, so their successes and failures are more likely to be judged according to beliefs about magical practices. Most people don't understand the very real connection between magic and medicine.'

My eyes widened. Medicine *and* magic?

'The rest of the story properly belongs to your mother. For my part in that episode, I was convicted and jailed, not for the practice of witchcraft, but for practising medicine without a licence.' He sighed. 'Perhaps I can best sum up my life for you by saying I've practised medicine without a licence and magic without a guide, striving always to push against the boundaries of the unknown. I've been imprisoned for my efforts more times than I've been rewarded. I've made mistakes and I have regrets.' His eyes were tired, and a little sad. 'Your mother is one of my regrets.' He rose and took my hand. 'Your arrival has reminded me that we touch more lives than we might imagine. I shall understand if you don't want to see me again. But whether or not you return, our paths are now linked.'

The log crumbled to embers in the hearth, sending a shower of sparks up the chimney.

'For all my faults, I've brought healing to many who have sought my aid. And I shall not be stopped.' He gave me an oddly twisted smile and tapped my ring. 'As for you, Rose – go with courage. And never lose faith in your gift.'

The image came to me of Mum in her storeroom, giving me the gold piece she had earned with her healing remedies, despite Da's warning, to support her daughter's gift.

Unstoppable.

I had found a common thread in my origins. But it didn't bind me closer to either of my birth parents. Instead, it scared me.

The more I wrestled with my own doubts and fears, the more I admired Cicely's confidence, radiant with motherhood. She told me Toby had settled down after he struck her. 'He was afeard I'd do what I said and throw him out. He needs me to keep the family strong. His own mum died giving birth to him and his da didn't know what to do with him, so he was passed round different families 'til he was grown. He always worked for his keep and didn't get enough love. That's why he needs me and the children.'

The truth that he needed her more than she needed him didn't put her off. 'Ye'll understand when ye have children, Rose,' she told me encouragingly. 'Mine are the world to me. They're all I need to be happy.'

I didn't think I'd ever have children, but I believed her. And the best way I had to show her my love was the gift of my skills. I told her I'd paint her a family portrait, like Master Gheeraerts had done for our lady and lord.

Cicely's deep delight at the prospect infected the children with such excitement that my initial sketches of the family were little more than wriggles of charcoal with dashes of chalk, for neither of them could sit still. Even Toby kept shifting from foot to foot, grinning in anticipation of a painting that would fix their family for others to see with new eyes.

'It won't be like Master Gheeraerts' portrait of our lord's family,' I warned them. 'I want to try something different, more suited to the life you share with each other.'

I sketched them together and also apart, capturing each member of the family at different moments during the day, in between my morning tasks as a lady's maid and my afternoon work in the still-room. In my emerging portrait, the family group was positioned at the centre of the frame. Each of them also appeared in one of the four corners, captured in a typical pose or pursuit – Toby standing proudly in full Pembroke livery, Cicely bringing warmth and light to her mistress's chamber while cleaning the windows, six-year-old Angelica folding handkerchiefs carefully beside her mother, and three-year-old Stanley romping with the spaniels on a walk with his uncle Peter. The family group was in full colour, painted upon an ochre underlayer that allowed me to render both their flesh tones and the light and shadow that bathed the composition, while the individual figures were painted upon a pale blue underlayer that suggested the quality of a dream, each defined by one stronger colour for emphasis: Toby with a deep blue cloak swinging from his shoulder, Cicely in a russet kirtle, Angelica with violet ribbons in her black curls and Stanley's dark brown eyes and reddish brown hair echoing the colouring of Pepper and Clove.

I hadn't expected Peter to appear in the portrait, but in his informal role as keeper of the spaniels he had grown quite close to his nephew, who loved the dogs. And after all, he was a member of Cicely's family too. Peter and I had settled into a comfortable friendship once he accepted that I wasn't interested in marrying him. I was happy to see that he was now courting Mistress Roberts's pretty niece, Margaret, who was in training alongside her aunt to become a housekeeper herself. Among the Wilton staff, there was no one besides Cicely that I trusted more deeply than Peter. Our shared trust brought us closer than his earlier courtship could ever have achieved.

'Thou'rt diff'rent, Rose,' he told me on one of our walks with the dogs.

'Different from what?' My mind was still full of compositional choices for the portrait, so I didn't expect what came next.

'Different from afore our last visit to London,' he replied. 'Ye're not the same.'

Indeed I'm not, I thought but didn't say. *And never again will be.*

My mother wasn't blind to the distance I'd kept between us since then. I knew it would be only a matter of time before she drew out of me what I still wouldn't volunteer to share.

That time came one morning when we were tidying the still-room after one of Master Gilbert's chaotic late-night experiments. I'd tried to settle myself and make peace with my origins many times over. In this effort I had failed, and I knew it showed. Suddenly, she put down her feather duster and gave me a level stare.

'All right, Rose – out with it. Whatever you're harbouring will only hurt you more if you keep it inside.'

It was time for truth-telling, easy or not. I swallowed the lump in my throat.

'I discovered I'm the daughter of a magus as well as a witch.'

My words lashed like a whip. My anger at what had been kept from me suddenly snapped into view, surprising me as much as Mum. The colour drained from her face.

'Is that what Simon told you?'

'He told me that the two of you used magic to help that woman deliver her child, and that he landed in jail for it. He said he made mistakes he regrets.' I let the silence pool between us, murky as London ditchwater after a storm. 'Why didn't you tell me the whole story, Mum?' Finally, the months of hiding my feelings of betrayal were at an end. 'What is the truth? Who should I believe?' My voice rose and cracked, despite myself. 'He told me there was more to the story. Are you a witch?'

'My child – the truth?' She clasped her hands together, her way of calling upon her inner reserves of strength. 'The truth is no fairy tale, such as I used to tell you on long winter nights. What I shared with you about the two of us learning to bring together my knowledge of herbs and his knowledge of the stars was true.' Her gaze fixed on a point beyond my head, as if seeing the memories enacted before her. 'What I didn't tell you was that I was enchanted not just by the stars, but by the possibility of magic in the everyday world. Simon showed me that we walk through a world inhabited by spirits that we cannot see. He'd been studying books about spell-casting and spirit-calling for as long as he'd been studying the stars. He believed that such practices, which he called *celestial magic*, work together for divine purposes, not evil.'

I could hardly breathe. My drawings of spirits embodying the healing properties of different herbs crowded into my mind. She was speaking a truth that my own art had made visible to me, thinking it was fancy.

Mum's words came faster now, stronger.

'Clearly God directs powers greater than humans can understand. Consider the Stones. The winter moon and summer sun halo those mysterious shapes every solstice, promising natural magic in the season's passing. What villager in Amesbury doesn't want to believe in such magic?' She paused, catching her breath. 'When Simon was still Martin's apprentice, a mother lost her child to an illness that neither of us could heal. A few years later, she came to me pregnant. She wanted my help, not only with the delivery to come, but in reaching the spirit of her dead child. With a new baby on the way, she wished to express her love and say goodbye. I promised I would help her.'

I could imagine Mum, always wanting to support others, trying to comfort the bereaved mother. But through what means? The answer came next.

'Before he left Amesbury, Simon had taught me some celestial magic. But I had never practised the calling of spirits. So I sent for Simon, who was still working as a schoolmaster in Salisbury, saving for setting himself up in London.'

'You asked his help to raise the dead?' A chill ran down my spine. Necromancy was no harmless spell.

'No, Rose. To reach across the boundary of death to connect with a spirit who had passed. Magic of light, not of darkness.'

But where to draw the line between them?

'Simon had been warned by the authorities not to return to Amesbury without a medical licence, for the local physicians saw his remedies as a threat,' she continued. 'But he came. Martin was at the market that day and would be gone many hours. Michael was with me, and you were being watched by my sister. Simon told me my presence was necessary, since the woman trusted me.'

I could hear Lady Catherine's voice. *Magic relies on belief.*

'That afternoon, Simon cast a circle and we lit candles for the points of the compass, facing in each of the four directions in turn. Then he asked me to call upon the elements of earth and water, due to my affinity for the natural world, while he summoned fire and air.' Mum wrapped her arms around herself, shivering at the memory. But it wasn't shame I saw in her face. It was wonder.

'As we spoke the summoning spell, the candles flared, not just once but four times. And the mother saw the spirit of her child – I could hear the joy and pain in her voice when she greeted him.' Mum's voice was triumphant. 'But the spirit disappeared before she could bid him farewell and then she went into labour, right there in the circle. The babe was born with a withered arm, and she blamed herself for giving attention to the child who was gone rather than the child who was arriving. She didn't blame me or Simon – at least not at first. But when her husband returned that night and saw the babe's arm, and the remains of the circle of candles, she told him what had happened.

'So casting the spell *did* cause—'

'No.' Mum's voice was firm. 'There was no connection between the babe's arm and our summoning spell. I'm certain of that. But that father wanted someone to be punished, so he accused me of witchcraft and sent for the Salisbury sheriff, Giles Estcourt, a hard man who had never trusted Simon and welcomed the chance to put him in jail.' Her face was as fixed as the Stones, only her lips moving. 'Simon told them it was all his doing, that I was innocent. But I was the one who had delivered the babe, and the poor creature's withered arm was enough to bring the charge of witchcraft down on me. When Martin found out, he checked his anger and simply told the authorities that he had released Simon from the apprenticeship and that we had nothing to do with him. Nothing could clear me by then except the trial by water. I knew I had done no harm, but in a way, I welcomed the test. After all, I had helped to cast the spell.'

Mum's eyes held mine, and she took my hand. I thought of the small puddles of wax I had noticed from time to time in the storeroom. I realised that I had always lived some portion of my life within the four points of my mother's compass.

'Because books on magic were found in Simon's possession, he was suspected of practising necromancy, but was finally only sent to prison for practising medicine without a licence. After he was released, he went to London, and I've not heard from him again.' Her voice wasn't regretful, but resolved.

'When I survived the trial by water, I knew I must protect your future. So I sent you to Lady Catherine. Martin made me promise never to bring magic into our family. I kept that promise and never spoke of it again, or of my own beliefs. But now Martin is gone, and you deserve to know the truth about Simon. And about me.'

Magic relies on belief. All these years, I had believed Mum innocent of the charge of witchcraft. Yet over those same years, my pen had taught me to recognise spirits that don't inhabit the visible world. I believed in more than I could explain, I could see what others missed. Could I trust in Mum's truth, which first led to my conception and then sent me away from her? Accept magic that embraced a world of portents and spells?

'When I described my birth as an accident,' I told Mum, 'he said there are no accidents under the stars.'

'You were no accident, Rose. I needed no stars to tell me that.'

The bitter lump of doubt that I had been carrying deep inside since hearing Simon's tale finally started to dissolve. For the first time, my visions made sense. But I wasn't yet ready to wear my astral ring, the magician's gift.

CHAPTER TWENTY-TWO

Mary, 1589

When calm returned to the nation, normal life at Wilton House gradually resumed as well. The approach of the Spanish Armada in the summer of 1588 had sent England into turmoil and Wilton into chaos. Servants rushed to prepare rooms and meals as the house was thrown open to members of Mary's and Henry's extended families, who gathered for comfort and protection.

Mary, too, had been energised. Finally, she understood her brother's eagerness to fight in the Netherlands, to defend a noble cause against daunting odds. And she was thrilled by Her Majesty's rousing address to her troops, mingling with the common soldiers and assuring them, *I know I have the body of a weak and feeble woman. But I have the heart and stomach of a king.* In the example of this Queen, undaunted by adversity, Mary had found the courage to end her self-imposed exile.

In the wake of Philip's death, she had turned to solitude as a means to survive the unbearable loss. Now she recalled the words Queen Elizabeth had once privately shared with her: *I am and not; I freeze, and yet am burned, since from myself another self I turned.* It was not simply *solitude's necessity for survival*, as she had guessed at the time – to which the Queen had responded, *You have grasped half of my riddle-in-verse.* The other half, Mary recognised, was about the obverse of solitude – protecting one *self* with another, the public face that was also necessary for survival. It was time to end her seclusion and re-enter the world.

As the threat of war receded following the nation's stunning naval victory, Mary felt her vital senses reawakening. She knew she must no longer allow herself to turn away, either from the world or from herself.

Philip, her beloved writing partner, was gone for ever. But collaboration, she realised, could take many forms. She returned with renewed energy to both Philip's *Arcadia* and Robert Garnier's *Marc Antoine.* Her engagement, here, was not with flesh-and-blood collaborators, but with their words. Nonetheless, she often felt the push and pull of partnership as she strove to fulfil the authors' aims with the fire of her own imagination. And sometimes, working with her brother's prose romance, she could sense his spirit guiding her pen.

After immersion in her brother's words each day at Ivychurch, turning in the evenings to Cleopatra – another female monarch with *the heart and stomach of a king* – refreshed Mary's creative energy. As in the still-room, she steeped existing material in the tincture of her own imagination, producing a more powerful solution. Mary went beyond literal translation, just as she and

Philip had done with the Psalms. She deepened motivation and heightened action to bring this unconventional queen and her consort to life. Her mother, Mary believed, would have appreciated her construction of a new sort of queen – leader and lover, powerful and vulnerable. There were so few who grasped the life force in that paradoxical union.

Mary took to reading her day's work aloud to Rose, testing the sounds of the words and the flow of the lines. As she read, her face came alight with the excitement of creation, and Rose caught her fire. The girl was captivated, eager to know more about Mary's process of composition.

One damp spring evening, as they sat before the fire in the library, Rose asked why the verse was called *blank*. Mary laughed.

'I suppose the label arose from the absence of rhyme,' she explained. 'Looking at your question from the point of view of an artist, I imagine the colours being supplied in traditional verse by the rhymes at the end of the lines. Blank verse is uncoloured by rhyme and uses the natural rhythms of speech. It's well suited to drama, where the players enhance the colours in the delivery of their lines on the stage.'

Rose took up her thought. 'Just as I might supply colour by painting an image already sketched in charcoal or ink upon a blank canvas.' Mary smiled in appreciation, and Rose beamed. 'You once suggested that I should draw what comes to me as I listen to you read,' she ventured. 'I might not see the whole picture, but I'd like to draw the pieces that become visible to me.'

At Mary's eager nod, Rose reached for her sketchbook, which she always kept close by. With quick strokes of charcoal, she began to render the images that came to her as she listened.

The images she drew were not illustrations of the story itself, but reflections of its power and significance interpreted through nature. The lovers' joyful reunion in Alexandria after long separation, *with exquisite delights and sumptuous pleasures*, Rose depicted as a waterfall fed by two streams, pouring over the cliff edge of the looming conflict in a spectacular torrent of light. When Cleopatra fled the disastrous battle of Actium with Antony in pursuit, Rose sketched the shattering of the waterfall upon the rocks below. But when the narrative reached the climactic scene – Cleopatra, under siege at Alexandria, enclosing herself in a high monument with her servant women – Rose set down her charcoal, mesmerised by the spectacle of the queen's heroic strength in raising Antony's half-dead body up to the monument with ropes so that he could be reunited with her in death. Then the artist applied her hand to envisioning their union beyond death as a double ouroboros – the two heroes connected by a never-ending love.

Gazing at the twining figures, Mary saw that Rose had chosen the best possible image for the completion and wholeness represented by the story's ideal of the hermaphrodite – male and female united beyond mortal constraints. Rose's vision invigorated her own, and Mary found herself considering how her translation might render the alchemical *truth of Cleopatra* Lady Catherine had described.

As she continued to shape the play, her quest for such a union simmered more urgently within her. The lines of verse seemed to function as a drawing and redrawing of Rose's images as well as Garnier's characters.

* * *

In the time since Philip's death, Mary had largely shunned the public sphere, turning from her other self. She had kept mainly to Wilton and the solitude of Ivychurch, wishing to tend his memory in private. Now, in the autumn of 1589, as the anniversary of his death passed and what would have been his thirty-fifth birthday approached, Mary invited several poets with ties to Philip to compose tributes to his memory.

On a dull November evening, some of the brightest literary minds in England gathered in the Great Hall of Baynard's Castle. Mary seated the men in a circle before a warm fire and plied them with cups of hot spiced ale and dishes of dates and ginger cakes studded with raisins. As her mother had said, *Success resides in the details.* Her voice radiated quiet ebullience, all the more powerful for being consciously constrained for this memorial occasion.

'I welcome you on behalf of my brother, whose spirit we commemorate with this gathering. He would have appreciated our coming together.'

Edmund Spenser rose. A tall, gentle man with large wide-set eyes that conveyed perpetual wonder at the world around him, the poet had captured Philip and Mary's admiration with his *Shepheardes Calendar*, a pastoral balancing the hardships and celebrations of country life. Edmund opened his poetic tribute with a dedication to Mary that celebrated the Dudley–Sidney alliance. Mary nodded appreciatively, but valued the poet's verse less for its strategic praise of her family than for the lines that mourned her brother: *He now is dead, and all his glory gone, and all his greatness vapoured to naught.* The image struck her ear as both an alchemical metaphor and a challenge. No, she would not let Philip's greatness dissipate into nothing. She would capture and distil it in literary vessels, publishing Philip's works for the world to share, from his sonnets to the Psalms to the *Arcadia*.

Fulke Greville, who had known Philip since their university days, offered an elegy that honoured *a spotless friend, a matchless man, whose virtue ever shined*. Mary had never liked him. His imperious glare down a long, sharp nose aroused her instinctive distrust, but she felt he had the right to participate in this tribute to his friend.

Disregarding her husband's insecurities and her own lingering yearnings, Mary had also invited Walter Raleigh to attend. His devotion to *truth in poesy* had inspired Mary's collaboration with her brother, even as his kisses had ignited her awareness of passion, and he belonged here too. Now, he shared an elegy for Philip, his face tight with suppressed emotion. Aware of the other writers in the circle, knowing that many of them sought to compete for her favour, in the form of patronage, Mary understood that such a convocation had its risks – jealousy among rivals, not to mention her husband.

It was Walter's urging that gave Mary the courage, among these established poets, to offer her own tribute:

> *These dearest offerings of my heart,*
> *dissolved to ink, while pen's impressions move*
> *the bleeding veins of never-dying love,*
> *I render here: Dear Soul, I take my leave.*

As she read aloud these lines so painfully composed, Mary could feel the lifeblood of her sorrow likewise *dissolve to ink*. With that offering, she relinquished her exclusive right to the grief that had governed her for the past three years. And from the ashes of her collaboration with her brother arose a new community.

Word of the gathering quickly spread through London's literary world. The idea of a circle of writers sharing their work in celebration of one of their own and, by extension, of each other's artistry fired the imaginations of established and aspiring poets alike. It also inspired Mary. She envisioned an informal, continuing group of writers, a literary community that could spark ideas and inspire new work. Mary made a careful selection among her literary acquaintances – authors willing to test the limits of literary forms as well as societal norms, and to learn from one another. Indeed, one of her goals in seeking new forms of collaboration was to encourage emerging talents. When Samuel Daniel, the tutor of her nine-year-old son William, showed her some sonnets with potential, she invited him to join what she had started to call the Circle.

The group gathered on an irregular basis, most often at Baynard's but sometimes at Wilton, when the participants enjoyed several days of shared fellowship away from the smoke and bustle of London. The meetings were marked by enthusiasm and collegiality, and the responses to new work offered for discussion were supportive, but not uncritical. The Countess herself often delivered the sharpest judgements, when she felt an author had disappointed her expectations or was simply showing off.

Heartened by the gatherings' initial success, Mary expanded her vision. She invited two scientists, Thomas Moffett and

Adrian Gilbert, to join the discussion, bringing the mysteries of the material world to bear upon the perspectives of poets. The Circle itself, she decided, was like an experiment in the still-room, materials blended and distilled until the union of like and unlike might yield more perfect knowledge.

Walter had the generosity to contemplate new possibilities, and vigorously supported her introduction of these men into the Circle. Edmund Spenser, too, welcomed a broad range of insights and ideas, as he demonstrated when reading from the manuscript of his wide-ranging epic poem in praise of Her Majesty, *The Faerie Queene*. Mary was proud to have such a scintillating imagination in her Circle.

Some in the group baulked, though, when the focus strayed from purely literary pursuits. Samuel Daniel, for one, objected to the newcomers – on those grounds, but also, Mary suspected, because he had savoured his position in the Circle as the only member of the Countess's household to be included. Sandy-haired, with active eyebrows over a lean nose, a sensuous mouth and a close-cropped beard, Samuel was a curious combination of earnest and touchy, awkward and bold, saying little in response to others' work but always eager to present his own. Mary thought his poems naive but promising, and found him intriguing, even endearing, but oddly unsettling.

CHAPTER TWENTY-THREE

Rose, 1591

I came to love what my mistress was pleased to call our *collaborative process*, drawing while she read aloud, and discovering that my visions, inspired by her words, could colour her work in turn. It was like what I imagined flying to be, with new vistas always coming into view. Lady Mary even had Brian clear out one of the storerooms beside the still-room to serve as a studio where I could grind pigments and mix paints from the materials she purchased for me. The waterfall I'd sketched for her play turned into a deluge of white, green and violet hues that streamed over boulders burnished crimson by the setting sun. In the double ouroboros of Antony and Cleopatra, I laboured to achieve the same shade of rosy gold as my mistress's ring.

Planting and gathering herbs alongside Mum in

preparation for our distilling medicines in the still-room was another kind of partnership, both old and new – recalling our work in the Amesbury garden, and newly healing as we slowly mended the rift between us. We shared a fascination with the connections between the tangible world and what Simon Forman termed 'celestial magic'. Mum unrolled the star chart he had given her, and between her memory of their practices and my reading of the chart, we were able to puzzle out many of the best times to plant, prune and harvest various herbs so as to enhance their power.

Mum drew the line at casting spells, though. She refused to consider any practice that could bring a charge of witchcraft down on our heads.

'The trial by water was like dying,' she told me as we pruned chamomile and mugwort by moonlight in the Wilton gardens. 'Darkness flooded my eyes and lungs as the river took me. After they pulled me back to the surface, I truly didn't know whether I was dead or alive. I cannot undergo such a trial again, Rose. Nor risk that fate for you.'

If part of me was disappointed at not being entrusted with the language of magic, another part was relieved. And I took pride in my growing expertise in the garden, the still-room and the studio.

One evening in the library, as I was collecting charcoal and blank paper from my oak box, preparing to make more drawings while my mistress read aloud, Lady Mary stopped me. 'May I see some of your other drawings?' Her voice was suddenly eager. 'I've been rattling on ceaselessly about my play without taking the time to consider your own work.'

I hesitated. Then I recalled Peter's words. *Thou'rt afeard of nowt.* It had taken time. I remembered my unease when I had shown the astrologer my painting of his sign, which would be viewed by any and all Londoners who passed by, and my pride at the appreciation in his eyes. But then I recalled Lady Catherine's voice: *Your sketches do more than render surface appearance – they bring your subjects to life.* Perhaps it was time to share my drawings with the mistress who had already shared her words with me.

I should have thought twice.

On the top of the stack of drawings in the box were my sketches for the family portrait of Cicely, Toby and the children. My lady laughed with delight to see Angelica folding handkerchiefs and Stanley romping with the spaniels. She scrutinised my drawings of the Stones and starflowers intently. 'Perhaps you will bring me to see the Stones myself one day,' she murmured, surprising me that, for all her travels, she had never seen this most ancient of mysteries at the heart of our local landscape.

Next, she found my drawing of herself, after her brother's death, standing proud and tearless before a window overlooking a storm-wracked world. She looked at that image thoughtfully, and said nothing.

Near the bottom she came upon my drawing of Cicely, illuminated by the sunlight in Lady Mary's own chamber. I flushed with embarrassment. This was a portrait executed in my mistress's bedchamber, without her permission, when we both should have been attending to our tasks as servants. But she placed her hand on my wrist and squeezed.

'I understand that the impulse to capture what you see isn't always convenient, or appropriate. This shows me the spirit that motivates creation.'

But my sigh of relief caught in my throat. Beneath the drawing of Cicely were sketches I had all but forgotten, placed at the bottom for safekeeping. Now they stared up at my lady – the faces and stances of the male courtiers who had surrounded her on our first visit at court, not only Walter Raleigh and her uncle Robert, but those many others who had sought her favour in vain. Across my mistress's face passed, first, a frown of confusion, then another expression that surprised me. From the start of my commission from Sir Henry, I had been dreading discovery. But her face didn't register the outrage that I had been expecting. Instead, I saw disappointment. Which was worse.

'Tell me about these drawings, Rose.' Slate grey, river grey, storm-cloud grey – her eyes were filled not with anger, but sadness.

'My lady . . .' I didn't know what to say.

'Did someone ask you to make them?'

Only the truth would serve. 'My lord.'

'How long ago?'

'Before I ever met you, my lady. Before you came to Wilton.'

She closed her eyes, her face pale beneath the dark red mass of her hair that I had bound that morning with pearls and lace.

'How often?'

'He asked me to draw what I observe. When he calls for me, I bring my drawings.'

Her lips pressed into a thin line, so firm that they seemed almost bloodless.

'I was fifteen when I married Henry – half my lifetime ago. He was forty-three. Not much can surprise me now. I don't wonder that he asked you to keep an eye on me, for he told me his father had warned him the same way about his previous wife. Men fear losing what they cannot control. So my husband controls what he can – if not a wife with her own passions and pursuits, then a maidservant who cannot disobey her master's orders.'

She was disappointed, I realised – not with me, but with him.

'What's surprising isn't that he asked you to spy on me, but that, in a court filled with deceptive posturing, your drawings expose the emptiness of such bravado.'

I had received forgiveness, of a sort.

After that, I hated the spying even more. But I understood that I needed to keep drawing what I saw, lest both my mistress and myself fall afoul of Sir Henry's temper. At least, I told myself, there was nothing of note to record for Sir Henry.

Until, one day, there was.

At dinner in the Great Hall at Baynard's, where my lady convened her circle of writers when she was in London, or on long weekends at Wilton, I could see Sir Henry warily eyeing some of her guests, all of them men. He declined to join her in the sessions where they read aloud from their works. That was the Countess's domain. The day after the gatherings, however, he expected a report from me, and I couldn't tell if he was disappointed or relieved when I had no special news to pass on. I attended my lady, and when she read from her own manuscripts I relished the sight of noble strangers hearing for the first time words that I had listened to already. I sketched some of their faces, adding elements from the stories or verses they read aloud, in a compact sketchbook that I created by sewing together smaller pieces of paper. This I set aside for Sir Henry's viewing.

William's tutor, Master Samuel Daniel, resided with the household and took most of his meals with the family. In her encouraging fashion, my lady had invited him to participate in the gatherings of the Wilton Circle, as it was coming to be known. Master Daniel took up the habit of walking with my lady in the afternoons, after his tutoring sessions with William were concluded. Because I was often in the gardens in the afternoon, tending or harvesting herbs, I watched the course of their strolls through the flower beds that bordered the herb garden. Master Daniel liked to recite his sonnets, addressed to a lady named Delia. I saw him pause expectantly after each poem, like a puppy hoping for a pat, which he usually received in the form of an indulgent smile from my lady. She seemed appreciative but not engaged – very different from the way she and Master Philip had discussed the shape and sound of a single line of verse.

One afternoon, I caught her voice carried by the breeze. 'Your sonnets would be more compelling, Samuel, if your language were more restrained and your images less predictable. Not all sonneteers must plunge to their deaths, like Icarus, from the melting heat of the beloved's eyes. Trust your voice, Samuel, and those of your characters. Let them speak for themselves, rather than with the voices of past poets.'

I didn't know who this Icarus was, but I gathered he came to a rather messy end. I also wondered who the Delia he celebrated in his sonnets might be. My answer came when Master Daniel knelt, suddenly, squashing some of the tulips, and pressed his lips to my mistress's fingers.

'You are my Delia, my muse, my heart.'

I crouched lower among the herbs, not wanting to be seen but unable to look away. Why didn't she pull away her hand and bid him depart? Her face, viewed through the silvery-green stalks of the rosemary bush shielding me from view, seemed more intrigued than annoyed.

'Samuel, I appreciate the tribute. But you needn't act out your sonnets for me.' Her grey eyes were kind, not disapproving. He sprang to his feet, his voice so loud and earnest that I couldn't have missed his words if I had clapped my hands to my ears.

'Mary, I want you to receive these sonnets from my heart, not merely as the efforts, however unworthy, of just another member of your Circle!'

I sat back on my heels, amazed. I couldn't hear my lady's next words, but I caught her tone, soft but firm. She spoke for only a few moments. Then Master Daniel left her side and strode rapidly towards the house, passing along the path without noticing me. But when Lady Mary turned towards the house, she saw me, crouching behind the rosemary bush, a branch clutched forgotten in my hand. She approached me with a steady pace.

'Those with highest hopes have farthest to fall.' Her voice was calm, her observation less like a mistress to her maidservant than one woman to another. I stared, blushing with unexpected pleasure. 'Shall we bring those herbs up to the still-room?'

she continued, gesturing towards the rush basket at my feet, layered with rosemary and hyssop, betony and sage. Together, we mounted the stairs, and for the rest of the afternoon we laboured together, distilling the bounty from the garden into fresh remedies as if the encounter between my mistress and Master Daniel had no significance.

When Sir Henry summoned me to his chamber the next day, I dropped a curtsey and handed him the sketchbook. He flipped through it quickly, then paused over the most recent images, from the previous evening's gathering. I had sketched several of the authors, matching each portrait with my visions of what they read.

From the manuscript in Master Spenser's hand emerged two tiny knights on horseback, one with a long plait of hair descending from the back of her helmet. Hearing that description in his poem had been a surprise – a lady knight on a quest! Then a sketch of Master Raleigh as he read from his account of an expedition to the New World, his figure framed by the outline of a sailing ship. Finally, Master Daniel, reciting another of his sonnets to 'Delia'.

'Where is your mistress, Rose?' I looked up at him uncertainly. 'Wasn't she present at this gathering?'

'Yes, my lord. But the gentlemen did most of the talking, so it was them I drew.'

'Of what did they speak?'

'It was mostly in verse, my lord. Beyond my learning, I'm afraid, though I tried to sketch what I heard.'

'Your imagination serves you well.' Sir Henry nodded.

As the painter had taught me, it is composition rather than subject that shapes what the viewer sees.

Then my lord surprised me.

'Marcus Gheeraerts has spoken to me of your progress in working with oils when you studied with him. And I've admired the sketches of the spaniels you have shown me. Anne and Philip are very fond of them. Would you be willing to take on a commission from me, to make paintings of the dogs for the children's quarters?'

I was astonished, grateful and fearful all at once. *A commission*! As if I were a real artist.

'Of course, milord. I'd be honoured.'

'If you will let me know what materials and how much time you will need, we can agree on a fee for your work. Catherine appreciated your gift for art, and Mary does as well. I shall be happy to see what you can accomplish in painting Pepper and Clove.'

Leaving his presence, I found myself trembling. I had been taken seriously as an artist. And I had deceived my lord, by omission. He couldn't ask me about what *wasn't* captured on paper.

And yet what I showed my lady that night was the truth.

'What did you draw for my husband last evening?' my mistress asked while I unlaced her stays by candlelight, as if she were simply curious.

I pulled the compact sketchbook from my pouch and handed it to her. 'Here's what I showed Sir Henry.'

Paging through my sketches of the Wilton Circle, Lady Mary paused at one of Master Raleigh, then raised one dark brow over a drawing of Master Daniel. 'Your drawings have the capacity not just to reveal what others may miss, but to record what you choose to make visible.' Her voice was wryly appreciative.

I dropped my eyes to the richly embroidered carpet beneath our feet, following the threads of colour across the landscape as they converged on a leafy tree in whose branches sat a small brown nightingale in full-throated song.

'I know you heard Master Daniel's profession of love in the garden, Rose.' I blushed, but she shook her head. 'At first, to be frank, I thought he was merely spouting the platitudes of all sonneteers. Until he disclosed that his sonnets to *Delia* are not only dedicated to me, but *about* me.' Her smile was surprisingly shy, combining amusement and embarrassment. She wasn't used to it, I realised – being appreciated not just as a patron, but as a woman.

She rose and went to the window. 'The marvel of how men deceive themselves in wooing women is surpassed only by how often they are able to deceive us.' Opening the casement, she breathed in the fragrant dusk. 'I believe that Samuel is a writer worthy of mentoring. He has the potential to be a fine poet and a worthy colleague. I've advised him that if he concentrates on writing instead of wooing, he'll have better chance of success.'

She straightened her spine. 'Courtship is a game played by men's rules. Only women with power can change the rules.' Women with power.

I thought of the kind of power wielded by Lady Catherine, Madame La Grande, my mother – of power shared between women, not yielded to men.

I had not intended to eavesdrop on Master Daniel's courtship of my lady. But hearing it had convinced me that a sketch of what I had actually seen would have missed the truth. And so, in the Circle, I had drawn the truth I knew — men offering words to a lady they could never attain.

CHAPTER TWENTY-FOUR

Mary, 1592–93

It was a slim volume, but to Mary it was huge: *Antonius – Done into English by the Countess of Pembroke*. On a crisp April morning at Baynard's, Mary held her first published book in her hands. Finally. Her words in print. Available to the public at the bookshop of her publisher, William Ponsonby, in St Paul's Churchyard.

But her satisfaction was tinged with unease. Publication posed a genuine risk. It was a bold, even brazen, decision for a woman to publish a play under her own name. While the drama itself explored the consequences of female power, its publication challenged the limits of female agency. For Mary, it was a necessary step, and she was satisfied with the work itself. Why, then, did she feel so alone? The flourishing Circle had offered a supportive space to share the manuscript. Mary had been heartened by Edmund Spenser's praise of her blank verse and Walter Raleigh's appreciation for her bold characterisation of Cleopatra. She asked herself if it was the exposure of publication, with its potential repercussions, that was fraying the edges of her confidence, despite the double authority of her identity as a Sidney and her title as Countess of Pembroke emblazoned across the title page. But it wasn't that.

Somehow the publication of her retrospective collaboration with Garnier, as she regarded it, had reopened the floodgates of abiding loss. She missed the intimate give and take of genuine collaboration with her brother – the double ouroboros, two minds meeting in a thrust and parry more electrifying, in her experience, than sexual intercourse could ever be – and with fruits more lasting, and rewarding, than children.

That truth had been brought home to her again by the latest challenge of her fractious son, now twelve. William had become a difficult child – demanding, moody and often plagued by splitting headaches. There was no question that Mary preferred wrestling with words on the page to channelling the boy's restless energies or absorbing his moody outbursts. Just this morning, he had stormed out of Samuel Daniel's study in the middle of a difficult lesson and demanded that his mother dismiss the tutor immediately. When she refused, he had fixed her with a withering glare.

'You hate me, don't you?' His voice shook. He clasped his hands together and ran his fingers against one another – a nervous habit. 'You've never loved me. And,' he added before stalking out the door, 'it's because of you my sister is dead.'

The accusation struck her like a spear. Little Kate had been William's darling, and her death had overwhelmed him as utterly as it had their mother. From that moment, his natural boisterousness had grown into unruliness and disobedience. Mary blamed herself, just as she still carried a residue of guilt for her daughter's death.

The door to the library opened and Henry entered the room, frowning, a copy of her play in his hands.

'What have you done?' He sounded less outraged than outmatched. Marriage had taken its toll on both of them. Never truly partners, their increasing distance after baby Philip's birth and Kate's death had settled into the compromise of simple coexistence, too easily disrupted, for Henry, by departures from the norm. With increasing age, he relied ever more heavily upon familiar routines to carry him through his days and grew annoyed when they were disrupted.

'I received this by messenger from Robert Cecil of the Privy Council,' he said, standing over her. 'He expresses concern about how Her Majesty might take your portrayal of Cleopatra's unconventional queenship, not to mention her love affair with Antony. It's sure to be controversial, seen as overtly political – and with your own name on the title page, Mary! Given your brother's difficulties when he presumed to advise the Queen on her marriage, I'd have expected better judgement. Once again, your choices complicate my path at court.' He sighed heavily, and she could see all too clearly the lines of age and care that marked his face.

Mary responded coolly. 'Should she honour me by reading

my play, the Queen may welcome its rendition of a female leader, from another age and country, who combines the courage and resolution of a hero with the passion and tenderness of a lover and mother. I don't believe she will assume I am associating her with the historical Cleopatra's flaws or misjudgements – she is too canny for that.' Making an effort to frame her *Antonius* in terms Henry might understand, Mary continued, 'I published this play to reach a wider audience than will ever read my works in manuscript, knowing it will never see performance on the public stage.' When Henry's expression remained unchanged, she added, 'The play is not about Her Majesty, nor did I intend it for her consideration. I do not fear her judgement.'

Without another word, Henry turned on his heel and left the room. Mary heaved a sigh. If only her husband could grasp that they could have mutual rather than competing dreams and ambitions, perhaps they could more comfortably inhabit a shared world.

For years, Mary had sought opportunities to establish common ground with Henry. One avenue that seemed hopeful was the theatre. Mary's interest in the stage was long-standing, and working on *Antonius* had only sharpened it. She often attended court performances of plays, but Henry accompanied her more out of duty, it seemed, than real interest. However, at Mary's suggestion he had brought several companies of players to perform at Ludlow Castle while serving as President of the Council of the Marches in Wales. He even took on the sponsorship of a company under his own name, the Earl of Pembroke's Men. The troupe performed on various London stages, and during times of plague, when the London theatres were closed, toured the countryside, where the earl's patronage brought invitations to perform at a number of great houses.

Henry's commitment, however, proved to be strategic rather than artistic. It was a show of a great man's largesse and benevolence, which would raise his standing in court circles and his reputation in the world at large. Mary's hopes of connecting with her husband through appreciation for his company were finally dashed when he warned her against associating with the players. 'Riff-raff, most of them – good for entertaining the household, or even the court, but not worthy of your notice.'

And yet she *had* noticed one of them – an actor named Will Shakespeare, some of whose sonnets had been passed in manuscript among the writers in her Circle. His verse disturbed and intrigued her. *Two loves I have, of comfort and despair*, ran one of them. An impossible ouroboros, binding opposites together. By the time her own play was published, however, the binding of opposites had become the abiding challenge of her marriage.

The Circle itself wasn't without problems. She had to admit she was flattered, though not aroused, by Samuel Daniel's attentions. His enthusiastic expressions of admiration for her work offered a welcome contrast to Henry's continuing disapproval. Yet the absence of subtlety and, even more, of any genuine originality in his own words, disappointed her and inevitably diminished the impact of his compliments. At such times, she found her thoughts straying back to Walter, who had once seemed to offer the prospect of a genuine partnership of the mind – notwithstanding his secret marriage, last year, to one of the Queen's ladies-in-waiting. But Samuel wouldn't leave her in peace.

'Mary, your bold Cleopatra has inspired the birth of my own!' he exclaimed one afternoon as they walked beside the River Wylye. With the literary world abuzz over Mary's audacious *Antonius*, Samuel was working on what he viewed as a companion piece, one whose very title would celebrate Mary's novel focus on the Egyptian queen: *The Tragedy of Cleopatra*.

Mary was delighted. 'I shall be pleased to support such an effort. I believe you have it in you to craft a play that soars.'

Samuel's face lit up and he pressed his fleshy lips to her fingers, as he had done when confessing that she was the *Delia* in his sonnets. She hadn't taken him seriously then, but had done her best to treat him kindly if firmly. As she had observed to Rose, those with highest hopes have farthest to fall. Rose's discretion had likely averted what could have been a damaging flare of misdirected jealousy on the part of her husband. More than ever, the last thing Mary needed was anyone playing the hopeful suitor.

Now, clearly emboldened by her praise, he was moved to recite a sonnet he had just composed and dedicated to her. Mary was alarmed by his fervent delivery and suggestive imagery, his verse depicted as a *quickening seed . . . begotten by thy hand and my own desire*. She was no maiden who might ignore innuendos with a blush, but a matron, not to mention a patron, who neither required nor desired such passion.

'Samuel, you must abandon this role of lover.' She had humoured him too gently for too long.

He once again dropped to his knees and reached out to her imploringly.

'I'm no actor playing a role, Mary. I'm the man who has desired to serve you since I first heard of how you sang your Psalm before the Queen. Such confidence and courage distinguishes you from most women. I'm the poet who, for love of you, began writing my sonnets to Delia.'

Inside, she flinched. Aloud, she measured her words carefully.

'I'm flattered, but unworthy of such an accolade, Samuel. I want to encourage rather than inspire other writers. My goal has always been to support the emergence of unique works of literature that might extend, rather than simply echo, the achievements of classical authors. I urge you to attend to your writing, not to me.'

Samuel's shoulders sagged and his expression crumpled. Then, slowly, his visage cleared. He rose to his feet and stepped so close to Mary that she could see the individual whiskers brushing his ruddy lips, the thick lashes fringing his eyes, their pupils dilated. His breath was hot and his words urgent. 'So be it,' he murmured into her ear. 'I shall accomplish more than you expect.'

Then, he bowed and offered his arm. No words were exchanged as they returned to the house.

When William matriculated at Oxford, Samuel remained at Wilton to tutor Anne and Philip, but attended the Circle only sporadically. He did not share his work on the play, and Mary welcomed the greater distance between them. She had more pressing matters at hand.

Philip's friend from university, Fulke Greville, had been responsible for the unauthorised publication of her brother's unrevised *Arcadia* manuscript, with editorial changes and additions that unmistakeably diverged from its author's intentions. Greville had attended the first gathering of what grew into the Wilton Circle, but had not returned. With the appearance of Philip's draft pages purporting to be sanctioned by both the author and his sister, Mary understood why.

She was outraged – all the more because, to legitimate his presumptuous publication, Greville had included Philip's own dedicatory letter to Mary herself, declaring the work as having been created *only for you, only to you*. Mary vigorously and publicly refuted the unauthorised edition, and the resulting controversy spurred public interest in seeing the actual narrative created by the nation's hero.

Now, Mary worked assiduously to complete her compilation of the revised *Arcadia* to counter Greville's version. Time was of the essence, but the process, Mary knew, could not be rushed. She was determined to bring her brother's truest vision to publication as he would have wished – a vision of heroism rooted in courage rather than magic, with love arising from choice, not enchantment. Weaving together the old and new *Arcadia* narratives, connecting the parts Philip had revised with the uncorrected pages, was like embroidering a single story across two different pieces of fabric while attempting to fasten the pieces together with the same thread.

Finally, she authorised the publication of *The Countess of Pembroke's Arcadia*. It opened with an address to the reader promising that the 'disfigured face' of the unsanctioned edition had been mended. Still, Mary was left with disappointment at the inevitably cobbled-together nature of the combined text. She didn't regret the attempt, but could only grieve anew the loss of her truest collaborator.

Mary now awaited the publication of Samuel Daniel's *Tragedy of Cleopatra* with a mixture of hope and apprehension. Since her attempt to redirect Samuel's romantic advances, their few exchanges had been limited to the children's education. He never spoke of the play, but she had heard it was to be dedicated to her. So when she received a copy at Baynard's Castle – not in its own volume, she noted with a wry smile, but included with a new edition of his *Delia* poems – she retired to the library to peruse it in solitude.

Sure enough, there was a dedication *To the Lady Mary, Countess of Pembroke*, proclaiming her his *Muse*, whose *well-graced Antony required his Cleopatra's company*. With what seemed to be refreshing humility, Samuel wrote that Mary's Antony would hardly recognise his Cleopatra, *in majesty debased, in courage lower*. Taking this for mere courtly modesty, Mary turned eagerly to the play, reading by the fireside as dusk fell, hoping to dive into a river of verse that would complement her view of the female monarch on whom she had lavished such care.

Instead, she found herself sucked into an undercurrent of diatribes culled from the classics, picturing Cleopatra as vain, lustful and irresponsible. No hero, but a self-centered seductress. Samuel had indeed debased her Cleopatra, like flipping a tapestry to reveal the inverse of the image, the knotted threads on the back depicting a fallen woman and failed ruler.

Mary was thunderstruck. Shadows clustered in corners and the wavering candlelight obscured her view. How could Samuel have done this? She recalled his feverish kisses on her fingers, his almost desperate insistence that he loved her, only to be turned away. So here was his revenge, putatively commissioned by her but in fact responding to her rejection of his advances. His whispered words came back to her. *I shall accomplish more than you expect*. Furious, Mary cast the book into the fire. Furious not only at him, but herself. Why did this feel like her failure rather than his? A failure of her own hope for him. *Those with highest hopes have farthest to fall*. Her words applied to herself after all.

CHAPTER TWENTY-FIVE

Rose, 1593

The members of the Circle never noticed Master Daniel's fantasy of romance with my lady. They were too enchanted by the sound of their own voices and the stories they devised. Of course I understood that what had happened between Lady Mary and her unwanted suitor was no romance, with all the desire on only one side. It would have been nothing indeed, were it not for the ever-present danger of my lord's jealousy. And as his trusted spy, I was the only one who could protect my lady from the consequences of her well-meaning but ill-advised attempt to help Master Daniel grow in skill as a writer. She seemed to have no practical understanding of the intensity of his longing for her favour, whether it was driven by ambition or passion.

But then Master Daniel published his play, which degraded the Egyptian queen my lady had celebrated in her own play, depicting her as a temptress and a coward. She cut him off, banishing him from her Circle and terminating his employment as her children's tutor.

'Foolishly, I had hoped for more, Rose,' she told me as I dressed her hair with green silk ribbons to match the gown in the colours of spring that she would be wearing to that evening's gathering of the Circle. I knew better than to ask her what she meant. Nor did I need to, knowing that the flow of her narrative could not be stopped once it commenced. 'Not for more courtship. For better writing!' Most ladies, confined in marriage to a much older lord, would have welcomed a wooer their own age. Not so my lady. It was words that mattered most to her – words revealing worlds.

I almost felt sorry for Master Daniel, losing what he most wanted to earn – my lady's regard. But mostly, I was relieved when he was dismissed from the household. And not a moment too soon. Sir Henry's summons was peremptory, brooking no delay.

I found him pacing the length of his own bedchamber one evening while the Circle assembled below. His valet was standing frozen in the shadows. I had been warned about my lord's temper when I first joined the household but had never seen it for myself. Now it was fully in evidence.

'I understand that my children's tutor was in the habit of accompanying my wife on afternoon strolls around the gardens.'

I cast a hasty glance at Toby, who looked away. What had he said?

'Not for some weeks, my lord,' I replied, as calmly as I could, though I was terrified of the consequences for my lady should I speak awry. 'And no more, of course, since he's gone.'

'Why did your drawings not record those walks?' he demanded. The vein in the side of his neck was throbbing, and he put out a hand to steady himself on the back of his chair. Toby stepped forward quickly and handed him the sturdy staff that had been more in evidence this past year. My lord was ageing. I wondered how much of this fury stemmed from his own awareness of that fact.

'I was tending herbs in the garden. I saw nothing amiss,' I insisted.

'Did he not kiss her fingers? Take her hand?' His voice trembled at the vision of his world collapsing around him.

'I think he was only playing the role of a poet, my lord. In the writers' circle, he was always showing off sonnets about someone named Delia.' I shrugged, to indicate their unimportance, from the distance of an unlearned servant.

'And your lady?' Here was the question all had been leading to. 'How did she respond to him playing the role?'

'She laughed, my lord.' I spoke the truth I knew. 'She told me he had much to learn.'

His colour was returning, his panting breaths slowing down. Toby took his arm to assist him into the chair. 'What did *you* think, Rose?'

I paused to consider my reply. 'He reminded me of Pepper seeking Mistress Anne's attention.' I saw Toby's eyes go wide with alarm. I knew I shouldn't compare a gentleman to a dog, of course, but clearly my lord needed to think of Master Daniel in a different way. I spoke as honestly as I would have to my lady herself, and he seemed to appreciate my blunt reply, despite it not befitting my station.

'Like a spaniel, eh?' A small smile quirked the corners of his mouth. 'So drawing my dogs is not dissimilar to drawing those members of the Circle after all.'

'Perhaps you'd like to see the paintings you commissioned, sir,' I volunteered, grasping at a chance to change the subject. 'I've nearly finished them.'

'I would welcome it,' he declared with relish, dismissing Toby and sending me to fetch the paintings.

I had painted not just the dogs, but the children with them, drawing on the lessons in composition I'd had from Master Gheeraerts. Pepper leaping into Master Philip's arms in front of the house, the boy standing up even straighter to bear the weight of the dog, his eyes gleaming with pride in his strength. Clove sitting patiently at Mistress Anne's feet, looking up at her face with utter fidelity. I had rendered the feathered tail blurred as it beat against the ground. The angle of the spaniel's chin, slightly raised, and the paws neatly paired, echoed the poised angle of the child's own chin and the tidy folding of her hands in her lap. The background was the verdant green of the Wilton lawns, running down to the River Nadder, its curls of foam picking up the curly foam of the dog's tail.

Sir Henry looked at the portraits for a long time, his eyes distant and moist.

'My father loved his spaniel, couldn't bear to be separated from him, and the dog returned that love. When he died, the dog wouldn't leave his body, but pined away and died beneath his hearse. That dog looked quite a bit like Clove.'

Sir Henry's expression was speculative, Master Daniel now far from his mind. 'I recall Mary telling me the painter Gheeraerts set you to reproduce the Eworth portrait of my father, to learn portraiture.'

I nodded cautiously, not eager to show him that first failed attempt. But he had something else in mind.

'I'm satisfied with your rendering of the spaniels – more than satisfied. Next, I'd like you to work a dog modelled on Clove into the portrait, to honour my father's affection. And to show that a dog's place is at the feet of his master.' His tone was unmistakable. Sharp and pleased at once. What was it my lady had said? *Men fear losing what they cannot control, and so my husband controls what he can.*

I curtsied in agreement, hiding my astonishment. To think of it – adding something into an existing painting by a master artist, to hang on the walls of Wilton for all time! I couldn't wait to get started. Before dismissing me, my lord reached into a leather purse attached to his belt and pressed two gold sovereigns into my hand, one for each of the paintings.

I fairly flew down to the servants' quarters, eager to show Cicely my lord's treasure. Approaching her door, I could hear the sounds of a disagreement. They stopped when I knocked.

'Now mayhap I shall learn summat useful,' Cicely snapped when she saw me standing on her threshold. 'Toby says milord's in a wuthering temper, but won't say what for.' Her Yorkshire lilt was always more pronounced when she was upset, or 'mithered'.

I stepped into the chamber and glared at Toby.

'What exactly did you tell him?' I didn't bother to soften my tone.

'Milord asked me to keep an eye on his lady.' So – Sir Henry had sought more eyes to feed his jealousy. 'When I told him I'd seen her walking with Master Daniel beside the river, he worked himself into a frenzy, and that's when he called for you.' Toby's voice was sheepish, apologetic. But I wasn't having any excuses.

'I'd hope you'd have the sense to keep quiet about what you don't understand!' I was furious. Toby took a step backward. My lady's efforts to discourage Master Daniel from his pursuit had gone for naught if any ignorant bystander could now pass on tales with no merit that would feed the ever-smouldering embers of my lord's unfounded suspicions. Yes, he had grounds to suspect the smitten Master Daniel, but no grounds to suspect Lady Mary.

'So there was nowt for him to fear?' Cicely now, frowning at Toby, but addressing me.

'Lady Mary refused Master Daniel's attempts to court her. She broke with him and sent him packing over his writing of a play. So there's nothing to tell.'

'Ask Rose afore you speak of our lady in future, Toby,' Cicely snapped. He scowled, but kept quiet.

One evening, before bidding my lady goodnight, I set on her dressing table one more drawing from the bottom of my oak box. Using only coloured chalk, I had captured the heel of my mistress's first pregnancy, from the crimson veins threading the creamy cord to the dark red afterbirth itself, its surface adorned with branching purple veins. Lady Mary raised her eyebrows to draw forth my explanation. 'The afterbirth from your first delivery, my lady. I had never seen one before, and was awed by its beauty. It seemed to me like a tree of life.'

She examined the drawing for a long time. I remembered the fog that had shrouded her after that birth. I guessed that calling it a tree of life must strike her as ludicrous. Then she pointed to the lively spirit peering forth from the end of the cord.

'Not everyone can see what your eye captures, Rose. For myself, I could see nothing after that birth but darkness. I'm glad to learn that my son was attended by such a life-giving spirit.'

The painting of Sir Henry's father was taken from the wall of the gallery and placed on an easel. Even approaching it was daunting – I was to *paint over* a section of Master Eworth's original. It felt like defacement, until I reminded myself that it was my lord's wish, and that he felt my addition would enhance the portrait, not diminish it.

Snatching every possible moment from my daily tasks of serving my lady in her chamber and the still-room, I set to work on the spaniel. I placed him in the lower right-hand corner of the frame, sitting obediently at his master's feet, looking up adoringly. I laid down a cool lime white for the underlayer supporting the spaniel's coat, so that its russet shade harmonised with the browns in the carpet. The more I worked with colour, the more readily I could understand the layering and mixing of shades in terms of my lady's alchemy, where painstaking combinations of dissimilar ingredients could produce a harmonious end result.

When Sir Henry came into the gallery to view the completed portrait, his wide eyes and raised eyebrows signalled that I had achieved greater success than he'd expected.

'No one would suspect that this composition wasn't the original design of the artist!'

I glowed with pleasure.

'What I like the most is that the image conveys an authentic bond between my father and his beloved dog.' His voice was warm with appreciation, and I could see that he took personal pride in the augmented image. Without his having touched a brush or my having seen the first Earl, the portrait now became a testament to our collaboration – a project of honour rather than suspicion.

Nonetheless, service to my master and mistress continued to demand vigilance, both protecting my lady from my lord's suspicions and protecting my lord by keeping his fears from her knowledge. There was nothing to be gained for either of them by sharing too much information, and much to be gained by achieving accord.

Meanwhile, I observed my lady's own explorations ranging in new directions, some of them surprising. In one of her more adventurous turns, she took to breeding stallions! This I learnt from Peter, the head groom. She designed what she called a *vidette*, akin to the viewing window in her athanor, through which she could observe the stallions mounting the mares. Peter blushed to confide this bit of intelligence, but I thought I understood my lady's actions. It was as if, having lost so many of those dearest to her, she craved the life force. In the stables as in the still-room, Lady Mary sought to advance creation.

And by serving her and my lord with my art, I could do the same.

CHAPTER TWENTY-SIX

Mary, 1600–01

Even before he was sent to prison, Mary's firstborn was her greatest trial.

As his father lay ill, weakened by age and his many years of duty to the Queen, twenty-year-old William had unaccountably delayed his return to Wilton from visiting the court at Greenwich. Did he feel no loyalty to family? To her?

Restless and volatile since boyhood, now ambitious and driven to prove his worth, William was not readily given to expressing affection for others. The only exception had been his little sister Kate, for whom he would have conquered dragons. Would William's capacity for affection have been otherwise, Mary wondered, if she had truly loved him from the start? After Kate had died, Mary recognised William's discovery that he was alone in the world, for hadn't she discovered the same when

Ambrosia died? The terrible truth was that she couldn't help him.

His other siblings, Philip and Anne, now sixteen and seventeen, had glided through childhood with sunny dispositions, easily beloved by their parents, the servants and the dogs. Not so their brother, whose years at school and university had polished his manners and sharpened his talent for the barbed riposte, without tempering his resentment. For William life was a battle, a contest of wills – with his father, whose efforts to advance his prospects at court he failed to appreciate, and with his mother, whose struggles with her firstborn admitted no show of vulnerability on either side.

But surely, thought Mary, he could have mustered the compassion to return home while his father suffered. She was all too aware that William avoided Wilton when he could, preferring to stay in London at Baynard's Castle, either alone or with his younger brother. When they appeared together at court, Philip's light-hearted verve and charm contrasted with his brother's more deliberately ambitious spirit. For his part, Philip was so clearly grateful that it was not he who was fated to carry the weight of their parents' expectations for the firstborn that he unfailingly supported William in any dispute. Mary had accepted early on that one consequence of this unspoken agreement between the brothers was her greater distance from her sons than her daughter.

Attending the Queen at Greenwich was hardly William's first solo venture at court. Born to be Earl of Pembroke, he had been in training to be a courtier from the moment of his birth. But Mary had a different dream for him, drawing on the illustrious legacy of his uncle. It wasn't the soldier's death for which she adored her brother, but the writer's life. *The Countess of Pembroke's Arcadia* was still enjoying brisk sales in the city's bookstalls, but William had not even read it. He preferred to find romance among the Queen's ladies-in-waiting than within the pages of a book.

Mary and Henry had been reviewing potential matches for their firstborn since he turned fifteen. The most recent prospect had been Bridget de Vere, granddaughter of the powerful William Cecil, Lord Burghley. But William had defied his father over this match, as he had several others, this time objecting to the girl's frivolity. It was true that William himself had an earnest, even dark, spirit that was not given to amusement. *More laughter would do you good*, Henry had urged, to no avail.

In her son's rebelliousness, Mary recognised her own girlhood. But having ultimately accepted the match arranged for her, she knew William would likewise have to make the best of an arranged marriage. As a man, in any case, he would have more choice in other matters of his life than she herself had ever enjoyed.

Mary understood that William needed help in order to be successful at court, unable to employ the charm that came so easily to his younger brother. He had a good head for politics but lacked the diplomatic gifts that promote advancement. So when his father's ill health required William to attend upon the Queen at Greenwich in his father's stead, Mary was glad that Philip would be there with him. She was hopeful that he would learn from the experience and expected him, at least, to comport himself with the dignity of his family's name. What she didn't expect was that he would disgrace it.

* * *

Over the long winter months of William's absence, Mary remained at Wilton by her husband's side as his health waxed and waned. Sleet crusted the tall windows only to be washed away by insistent rain, as if the weather itself couldn't make up its mind. She was assisted daily in Henry's bedchamber by Anne, whose loving smile could be counted upon to restore her father's spirits, however briefly. Philip balanced regular visits to Wilton with attendance at court, and volunteered news for Henry's interest when he was home. He mentioned his brother only briefly, and his mother understood that pressing him for more information would inhibit his otherwise easy flow of stories. Henry couldn't listen long in any case.

Doctor Moffett had made plain that there would be no cure. Henry's weakened frame was subject to passing fevers and increasingly serious ailments, and a purging induced by flowers of antimony had only worsened his state.

'For his pain I can administer a tincture of opium in small doses. Making him as comfortable as possible in these final weeks is the best we can hope to achieve,' the doctor explained. Although the tincture reduced Henry's discomfort, it also dulled his senses, so there were few opportunities for genuine communication. To counteract the effects of the laudanum, Rose prepared a remedy according to Joan's prescription, and Mary was rewarded by almost a full day of calm and clarity with her husband.

'I realise it won't be easy for you to carry on the management of our properties,' Henry told his wife that afternoon. *Indeed it won't*, thought Mary. In addition to Wilton and Baynard's, the family's holdings included the castles at Ludlow and Cardiff, as well as multiple properties in the south of England and Wales. 'But proper oversight will be necessary.' Mary didn't relish the responsibility of managing William's inheritance, not merely until his majority at the age of twenty-one in three months, but until he'd achieved genuine maturity – a more distant prospect.

For Henry's benefit now, Mary simply nodded, and he closed his eyes. She had learnt, in nearly two dozen years of marriage, the necessity of managing Henry's expectations apart from her own. There was little to be gained by speaking openly in a marriage where they had both perfected the art of communicating less than they kept to themselves. Mary felt the sheer weight of their years of marriage, which had brought her from the age of fifteen to thirty-nine.

Over those years, Mary had forgiven Henry for his limited notions of a woman's skills in court politics in exchange for his approval of her skills on the page and in the still-room. In the solitude of her marriage, she had decided not to hold his deeply ingrained assumptions against him. He had not often been able to engage with her in difficult matters of the mind and heart, but he supported her work as an author and an alchemist. A marriage of cooperation was better than the experience of most noblewomen she knew. If she had once longed for more, she understood that it could have been much worse.

But the truth was that she had never felt so alone as in marriage. They had experienced many of the same losses and the same griefs – but separately. What more could she say to him now? She looked at Henry's form on the bed and realised that he was awake. His eyes were fixed on her face.

'Do you remember discussing Boethius the first time we met?' His voice was so low that she had to bend towards his lips to catch each word. 'I observed, speaking from the ignorant confidence of my vastly greater age, that I feared no consolation for grief could be discovered. I've never forgotten your response.' His voice grew stronger. 'You told me that, faced with grief, you sought to pursue *things of the mind*.' His chest rose and fell with a slow sigh. 'That has ever been the difference between us – and it is that comfort that I leave you with now. If I can hold one glimmer of hope before me as I depart this world, it is the conviction that you shall always be able to rely on things of the mind.'

Picturing the kind and reserved widower that she had met so long ago in the gardens of Kenilworth, Mary recognised that, for all their differences, Henry's fundamental generosity had endured.

Henry Herbert took his final breath the next morning in the presence of his wife, his daughter and his youngest son. The son whose birth ensured the longevity of the Pembroke legacy was not there.

Later that day, Mary entered Philip's chamber in search of him. Finding it empty, she turned to go when she spied a crumpled paper by the door. She stooped to pick it up, thinking to place it on her son's desk, when she noticed the writing – William's hand. Curiosity overcoming propriety, she smoothed it out and read.

Dear brother –
There's more to tell you than I have paper and ink to use. What can I say? Let me write plainly what no one else must ever hear.

Her gaze hooked me from the start. And her voice, like a siren. Escape was out of the question. Her passion was the bait for my desire. She pulled me in like a fish on a line until I was dangling at her mercy.

She dressed as a boy – a boy! – and came to me at Baynard's wearing a doublet and breeches. When the breeches came off, I had no choice.

Mary is her name. Mary Fitton. One of the Queen's maids of honour. Although not much honour was in evidence during our coupling.

All I ask of you is please don't tell Mother.

Henry's firstborn son and heir arrived home three days later, accompanied by Mary's brother Robert to assist in carrying out the Earl of Pembroke's bequest. Before she had any words with her son, she drew her brother into the library.

'How much did you know?' Her question hung in the air as Robert studied William's letter to Philip. She had no doubt that William was here now only because her brother had commanded his presence.

'I heard about the affair. Truly, I was hoping to bring it to an end before I journeyed to Wilton. I didn't want to disturb you with the news while there was any hope that Henry might recover. I knew he would take it hard.' The lines on Robert's face belied his lithe and still-youthful appearance. Mary saw the fine scattering of silver within his auburn curls, even more visible in his close-cropped beard. At thirty-seven, her little brother was no longer young. A widow of nearly forty, she herself felt ancient.

'She's older than William, this Mary Fitton, and apparently pursued him shamelessly. She liked to call herself Moll, after the notorious cutpurse Moll Frith, who's known for wearing a doublet and breeches for her escapades.' Robert shrugged. 'It could be said that young William had no chance against her wiles, Mary.'

'He had a choice, Robert. Men always have a choice.' Her voice was cutting in its conviction.

Robert led Mary to a chair. He had more bad news. 'The young woman is pregnant.'

For many moments neither of them spoke. Mary had feared this from the moment she read the letter.

She shook her head slowly. 'I'm glad that Henry never had to learn of this shame. It would have broken not just his heart, but his hope for the future. He always believed in William's potential.' Then, after another grim silence, 'Perhaps if I had believed in our son as well, he wouldn't have arrived in this mess.' Her mind kept working, reviewing the possible consequences. 'What does the Queen know?'

'She knows all.' Robert's sigh was a muted groan. 'The news reached her ear the day after Henry's death. William confessed the liaison, but refuses to marry the girl. Her Majesty has ordered him to prison.'

Mary's shock settled sickeningly in the pit of her stomach. Heedlessly pursuing pleasure, William had darkened both the Sidney and Pembroke family names.

As if reading her mind, Robert went further. 'With this foolish affair, I fear he has thrown away his chances for a career at court.' His next words were careful. 'Unless, that is, your relationship with the Queen can repair some of the damage.'

He bowed his head. 'I regret that William's behaviour requires your intervention at this heavy moment of your loss.'

Mary rose and embraced her brother. 'My most grievous losses have already occurred.' Ambrosia. Her daughter Kate. Her parents. Philip.

As executor of Henry's will, it fell to Robert to inform Mary that her husband had left her well-supported, although not as wealthy as during his life, after generous bequests to the poor in the parishes near his primary residences. 'You shall want for nothing during the remainder of your life. The only constraint upon you, according to Henry's will, is that, if you marry again, you shall lose access to all funds.'

Unsurprised, Mary nodded. The constraints and jealousy of marriage extended beyond death. It was his right. And yet, as always, he was fair. Remaining unmarried, she would be cared for. And why, she thought, would she ever want to marry again? That part of her life was over now, as dead as her husband.

Reflecting on that new reality, Mary marvelled, not for the first time, that Rose had never married. At thirty-six, she was now far beyond marriageable age, and her unprepossessing looks and self-sufficient spirit had hardly drawn swarms of admirers. Mary remembered that years ago Cicely's brother, Peter, had seemed to be sweet on her, but nothing had come of it. Indeed, Rose had been, and still was, closer to Cicely than to anyone else. Except, Mary hoped, her mistress. For years now, Rose had been more than a maidservant. She was a companion, a collaborator in the still-room, a wise interpreter of words through images – almost, despite their difference in station, a friend.

Henry's will specified that he was to be buried at Salisbury Cathedral, *without any sumptuous funeral or use of heraldry*, alongside his daughter Kate. Unexpectedly, the very simplicity of Henry's final wish opened Mary's heart to a grief that merged the loss of her daughter and her husband, buried in a shared tomb in the churchyard.

How Henry would have responded to what must come next Mary couldn't imagine. His exultation at William's birth, by contrast to the misty vapours of her own dark fog, had inflated his hopes for their firstborn. But the consequences of William's actions were now hers to address alone.

Mary wrote to the Queen before the funeral, imploring mercy for her husband's heir and predicting that William would prove a loyal servant now that he had suffered her censure. But Her Majesty would not be moved. William was to return to London immediately after the funeral – to be committed to Fleet Prison. Not the Tower, anyway, but still prison. Mary swallowed her fears with difficulty.

William expressed neither remorse nor regret.

'I am the next Earl of Pembroke.' His voice was strong, proud, defiant. Too defiant, thought Mary, and proud without cause. This son of hers had so much to learn. And her husband had left it to her to teach him.

'Being the Earl of Pembroke carries obligations,' she countered. 'We tried to raise you to appreciate those obligations. Your actions now hardly demonstrate your worthiness for your father's title.' For all the constraints and disappointments of her marriage, Mary had never questioned her husband's fundamental commitment to decency. Her son's behaviour was an affront to his father's honour.

'All my life I've been trained to advance the Pembroke position at court, to uphold the Sidney legacy, to represent my family rather than myself. What about my own satisfaction?'

'What about your own honour?' Mary's voice was hot, her patience at an end. 'And what about the maid of honour? Did you consider her position?'

'She had no honour.' William's rejoinder was cold, but Mary caught a flicker of uncertainty in his voice. 'That's why I would never marry her. I realised too late that I had been hooked by a woman's wiles. She took as much pleasure as she gave.'

Hooked by a woman's wiles? Mary recoiled from his words. This was the long-awaited heir to the Pembroke line, the child whose birth had overwhelmed her with darkness. But she couldn't avoid her own responsibility, couldn't simply turn aside from her son any more than he could turn aside from his actions. He was still her child. And he didn't know as much as he thought.

'So you took what you wanted – the pleasure of being desired, even admired. But what did you give in return? Any one of us likes to be appreciated, but only a mutual meeting of minds can bring joy.' Would he ever know what she meant? Despite his actions, he had to learn there was more to aim for than he had yet known. 'That is still my hope for your life – that you shall come to find that genuine exchange with another.'

William was listening to her now, but his face was unreadable. He was compulsively releasing and reconnecting his fingers in the nervous habit he had developed after Kate's death.

338

'Who do *you* most admire, Mother?' His heated glare bored into her. Then, the blow. 'Walter Raleigh?'

Mary gasped. Of course Walter had been a frequent guest at Wilton and Baynard's, as a family friend and fellow writer, and William must have drawn his own conclusions from their animated exchanges. Was she always to be defending herself from the suspicions of men? Her gorge rose. In her ears, the echo of Lettice's poisonous warning. *Never underestimate a man's capacity for jealousy.* Apparently as true of a son as a husband.

Yet her heart smote her. The most painful irony was that she had never tasted more than a tantalising promise of what a bond between herself and Walter might have been. She drew a breath.

'Once, William, I would have said that I most admire truth in words, language that can convey not just the ideal, but the real. That's why your uncle and I spent so much time putting the Psalms into English, striving to achieve both truth and beauty in our verse.' Then she shook her head. 'But Philip is dead, now. Henry also.' Shuddering, she added what she knew to be his most painful loss. 'Kate.' Their eyes met. 'Now, I find myself seeking consolation in words that might successfully render life, in all its hopes as well as disappointments.' She took her son's hand, then, and he didn't pull away. 'What's important isn't avoiding failure, but accepting responsibility.' He deserved honesty, not simply platitudes. 'For all my aspirations, I've failed more times than I've succeeded, William. In marriage.' She swallowed, hard. 'In motherhood. On many different occasions. No single thread carries the entire story.'

She fell silent, hoping for some acknowledgement of a lesson learnt. But William released her hand, stood, and strode from the room.

Early on the morning following his father's funeral, William set out for London, to prison. He did not come to his mother's chamber to bid her farewell. From her window, Mary watched the carriage pull away.

No single thread carries the entire story. Mary sighed. But a single knot can change it irreparably.

CHAPTER TWENTY-SEVEN

Rose, 1603

The final year that England had a queen on the throne, I learnt the magic that can result from an artist's sleight of hand. My mistress insisted that I continue my studies in Master Gheeraerts' studio whenever I accompanied her to London. Even as I grew more expert in colour and composition, I came to understand a visual paradox – that the life of a portrait may reside as much in what is not painted as in what is shown.

Over time, I had observed the monarch's ageing features when Lady Mary attended the Queen and marvelled at the magic of the painter's royal portraits in which no signs of age were visible. While my lady had complimented my gift for creating images where *the imagined coexists with the visible*, Master Gheeraerts was expert at turning the visible into the imagined, so convincingly that one could believe the Queen for ever young. His stunning portrait of Her Majesty standing upon a map, with storms giving way to sunlight, celebrated her goddess-like powers with an image drawn purely from the painter's imagination, but one that would convince anyone of Her Majesty's invincibility.

Thanks to Master Gheeraerts' instruction, I could appreciate my lady's insistence that principles of alchemy could be applied to any work of creation – in this case, I thought as I looked over his sketches for a new royal portrait, the stages of transformation that a successful portrait must undergo between initial drawings and final image.

'It begins with the outward gaze.' I looked up to see the painter standing beside me, his high forehead furrowed in concentration. 'All the details of the composition substantiate the message of the gaze. In painting the Queen, success depends on convincing the viewer that you are in the presence of majesty, admitted to an imagined intimacy that only the picture frame allows. I paint the details to please the eye of the Queen, but it is her gaze that mesmerises the viewer, who can never hope to approach the monarch herself.'

We stood side by side in silence for a moment, the sketches spread before us, while around us the studio buzzed with the work of apprentices painting copies of a royal portrait that would be hung in the various estates visited by the Queen on her annual progresses.

Now he turned to me. 'I was very pleased to comply with your mistress's request that I instruct you in the art of painting in oils.'

Inhaling the familiar heady paint fumes in the workshop, I

recognised that I occupied an unusual position, and shifted on my feet. I ventured a response.

'As you know, at Lady Mary's request I often produce images arising from the subjects that she writes about, drawing imagined rather than actual scenes, to supply her with another viewpoint.' His expression invited me to continue. 'In those cases I find that my greatest challenge is grounding the imagined sufficiently in the real.'

Master Gheeraerts nodded, his worn face creasing in a smile of recognition. 'That challenge is the hurdle of art itself, Rose. No matter how faithfully we may strive to render a subject, the results stem from the mind's eye, which may tip the scale of a canvas between the imagined and the real with no greater provocation than whether or not we're hungry at that moment.' Another reminder that circumstances can limit vision, or liberate it.

What I liked most about Cardiff Castle was the breathtaking view. Perched on a promontory above the River Taff beneath the pure blue of the Welsh sky, it had me itching to use my ultramarine pigments on canvas. At Cardiff, which my lady now frequently visited when attending to the management of her husband's estates, I was happy to paint the vistas before my eyes, without inserting imagined details according to my fancy. Those required an intimate focus, the gaze of a beetle. The view from the castle keep was that of a bird.

But this time, my enjoyment of Cardiff quickly turned to dread.

Sir Henry's death had set long-simmering resentments over English rule to the boil. Now, the town erupted into riots as an unruly mob of Welshmen challenged the Pembroke authority over the town. My lady believed herself secure within the castle, but I was less confident. One of her private walks, in the outer bailey, had recently been torn to pieces, the paving stones hurled into the apple orchard that Sir Henry had planted between the keep and the Shire Hall. Out of my lady's hearing, some of the local servants insulted members of the Pembroke household, including me. Brian was knocked down in the stables and had to use his fists to defend himself.

The Cardiff Castle steward, Edmund Mathew, turned a blind eye to these disturbances. A stick of a man with the tongue of a viper, who also owned extensive lands around Cardiff, this man had crossed the Countess before. He took his responsibility for overseeing the household as licence to undermine her authority and now was emboldened by the disturbances in the streets. But if he thought to cow my lady, he underestimated her. Crisis only stiffened her spine. When Brian brought her news of the attack in the stables, she dismissed Master Mathew, barred him from the castle and gave the stewardship to Hugh Davyd, a Welshman who had served her own father, Sir Henry Sidney, when he had been governor of Cardiff. Even so, none of us felt safe.

Those who served our lady in England as well as Wales learnt to keep together and never walk alone.

Though Master Gheeraerts' royal portraits had made her seem ageless, Her Majesty was mortal after all. Holding the letter from her brother Robert, Lady Mary turned even paler than usual and swayed slightly on her feet. Her voice was flat. 'Her Royal Majesty is dead. James VI of Scotland has been named King of England.' She pressed the letter to her forehead as if to still a sudden ache. 'Ah, Rose, this is the end of an era. We shall never see the like again. The Queen's circle will be displaced by new courtiers who already have the favour of King James from his years as the Scottish monarch. But we must be visible to the new Queen. We shall return to London immediately for the state funeral.'

I couldn't imagine our country without the Queen who had ruled for longer than I had been alive. As I watched the anxiety that darkened my mistress's face, I wondered if Her Majesty's death might change my life as well, even as Sir Henry's death had put the lives of the Pembroke servants in jeopardy in Cardiff.

'Wales has welcomed my family ever since my father's governance,' she murmured the night before we departed. 'Now it has become enemy territory.'

To hasten our departure, we travelled with only what we needed for the journey itself. Steward Davyd was commissioned to follow with the rest of the household possessions, including her money, plate and jewels, accompanied by a mounted guard.

'I shall return,' she promised her bailiffs.

For the first time, I was glad to be leaving Wales.

The day after our arrival at Wilton, I was putting my lady's belongings into order when there was a sharp knock at her chamber door. Master Wilkins apologised for the intrusion in a voice tight with panic. 'Your man Gareth has just arrived from Cardiff.'

At the foot of the stairs stood the castle porter, filthy and dishevelled. 'My lady,' he gasped, shaking. 'Hugh Davyd has been murdered on the road.'

Lady Mary led him to a chair. 'Speak the truth without fear,' she told him, after sending a footman for food and drink.

'We set off after you with your valuables, mum, travelling quick and keeping to the main roads. But we'd barely reached the New Park Wood, look you, when we were set upon by three ruffians with dagger, pistol and cudgel. They pulled Hugh from his horse and beat him about the head 'til blood ran from his skull. When he wouldn't give up the keys to the chest of treasures, they chopped off his hand and rode off with everything, shooting at the rest of us as they went. I dragged Hugh into shelter in some bushes and tried to bind his wounds while the other servants ran to Newport for help.'

Gulping down his distress, the man blurted out, 'I couldn't stop the bleeding.' I shuddered at the image. A servant appeared bearing a plate of bread and cheese and a pot of ale. After taking some refreshment, the man continued.

'When we were still at Cardiff, Hugh told me Edmund Mathew had tried to bribe him to hand over the valuables. He refused, and Mathew threatened to kill him. But Hugh believed our own countrymen wouldn't attack us. He judged wrong. The man who beat him was Philip Llen, one of Mathew's men.'

The man sobbed out the rest, his words muddled but his meaning clear. 'With his dying breath, Hugh said it broke his heart to fail you, my lady. Many in Wales love you and are loyal to Lord Pembroke still. It's villains like Mathew who mar the honour of our land.'

My lady's face was stone. If the Countess of Pembroke's own man could be murdered on the demand of a Welshman, what order remained in the kingdom? After putting Gareth under

Doctor Moffett's care, she wrote out his testimony and placed it with an order to bring charges against Edmund Mathew in Wales.

The Welsh uprising wasn't the only crisis confronting my lady as she prepared to attend the royal funeral. The plague had erupted again in London. We were safe in the fresh air of Wiltshire, but Lady Mary was resolved to pay her final respects to the Queen she had loved.

Upon the recommendation of Doctor Moffett, as soon as we arrived at Baynard's my mistress called for a plague doctor to advise the household before we participated in the Queen's funeral. I had never seen such an alarming apparition. Looming over the butler who ushered him into the drawing room, he wore a broad-brimmed leather hat and his entire face was covered by a mask with a long beak projecting in front of his nose, like a giant bird.

'Because my duties take me into houses infected by the plague, this mask protects me from the contagion and yourselves from any infection I may be carrying,' he explained in a hoarse voice, muffled by the mask. 'The beak holds medicinal herbs and spices, and a vinegar sponge, to ward off the disease.' His advice was blunt. 'This plague has been spreading like wildfire, milady. You will not be safe outside the walls of this house.'

'Plague or no, I shall be in the funeral procession,' my lady declared. But she was not above taking counsel. On the plague doctor's advice, she arranged for those of us accompanying her to the funeral to wear cloth coverings that wrapped across our faces, to protect us against what the doctor had termed *the*

347

miasma of illness in the city's air, and to carry pomanders of rose musk, cloves and mint.

I accompanied Lady Mary and her daughter, Anne, as they travelled upriver from Baynard's to Whitehall, merging with a succession of other noble barges as well as scores of watermen and their wherries carrying common folk. Crowds of Londoners, apparently heedless of the plague, thronged the streets to witness the funeral procession from Whitehall Palace to Westminster Abbey. The chilling sight of so many masked figures made the plague seem both mysterious and suddenly real. Even more alarming, many in the crowd wore no masks at all.

I had dressed the Countess of Pembroke in garments of mourning – a heavy gown of black brocade shot through with silver and a hood of black silk weighed down with beads of jet. My lady's thick red hair, lately streaked with silver, was bound with black lace ribbons beneath the hood so that no colour could be seen. Yet her pale face above the mask was so striking, her dark eyes so fierce with sorrow and her bearing so regal that I noticed many of the onlookers gawking and whispering. Carrying her train, I was reminded of my earliest days in her service, a leaf bobbing in the wake of a swan.

The royal hearse was topped by a crowned wax effigy of Queen Elizabeth in her crimson Parliament robes. Lady Mary had not participated in her brother's funeral procession, but now she joined the other peeresses of the realm in their black mourning cloaks and hoods. By the time we arrived at Westminster Abbey, I was breathless from the weight of my lady's train and from panting for air beneath my own mask. I marvelled at her ability to walk such a distance in the heavy gown. As I waited with the other servants, I pressed the fragrant pomander against the linen covering my face, inhaling its bracing scent. Eyeing the throng, I wondered despite myself if I might catch a glimpse of my birth father, the magus. But too many faces were masked, his most likely as well. I hadn't yet worn the ring that was his gift. Finally putting it on would signify accepting his role in shaping my path. And I wasn't ready to take that step.

Now thirty-nine, I had long ago accepted that I would have no children of my own. I couldn't lament my lack of offspring, given how close I was to Cicely's children. And I had seen enough of childbirth at close hand not to regret escaping that labour. Certainly I appreciated the many opportunities for exploring art and alchemy that would not have been my lot in marriage. Children brought many trials, too, as I knew only too well from my mistress's experience. I was happy, instead, to serve as an informal godmother for Angelica, while Peter, whose marriage to Margaret, the housekeeper's niece, had not produced any children, was godfather to his nephew Stanley. It seemed fitting that Peter and I should perform these roles for Cicely's children, since she was the origin of our connection and still the centre of our world.

But after our safe return to Wilton, my dismay over the state of Cicely's marriage to Toby only grew. Toby was more and more sullen since he'd lost his position as valet upon his master's death and been demoted to footman. It was only thanks to his marriage to Cicely that he had not been dismissed outright.

Even Cicely, who believed the best of everyone, confessed to me one afternoon that she couldn't make any headway with

Toby's increasing bleakness and bad temper. 'After Sir Henry died, Toby wanted the position of assistant steward. And when Master Wilkins decided to train Stanley instead, Toby took against our own son. He gets more miserable and mardy every day!'

Usually troubles rolled off Cicely like water, but no longer. Not when her children were involved. I listened with growing concern, but knew better than to criticise Toby myself, for that would only bring her to his defence. I didn't like leaving Cicely at Wilton when I accompanied my lady to London, but she assured me she could handle Toby as well as ever she had.

Less than a month after the Queen's funeral, my lady informed me that we would be returning to London in July for the coronation of His Majesty James I and his consort, Queen Anna. I was shocked – while the plague still raged there? She explained it was an essential journey, for the purpose of greeting Queen Anna, whose favour might shape Lady Mary's future, particularly now she was a widow.

'My aim is to serve the new Queen as one of her senior ladies-in-waiting, just as my own mother attended Queen Elizabeth,' she confided in me, as she did ever more frequently since our return from Wales.

When we arrived in London, I sought Lady Mary's permission to take an afternoon away from Baynard's, thinking to pay another visit to Simon Forman. But my lady said no. With plague now sweeping the city with redoubled ferocity, it would not be safe to go anywhere on foot. We travelled by enclosed carriage past houses whose doors were sealed and marked with red crosses signalling the presence of plague.

Infected inhabitants were ordered to remain in confinement for six weeks, to limit the contagion. From the Baynard's servants, we heard horrible tales of inflamed buboes and bursting boils that no treatments could heal. I couldn't help wondering about the astrologer's fate in the crowded streets of Billingsgate. But I didn't dwell on such thoughts overlong. My true family, I knew, was my mother, my lady and Cicely.

The royal court had undergone a change as striking as the sleight of hand achieved by the painter in the past Queen's portraits. When she died, Queen Elizabeth was surrounded by noblewomen who had served her since the start of her reign, assisted by others from the generation of my mistress, who was now forty-one. The new Queen, only twenty-eight herself, had selected a flock of fresh-faced maids of honour the age of my lady's daughter. Our first visit to the new court was a study in contrasts.

Queen Anna was stunning – a Snow Queen whose fair hair, swept up and back from her face, was piled higher than a crown, while the expanse of her white bosom, edged with scarcely a breath of filigreed lace, left little to the imagination. The painter's final portrait of Queen Elizabeth had achieved a suggestion of modesty in the multiple strands of jewels draped across Her Majesty's chest. Not so this Queen. Where her predecessor's red hair and vividly coloured silks and ribbons had commanded attention, this Queen was as pale as a 'dishful of snow', a sweet concoction whipped from cream and rose water I'd tasted once after a banquet at Wilton. All of this made the contrast with the ungainly bulbous-nosed King, clothed in forest green and black velvet, only more striking. Beauty and the beast, I thought uncharitably. The princess and the toad. I could never voice such judgements in the court, but I couldn't wait to share them with Cicely.

To my dismay, Queen Anna barely acknowledged the presence of Lady Mary or her good friend Lady Margaret Clifford, the Countess of Cumberland, when they arrived to pay tribute to Her Royal Highness in the Presence Chamber at Hampton Court. Fortunately, my lady's brother, Robert Sidney, had been promoted almost immediately by the new King to the position of Queen's Lord Chamberlain. Only when Sir Robert gestured to his sister did the Queen beckon her forward, though she seemed to have little to say to her after they were introduced. I could see from the tight line of Lady Mary's jaw and her rigidly erect posture as she departed the Queen's presence how sharply her disappointment cut into her hopes. But my lady was not one to dwell on setbacks. If anything, I guessed that the polite indifference of the Snow Queen would only intensify Lady Mary's resolve to advance her position at court by other means.

That opportunity arrived in autumn, when King James took the court on a royal progress away from London, where the plague showed no sign of slackening. Wilton House was his first stop. My lady's sons had already captured the liking of the King, who apparently took pleasure in choosing young men as favourites. If anything, William's disgrace under Queen Elizabeth only recommended him more highly to this King, who took every occasion to distinguish himself from his predecessor. My lady devoted her efforts to entertaining both the Queen and the

King, though their tastes couldn't have been more different.

'Where the King prefers the hunt,' my mistress explained, 'the Queen favours the theatre. I've encouraged William to bring the Lord Chamberlain's Men here to entertain their Royal Majesties with a new comedy by Will Shakespeare.'

That was how I came to see a performance of a play about shepherds and courtiers that unexpectedly awakened a longing in my heart for another life than the one I had. Unlike the tragedy translated by my lady, Master Shakespeare's *As You Like It* was indeed, as its title suggested, a merry comedy for each viewer to take as he or she liked. The cousins Rosalind and Celia, *like Juno's swans, coupled and inseparable*, reminded me so closely of myself and Cicely that I could picture us striking out together in the world. I laughed, though with a lump in my throat, at the hopeless love of the shepherdess Phebe for Rosalind disguised as a boy, who she clearly loves not just for her sex but for her spirit, in contrast to the mooning love-struck shepherd who has been courting her. Rosalind's confession to Celia that *my affection hath an unknown bottom* spoke to me not of her feelings for Orlando, but of my own feelings for Cicely. This was the world I wanted – not a husband and children, but a companion of the heart to share laughter and tears, hopes and fears. I understood when Phebe settled for the shepherd in the end, because she could not have Rosalind, and I thought of Cicely marrying Toby when I wished the outcome otherwise.

After the performance, I noticed my lady in animated conversation with Master Shakespeare, a pale, studious-looking man who, like my mistress, had a piercing gaze and ink-stained fingers. I couldn't hear their words, and in any case didn't care to as I was too wrapped up in the feelings the performance had provoked. It wasn't that the play showed me a world I could actually live in, but it brought my own hopes and dreams to the surface, conjuring me to imagine life as I might like it. Even now.

Cicely and Angelica were far too busy that afternoon tending to our visitors to watch the play, so I told them the entire story that evening, reciting some of my favourite lines from memory. I wanted Cicely to see my vision, but after laughing with me, she sighed.

'All of those fancy words would've flummoxed me. The larking of those lovers is best in thy telling.'

'But were the lovers happy in the end?' Now of marriageable age herself, Angelica wanted a love story to turn out as *she* liked it.

'Well, everyone gets married in the end, but we don't really know,' I admitted. 'In some ways, their real lives are just beginning. I'd guess Rosalind and Celia remain friends for ever, and their husbands learn how to live from them – and with them.' When Cicely smiled, I realised she had seen my vision after all. It was a matter of grounding the imagined in the real.

INTERLUDE: THE STAGE

William Shakespeare

Age cannot wither her, nor custom stale
Her infinite variety. Other women cloy
The appetites they feed, but she makes hungry
Where most she satisfies.

Will Shakespeare drops his quill pen upon the table and rests his broad forehead in his hand. Growing radiance from the waxing moon silvers the leaded windows of the George Inn in Southwark. The half-timbered walls are dark with smoke, but sufficient light flickers over his table from the single candle that he can see the pages. Long past the chimes at midnight, it's quiet enough, now, to write in private, without the players who throng the place at suppertime. He doesn't want anyone to discover he's writing a new play for the Countess of Pembroke.

He still can't believe his luck in receiving her patronage, which he knows can turn in a moment.

The previous autumn, at the Countess's request, her son William had commissioned a performance of Will's *As You Like It* at Wilton House. Once again, the theatres were closed due to plague by order of the Privy Council. But the show must go on, and the players embraced this chance of escape. After London, where body collectors' carts plied the streets and the air was rank with death, Wilton was paradise.

Will was particularly delighted at William Herbert's invitation to bring the Chamberlain's Men to perform at Wilton – not just the honour, but the opportunity to meet Mary Sidney Herbert herself. At that performance, he heard the Dowager Countess laugh aloud more than once, and most heartily when the actor playing Rosalind, a boy playing a girl playing a boy, delivered the Epilogue.

As the audience dispersed, she sent for him. He didn't know what to expect. He had heard of her brilliance, and her acerbity, from bits of gossip passed like currency among writers in the tavern. None had met her in person, but many claimed to know at least one of the fortunate writers in the literary circle that she gathered around her. *She can sharpen a verse on the whetstone of her intellect, or puncture an ego with the needle of her wit.*

Dispensing with formalities, the Countess addressed him crisply. 'Your Rosalind is the finest character I've seen in a dramatic comedy. *Men have died from time to time, and worms have eaten them, but not for love*, she says, putting the lovesick Orlando in his place. A sentiment more sonneteers should keep in mind!' At once bright and dark, the piercing eyes beneath her raised brows beggared all description, a paradox that lodged in his mind even as he was swept away by her praise. This he had not expected.

'Your play reveals a woman's skill in conjuring concord from discord. Rosalind fashions couplings out of conflict with patience and humour that conceal the grasp of human nature informing her art. Well done, sir!'

Her eyes sparked with evident delight. Then her tone shifted. 'But *I am for other than for dancing measures.*' His words again, from the play's pensive philosopher.

'Having outlived my beloved brother as well as my husband, what increasingly captures my interest is the possibility for love rooted in maturity rather than youth. The lovers in your comedies are very young, Master Shakespeare. Have you considered letting them grow up and fall down, love and yet lose?' It was more of a challenge than a question. And so was the next one. 'You know my translation of Garnier?'

He felt a surge of anticipation. Of course he knew her play. He had purchased it from a Southwark bookseller almost a decade earlier. The Countess of Pembroke's *Antonius* infused his consciousness from its opening speech, a paean to a goddess in the voice of a general willing to risk all for love. While her adept verse drew him in from the start, it is her characterisation of the indomitable Queen that still holds him in thrall. A Cleopatra of head-turning complexity – lover and mother, seeker and ruler, coward and hero, flawed and yet complete. He has mulled over the tragedy and wrestled with its contradictions ever since, tempted to take on the story himself.

No such character has ever appeared on the English stage. Nor is likely to unless he writes her himself, for the Countess's convention-breaking *Antonius* was composed not for the public stage but for a courtly circle more primed for paradox than the larger public, who tend to like their villains dark and their heroes dazzling. Indeed, the queen in the tragedy he has just drafted will be his most fully realised thus far, but also his darkest: Lady Macbeth, who provokes a regicide then descends into madness.

What a challenge rendering a Cleopatra inspired by *Antonius* would be – to show the public a female monarch who rules both an empire and a Roman general's heart, with a touch as deft as it is ruthless – and to make the audience fall in love with her for the invincible wilfulness that is her greatest strength and vulnerability in one.

The Countess was awaiting a reply.

'I recall your Cleopatra declaring, of Antony, *He is my self*,' Will ventured. 'Surely that union arises from their conflicting natures?'

Receiving his words, the lady took a quick breath, then slowly exhaled. Mercurial emotions crossed her face – pleasure, recognition, hope, doubt.

'Alchemists,' the Countess observed, 'strive to unite what is opposed. They aspire to bring spirit and matter, male and female, Sol and Luna into what I call a hermaphroditic ideal. I see that ideal in this story. What do you think, Master Shakespeare?'

Not just a question, but a challenge. Now Will took a breath of his own.

'Indeed. Were I to endeavour to place this tale upon the public stage, I would want to show compelling power on both sides. Sol and Luna, in your words. What interests me is the reciprocal attraction and inevitable conflict that drives tragedy.' He had no plan yet, only possibilities.

'A tragedy of Antony *and* Cleopatra, then?'

'None other.'

With that, Will Shakespeare acquired a new patron for a fresh project. But he hasn't forgotten the cautionary example of Samuel Daniel, whose *Tragedy of Cleopatra* had drawn not approbation but her ire. An author who undermines the eloquence of the Countess of Pembroke is liable to end up short on funds as well as reputation.

Now, embarking on a venture fraught with such possibility and peril, he finds himself apprehensive as well as exhilarated. In exchange for her sponsorship, he has agreed to show her his drafts as he writes – a perilous bargain, indeed. How will she regard the pages he is taking to Baynard's Castle tomorrow? He has determined not to show her the passages she herself has inspired until he can gauge her reaction to the opening scene he has just drafted in the flickering candlelight. For even as her play captured his attention, so must his own transmutation of the story capture hers. He's convinced that any celebration of this queen's infinite variety must commence with dark before light, shadows before bright possibility.

His choice of that starting point might prove the sticking point. But as the old saw has it: nothing ventured, nothing gained. It remains to be seen how she will treat a playwright who aspires not to contradict his patron's vision, but to complicate it.

As he gathers his papers and douses the candle, Will is anxious, but eager. This Countess makes hungry where most she satisfies.

PART THREE: 1604–12

RUBEDO (*projectio*)*:* the final red stage, representing completion and release, synthesis, unity of masculine and feminine.

PART THREE: 1904–12

CHAPTER TWENTY-EIGHT

Mary, 1604

Surely she had learnt her lesson. No good could come from trusting her story to a man. Her vision of Cleopatra, transmuted from Garnier's raw material through multiple distillations to intensify the force of the female hero, had been so degraded by Samuel Daniel that when he had the temerity to appear at the next gathering she had frozen him with silent disdain and later informed him that he was no longer welcome. Expecting more than Samuel had the capability, or will, to achieve had been a miscalculation, and Mary felt a disquieting pang of failure.

She also dismissed him as tutor to her younger children. However, she could not deny that in that realm, at least, he had been truly gifted. She swallowed her rage long enough to pass him on to her friend Margaret Clifford, whose daughter, Anne, required tutelage.

'You crushed his romantic aspirations, Mary,' Margaret remarked.

'Social ambitions would be more accurate. Samuel fancies himself a love poet, but his *Delia* sonnets are like stale sugared almonds – coated with sweetness but without lasting flavour.' Warming to her subject, seeking the right words, she continued, 'True passion has an edge, whether it's the Psalmist's wrestling with God's inscrutable love or a far more provocative sonneteer's disarming confession that *My mistress' eyes are nothing like the sun.*'

Mary had noted Will Shakespeare's voice with interest ever since first reading a few of his sonnets that circulated among her friends. Always an edge there and sometimes quite sharp: *When my love swears that she is made of truth, I do believe her, though I know she lies.* That, and the intriguingly dark undercurrent that grounded the bright humour in his comedy set in the Forest of Arden, had inspired her proposal of patronage when they had met at Wilton the previous month.

It was a calculated risk offering sponsorship to Master Shakespeare to distil the tale of Antony and Cleopatra for the public stage. Mary was excited by the potential pairing of this playwright and this story, but wary lest yet another man devalue the Egyptian queen. That was why, in exchange for her patronage, she had exacted Shakespeare's agreement to show her his drafts as he worked. She had learnt from the disaster of Samuel's *Cleopatra* to trust nothing wholly to chance.

She was wagering that the playwright would construct a riveting tragedy of two lovers who were also leaders, two serpents biting one another's tails in an unbroken loop. But she feared he might succumb to the ready temptation to elevate the male hero by darkening the lady, as others had done.

The most successful experiments in her still-room required multiple iterations, with ingredients newly mixed, balanced and subjected to the furnace. There was a chance, if the vessel didn't explode, to arrive one step closer to the hermaphroditic ideal that Catherine had called *the truth of Cleopatra*. But the risk of disaster was all too real.

Will Shakespeare brought the draft of his opening scene to Baynard's Castle, a rolled-up sheaf of papers tied with black string, carried in one slender hand. After acknowledging his deep bow with a smile and taking the proffered manuscript, Mary ushered him into the library, where quill pens and inkpots sat on either side of the oak table, flanking a stack of clean sheets of paper. This was how she and Philip had worked together, facing each other. He registered this arrangement with a quizzical lifting of brows over his hazel eyes. Although his figure was slight, an almost palpable aura of energy surrounded him like a chameleon capable of many hues.

Mary seated herself on one side of the table and gestured to the playwright to sit across from her. Slowly, deliberately, she read through his pages. Then she raised her own brows.

'I recall you professed your intent to explore *the reciprocal attraction and inevitable conflict that drives the tragedy*, Master Shakespeare.' She let her challenge register in her voice. 'All well and good, and yet in the very first speech here, the *captain's heart* of the hero becomes *the bellows and the fan to cool a gypsy's lust*. Where is the reciprocity in that transaction? Antony sounds like the servant who mans the bellows in my still-room.' Though her tone was dismissive, her eyes were not. Could he rise to the challenge? Or did he see Cleopatra as a strumpet and Antony a fool? In which case there was no tragedy at all.

'Consider who is speaking, my lady.' His words were measured, as if he, too, was aware that their association might founder right here. She had told him she did not seek control over his creative process. What she had not said and had not fully recognised until this moment, was that what she wished for was genuine collaboration, an intellectual exchange. True, it was founded in financial remuneration, but also in the playwright's eager response to her *Antonius*. She had explained the process she valued in working with her brother, and now she sought the chance to match Will's ideas with her own. This ugly description of Cleopatra at the very start of his play took her aback, recalling the sharp disappointment of her encounter with Samuel's degenerate queen. But his calm response spoke to the importance of point of view.

Consider who is speaking. Of course – not Antony himself, but one of his soldiers. 'I see. He's expressing the Romans' disgust at their general's passion for this foreign queen.' Still, Mary remained sceptical. 'Next, you bring in a soothsayer and a eunuch with the Queen's attendants, creating an image of Egyptian superstition.' She paused. Then she took the plunge. 'Perhaps what's needed at the outset is a scene between Antony and Cleopatra together, where the audience can experience the vivid intensity of their love and glimpse the inadequacy of all frames.'

Mary held her breath. The couple's passion, the basis for all ambition as well as the touchstone of tragedy, must come alive for the audience at the outset. Then his eyes lit up. He seized a sheet of paper, dipped a quill into ink, and dashed off his response. As she had guessed, he could think more clearly as he wrote. And seeing his nod of pleasure at having the tools he needed at hand, she smiled at his realisation that this was why she had prepared the arrangement on the table because this was how she, too, worked.

He explained his scrawl. 'I hear a bantering exchange between them, measuring each other's loves. The Queen coyly demands, *If it be love indeed, tell me how much*, and Antony parries, *There's beggary in the love that can be reckoned.*'

Now it was her turn to embrace the challenge, taking up her own quill and writing on a fresh piece of paper before sharing her thought. 'Then, what if Antony goes further? If she would set a boundary on his love, *Then must thou find out new heaven and new earth.*'

She held his gaze, her face luminous with the joy of finding new language for a new Antony. Risking all, she had hoped for no less.

The man was on his feet, pacing around the table. 'But Cleopatra is still doubtful. She has seen other men profess devotion, only to prove false.'

Mary understood that experience only too well. '*Excellent falsehood!*' The line escaped her lips unbidden, and she feared she'd gone too far. But then his eyes flashed and he seized another sheet of paper.

'To which Antony responds, *Let Rome in Tiber melt, and the wide arch of the empire fall!*' He paused for a moment, fingering the gold loop glinting in one ear. Then: '*Here is my space.*'

His actor's voice thrilled her, shivering her bones. The scene was a fire sparked by their exchange of words, all light and heat. '*A mutual pair who stand up peerless*,' he added.

'Each of them larger than life, yes! That's why love veers so quickly into jealousy on both sides.' She paused. 'To be honest, I hadn't understood that when writing *Antonius*. My vision of Cleopatra then was one of unwavering constancy, like marble, to discredit all those historical slurs. But I see now that for their love to be mutual, they must both be flawed.'

He met her words with his own. 'And so responsive to each other that they swing from one extreme to another, carrying the audience with them – the Roman audience, the Egyptian audience – and soon, the audience at the Globe.' The air between them shimmered with possibility, and the pressure that had bound her chest in anticipation of reading Will's draft melted.

'Carry on, Master Shakespeare.' Mary's voice was alive with anticipation. 'This drama deserves the widest audience possible. And I like reframing the story this way.'

'Your *Antonius* inspired it.' His voice was appreciative, and something more, threaded with bright wonder. 'I've worked with other source texts, but what we've done today is new to me. I'm beginning to think of our arrangement as not only patronage, but partnership.'

Mary's breath caught. He went further. 'To speak truth, your ladyship, I would never normally countenance a patron as collaborator. But then, I've never before experienced a mind like yours.' He paused, struck by a thought. '*Infinite variety* – that's the term that applies.'

Mary had a new request, no, an invitation. 'If I am to be your collaborator, I cannot be *your ladyship*. You must call me Mary.'

'And I,' he replied, 'am Will.'

Henry would undoubtedly have been jealous, she mused, but for no cause. Or no cause that he could measure. More transformative than any act of bodily union, this was the communion of minds that she had sought ever since her brother's passing.

Thomas Moffett's death marked the close of an act. After Rose's friend Cicely suffered that dangerous miscarriage that Mary had been unable to palliate, Henry had brought Doctor Moffett from London for his expertise with Paracelsian treatments. Over time, the doctor's knowledge had served to expand her own. Now, having attended the births of each of her children and the death of her husband with skill and compassion, he was gone.

Mary's brother Robert lost no time in sending along another court physician, educated, like Moffett, at Oxford and Basel, and as expert as his predecessor in chemical and Paracelsian remedies. Mary had been prepared to see to the medical needs of the household herself with the assistance of Adrian Gilbert, but Robert insisted. *Matthew is an excellent physician and a good man*, he wrote, telling her to expect Doctor Lister by the end of the month. He added a postscript: *You may appreciate his presence in your Circle*.

Young and vain, and probably closer in age to her son William than to herself. Those were Mary's first thoughts when the new doctor presented himself at Wilton. He was indeed ten years younger than Mary, as attested by the credentials he presented, and striking to look at – an abundance of golden curls above a carefully trimmed beard, dark brown eyes flecked surprisingly with gold beneath fair lashes.

What had Robert been thinking commending such a dandy for service at Wilton, let alone for inclusion in the Circle? He was polite and formal, with a touch of Yorkshire in his speech, putting no great effort into making a good impression. Mary's instinct was to dislike him heartily and send him packing. Yet his seeming indifference to her favour intrigued her. Mary was used to turning men's heads, not so much with her beauty, now that she was forty-two, as through wit and force of will, although her hair, now darkened to a glossy auburn, still drew admiring glances. No, she decided, this new doctor was not the replacement she was seeking. However, out of respect to her brother, she graciously welcomed him to Wilton House and invited him to join her Circle in its next meeting.

Mary had urged Will Shakespeare to join the Circle, but he declined, with thanks. 'Please don't take offence, but I have little use for it. My circle is the Globe, my world the stage. My life, as both player and playwright, is there. The hope of meeting you was what brought me to Wilton. What has followed I can only describe as the happiest of accidents as a quid pro quo become a partnership.'

The Circle was evolving, Mary mused, as its members gathered in the Great Hall at Wilton a week after Doctor Lister's arrival. For one thing, the charter member dearest to her heart was missing. Arrested on hearsay and convicted of treason in a plot against King James, Walter Raleigh was now imprisoned in the Tower of London. Despite Walter's marriage to another, over twelve years ago now, the ouroboros of their bond had endured. In the depths of her soul, Mary was convinced of his innocence. She had done her utmost to convince, and then cajole the King on Walter's behalf. After the trial, with a date set for his execution, she had arranged for a performance by the King's Men of one of Will Shakespeare's most popular comedies, *Much Ado About Nothing*, hoping that its title might suggest leniency. She understood that the new King liked to be entertained and was more likely to look favourably upon a petitioner who brought him pleasure.

To her enormous relief, after that performance the King had decided to spare Walter's life. Ever resourceful, Walter had proceeded to strike up a friendship with the Warden of the Tower, who allowed him to continue his alchemical investigations, complete with a furnace, and to assemble a library that soon numbered several hundred volumes. Mary missed his presence terribly and comforted herself by rubbing her ouroboros ring, the only physical token of their bond.

Walter's absence from the Circle was palliated by Mary's happiness that her son William had joined it. After three months in prison on Queen Elizabeth's command, William had fallen ill of an ague, and Doctor Moffett's corroboration of his illness had been sufficient to prompt Her Majesty to modify his sentence. He had been banished to Baynard's Castle, and then to Wilton, forbidden to visit the court or to travel abroad. During his confinement, his baby son by Mary Fitton had died, without meeting his father. A dark end to an ugly story, thought Mary.

With the death of the old Queen in 1603 and the advent of a new ruler, William had also been released from disgrace. He had arranged a politically advantageous marriage to the eldest daughter of the powerful and wealthy Earl of Shrewsbury. Plain and timid, Mary Talbot was as different from Mary Fitton, his mother judged, as a mole from a magpie. Apparently ambition overmastered passion, at least in her son's choice of a wife.

William had lost no time to ingratiate himself with the new monarch and his circle. Although he lacked his brother's easy charm, he was able to impress the other nobles at court by sheer force of intelligence. Hoping to achieve a reconciliation with her recalcitrant son, Mary sought ways to advance his interests and urged him to join her Circle whenever he was at Baynard's or Wilton. Stressing the group's intellectual variety, she explained that the works offered for discussion ranged from romances and love poems to medical and alchemical theories. His acceptance had been half-hearted, and he attended only sporadically at first. But before long, to Mary's deep pleasure, he was joining in the avid give-and-take of the conversations, matching wits with the keenest minds in the group. If he could continue to apply himself to satisfying his intellect as readily as his passions, Mary thought, he might yet grow to be a worthy Earl of Pembroke.

Now, as Mary took her place in the circle of chairs, she motioned Doctor Lister to sit beside her. He carried himself with quiet reserve, saying nothing to her or the other members. But his watchful eyes never left her, and she had an uncomfortable sensation of being measured, with judgement yet to come. Mary shook her head to clear it.

'We are joined tonight by a new visitor, Doctor Matthew Lister, who will be taking Doctor Moffett's place, for now.' The other members of the Circle nodded courteous greetings.

He nodded in return, offering a slightly lopsided smile to all. But he said nothing, and Mary moved on. The proposition she planned to offer tonight had the potential of either completing her Circle in ways she had only dreamt of, or breaking it irreparably.

For many years men had listened when she spoke and sought her favour because, as Henry's wife and Countess of Pembroke, she could wield considerable influence in court circles. Although her title in marriage had now passed to her daughter-in-law, the Dowager Countess commanded both respect and a considerable income. She had recently designed her own seal – two Sidney pheons in the shape of arrowheads interlocked to form an M crossed by an H, surmounted by the Dudley bear and Sidney porcupine. With that, she had reframed herself as an independent woman, as a published author and founder of a prestigious Circle of writers and thinkers.

Working on the play with Will Shakespeare, which gave equal space to hero and heroine, to mutual ambition as well as desire unconstrained by conventions of gender, Mary had begun to ponder a new possibility, of reframing the Circle itself to reflect what she had come to understand was not only possible, but essential, to *the truth of Cleopatra*.

The firelight in the Great Hall illuminated a gathering of authors whose voices she had come to trust and appreciate. There was Jack Donne, his keen intellect suggested by a sharp nose and chiselled beard, who had caught Mary's attention a decade ago, when he himself was scarcely twenty, now grown into a mature poet whose scintillating metaphors shed light on mysteries of body and spirit alike. Stocky, tousled Ben Jonson, the same age as Jack and of the same vintage in the Circle, whose masques for the court were themselves miracles of illumination, but who used his rapier wit more often to thrust and parry than to banish shadows. John Davies, the fleshy, imperious lawyer-poet and one-time secretary to Sir Henry, whose *Hymns to Astraea* celebrated his friendship with the late Queen. Edmund Spenser, one of the original members, fastidious and dignified, who in his *Faerie Queene* had created the warrior-heroine Britomart, the most genuinely hermaphroditic character Mary had yet encountered. And a dozen others, many of them equally celebrated authors.

Mary drew a deep breath and began. 'In alchemy, the possibility of perfection arises from conjoining disparate elements. By that measure, then, the feminine gender should be judged not as inferior or defective, but as essential to the ongoing process of perfection. Only by embracing both genders may that goal be achieved.'

She paused to let her words register. Then she continued.

'That being so, gentlemen, I am considering the prospect of admitting women authors to our Circle.' A stark silence ensued. On some faces she detected scepticism, even hostility, on others curiosity. There was no telling if her decision would unite the Circle, or dissolve it.

She knew it would take time – time for these men to digest her radical proposal, and time for Mary to cultivate the talents of the young women she hoped to introduce, including her niece and goddaughter, Mary Wroth, and her own daughter, Anne.

Silence hung in the air for another long moment.

'I believe that bringing different minds together into collaborative thought and writing can achieve marvels. I'm honoured to be present for this venture.'

So Matthew Lister had a voice after all.

CHAPTER TWENTY-NINE

Rose, 1605

'I need thy help, Rose. I've nowhere else to turn.'

Cicely's voice was shaded with sadness and regret. Trying to sort a path for herself through Toby's rages, she seemed on the verge of losing her way. Cicely – my model for forging ahead confidently no matter what the challenges.

'Anything.' My reply was heart-given. I pressed my cheek to hers and she wrapped her warm arms around my neck. I wished for more happiness for her, more time with her, more Cicely in my life in every way. 'What can I do?'

She took a breath and blew it out. 'I know tha sees 'tis getting harder with Toby. He flies off the handle at the slightest cause, and he's always down at the tavern of an evening. I need to find ways to earn wages he can't drink away. Happen there's work for me in the still-room? It steadies me to work with thee, it does.' She caught my frown and added hastily, 'I'd do all me other work too, of course.'

'That's not what I'm worried about,' I reassured her. 'It's just that with Mum helping Lady Mary in the still-room, there's not much extra that needs doing.' Seeing her expression droop, I added quickly, 'But our mistress is becoming known throughout Wiltshire for her herbal concoctions. She'll surely need more help when summer comes and the herbs need harvesting and distilling.' Then suddenly I guessed what she might not want to say. 'Are you keeping safe, Cicely? Do you need somewhere else to stay? There's always a place for you with Mum and me.'

But she shook her head, mustering a smile that fooled neither of us. 'Nothing like that! Toby'll settle, I'm sure. I'm just less mardy when I'm with thee.'

Soon enough, Lady Mary invited Cicely to help me in producing her herbal concoctions. We spent hours together, chopping herbs and distilling tinctures.

'If only I could read,' she sighed one day, as I reviewed the instructions for remedies stored in Lady Catherine's black walnut box. 'Happen someday ye'll teach me as Lady Catherine taught thee.'

When Cicely's son, Stanley, proposed to his sweetheart, Sophia, one of the chambermaids, Cicely asked me to help her select flowers for the wedding bouquet. 'Remember how mithered tha wast over the backend flowers at me wedding?' But her chuckle was only a shadow of the familiar burble of merriment that always lifted my spirits.

Devoting herself to her children's well-being brought Cicely great comfort. But even as they bloomed and found their own paths, I watched the distance between Cicely and her husband widen from a rift to a ravine. Toby's disappointed hopes for advancement were driving him to drink beyond his capacity. Cicely didn't complain, but I was alarmed when Toby's behaviour turned from sullen silence to outbursts of temper. Though Cicely bore the brunt of his anger, increasingly he snarled at Stanley, whose cheerful hard work as assistant steward had displaced his father in Master Wilkins' favour. As for me, he had resented me ever since I stood up to him when he fanned the flames of Sir Henry's jealousy over Samuel Daniel.

Toby would have kept me from Cicely if he could. But there was no chance of that. The more erratic he became, the more Cicely turned to me for the steadiness of spirit I had always sought in her. On the worst nights, when Toby drank himself into darkness, Cicely took to sharing my bed in the comfortable chamber where Mum and I slept. Remembering how I had huddled into her warm embrace as a lonely young chambermaid, I welcomed Cicely into my own bed whenever she needed comfort.

I longed to release her from the captivity of her marriage. But whenever I urged her to leave Toby, she wouldn't consider it, insisting that he was a good man at heart, and that all he needed was enough patience and care to settle him back into his old ways. Those old ways had never offered her much by way of comfort or pleasure, I thought but didn't say.

Racking my brains over Cicely's trouble, I missed the trouble that was right before my eyes. From time to time, Mum put her hand to her chest and steadied herself, especially when climbing the steep stairs to the still-room. She brushed it off. ''Tis only an ache in my legs, love. Don't worry yourself.'

And so I didn't, until one day she collapsed among the bushes in the herb garden. 'I believe it's a matter of her heart,' Doctor Lister told Lady Mary after examining Mum in our chamber. She lay stretched beneath a sheet on the bed, her wrist limp in the doctor's gentle hands. 'I recommend a tincture of hawthorn with turmeric to improve the blood flow. But I cannot predict the course of her illness. I fear that the weakness in her heart may prevail if the tincture does not have the desired effect.' When my lady turned to look at me, the compassion in her eyes frightened me even more than the doctor's words.

That evening, I slid into bed beside Mum. Cicely insisted on sitting up beside us all night. She prepared a tisane using galangal root from our stores, Mum's own final prescription for Lady Catherine, as she had said, *to bring ease when no clear cure is at hand.* I took her wrist the way Doctor Lister showed me, to check for her heartbeat during the night. Her raspy breathing sounded like river pebbles lapped by water in her chest. Cicely squeezed my fingers, but I felt numb.

I had been carrying a residue of resentment towards my mother for so many years that I had almost ceased to recognise it. Learning that she had hidden my origins from me for so long had felt like a betrayal. But did I really think knowing about my birth father would have changed my life? It was time to let it go.

She was my source. And now, it was time to let her go too.

As morning light slid gently into the room, her pulse was so faint that a whimper escaped my lips, watching the vein that ran like a green stem from her arm into her palm. Mum's eyes opened. She smiled when I held the fragrant tisane, now cool, to her lips.

'Rose, you're here. I wanted to see you, before—' She reached out to touch my cheek, wet with tears, and I kissed her fingers, then buried my face in her shoulder.

'I know I hurt you by waiting so long to tell you the truth about your father. I haven't done a good job of explaining why.' Her gaze was clear, but with that dark undercurrent running always beneath the surface.

'You were Simon's truest work, and even that was by accident. It was mothering you that taught me who I was.' She closed her eyes.

The silence stretched out for so long that I thought she had drifted asleep. Then she breathed in and opened her eyes.

'He never had a chance to be your father, and for that I was grateful. Not because Martin was a better father, but because Simon would have tried to anchor himself in you and make you need him. He craves the illusion that he's necessary.'

Mum squeezed my fingers, so strongly that I felt a moment of hope in her recovery.

'You may have his eyes, but otherwise you couldn't be more different. From either of us. You're stronger than me as well.'

Mum must have read the silent protest in my face, for she pushed on. 'It took me my entire life to understand that our fates are not a matter of the stars, but of the choices we make. Simon was so obsessed with reading the astral signs that he missed connections of the heart. But recognising those has always been your most powerful gift.' Her smile, suddenly, was radiant.

* * *

We buried Mum in the Amesbury churchyard, beside her husband. With my brother, Michael, and his wife, Elizabeth, I planted flowers on her grave. White starflowers.

Lady Mary attended my mother's funeral – a mark of respect and appreciation not often given to a servant.

'Joan was like the North Star,' my lady told me that night as we stood in the herb garden under the waning moon. She gestured to the brightest star on the horizon. 'With her guidance, one could always chart a true course.'

Finally, I understood. I knew myself because my mother had always known me.

CHAPTER THIRTY

Mary, 1606

Adding women was an experiment – as calculated and considered as any selection of new ingredients for trial in the still-room, and at the same time as imbued with hope and prone to disaster as the effort of a first-time alchemist. She couldn't predict the results. Except that this time, the alembic was her Circle and any explosion due to excessive heat or the reaction of incompatible ingredients might shatter the vessel irreparably.

She spent the morning before the meeting, this one at Baynard's Castle, considering how to introduce the women she had invited. The new members represented a mix of generations. Aemilia Lanyer at thirty-seven was in the same age cohort as regulars in the Circle such as Ben Jonson and Jack Donne, while Mary's niece was just nineteen. Aemilia's poem cycle dedicated to women and her niece's love sonnets were certain to produce a stimulating response, Mary thought with a smile.

In the two years since she had stated her intention of admitting women to the Circle, Mary had nurtured the developing talents of several exceptional young noblewomen whose work, she felt, would add spice and savour to the group's discussions. In addition to her niece, they included Mary's own daughter, Anne, whose thoughtful reserve she believed would flower into confidence, and Elizabeth Cary, whose lively mind was perpetually questioning assumptions – both of them already promising poets. If they all spoke this evening, she would be happy, but even if they were simply seen she would be satisfied. Seeing, after all, is believing.

Mary had also spent countless hours deflecting doubts and repelling objections from present members, some of whom questioned the propriety of the proposed arrangement, others the women's capacity for producing work that would meet the Circle's high standards. Even so, a number of authors had declined to attend tonight's gathering, some expressing outright disapproval, others' excuses subtly conveying their scepticism. Some of those who did appear would come for the spectacle, perhaps hoping to witness an explosion. The evening seemed destined to either fizzle or flame.

To Mary's surprise, her son William was one of the first to arrive. She hadn't expected that the voices of these particular authors would appeal to a man *hooked by the wiles* of a woman such as Mary Fitton. Mary was not surprised that all four newcomers chose to sit flanking their hostess in the circle of chairs, as the men in the group studied them – eagerly, curiously, dubiously, according to their expectations. She noted that William took a seat beside his cousin, Mary Wroth, as they continued an animated conversation.

'I am pleased tonight to introduce four new members to our Circle,' Mary began. 'Some of them you know by name and family connection. All of them you will come to know and appreciate through the work they will share.' Her pride and confidence in each of these writers welled so powerfully within her that she had to swallow a lump in her throat. 'And from you I hope they might gain wisdom and skill.'

Mary had asked Aemilia Lanyer to open the evening by reading from the manuscript of her biblically themed cycle of poems, *Salve Deus Rex Judaeorum*. A risky choice, she knew, but better tread than tiptoe. When she introduced her friend, the expectant murmur around the Circle faded. All eyes were drawn to Aemilia's confident stance as she stood to read, her strong jaw and prominent nose surmounted by piercing black eyes that could sparkle with wit or level with scorn. Her curly black hair capped by a white lace coif and her long neck adorned with simple beads of jet, she conveyed both confidence and conviction.

'I plan to dedicate my work to *all virtuous ladies and gentlewomen of this kingdom*' – she paused and looked around the Circle – 'and not to *evil-disposed men who, forgetting they were born of women, nourished of women, and that if it were not by the means of women, they would be quite extinguished out of the world, do like vipers deface the wombs wherein they were bred*.' A shocked silence followed several audible gasps, as all eyes turned to the Countess.

Mary returned their looks. She missed Walter's presence. He surely would have validated such a frank assessment with a ready smile, tempering the outrage simmering among some of the men like a stew approaching the boiling point. John Davies, for one, fixed her with a glower and pursed lips.

With a small smile, Aemilia calmly continued with verses from her poem. In one, Eve's sharing the apple of knowledge with Adam, and thus with all mankind, was deemed not a sin but a gift, motivated by *too much love* – the consequence of this generosity being a debt owed by men to women, not the other way round. This she distilled in another verse, an argument by the wife of Pontius Pilate against her husband's terrible miscalculation in crucifying Christ, and against men's foolish arrogance in general. Her voice sounded in the chamber like a bell: '*Then let us have our liberty again, and challenge to yourselves no sovereignty. Why should you disdain our being your equals, free from tyranny?*'

Mary eyed the men as they listened, intrigued to observe their reactions to this unfamiliar voice and uncommon, nay radical, perspective. While Jack Donne narrowed his eyes, Ben Jonson nodded appreciatively. Matthew Lister smiled. Her daughter, Anne, her niece Mary and Elizabeth Cary positively glowed in the blaze of Aemilia's words. Both Mary and Elizabeth were married now, and possibly as starved for a genuine communion of minds as she herself had been in the early years of marriage. She wished for each of their futures a collaboration as lively as her current bond with Will Shakespeare.

When Aemilia concluded, there was a brief, awkward silence. Then, voice by voice, the room filled with animated conversation. Several of the men praised Aemilia for her ingenious conception, using Pilate's wife to comment on his error of judgement. Others remained silent, clearly uneasy with her bold call for equality. But with such materials, the alchemical vessel was bound to crack.

John Davies lurched ponderously to his feet. 'Heresy!'

'What heresy, John?' rejoined Mary. 'Pilate's wife exposes her husband's folly in crucifying our Saviour. Do you mean to defend Pontius Pilate?' Scowling, the poet subsided into surly silence, his challenge checked. This was her chessboard, after all. It was good for the men's comfortable assumptions to be rattled. And long overdue.

Mary next introduced her young niece, Mary Wroth, whose poetry deserved an audience. Following Aemilia's example, Mary stood straight and tall during the Countess's introduction. Her red hair, sharing the family hue, was even curlier than her aunt's, and a few tendrils escaped their binding to tremble beside her cheeks. Seated close to the young woman, Mary glimpsed a sheen of sweat across her forehead. The sheet of paper in her goddaughter's hand trembled slightly, but when she opened her mouth, her voice was strong and clear.

The poem she offered captured the anguish of disappointed love:

False hope, which feeds but to destroy and spill
What it first breeds; unnatural to the birth
Of thine own womb; conceiving but to kill.

A love sonnet crafted around miscarriage! No male sonneteer would even think to convey the pain of love through one of women's most common experiences of death. Mary saw several of the men shift uneasily, and marvelled to find greater discomfort on some faces than Aemilia's more explicitly radical verse had produced. For them, the love sonnet was a familiar and reliable form – but not in this voice. Men were supposed to be the lovers, women the objects. Male sonneteers weren't concerned with women's experiences in love, only with their own successes or failures. She saw Ben Jonson, his eyes alight, fixed intensely on her niece. But William was looking at his knees. As the hoped-for future leader of the Circle, could her son appreciate the language of a battered heart? Value the courage of a voice writing through loss, no matter man or woman?

False hope . . . conceiving but to kill. Mary wondered at the evident passion and pain in the verse. She realised, now, that she knew so little of her goddaughter's life, of her loves and losses. This child, whose conception she had brought to pass with the remedies she had made for Barbara and Robert Sidney, had grown into an accomplished young woman with an arresting imagination.

Will came one last time to the library at Baynard's, to work with Mary on the final scene of their play – *theirs*, as both of them now considered it, a mutual creation.

Mary had asked Rose to join them this time, to listen and sketch as they worked, as she had when Mary was wrestling with passages in her own play. 'Her artist's eye often sees connections that I only recognise once she has sketched them upon paper or painted them on canvas,' Mary explained. She showed him Rose's drawing of the double ouroboros, signifying the union of Antony and Cleopatra in her *Antonius*.

'I see death not as the ending of their story but as a fitting climax to a tragic union, one that requires, as Antony says, *new heaven, new earth.*' Will looked closely at the image, then at Rose, and nodded.

When they took their places, facing each other across the table, Mary tugged at the ribbon that Rose had used to bind back her hair. When she wrote in private, she liked to feel her body as free as her mind, loosening her bodice and her hairdressings. As the ribbon came off now, her heavy auburn locks tumbled past her shoulders.

Will had been staring thoughtfully out the window as evening sunlight gilded the Baynard's library, his pen poised. Drawn by her motion, he turned and looked at her.

'*To die with thee, and dying thee embrace, my body joined with thine, my mouth with thine.*' Words from her own play. Hearing them spoken in Will's voice was an embrace that dried Mary's mouth and accelerated her pulse. Will tilted his chin, half closing his eyes, his familiar posture when working through an idea. 'In our scene, I hear Antony declaring, *I will be a bridegroom in my death, and run to it as to a lover's bed.*'

Mary closed her eyes in turn. Such a bridegroom she was unlikely ever to meet.

'You close your play with Cleopatra's *thousand kisses* upon Antony's dead body,' Will continued. 'What if we give those kisses to both of them, to achieve the mutuality you want to see?' Now he was writing his own words on the draft. 'So first Antony moans: *I am dying, Egypt. Of many thousand kisses, the last I lay upon thy lips.*'

Her quill poised, Mary completed Will's thought. 'And Cleopatra greets his kiss with hers: *Die where thou hast lived, and quicken with kissing. Had my lips that power, thus would I wear them out.*' She lifted her head, pushing back her hair and raising her own chin. '*Husband, I come! I am fire and air, my other elements I give to baser life.*' She passed the draft across the table. 'Alchemy demands a balance. This speech aspires to that.'

Will breathed out heavily, and nodded.

Their eyes met and they shared a long look. Too long.

Mary called to Rose to bind her hair back up again. Will stood and moved to the window, then turned back with a smile.

'Together, Mary, we have crafted a play unlike any I have written before – a play of communion across boundaries.'

Indeed. She was satisfied that she had expanded the boundaries of her own vision while connecting with his. A suitable ending, she thought. A worthwhile experiment.

Mary caught a twinkle in his eye. 'With your permission, I will submit it to the newly appointed licenser of plays, for performance at court.'

She made the connection instantly. 'Samuel Daniel, I believe?'

Will laughed. 'Do you suppose he'll recognise it as a collaboration, if it's not spelled out?'

'Not a chance. Samuel doesn't read between the lines.'

CHAPTER THIRTY-ONE

Rose, 1606

The alchemy of their partnership was unmistakable. Anyone could have seen it. But I was the only one watching.

My first reaction was happiness for my lady. It was plain to me that she had never before known such a bond. My second thought was concern that she would never know such a bond again. Master Shakespeare was a player, not a noble. It was no accident that they were keeping their partnership invisible even to the Circle. Whatever happened to the product of this partnership – the tragedy of what they called a *mutual pair* – the joy they took from working together was between them only, not for the eyes of the world. My third feeling was relief that I was no longer reporting to Sir Henry.

* * *

'I'd like you to be there, Rose,' my mistress told me before her final writing session with Master Shakespeare. She trusted my eye for details that no one else would think to see. It's not that I followed all the words that spilled forth from their pens as they wrote, drafting some passages in turn, others side by side. For me, it was a matter of listening and looking at the same time.

My lady showed Master Shakespeare the double ouroboros I had drawn – two snakes seizing each other's tails for dear life. 'A fitting climax to a tragic union,' Lady Mary explained. But he didn't need her words to understand. When he nodded at my drawing, I imagined that he saw beyond the characters to what I had actually tried to capture – the bond between the authors of this new play. And when my mistress loosed her hair from its bindings, his eyes lingered not on the page, but on her face.

That night, I set to work by candlelight, seated at the oak table of the Baynard's library, where they'd been working, and looked over the hasty sketches I'd made. My lady's final speech for the queen gave me my first idea. *I am fire and air* – which is how they seemed to me. At the bottom of a sheet of dun parchment, in black ink, I drew their figures sitting at the table. I used red chalk for the fire that lifted from the page Master Shakespeare was writing, white chalk for the smoky air that floated above my lady's words. Within those clouds of fire and air I placed outline sketches of the characters: Cleopatra on my lady's side, drawn in red chalk, Antony's outline in white above Master Shakespeare.

Antony was a warrior, his captain's heart plain to see in his features, yet with tenderness in his expression as he looked across the page to Cleopatra. Cleopatra was a lady with the features of my mistress but the bearing of Queen Elizabeth, standing atop a map with one foot on the boot of Italy and the other across the water in Egypt – an echo of Master Gheeraerts' portrait of the Queen.

Time evaporated. My candle had burned down to a stub when Lady Mary opened the door of the library, her face whiter than my chalk.

'Rose, it's Anne.' She seemed unsteady on her feet, but when I tried to lead her to a chair she gripped my arm instead, her voice sharp with panic. 'I need you to fetch Doctor Lister from the west wing.'

Lady Anne was never strong. All through her childhood she had been plagued by fevers and headaches, though unlike poor little Kate, she had always recovered. But now, in her twenties, she lacked the ever-present energy that so vividly marked her mother.

Doctor Lister was new to the household, but he had already earned my lady's respect. She had even invited him to work beside us in the still-room to manufacture chemical medicines. Unlike Master Gilbert, whose careless exuberance seemed to result in as many failures as successes, Doctor Lister was patient and meticulous. Despite his medical degree, he recognised that my lady, and even I, knew more than he did in this domain. *Hierarchy in a work-room should be a matter of experience, not station*, he'd said.

These useless thoughts raced through my mind as I pounded on the door of the doctor's chamber until it opened. His sandy hair dishevelled, Doctor Lister drew a robe about his nightclothes and hastened alongside me to Lady Anne's chamber. My mistress knelt beside the bed in prayer while her daughter shuddered with fever. Lady Anne's face was grey, her cheeks sunken, her hair drenched with sweat. The doctor was aware of her repeated illnesses, but she had not needed his attention, until tonight. He raised my mistress into the chair I drew forward and asked her about the history of these complaints.

'I've retrieved the notes from my closet. Let me show you.'

She handed him her record of the household ailments she and Doctor Moffett had treated, together with the remedies that had been applied and their outcomes. They recorded her daughter's bouts of illness, recurring at different intervals but always with the same symptoms.

'They begin with a blinding headache, which often subsides but is sometimes accompanied by a high fever,' my lady explained. 'She has usually responded well to an infusion of guaiacum, sassafras and syrup of roses. But tonight she did not.'

'Your register of treatments is impressive,' Doctor Lister told her. 'Would that all households kept such records and such an array of remedies.'

'I have followed the example of my predecessor, Catherine Herbert,' my lady admitted. Suddenly my first mistress's presence was in the room and I was a child again, awed by her wisdom and terrified that she would die.

'Even the most meticulous records of the past cannot predict the future course of an illness,' Doctor Lister observed softly, squeezing Lady Mary's hand. Silent tears were running down her face.

He prescribed oil of antimony, two drops mixed with a syrup of violets, to purge the humours in the stomach. But even I could read his prognosis in my lady's eyes.

Within the hour, Lady Anne was gone. My lady clasped her daughter's body in her arms and wailed. I knelt by her side as she wept through the night. Then, as the black heavens beyond the windows faded to grey, I brought a basin of water and clean cloths to the chamber. Together, we washed Lady Anne's body and wrapped her in a linen sheet. In its folds my lady laid sprigs of rosemary, for remembrance.

At the other end of the room, Doctor Lister worked as well, quietly adding his own notes to my lady's record of the illness that had taken her daughter. I wondered how his notes could make any difference, now that death had arrived. But Lady Mary seemed comforted by his silent presence.

As dawn coloured the wind-blown surface of the Thames, the doctor came to my lady's side, took her hand, and led her from the room.

CHAPTER THIRTY-TWO

Mary, 1606–07

Words from one of Will's edgy sonnets circled her mind: *That thou art blamed shall not be thy defect.* Except that she blamed herself. Her defects were more shocking than the deadly Lady Macbeth in Will's most horrifying tragedy. She, at least, could say *I have given suck and know how tender 'tis to love the babe that milks me.* But Mary had never nursed her babes and had loved them the most dearly when they were lost to her for ever, as if her own milk had been gall.

Mary's grief at the loss of her only remaining daughter was as cold and impenetrable as the icy blackness that had overtaken her after each childbirth. For weeks she refused all visitors, barely tasting her food and telling herself she was only reaping what she deserved. She could remember, all too vividly, holding each tiny newborn in her arms and feeling nothing. Defective.

Indeed, Cleopatra, that powerful queen Mary so admired, was herself a failed mother, abandoning her children to pursue union with Antony in death. Cleopatra's words in her own *Antonius* returned to haunt her: *Farewell, my babes, farewell, my heart is closed with pity and pain, myself with death enclosed.*

Only one person had refused to be turned away. Later, Mary could remember the very day the blackness started to dissipate, the day Matthew Lister brought her not medicine but a manuscript. Knocking and entering her chamber without permission, he placed it in her lap as she sat at the window, gazing vacantly over the Wilton gardens sheathed in frost. After months of patient nurture, seeking to bring her back to health by degrees, as Doctor Moffett had done after her traumatic childbirths, Doctor Lister had changed tack and simply ignored the boundaries she set.

Her indignation at his intrusion flared, then her eyes rested on a title, *Égalité des hommes et des femmes*, and below it, a name: *Marie de Gournay*.

'One of my colleagues in France sent me these pages.' The gold flecks in his eyes were even brighter than she remembered. 'Mademoiselle de Gournay is a gifted alchemist. Her writings explore connections between theories of alchemy and the relations between the sexes. I thought you might want to bring her notes on the equality of men and women to the attention of our Circle.' *Our* Circle. 'Of course, you will want to read them first.'

And with that, Mary felt her frozen solitude begin to thaw.

* * *

Mary found herself swept forward by the manuscript, a tumbling river of ideas. Marie's ideal was the hermaphroditic human. Dismissing the *chirping dolts* who maintain that *the supreme excellence women may achieve is to resemble ordinary men*, she made a case for the extraordinary. *Man and woman are so thoroughly one, that if man is more than woman, woman is more than man*. For Marie, friendship between the sexes was akin to alchemical transformation, uniting disparate elements. This, Mary realised, was *the truth of Cleopatra*.

Matthew and Mary fell into a pattern of discussing a new passage from Marie's treatise during each midday meal, until Mary realised, some weeks on, that she was eating her food with relish once again, and that she and the doctor had slipped into a companionable first-name friendship.

Mary reconvened the Circle, for the first time in a year, and introduced the manuscript, asking Matthew to read aloud the passages for discussion that they had selected together. In response to the Frenchwoman's bold case for sexual parity, the men in the group didn't have much to say. But the women fairly erupted.

'Believing this would change the premise of all romance!' Mary Wroth's voice was alight with the possibilities.

'Believing this would change the premise of all *marriage*,' piped up Anne Clifford, the newest member of the Circle. Inviting the seventeen-year-old to take her daughter's empty chair had been hard for Mary. She did not want to efface the memory of the dead, nor have the other members think the newcomer was simply a replacement. Raven-haired, with eyes to match, she was the only daughter of Mary's close friend Margaret Clifford and, while not a poet herself, was possessed of a bright intelligence and wit that enlivened the group's discussions.

'Does anyone believe that friendship between a man and a woman can be a bond between equals?' asked Elizabeth Cary, the sceptic.

'Indeed, it would change the premise of the very society that shapes our daily lives,' added Aemilia Lanyer dryly, with a sidelong glance at the Countess.

Mary's own sidelong glance was for Matthew, who had brought her this audacious manuscript in the first place. Exploring it with him had opened a window that allowed light and air back into her life. A bond between equals.

Apart from the Circle, however, Mary felt even more disconnected from the world at large, especially at court. Empty words and emptier smiles, she thought, remembering Rose's early sketches of young men posing for attention and older women masking their insecurities. Now she was one of those older women. Rose, always at her side, could anticipate her needs so readily that Mary found herself regularly confiding in her maidservant. With Rose and, increasingly, with Matthew she shared her fears and disappointments. There were no remaining joys to share with anyone.

That is, until an invitation arrived, announcing the performance, at the Banqueting House in Whitehall, of a play by William Shakespeare: *Antony and Cleopatra*.

The old Banqueting House, which had fallen into dingy disrepair in the days of Queen Elizabeth, had been demolished by order of King James and replaced by a new and much larger structure. Fitted up like a theatre, it had a raised stage at one end, facing Their Majesties' chairs placed beneath a canopy and surrounded by well-appointed boxes for the noble audience. Mary found the new building breathtaking. Rows of gilded pillars supported a roof festooned with plaster flowers and sculpted angels, the whole illuminated by tiers of mullioned windows. Mary was thrilled to realise that this grand room was the setting for a play that she herself had helped to create, and happy that Matthew was at her side.

Will came to greet her, pushing through the gathering crowd of courtiers. He had written to her when he learnt of Anne's death, sending a sonnet. *No longer mourn for me when I am dead. I love you so that I in your sweet thoughts would be forgot, if thinking on me then should make you woe.* Anne's voice, transmuted. He, too, had lost a child, she knew. And a sister. Mary appreciated the embrace of his verse.

Tonight, however, he seemed on edge. Mirrored in his face she saw some part of her own wonder, tinged with apprehension, on arriving at Whitehall to see a play that, for her, had started as a dream in the first draft of her *Antonius*, then had become a vision shared by a countess and a player.

'The boy playing the Queen has been taken ill, so I'll be playing Cleopatra tonight.' That explained his jumpiness and his clean-shaven chin. But was that the truth? Or, Mary mused, was he taking the role for her benefit, to show her in his person the queen they had wrought together? Mary was nervous as well. Not only had she never heard her own verse spoken in public, she had never read the final script. In the dark aftermath of Anne's death, she had not seen Will bring their drafts to completion.

What she witnessed was a tragedy of even greater extremes than she had seen in her work with Will. This Cleopatra was by turns wavering and wily, frightened and fierce, captivating and cruel. Her glimmering presence, acted by Will with convincing passion, kept the audience rapt, as eager to believe the Romans' harsh mockery of Antony's *Egyptian dish* and *ribald nag* as the awed tributes to a queen who was admired even by *the air, which had gone to gaze on Cleopatra too, and made a gap in nature*.

When Will delivered Cleopatra's final words, he looked directly out at Mary, his voice caressing her lines in tribute to their partnership: '*I am fire and air; my other elements I give to baser life.*'

'One would almost think,' whispered Matthew, 'Master Shakespeare to be an alchemist.' But Mary wasn't really listening to him. She was watching the audience.

Some were moved to tears while others shifted uneasily, perhaps attempting to shrug off their discomfort with this queen's powerful sexuality. At the end, as the actors took their bows, the response was muted. But when, after an unnerving pause, Queen Anna rose to applaud, followed a moment later by a brusque nod from her husband, the room resounded with cheers, even as a few courtiers discreetly turned away. Mary understood that the play's success was due precisely to what made it disturbing – its compelling attention to both sides of the spectrum of tragedy, with lovers at once unquestionably heroic and deeply flawed. One serpent biting the tail of the other.

And Her Majesty, Mary was heartened to discover, was not, after all, the *Snow Queen* that Rose had termed her after Mary's icy reception on their first meeting. She clearly understood and even appreciated the intriguing complexities in this incarnation of Cleopatra. Here, perhaps, was a queen of infinite variety.

CHAPTER THIRTY-THREE

Rose, 1609

Lady Mary and I had become so close that it seemed, at times, we were reading each other's thoughts. And yet she still amazed me. I marvelled at what she could not only envision but achieve, such as a collaboration with Master Shakespeare that could bring her words to the public stage. And also what she could miss. How she could be so perceptive in the realm of ideas, and yet so unaware of people's hearts, was truly a mystery.

Spurred by the success of the Egyptian play, she plunged into a new project that kept both of us busy – a performance of *Antonius* at Wilton. She wanted the sketches I had made of the play she wrote with Master Shakespeare to be used by her dressmaker for the costumes.

'I want to see my vision performed before an audience, all the more for having relinquished any public connection to the play I collaborated on with Will.' On her face I saw resignation, but also resolve. This story wasn't finished for her yet. 'I shall cast my play from members of my Circle and perform it for family and friends. Apart from the ladies who have appeared in masques, where women have only non-speaking parts, most of the participants in this production will have no experience with theatre. So anything is possible!'

Only my lady would take a lack of experience as evidence of possibility and not a predictor of failure. I marvelled. She had lost her sister, her brother, both parents, two daughters and yet she was still moving forward.

So began weeks of preparation that involved almost every member of the household staff, from carpenters building a tower for the final scene to seamstresses stitching costumes. To my lady's delight, and the dressmaker's dismay, my drawings of Antony and Cleopatra included alchemical symbols and signs of the zodiac in their costumes. But after the woman understood that the Countess was determined to include every detail, and resolved to spare neither time nor expense, she engaged several assistants and spent the next weeks creating costumes worthy of the legendary lovers.

With all the preparations for the approaching performance, the household seemed like a hive of bees in service to their queen. Cicely was busy training the new chambermaids hired for service as more experienced servants helped with the production, and I was busy with multiple tasks assisting my lady as she rehearsed her play. Hastening to the kitchen one day to increase the order for the day's meals to feed all the actors and helpers, I collided with a comely young woman who had the look of someone I knew. Catching my breath, I viewed her curiously. 'I don't believe I know your name.'

'Alice, miss,' she explained, bobbing her head hastily. 'One of the new maids.'

'Welcome to Wilton,' I replied, still trying to place her features. 'As you can see, we've need of all hands.' At that, her mouth twisted in a puckering of anxiety and discontent, and I could see the resemblance to the spiteful scullery maid I'd struck on that long-ago day for insulting Mum. 'Are you any kin to Sarah?'

'Her niece,' was the reply.

'I'm Rose,' I offered.

'I know.' Again, that wince, like tasting something sour. There was no love lost between her aunt and me, so perhaps Sarah had used dark tales of my mother the 'witch' to scare her niece. If so, it wasn't my place to reassure the lass. As she scuttled away down the corridor, I wondered if she'd fit in, since her aunt had never settled into the friendly give-and-take of the household. But there was a softness to Alice's demeanour that differed from Sarah's sharp edges. And with Cicely to train her, I reassured myself, she'd soon be set right.

Lady Mary seemed to be doing everything at once. I listened to her rehearsing lines with actors who had no experience with spoken parts and watched her directing stable boys turned stagehands about placing elements of the set in the Great Hall, which would also contain seats for all the audience.

Observing live actors rehearsing their parts was entirely different from hearing the lines read aloud by my lady when she was composing the play. She cast Doctor Lister in the part of Antony, and as Cleopatra her own niece, Lady Mary Wroth, who had inherited her aunt's red hair but a more even temper. Lady Elizabeth Cary, keen-eyed, sharp-edged and strikingly fair, was playing Iras, one of the Queen's attendants, while Lady Anne Clifford, her face framed by a profusion of dark tumbling curls, had the part of Charmian, the maidservant who refuses to surrender her queen to the forces of grief and despair. I was silently amused to see titled ladies learning to play servants.

The other Wilton servants, overhearing the rehearsals, must have wondered at this queen's outspoken attendants. When Cleopatra laments that her flight from battle spurred Antony to flee as well, Iras sternly demands to know *Why with continual cries do you exasperate your grief?* The ever-practical Charmian cautions Cleopatra that it's *ill-done to lose yourself, and to no end*, and reminds her that *our first affection to ourself is due*.

My lady had certainly never heard such bold words from me. But, I pondered, perhaps she should have. Hearing these imagined maids challenging their mistress to see herself more clearly, I wondered about my own role in her life. By the end of the play, when Cleopatra implores *My sisters, hold me up*, I understood that her maids have become the sisters of her heart. And I came to see that the double ouroboros I had drawn for the union of Antony and Cleopatra in death embodied less visible aspects of what my lady called *the truth of Cleopatra*. She had spoken often of *a union of opposites* – spirit and matter, male and female – perhaps even mistress and maid?

As my lady rehearsed the actors in the Great Hall, I drew what I saw. With no audience there, I was free to observe the performers from multiple vantage points, as she herself did. She surveyed some scenes from a distance, such as the entrances and exits of the Chorus, cast from young men in her Circle, but she stepped in close to share thoughts with individual actors.

In one of the final rehearsals she was on the stage, directing the last moments of the play where Cleopatra holds the dead Antony in her arms while her attendants look on. She was speaking to her niece about the queen's final moments before her own death, as Doctor Lister lay still, cradled in Cleopatra's lap. As usual, I drew what I saw.

At the end of the scene, Lady Mary applauded the performers and spoke some encouraging words to Doctor Lister as he got to his feet. He looked as if he would say something in response, but she was on to Cleopatra herself now, arranging the folds of her goddaughter's costume and settling the helmet-like crown carefully atop those flame-coloured curls. With her brave bearing and quiet gaze, Lady Mary Wroth embodied the puzzle of Cleopatra: her beauty and courage, vulnerability and resolve.

It was only later, looking over my sketches, that I glimpsed what my lady hadn't noticed. And it wasn't until after the performance that I recognised the pit she was digging for herself.

CHAPTER THIRTY-FOUR

Mary, 1609

Inspired by the performance of Antony and Cleopatra *at the Banqueting House, I have decided to revisit my original vision by staging a private production of* Antonius *at Wilton. I dearly hope you will attend.*

To Mary's invitation, Will had replied that he wished he could see it, but was prevented by his commitments at the Globe and his company's newly renovated Blackfriars Theatre. He was working on a new play that he called his *winter's tale*, about a queen who dies of a broken heart but is brought back to life by her resourceful maidservant. Mary swallowed the twinge of loss. She missed the free-flowing channel of ideas that had run between them. Sharing language, they had shared a world. She missed working at his side, though not as keenly now that she and Matthew had found a similar bond between equals. And besides, this performance was all hers.

Casting her namesake and goddaughter as Cleopatra had been Mary's plan from the start. Mary Wroth had a spirit too bright to be confined to a supporting role. She asked Matthew to take the part of Antony. As her friend and confidant, he shared her desire to make a success of this play, published over her own name but never yet performed. When he protested that he'd never acted a line, she swept away his objections as imperiously as Cleopatra herself.

'You're the one who brought me back from darkness to re-engage with the Circle,' she told him, lifting her chin and tilting her head the way Will had done. 'You cannot say nay.' He gave her his lopsided smile and didn't argue.

The weeks of rehearsal passed in a frenzy of activity. Never having directed a play before, Mary found the experience invigorating and addictive. The hardest part was letting go and allowing the actors to carry the play forward on their own. Learning to collaborate with Garnier through translation, she had found a way to realise her vision for Cleopatra in her own voice. Now she needed to allow the actors to embody that vision.

The preparations took up most of the late-arriving spring. But finally, as blossoms brushed the branches of the trees along the river and early blooms poked boldly from recently frozen earth in the Wilton gardens, the Countess assembled her audience of friends, fellow authors, family members and servants in the Great Hall for the first performance of *Antonius*. No raised stage here, but the smooth flagstones at one end of the hall, with the arches on either side serving for entrances and exits. Mary Wroth was stunning in a crimson gown sparkling with alchemical symbols in gold thread from Rose's design. Matthew's Antony wore a short white tunic trimmed in gold, with signs of the zodiac set into the gold crests that studded his warrior's breastplate.

A fanfare from the musicians seated in the upper gallery quieted the audience, and Matthew walked alone to the centre of the stage. His voice, shaky at first, steadily gained in strength as he expressed Antony's resolve. '*Since cruel heaven's against me obstinate, and since my queen herself, the idol of my heart, doth me pursue, it's fitting that I die.*'

As the performance continued, from her seat on the aisle Mary could see Ben Jonson's raised eyebrow, always a sign of approval. Aemilia Lanyer turned around to catch Mary's eye with an eager nod.

Late in the play, when Charmian urged Cleopatra, '*Live for your sons*', only to be rebuked by the queen – '*Nay, for their father die*' – Mary couldn't take her eyes from her niece. And when the maidservant argued spiritedly that '*our first affection to ourself is due*', Cleopatra's declaration of her love was heartfelt: '*He is my self.*' Mary Wroth delivered her lines as if born to them, with a conviction that brought Mary's own verse alive beyond her most ambitious expectation. She remembered Matthew watching this scene during a rehearsal and guessed that even now, backstage, he was just as transfixed as Mary was in the front of the hall.

Now Mary recalled Matthew stepping forward after that

409

rehearsal and murmuring something to her goddaughter, as young Mary's eyes lit up. Was that where his interests lay? Was that his reason for participating, however reluctantly, in this venture?

Recently, in meals shared with Matthew and lively conversations ranging from friendly debates over Paracelsus and Plutarch to consultations over still-room strategies, Mary had sensed, through their growing closeness, that something was missing. And now, with an involuntary pang, she believed she understood why.

Mary pulled her mind back to the stage just in time to see her goddaughter bestowing '*a thousand kisses, thousand, thousand more*' on Matthew's face, his head clasped to her breast. Then Cleopatra sank back upon the floor, joining her lover in death, while the audience erupted into enthusiastic applause.

The play was a success. But Mary's pleasure was mixed with something dangerously close to pain.

'I believe the good doctor has his eye on my niece,' she observed to Rose that evening in the bedchamber with an attempt at nonchalance.

Rose continued to run the brush through her hair without speaking. Her maidservant could keep her own counsel as effectively as the doctor. Perhaps, Mary thought, that was how both Rose and Matthew had become her confidants over the years, although a more unlikely pair of friends for herself she never could have imagined. The artist and the alchemist, the attendant and the healer. Their outlooks on the world were so different from one another's. And yet she trusted them both to receive secrets that, in the world she had once inhabited, would have been shared only with her sister. But that world was long dead.

'I know she's married to Robert Wroth,' Mary continued, 'but that was an arranged match, and he is unworthy of my goddaughter's intellect. Matthew would be worthy.' Catching the sudden pause in Rose's rhythm with the brush, she added bluntly, 'It wouldn't be the first time a wife has sought companionship outside marriage.'

'No, my lady.'

Mary caught Rose's wrist, halting the brush. '*No*, because you have known of such behaviour? Perhaps my working relationship with Master Shakespeare? I'd be happy if my niece could find such comfort with Matthew.'

But Rose was shaking her head. '*No*, because you're wrong.'

Mary was stunned into silence. Rose had never before addressed her thus. Then Ambrosia's voice entered her head. *Listen to her – this one doesn't waste words.*

But Rose said nothing else.

'You've been with me for over thirty years now, Rose. Please, speak.'

Rose put down the brush. 'I have observed Doctor Lister as closely as ever I observed your suitors at court under orders from Sir Henry. I don't believe he's courting your niece.'

Mary waited. Hadn't she always told herself that Rose saw more than others? But what had she herself missed?

'The young Lady Mary has a different bond, one that cannot easily be shaken.' When Mary frowned her question, Rose responded steadily, 'With your son, Master William.'

411

'My *son*?' She had not noticed any particular connection between the cousins, beyond friendly camaraderie. She was appalled. Any such bond would harm her niece more than her son.

'Yes, my lady,' Rose confirmed.

Mary took a deep breath. 'Well, then . . .' Now she couldn't help herself. She needed to know more. 'Have you observed Doctor Lister to be interested in one of the other young ladies in the Circle instead?'

Rose took a breath and blew it out. 'I made some sketches during rehearsals of your play this past month. With your permission, I'll retrieve them from my chamber.'

Awaiting her return, Mary sorted restlessly through the images that Rose had made for the dressmaker, still stacked on her table. The largest was a drawing of the Egyptian queen in full costume. Mary had been so taken with the alchemical patterns on the gown that she hadn't paid attention to the face. Now she realised it was a combination of her own features and those of Will Shakespeare, with her red hair and high cheekbones coupled with his hazel eyes and sharp nose.

A *hermaphrodite*. So her musings about *the truth of Cleopatra* had taken root in Rose's mind

Then she noticed Cleopatra's tower in the background, the place of final reunion with Antony, shown as a tall, cylindrical structure with a peaked roof from which white plumes billowed. Unmistakably a version of the athanor in her still-room.

Rose returned to find her mistress scanning the image in the candlelight.

'I shall frame this for the still-room!' Mary's voice was

412

exuberant. Rose beamed, then handed Mary the drawings she had brought. In one of them, Mary saw the fair-headed Matthew, as Antony, declaiming from centre stage. Another showed the red-haired Mary Wroth, as Cleopatra, flanked by her weeping attendants, holding the expiring Antony in her arms. The third drawing included Mary herself, directing the actors in that very tower scene. With Antony lying in the arms of his queen, Mary was focused on Cleopatra, urging her to release her tears. In this scene, Antony's eyes should have been closed in death. But they were open, and Matthew's gaze was fixed not on Cleopatra, but the Countess. On his features Rose had captured what looked almost like devotion. Mary frowned. This could not be right.

'Your fancy?' she asked the artist slowly, not daring to trust her eyes.

'No, my lady. Not a matter of fancy at all.'

Mary blushed, heat rising from her chest to her neck and suffusing her pale cheeks until her face in the glass glowed with the rosy hue of a begonia. Rose touched her shoulder. 'It has been thus almost since his arrival at Wilton House, my lady.' Her calm voice carried the undeniable weight of truth.

The next morning, when Mary strolled with Matthew along the river after breakfast, as they liked to do now that spring had softened the grounds, she found herself with no words. But Matthew was eager to talk.

'The performance was quite a success, nay, a triumph, wouldn't you agree?' His jubilant tone brought a smile to

Mary's lips and loosed her tongue.

'You were marvellous as Antony, and my niece as Cleopatra. I like to believe the union of those two heroes in the final scene might be at least as moving as the climax of Will's play at court.' Speaking of the play was a relief, a concrete subject that could distract her from the previous night's revelations.

'I believe your play, ending with the kisses of Cleopatra as she joins Antony in death, offers more satisfaction than Shakespeare's solemn coda,' Matthew responded. 'Or at least, more satisfaction to me.'

Mary froze. *The kisses of Cleopatra* . . . Had Rose been wrong? But those gold-flecked eyes were even brighter now, and fixed on her. She shifted awkwardly. Then she spoke, bluntly, needing to get to the truth of the feeling that had been tormenting her since the performance.

'Watching you perform last night, I thought you agreed to play Antony in order to gain the company of my niece.'

Matthew's jaw dropped. Then he took her hand in his own. 'I believed your collaboration with Will Shakespeare was a bond I could never hope to match. It was only in rehearsing for *Antonius* this month that I came to appreciate the necessary connection between characters and actors, and the inevitable distinction between characters and their creators.' He paused, like a diver preparing to launch himself into a fast-flowing current. 'It was you I sought all along.'

Their lips met lightly at first, a brush of a touch like two leaves pushed together by the breeze. Mary closed her eyes. When his lips returned to hers, she opened her mouth for the first time. No more words. Only sensations, her heart pounding, her tongue caressing, her body aflame. As the leaves touched, two dew drops merged into one. No mere kiss. This, finally, was communion.

That night, in her chamber, they took their time. With Henry, Mary had found the mechanical act of coupling utterly unremarkable. But now, slowly, as her body unfolded with Matthew, she discovered sensations she had never dreamt could exist.

'*New heaven, new earth*, Matthew,' she whispered in her lover's arms as they watched the sunrise creep across their bed.

'*Here is my space*,' was his reply. When she curved her back into his embrace, his hand cupping her breast, she understood what that meant. For the first time.

Spring gave way to summer and sunlight suffused the dark corners of Mary's spirit. Curling into Matthew's body each night, awaking on his shoulder each morning, breathing in the warm musky smell of his essence, more potent than any tincture, she was convinced that she'd wake from this dream at any moment. *Past the size of dreaming*, Will's Cleopatra had said. That was how she felt. That this union was deeper than any dream, more fantastical than any fable, and liable to vanish without warning, because it hadn't been written down. Writing was how she had always captured the real, but this bond of the heart didn't require documentation. Or so she hoped. She hadn't recognised his love over all the months that Rose had sketched its presence, so how would she see the end coming?

When the note arrived, she was almost relieved to receive

the blow.

The renowned Doctor Lister is not quite the paragon you
might imagine. Five years ago he was culpable in the death of
his own brother and faced charges of manslaughter. Be wary
of entrusting the well-being of your household to that man.
Your friend, Samuel

CHAPTER THIRTY-FIVE

Rose, 1610–11

'I want to commission a painting from you, a picture of the *Rosa Mundi*,' Lady Mary said as I dressed her for a gathering of the Circle, fastening new sleeves of starflower blue to her silver-embroidered indigo bodice. Dressing her now was more pleasure than labour.

'The Rose of the World isn't a flower,' I objected. 'No single image will serve.'

'Precisely.'

My lady had never paid me for an individual piece of work, though she usually added an extra sovereign to my quarterly wages as a reward for my drawings. I had set these extra payments aside, as I had part of Sir Henry's, with a clear goal in mind. Thanks to her generosity and my thrift, I had saved almost enough to buy my own cottage in Amesbury. I visited my brother twice a year, and loved my six nieces and nephews, but I knew my future must include Cicely. Someday, I vowed, once she broke free of Toby, we would live together in Amesbury and share her grandchildren. Stanley now had a fine brood of three, with baby Dorcas just arrived, though Angelica, now in service to Lady Mary Wroth, had never married. Like me.

In all these musings, it never occurred to me to question that my vision for the future didn't include Toby. He didn't deserve to inhabit Cicely's future, no matter how visible he was in her present. His behaviour only bore that out. And I never wondered if Cicely's own vision for the future included me. From the first, we had been like paired herbs planted in the same pot, sharing the same needs for water and sunlight – rosemary and lavender, sage and thyme. Before Toby had entered the picture, we'd shared tasks and confidences, work and life, and I couldn't envision any other possibility.

I had become so accustomed to reading my lady's desires and meeting her needs that I believed myself to be indispensable. What I didn't realise until later was that I needed my lady as much as she needed me.

'I've decided to travel to France with Matthew for an extended visit,' she announced abruptly. 'I seek to encounter new ideas abroad, and new authors, women as well as men, whose voices might help our own writers here in England to explore new paths. In Paris, I look forward to meeting Marie de Gournay, whose ideas have so enlivened my own Circle.'

I laced the points on her bodice, hearing everything she wasn't speaking aloud. Here in England, the Dowager Countess of Pembroke could not openly carry on a relationship with a man who was not her husband. And I knew Sir Henry's will forbade her remarrying. Europe would offer space to enjoy not just a new life of the mind, but a new life of the heart and body.

She placed her hands over my own, stilling the lacing. 'Without you, I might have missed, well, everything. Really, it's thanks to you, Rose, that this trip is taking place at all. You opened my eyes to a joy I had neither known nor thought to imagine.' Her grey gaze held mine without wavering.

As usual, she shared the big ideas first, saving details for later. But my lady never lacked a plan. My thoughts rushed forward. How would a long absence affect the household?

Lady Mary smiled. 'I'm learning to hear what you don't speak, just as you see what isn't always visible. I shall engage an attendant in France. I need you to remain at Wilton. You shall have charge of the still-room.'

Have charge? Until now, I'd not been in charge of anything except my lady's petticoats. A wave of doubt flooded me. Under Lady Mary's direction, I could do anything. But I could imagine all too well how I might go awry on my own.

'Adrian will feel slighted, but he's getting older now, and I don't trust his memory. He can continue with his experiments, but I'm putting the manufacture of healing potions and cordials in your charge. And the cabinet of special remedies will be in your exclusive care.'

I was stunned. How would I manage all that? But again, she read the question trembling on my tongue. 'I trust that your experience, combined with your mother's instincts, Lady Catherine's book of remedies and my own store of medicines

419

will allow you to care for the household while I'm not here.'

Lady Mary handed me the ring of keys that I remembered so well: the large brass key to the still-room door, the small silver key to the cabinet and the tiny golden key to the black walnut box of medical recipes.

'I have allocated three sovereigns for your oversight of the still-room and the cabinet of medicines during my absence, and two more to support your continuing work as an artist.' *Five sovereigns!* Truly a princely sum, which would make up the remainder of what I would need to purchase a cottage of my own.

'It will take some time before we can depart, perhaps not before the end of the year. I have commitments at court that must not be ignored.' She took my hand. 'But I wanted to tell you well in advance of our departure, as there will be much to do in preparation for assuming your new duties. I'm confident that the still-room will be in your capable hands.'

Hearing her affirmation, I started to regain my bearings. My lady was preparing to enter upon a new stage of her life, and so, perhaps, would I. Without my daily attendance on our mistress, I could devote more of my attention to art.

I could scarcely wait to let Cicely know what was to come. But first, I visited my oaken starflower box. Having charge of the still-room was a weighty responsibility, greater than any I had taken on in my life. In a corner of the box, wrapped in a scrap of silk left over from Da's stores and tied with a purple ribbon, was the object I sought. The astrologer's gift to me.

When I fingered the ring, the precise engravings upon the

deep rose of the stone caught the light. I could hear Simon Forman's voice, explaining the symbols. *Pisces ascendant, ruled by Jupiter, the Moon in Virgo, and the rising arrow of Sagittarius.* I understood that my adaptability under the rising sign of Pisces was balanced by my appreciation for structure and detail under the Moon in Virgo. The arrow of Sagittarius, *which will bring you luck, growth, and wisdom,* kept me searching for new directions. The astral ring fairly glowed with life and promise. I started to slip the ring onto my finger, then I hesitated. Now, more than ever, I had need of its promise, but I wasn't yet ready to fully claim this part of my heritage. Rewrapping the ring carefully, I returned it to the box.

When I began telling Cicely my news, flushed with excitement, she seemed preoccupied, rubbing her temple as if to still an ache. She'd always been interested in hearing the latest news from my lady's life and eager to tell me the latest exploit of one of her grandchildren. And I had long depended on the comfortable warmth of her spirit. Now, something was pulling her attention away from our bond.

Concerned, I drew her into the herb garden. I had maintained the order of Mum's design for the garden, which she had taken in hand after coming to work at Wilton. Weeding and pruning what I still thought of as Mum's herbs was my favourite task, whether by sunlight or moonlight, because I could hear her voice, directing me, encouraging me, maintaining order in my world.

A robin hopped away as we squatted, a fat worm wriggling in his beak. For a time we worked together in silence, Cicely digging up weeds to create more breathing space for the herbs while I harvested some of the best leaves from the fragrant basil plants and pinched the dark purple blossoms from the stems to encourage each plant to branch and make more leaves. A breeze from the river caressed our faces. My sense of well-being and hope for the future was so strong that it took me a moment to notice that Cicely's deep blue eyes had filled with tears. I stopped what I was doing and rocked back onto my heels, digging my fingers into the damp earth beside me for support.

''Tis Toby,' she admitted. 'He halted Master Wilkins in his tracks yesterday and demanded, again, to be allowed to serve as assistant steward. When Master Wilkins explained, again, that Stanley has a better spirit for the job – and is more reliable – Toby exploded. Not at the steward, thank goodness – at me.' She meant to reassure me, but suddenly I recognised the purpling bruise on her temple beneath her fingers. I'd always believed that Cicely deserved better than Toby. But I hadn't been truly worried until now.

Just as my own path was opening before me, it appeared hers was taking a turn for the worse. The drinking was getting out of hand. Toby's increasing surliness kept the other servants at a distance. Because he couldn't compete with Cicely's warmth and his own son's competence, he'd stopped trying and turned mean.

I hoped her resolute calm in the face of his temper would settle him down. Instead, as summer faded, he started breaking things – plates, bowls, whatever was at hand. When an 'accident' broke her wrist, I fetched Doctor Lister, thankful he and my lady had not yet departed for France.

Cicely liked talking with the doctor because he'd been born and raised in West Yorkshire in a village not far from Cicely and Peter's, and when he spoke to her he let his own Yorkshire lilt come out. I saw her warm appreciation as he wrapped the wrist and fashioned a sling for her arm from a long linen cloth. For the pain, my mistress gave her a tincture of valerian root with ginger to add to a tisane brewed from dried feverfew leaves. When the doctor questioned her about the injury, she insisted she had missed a step on the stairs leading down to the servants' quarters and had injured her wrist in the effort to break her fall.

I knew better, and Peter wasn't having it either. He extracted the true cause of the injury from his sister in less time than it took Toby to polish off a flagon of ale. Then he sought the man out and pummelled him, knocking him to the floor.

'I'll kill thee, I will. Don't give me another reason,' he warned, as Toby scrambled to his feet and took off for the village, stumbling and cursing.

'Are you frightened?' I asked Cicely that night in her chamber. Just then, the door slammed back against the wall, but she didn't flinch. Stomping into the room, Toby glared at me blearily and then pitched onto their bed, insensible. Cicely covered her husband's inert form with a quilt.

'Nay, Rose, there's nowt for me to fear,' she whispered. 'Inside, Toby has a kind heart.'

'But he has harsh hands,' I persisted. 'You must leave him.'

She shook her head. 'He'll fall apart, he will. I can't do that to him. He's still me husband. The drinking gets him maddled is all.'

Sure enough, the next morning he was on his knees begging for her forgiveness, kissing her bandaged wrist and promising never to lay a hand on her again. For a few weeks, he seemed better. And then, for no reason I could tell, it started all over again – the drinking, the cursing, the violence. She made me promise not to tell Peter about the marks on her arms from Toby shaking her. The black eye was harder to conceal, but when she begged some of Lady Mary's face powder from me, I applied it, though I hated myself for doing it. But I'd never been able to say no to Cicely, for she had never said no to me.

I took what steps I could. When Lady Mary began to organise the still-room in readiness for me to take charge of the medicines, I proposed Cicely as my assistant. 'She's trusted by the entire household,' I explained, 'and better than I am at keeping track of their various ailments.'

'Of course, Rose,' she agreed immediately. 'Train Cicely in the remedies for common ailments, by all means. It cannot hurt to have more than one in the household who's knowledgeable. But never prescribe a cure without consulting the box of recipes that we store in the cabinet. These supplies can be dangerous if misapplied. Cicely cannot read, so you're the only one I'm trusting with the keys.'

I felt a twinge of regret that I'd never had time to teach Cicely her letters as I had promised. Seeing me bite my lip, Lady Mary added, 'Should you encounter an ailment for which you can identify no remedy, send for Doctor Scott in Salisbury. He and Matthew trained together at Cambridge, and he can be here almost immediately should the need arise.'

An ailment with no remedy. A thin flicker of worry snaked into my chest. That night I flipped through my own drawings of herbals, to refresh my memory and give myself courage, calling to mind the zodiac symbols on my astral ring. *Luck, growth and wisdom.*

To build my confidence, and to keep Cicely away from Toby, I took to bringing her with me to the still-room every afternoon, after Lady Mary and Doctor Lister's regular work together there in the mornings. Master Gilbert, now seventy, came in to putter with his concoctions only every few days, though from his occasional eruptions of enthusiasm in the Circle, one might think he was ever on the verge of achieving the Philosopher's Stone. So Cicely and I had the still-room mostly to ourselves.

But one afternoon, as we opened the door, there was Master Gilbert in the thick of things. When I greeted him, he glared at us with such hostility that I stopped in my tracks. Until now, he'd grudgingly accepted my presence, and had long ago learnt to keep his hands to himself, after I'd laid a sharp slap on his face.

'No place here for those with no learning,' he growled. 'You shouldn't be bringing such as the likes of her near the precious materials in this room. Who knows what sort of disorder she might cause.' Beside me, Cicely stiffened. I squeezed her hand.

'Lady Mary asked me to instruct Cicely in the still-room so she can assist me in making and dispensing remedies while our mistress is abroad. I'm sure she wants to protect your time for expert experimentation rather than simple production, Master Gilbert.' Flattery was a tool I'd learnt at court. It was strangely satisfying to use it now. I dropped a curtsey and was relieved to see his anger subside. Soon enough, with a shrug and a grunt, he departed for his afternoon nap.

'Master of disorder himself, that's what he's best at,' I assured Cicely. This set her laughing, her good humour restored.

As afternoon sunlight warmed the shelves of copper alembics and glass aludels, I guided Cicely through an inventory of the household medicines. Opening the cabinet of remedies, I explained the uses of the various cordials and distilled tinctures, and their hierarchy on the shelves, from the mild herbals on the lower levels, suitable for everyday complaints, to the most potent distillations on the top, beneficial in extreme cases and small doses but lethal if misused.

On the following days I read aloud to Cicely the lists of ailments and remedies prepared by my past and present mistresses. I discovered that her remarkable memory extended not just to individual servants' hopes and worries – making her the best source for knowing why anyone was out of sorts – but to what I read aloud as well.

'For remedy of the headache, whatsoever kind it be, according to the signs of the offending humour, apply cordials or coolers inward or outward,' she recited. Then, with a rich chuckle, 'And Master Gilbert makes some of these – really? I find it hard to believe that fellah knows owt from nowt!'

'Well, for all that, I can tell you that Master Gilbert has eased many an aching head.'

Those afternoons were the best times we had that autumn – me reading, Cicely reciting, and both of us laughing until we cried. Those were good tears.

By the time Lady Mary departed, Cicely seemed almost

content. When we returned to the servants' quarters after spending an afternoon in the still-room, Toby was generally seated at the table in the long kitchen waiting for his supper, ignoring the other servants' chatter. But then he'd never been one for talking. He'd eat whatever Cook prepared and leave without a word. Some nights he didn't reappear. Rumours abounded. One of the chambermaids was apparently only too willing to share her bed with him. To my surprise, Cicely didn't care to know which one. She was happy to have her grandchildren to visit on those nights and put them to bed in her own chamber with no shouting to disturb them.

'It's a relief not to be sweeping up broken crockery so often,' she told me. 'If someone else can settle him, I'm not the one to complain.' And so, for a time, our lives settled into a steady rhythm. Some nights when Toby wasn't home, we resumed our earliest habit of sharing a bed. With Cicely curling herself around me, I knew greater contentment than I would have dreamt of finding with a husband.

One night, arranging ourselves before sleep, I stroked her back lightly through the thin linen of her smock. Once started, I kept going, encouraged by the warmth of her flesh beneath my palms. When Cicely rolled over to face me and touched my lips, I met her mouth with my own. My body blazed with colour and heat. Finally pursuing what I wanted, I gave myself wholly to Cicely and received what I'd never dared to hope could be mine in return. From that night forward, my days might not have seemed different to anyone watching me. But everything I did was brightened by an underlayer of joy.

* * *

427

When I first put charcoal to paper on the day Lady Mary left Wilton for the Continent, I had no idea where it would lead. But I was ready to venture into new territory. First, I removed the silk-wrapped ring from my box and examined, once more, the symbols engraved upon the stone over two decades ago by the man who had fathered me. And on the inside of the ring, the name *Rosamund* and the initials *SF*. I had told him my name was Rosamund when I wasn't ready to disclose our relation. But in revealing the name that Lady Catherine had bestowed upon me when she first told me the tale of the *Rosa Mundi*, I had allowed him entrance into a part of myself that I had shared with no one else.

Simon Forman had walked away from my mother and myself to build a career as an astrologer-physician in London. Yet with this ring, he left me with a tangible sign of his legacy – the practice he called *celestial magic*.

Lady Catherine had described the *Rosa Mundi* as signifying *the culmination of alchemical perfection that brings contrasting forces into union*. From Lady Mary I had learnt the stages of alchemy, through which all base substances must move before that perfection can be achieved. Finally, I was ready to claim who I was – all of me.

Slowly I twisted the astral ring onto my finger. Then I began to execute the picture my lady had commissioned but, until now, I'd been unready to produce.

First the earth, black as ash, around the base of a rose bush – *Nigredo*. Heavy cross-hatching in black charcoal.

Next, moving the eye up the stem, the first bud, white as snow – *Albedo*. White chalk for this one, fleshing out an outline

428

of petals marked over with a silver stylus to preserve the lines of the drawing under the subsequent laying down of paint.

And finally, the fully blooming red rose at the top of the bush – *Rubedo*. Here, I let my fancy drive my hand. Red petals in red chalk that were also red curls surrounding the features of my lady, inked in black.

If I was the white bud, she was the red rose. More than any other viewer, she would understand that, together, we formed the *Rosa Mundi*.

I added one last sketch to the underlayer before applying paints – an image that no one but myself would know was there – a sprig of rosemary. *Rosemary*. For the first time, I recognised the merger of our names, a union of contrasts beyond the visible. When I had sprinkled rosemary needles across the floor of the still-room on my first visit there, so many years ago, I had thought I was commemorating the past. It turned out I was anticipating the future.

CHAPTER THIRTY-SIX

Mary, 1611

Paris was a revelation, as dirty and crowded as London but somehow more elegant, its rhythms unruffled. Mary and Matthew had settled into comfortable accommodations on the Île de la Cité, let from a long-time Huguenot ally of the Sidney family. A small staff catered to their needs, which were refreshingly modest compared to the grand scale of life at Wilton and Baynard's.

The overriding purpose of coming to Paris, to Mary's mind at least, was the opportunity to meet and converse with the woman whose words had lifted Mary's fog of despair after Anne's death and had roiled the Circle with her shocking assertions of sexual equality. Marie de Gournay. So Mary was disappointed to learn, when Matthew had enquired on their arrival, that she had removed to the country and was not expected to return to the city for a month.

In the meantime, Matthew conferred with French physicians whose friendship he had cultivated during their shared medical training in Basel, and Mary began to make acquaintances with other members of the city's literary circles. Breathing more freely with distance from the curious scrutiny of the English court, Mary found it easier to understand how women authors in France and Italy published works that would scandalise English audiences if associated with the name of a woman.

But Samuel's letter accusing her lover of murder gnawed at her. When she had received it, their love was so fresh and invigorating that she had managed to discount its message and put it out of her mind. It had never been far from her consciousness, though, arising unbidden in those moments when she felt her happiness could only be a dream.

Of course, Samuel had every reason to lie. Mary had severed his connection to the Circle after he'd published his scurrilous *Cleopatra*. She hadn't bothered to respond to, or even look at, his subsequent revisions of the play, which he had sent to her accompanied by long letters in which he pleaded for readmission to the Circle, swearing he had *renewed the vows I owe your worth*.

What rot. Those words meant nothing, and neither did those in his slanderous letter. Since he couldn't win her, he wanted to hurt her. The letter had arrived just as hints of her relationship with Matthew were starting to percolate at court, providing ripe gossip for tongues always eager to babble over secret liaisons. That unwelcome chatter had only served as further impetus for flight to France.

And yet, against her will and her deepest instincts, Mary wondered. Could Samuel's accusation be true, at least in part? After reading and then rereading the letter, Mary had held it to a candle until the paper was ash. But the words still burned.

'Marie has returned to Paris!' Matthew announced one afternoon, holding aloft a message just delivered. 'She has learnt we are here and is anxious to make your acquaintance. We are invited to visit her tomorrow.'

Matthew was as excited as Mary at the prospect. 'Marie was a close friend of Michel de Montaigne, the philosopher. She edited and published his *Essais* after his death, and she is a deep thinker in her own right, as we have discovered in her *Égalité*. You and she will be a perfect fit. You share not only a name but a passion for alchemy and authorship, transmuting disparate elements into new forms.' That last was accompanied by a wink, a frank appraisal with a touch of wit. 'What's more, both of you hold yourselves and others to a bold standard of truth that brooks no falsity.'

Marie de Gournay lived in a neat cottage in the village of Montmartre, just outside the limits of Paris. When Matthew pushed open the gate in the worn stone wall, Mary was struck by the heady fragrance of a well-tended herb garden. Golden fruit weighed the branches of a fine pear tree.

The woman who opened the door to Mary's knock was small and sturdy, her stained apron suggesting that their appearance had interrupted work on a meal. 'Nicole,' she introduced herself tartly. As Mary began to explain the purpose of their visit in French, their hostess appeared, a bundle of apricot fur purring in her arms while two black kittens chased each other around her skirts. Mademoiselle de Gournay greeted them with a smile. Brown-skinned and sinewy, from work in the garden, Mary guessed, displaying bright black eyes over a long nose and sharp chin. '*Mes chats*,' she explained with a shrug. 'My companions.' This woman wasn't one to stand on ceremony. 'I have been awaiting your arrival with interest ever since Matthieu wrote me of your plans to come to France. You shall join me for *déjeuner, oui*?' And then, without a pause, 'Your translation of my countryman Garnier's *Marc Antoine* reveals a new side to the queen of Egypt.' So she knew Mary's play! 'Editing the essays of Monsieur Montaigne, who was pleased to call me his *fille d'alliance* – his daughter by adoption – I've had to find my own words as well.'

'Your treatise on the equality of men and women brought me back from the dead,' Mary confessed softly. When the memory of Anne's death reduced Mary momentarily to silence, her new acquaintance took up the thread of conversation and passed it on to Matthew with ease, enabling Mary to breathe again without needing an excuse.

Nicole produced a mouth-watering midday meal that included a hearty stew with fresh crusty bread, followed by thinly sliced pears and creamy cheese. Marie's three cats took turns receiving morsels from her plate, while she and Mary conversed in a rapid-fire exchange of French and English, augmented by interjections from Matthew. By the end of the meal, Mary was invigorated, exhausted and hungry for more. A woman who could match wits with her so fluidly would add immeasurably to the exchanges in the Circle, challenging the men and encouraging the women to consider fresh ideas.

Marie responded to Mary's invitation with a sunburst of a grin and a single upheld finger. 'I would be more than delighted to visit you at Wilton, *ma chère amie*. But now, you must spend some time with me here in Paris. There is much I wish to share with you, if you will not mind me sometimes taking Mary from you,' she added, turning to Matthew, then, at his ready assent, back to Mary. '*Un homme exceptionnel.* You are fortunate in having each other.'

That night, Matthew brought two cups of wine to their chamber. 'To toast your friendship with Marie.' His voice was warm with affection and happiness.

Mary took the cup, but set it aside. She had hoped that being in another country, away from all that was familiar, would banish her nagging doubts about Samuel's letter. But it had only sharpened their potency. Loving Matthew no longer seemed to offer security, when love, in her experience, invariably led to loss.

'You know a lot about my family, Matthew,' she began. 'I've shared my feelings about the deaths of my sister Ambrosia and my brother Philip.' Pressing a fist against her chest to still the uncomfortable thumping, she continued, 'But I know almost nothing of yours.'

Matthew's eyebrows drew together. 'My brother Edward is dead, and my father and I are estranged.' *Estranged* indeed, if Samuel's accusation was true, Mary thought. His voice was tight. 'I stay in touch only with my mother now. I was thinking, recently, that once we return from the Continent, perhaps I can bring her to Wilton to meet you.' He touched

Mary's cheek. 'I'd like my mother to know the woman I love.'

Mary took his hand from her face and held it in her own.

'How did Edward die?'

His face registered her question as a blow, eyes widening in shock. But it was too late to take it back.

Regaining his composure with an effort, Matthew replied slowly, deliberately. 'He fell ill with a wasting sickness, seven years ago, when I returned to Thornton after completing my medical training in Basel. My father boasted to all the villagers that Edward's brother the doctor would surely cure him.' He broke off, then, and when he resumed, his voice was choked. 'Edward himself had so much hope at the start, and we all believed he'd make a recovery, especially because he hadn't one of the more commonly known dangerous diseases, such as plague or smallpox.' He dropped his head, his hand limp in Mary's grasp.

'I couldn't save him, because I didn't know what was wrong. I had no cure to offer.' The rest of the story came tumbling out. 'But it's worse than that. When Edward died, my father said I'd poisoned him. My mother insisted it was his grief speaking, but I was charged and stood trial.' He rose and paced to the window, black with night, before turning to face Mary.

'I was acquitted for lack of evidence. But my father was right.' Tears were running down his cheeks. 'I killed my brother.'

Mary gasped. Samuel's words rang in her head: *The renowned Doctor Lister is not quite the paragon you might imagine. Be wary . . .* No – it wasn't possible.

'You condemn yourself for not having a cure,' she whispered, grasping for an explanation. 'That's not the same as killing. You mustn't blame yourself.' But Matthew was shaking his head, vehemently.

'He was in so much pain, at the end. He couldn't even sit up in bed. The disease, whatever it was, had riddled his body, taking over his muscles, his lungs and his spirit. My mother wept every day, and my father raged, pressing me to make use of my *fancy medical training* to do some good. Edward begged me to make it stop, to free him from the terrible pain.' He broke down, sobbing into his hands. Now she understood, both what Samuel had conveyed out of malice, and what Matthew had concealed out of grief. 'I violated the Hippocratic Oath.'

Mary recalled what Joan had told her. *When no clear cure is at hand, the truth can bring more comfort than false hope.* Matthew, as a physician, had not only recognised that truth, but employed his learning to do something about it. To help, not harm.

She took his hand. The hand of a healer. 'A merciful ending must be the hardest task. I think you accompanied your brother on a path not everyone can recognise.' Matthew raised his head, his eyes red and swollen.

'So you don't abhor my action?'

'I love you,' she answered simply. And this time it really was simple. And it was enough.

When Mary held him that night in bed, she let Samuel's poisoned accusation wash away in the tears she and Matthew shared. For their siblings.

The next morning, Mary had a confession of her own. 'Samuel sent me a letter. About your brother.'

On Matthew's face was a look of such sadness that she

regretted for a moment having revealed it. But no, their bond must be founded in truth, no matter the pain.

'I dreaded the time when you would find out,' he murmured. 'My responsibility for my brother's death hasn't ceased to haunt me for a single day. I should have shared my secret with you before now. But I've been so happy that I didn't want anything to destroy what we've found together.'

Mary nodded and held him tighter. 'When I received Samuel's message, even as I recognised its origins in jealousy, I feared that its truth might be an ending.' She shook her head. 'Instead, we shall begin anew. We must not hide anything from each other. Life is too precious for half-truths. Too short for half-measures.'

Released from the doubts and fears that had bound her heart, Mary felt liberated. And she needed to tell someone. She couldn't call for Rose and bend her ear, so the next morning she picked up her pen and began to write – to Ambrosia.

You wouldn't dream what I've done. Taken a lover! So much better than a husband.

By the way, I was wrong about my first kiss – the one with Jake, the story I never got to tell you. And yes, dear sister, I have been kissed since then. But never truly, until now.

My first true kiss was with Matthew.

To her surprise, Mary found that one of the things she most enjoyed in her conversations with Marie de Gournay was their disagreements. In one of their spirited debates, Marie observed that conflict is inherent in the relationship between a man and a woman as two separate beings. As evidence, she offered the *strokes of contempt* visited upon women who threatened men's sense of self-worth and superiority. '*Pas toi, Matthieu, bien sûr,*' she assured her friend's companion with a smile. 'But too many others, who must be opposed daily.'

'Is opposition always necessary?' Mary countered. 'I've found that genuine collaboration can move beyond opposition to reconciliation.'

Marie lifted her shoulders in what Mary had come to recognise as a peculiarly French shrug.

'For those who can find it, I celebrate them. For myself, I seek another way.'

Mary treasured these exchanges, which exceeded her expectations. What she didn't expect was the outings with Marie, into adventures she had never imagined, a giddy round of experimentation.

First, Marie took Mary to the shooting range where she practised marksmanship. Marie placed a long heavy pistol into Mary's hand and insisted she give it a try. 'Why should men be the only ones to enjoy weapons?'

She aimed her pistol at the target and pulled the trigger. The recoil from the explosion of gunpowder knocked the gun from her hands. Undeterred, Mary tried again, and with practice she learnt to appreciate, if not precisely enjoy, the skill involved in shooting.

Next, Marie introduced her to the practice of taking tobacco. 'I've added mugwort to the tobacco, to enhance your dreams,' explained her new friend. Mary's first puff of the aromatic mixture produced a raw burning sensation in her chest and a bout of coughing. Slightly giddy from the languorous curls of smoke that escaped her lips, she opened a casement window for a breath of fresh air and found herself drinking in the scent of Marie's garden as if it were a distilled liquor. Mary started to grasp Walter Raleigh's enthusiasm for tobacco.

'It's the absence of prohibition that I enjoy the most,' Mary told Matthew that night in bed. 'I find that I can appreciate the materiality of life more easily in France than in England. When I'm here, I don't need to live in my head.'

In the dark of midnight, as Mary slept curled on Matthew's shoulder, there came a pounding at the outside door. A panting messenger stood on the threshold, his steed lathered with sweat.

Mary's heart plummeted. Had someone died? The prospect of another loss was unbearable. Trembling, she unfolded the message and scanned the spidery lines in the Wilton steward's hand.

'We must return to Wilton at once.' Her voice came out in a harsh whisper. 'Rose has been arrested. For murder.'

CHAPTER THIRTY-SEVEN

Rose, 1611

I never saw it coming.

I was tidying the still-room that morning after a distillation of hyssop, which I'd learnt from Mum could be used to combat a remarkable range of ailments, from sore throats to the plague itself. She herself had placed further value on the herb, adding hyssop oil to her own tisanes while she was still well. When I asked, she simply spoke of it as a cleansing aid. It was only after she was gone that I came upon an entry in Lady Catherine's papers, which I still often consulted, noting the belief in hyssop's power to *purify and forgive sins*. That was when I grasped that Mum must have been doing penance ever since I was conceived. Atoning for a sin that she alone took responsibility for. *Our fates are not a matter of the stars, but of the choices we make*, she had told me.

I was sweeping the curling fragments of tiny purple hyssop blossoms from the floor beneath the worktable when there came a pounding of heavy boots on the stairs and a sharp knock on the still-room door. Before I could answer it, Master Wilkins stepped inside, followed by a constable with a menacing glare and a stolid watchman wielding a club.

'We're taking you into custody, Rose Commin,' rasped the constable, his wiry frame supporting a powerful grip on my upper arms. 'You've been accused of murder.'

My broom clattered to the floor, scattering the pile of petals. It made no sense. What murder? No one in the house had died. When I struggled in the constable's grasp, the deputy brandished his club in my direction.

Master Wilkins stepped forward. 'See here, there's no cause for force. Rose is a good woman and a skilled healer who her ladyship has trusted with the care of the household in her absence.'

The constable shouldered him aside. 'Murder is cause enough,' he replied, and pushed me to the door. My mind was blank as the stone slab I had just washed after chopping the hyssop. *Murder.* The officer half shoved and half dragged me down the stairs. My ankle twisted during the bumpy descent so that I cried out in pain when he shook me upright at the bottom.

Peter and Cicely were standing at the foot of the stairs with a cluster of servants. Peter reached out to me, but the deputy knocked him back with an elbow to the throat.

'Rose, we'll sort out this mullock! Be not afeard—' But Cicely's words were interrupted by a shrill cry.

''Tis her, all right! She's the witch that murdered Toby.' It was Alice, Sarah's niece. The conviction in her voice was a torch, setting whispers among the watching servants ablaze. Momentarily the constable stopped in his tracks. I stared at Alice, but she wouldn't look at me, her mouth twisted in that sour pucker I recalled from the first time I met her. But something else darkened her face. *Fear*. Why was she accusing me of murder? And – *Toby*? Now I saw that Cicely's face was streaked with tears.

'Toby's gone, Rose. He didn't wake this morning.'

Before I could gather my thoughts, I found myself dumped into a cart and taken away to the Salisbury jail. Like my birth father before me.

The cell was dark and dank, its dimness unrelieved by the single barred window, set too high in the wall for me to look out. Before the door clanged shut, smothering all light, I glimpsed a straw mattress on the earthen floor with no blanket. Shivering, I crouched in the darkness, rubbing my swollen ankle, too shocked even to cry.

The truce between Toby and Cicely couldn't last for ever. He'd lately been fuddled by drink almost daily and had finally been taken to task by the steward.

'You dishonour this household. Any further lapses and you shall be dismissed.' Master Wilkins' warning was a serious matter – not just a threat, but a vow. Every servant knew what had been said. Father and son had words as well. Last evening, Stanley had called his father a disgrace and Toby, predictably, had stormed out to the tavern.

Roused from sleep at midnight by hammering on my chamber door, I found Cicely cradling three-year-old Dorcas in her arms, her face white with fury. With one palm, she supported a chubby hand bent at an impossible angle from the child's wrist.

Cicely told me she had put the grandchildren to bed in her chamber, as she often did, to give Stanley and Sophia some time together. When Toby returned to find his bed occupied, he let loose a volley of oaths. 'I'll not have that bastard's litter in my bed,' he shouted, and threw the children roughly to the floor.

'For meself, I care not what he does, but what he has done to the child I cannot forgive,' she whispered. The same break that Toby had given her, but far worse against a child. 'Can ye mend it for now, afore Stanley learns what his da has done?' Her voice choked with painful sobs that frightened even Dorcas into silence.

Recalling Doctor Lister's binding of Cicely's wrist, I cast about for something to wrap the break. I tore a length from the bottom of my petticoat, but soon realised I needed more material to fashion a sling. I laid the child on my bed, covering her with extra blankets for the shock.

'Go to the still-room,' I told Cicely, handing over the ring of keys. 'You'll find more linen on the shelf inside the door. Bring me one and remember to lock the door when you leave.'

As soon as her grandmother left the room, Dorcas started to wail, and my attempt to bind her wrist produced full-blown shrieks. I scrabbled through my belongings for the sack of candied ginger Mum had kept always on hand for the children of her patients. I offered Dorcas a piece, but at the sight of the brown cube she started screaming so loudly I feared her cries would wake the entire servants' wing. I quickly pressed the ginger between the child's lips, and her wails stopped in surprise at the sweetness. Then she opened her mouth to allow me to place the treat on her tongue and began sucking with pleasure. But as soon as she tried to sit up in my bed, the pain in her wrist brought on more tears.

Where was Cicely? *Surely she must have found the linens by now*, I thought. Brushing Dorcas's damp curls from her forehead, I cursed Toby for the harm he had caused those I loved. And then, finally, Cicely was at the door, bearing a sheet of clean linen.

I bound Dorcas's wrist more evenly, and fashioned a sling to support her tiny arm, as I had seen Doctor Lister do for Cicely.

'I'll send for Doctor Scott as soon as it's light,' I assured her. 'Will you be safe returning to your chamber?'

She nodded, no longer offering to make excuses for her husband, her face drawn with weariness. 'I'll bring the child back to her mum, and then see to Toby, who's likely sleeping off the drink.' She was not angry so much as resigned. And resolved. 'He shall never do this again.'

I crawled back into my bed to capture an hour of sleep before dawn.

When I arose, the servants' hall was humming with rumours. Master Wilkins was going to toss Toby out if Stanley didn't kill him first. Cicely would be forced to plead for her husband lest he beat her black and blue. She need plead for nothing, I thought. Certainly not for Toby.

But as it happened, later that day it was me she turned to on Toby's behalf.

'Took ill after his dinner,' she told me quietly. 'Can't keep anything down. I've seen this afore, after he drinks himself senseless, but this time he insists is different. He asked me to call for thee.'

With a sigh, I agreed to consult the remedies in the still-room, and only then did I realise I'd not received the keys back from Cicely.

'I forgot.' As she handed over the keys, I could see new lines of sorrow and fatigue pulling down her mouth. Cicely deserved better than Toby. Always had. I only wished there was more I could do.

In the still-room, I unlocked the inlaid cabinet and removed the black walnut box. I was so tired that it took me some time to sift through remedies for stomach ailments. Finally I settled on a prescription for an infusion of peppermint leaves steeped with crushed garlic cloves, fortified with elderberry syrup and a tincture of birch leaves, to be followed by chewing fennel seeds. I resented Toby asking for a cure after what he had done to Dorcas. But my lady had put me in charge of healing, not punishment. So I sorted through the cabinet of remedies for the ingredients and made my way to Cicely's room.

By the time I arrived, Toby was vomiting blood. Cicely sat quietly beside the bed, holding a basin for his retching and wiping his forehead with a damp cloth between heaves. I brewed the infusion and watched while Cicely gave him the first dose.

Doctor Scott, called in to examine Dorcas's wrist, came by to check on Toby as well and advised him to follow my prescription. 'Peppermint and fennel can do no harm and might indeed ease your discomfort,' he explained. Before he left, the doctor complimented me on my binding of the child's arm.

'There's a good chance it will heal straight rather than awry, thanks to Rose,' he told Cicely, who brightened for the first time since she had carried Dorcas to my chamber.

'As for your husband, I advise watching him through the night to ensure that he doesn't choke on his own vomit. He'll likely be better by the morrow.'

The doctor's assurance had given me no cause for concern, so I hadn't thought to check on Toby before I mounted the stairs to the still-room early the next morning to prepare the hyssop tincture. Now, alone in the chill cell, I frantically reviewed the ingredients in the remedy I'd used to treat his stomach ailment the night before. Had I accidentally included something harmful? I didn't think I could have. But a stone was forming in the pit of my stomach.

My last thought that night was the cry of *Witch!* when I was nine years old, followed by Mum's voice as she was led away. *Don't be afraid.*

Alice's accusation was only the start. The constable returned to Wilton the next day to search for damning evidence. Alerted by one of the servants, he asked to see all my drawings, and found what he was looking for. First, sketches of the spirits I had associated with different herbs. Then the red chalk drawing of the afterbirth of William, with the spirit peeping from the baby's cord. Finally, in my painting of the *Rosa Mundi*, a full-blown rose with my lady's face.

'Dreadful,' the constable muttered as he pieced through the offending images. 'Fearsome. Not of this world.' The murmurs of witchcraft multiplied, feeding rumours that I not only made drawings of evil spirits, but called upon them as well.

All this I learnt from Cicely when she visited me two days after my arrest. She was not permitted entrance into my cell but spoke to me through the small grille in the door.

'I should never have asked thee to treat him,' she repeated, over and over. 'This is all me own fault. I wanted the household to see he'd been properly cared for. I never thought ye'd be accused of witchcraft!' She was shaking, her usual cheery confidence in tatters. All her concern was for me, all her guilt for the charges against me.

'This is not your fault. Toby was the one who drank himself mad and broke Dorcas's wrist,' I reminded her. 'But why would Alice accuse me?'

'Alice is but a child. I think she fancied Toby, and this has flummoxed her. She wants someone to blame.' Now I recalled seeing the girl hovering outside the door when I'd taken the remedy to Cicely's room. 'But to cry *Witch!* What must she be thinking? Death needs no spells.' She sighed. 'Any road, no one'll believe her.'

But they did.

The next morning, the constable came to my cell, grim-faced and tense. He bound my wrists with a stout cord and led me, limping, to the Salisbury magistrate's office. In a large, high-backed oak chair, its arms black with age, sat a thin, white-haired old man. Justice Estcourt. His robe of office hung loosely from his shoulders, but his carriage was erect, his dark eyes clear.

'Rose Commin, Your Honour.' The constable loosed my bonds and pushed me forward, nodding respectfully to the ancient, who fixed me with a keen gaze. Spread across the table before him were my drawings. Evidence.

'Rose Commin, a servant in your household told the constable that you wear a ring marked with evil symbols.'

I pulled off the astral ring and dropped it into his palm. 'Look for yourself,' I said bluntly. 'The markings are star signs. Harmless!'

He turned the ring in his bony fingers, squinting suspiciously. 'How came you by this?'

'It was payment from a London' – I paused, the word *astrologer* on my tongue. It was then I realised I might be in greater danger than I thought – 'physician, for my services in painting him a sign.'

'What is this "SF"?' he demanded, reading the initials on the inside of the ring. When I voiced the name *Simon Forman*, his eyes hardened. Clearly that name still held some dark resonance hereabouts. 'I was sheriff here when one Simon Forman was arrested on a charge of necromancy.' The magistrate's voice was scratchy, so soft that I could scarce catch all his words, but his eyes were bright with speculation. 'I remember that villain and his association with Joan Commin.'

He saw me flinch, hearing Mum's name on his lips, and narrowed his eyes. Mum had almost died due to her bond with the astrologer, and now I was blackened with the same brush. 'I see your name's Commin also. Any relation?' His voice was steel, sharp enough to cut.

'My mother,' I replied, determined not to reveal more than I had to.

'I want the truth about how you came to possess a sigil

from Simon Forman.' No ignorant countryman, he used the ancient name for the magical symbols engraved onto my rose quartz stone. Clearly he believed I was concealing a darker bond and was determined to drag it out of me. 'How came you to know him in the first place?'

I wasn't about to darken my mother's reputation by revealing the story of my origins. I replied, coolly, I hoped, 'I had heard his name, and sought him out of curiosity when I was in London with the Earl of Pembroke for the funeral of Sir Philip Sidney.' I guessed my ties to that powerful family could only help my standing. 'When I offered to paint him a new sign for his business, he gave me the ring in return.'

'And that was the extent of your dealings with this Forman?' His eyes were shrewd. For all his white hair and the trembling hands resting on the arms of the chair, this was no rambler, but a hound on the scent of the hunt. 'And you are wearing his ring, while dispensing remedies for the Wilton household. Why would that be?'

Why indeed? Scrambling for an answer, I stumbled into the trap. 'I thought it wouldn't hurt to have protection under the zodiac.'

'So you believe in astral magic, then?' With my parentage, how could I not? But I knew better than to speak what would only harm my case.

'I employ the medical remedies developed by my mistresses, Lady Mary and Lady Catherine Herbert.'

'Magic and medicine sometimes are separated by only a thin line, girl,' the judge observed. His voice hardened. 'Did you use medicine to kill Toby Saunders on Tuesday last? Or magic?'

'No, Your Honour. I used no magic. I prescribed a herbal treatment for healing.'

'Did you wish him dead, for his ill treatment of your friend, Cicely Saunders?'

'I wished him gone away,' I replied honestly, those dark eyes demanding the truth from me, 'but I never sought to kill him. I sought to heal.'

'That's as may be. It appears someone wanted him dead.'

'Wanting is not the same as doing, Your Honour.'

It was only after hearing my own words that I started to wonder.

CHAPTER THIRTY-EIGHT

Mary, 1611

When they disembarked in Dover, another message was waiting. Mary handed it to Matthew without a word.

Rose was to stand trial by water as a witch. Just like her mother.

Mary understood all too well that fear of witchcraft was even fiercer than panic over plague. The accused was quarantined in prison, separated from family and friends whether the charges were true or false. Worst of all, when linked to murder, the label of 'witch' could end Rose's life.

'I know she's innocent,' she told Matthew as the carriage hastened overnight towards Wilton. When she closed her eyes, she could see Rose's watchful face and observant gaze, and recalled her care for little Kate, for Cicely. For Mary herself. This death, at least, she was determined to prevent.

Early the next morning, Mary and Matthew alighted from the carriage only to discover from old Humphrey Wilkins that the entire household had gone to view the trial by water, at the confluence of the Nadder and Wylye rivers. After so long away, the damp English chill penetrated Mary's bones. A deeper chill penetrated her heart. Re-entering the carriage, she ordered the coachman to make haste.

'Let me address the magistrate,' Matthew urged.

'This is my responsibility,' Mary replied, her grey gaze glinting like forged steel. The throng of onlookers crowding the riverbank parted before her urgent advance.

Rose, bound hand and foot and blindfolded, had been bundled into the rowing boat that would take her to the deepest water to be immersed. Even from a distance, Mary could see she was white to the lips, but holding herself upright.

'Halt these proceedings immediately!' Mary's voice filled the air as powerfully as when she had sung before the Queen. The muttering mob of villagers and servants hushed, and the magistrate slowly turned, amazed. For a long moment, time stood still, as a wedge of swans, startled by Mary's command, lifted off from the river. At first they seemed to be running on the surface of the water, until, their long necks reaching forward and their wings stroking rhythmically as heartbeats, they gradually ascended. White birds against a grey sky, calling to each other as they rose.

'On whose authority?' Justice Estcourt demanded.

'On the authority of the Pembroke title,' Mary rejoined. 'I have returned to Wilton to repudiate this charge against my trusted friend and companion.'

The crowd, silenced by her appearance, now erupted into excited chatter. *Friend and companion*! No other servant would be so named, nor by any other countess.

'You may release her into my safekeeping while I personally investigate these charges.' Mary's voice admitted no other choice. But the magistrate stood his ground.

'Accused of murder by witchcraft, the prisoner shall remain in custody while you conduct whatever *investigation* you deem necessary. This trial shall be postponed, and I will review your findings before proceeding.' No yielding there. And no room for error.

Still bound when her mistress removed the blindfold, Rose opened her eyes to Mary's embrace.

In the days that followed, Mary's careful and persistent enquiry revealed that the scullery maid Sarah had been Toby's childhood sweetheart before they entered into service together at Wilton. Toby's infatuation with Cicely, leading to her pregnancy and their subsequent marriage, had dealt a death blow to Sarah's hopes and plans. As the years passed, Sarah's bitterness had only intensified, directed at Cicely and all of those Cicely cared for. Among these most of all was Rose, who was Cicely's closest friend and, Mary discovered, had once struck Sarah for calling Joan a witch. By now, Sarah's only ally in the household was Alice, who had apparently taken her aunt's word that Cicely had first entrapped Toby and then ruined him, and that Rose must have cast a lethal spell on him in order to have Cicely for herself.

When the Countess interviewed Sarah and her niece, Alice

was too terrified to speak, afraid, according to Sarah, of what Rose could do to her if she bore witness against her. So Sarah spoke for them both, disdaining Rose's supposed power to harm her.

'That woman drove him to drink,' Sarah hissed. 'My niece knows the truth and she—'

'What evidence of witchcraft on Rose's part did Alice witness?' Mary cut in, losing patience with the litany of accusations.

'Any witch can hide her trade,' retorted Sarah. 'And that one's mother was a witch, so she has all the craft she needed! And she can read. She knows the spells and potions in them black-magic books. She wanted revenge for Toby raising a hand to her *beloved* Cicely. 'Twas that potion killed him. And Alice herself saw Rose bring it to him.'

There were gaps of logic here, but reason wasn't driving the accusation. She could understand Sarah's enmity and Alice's loyalty to her aunt. What wasn't clear was what had driven Alice to make such a deadly accusation.

'Perhaps you can make sense of what I cannot,' Mary told Rose when she went to the prison, insisting the guards let her out of the rank cell so they could speak together. With a standing claim of witchcraft, a compelling case had to be made to refute the accusation and dismiss the charge. If not, the trial by water would proceed, and Rose could die.

When Mary presented the meticulously penned summary of her investigation, Justice Estcourt looked over the findings and perfunctorily dismissed them.

'I'm not convinced by backstairs jealousies and gossip. The fact remains that Rose administered a dose of what she said was a healing potion, and the next day the man was dead. If your *friend and companion*' – the words were heavy with scorn – 'didn't kill him, who did?'

Mary grasped at a straw. 'That I don't know, yet. But I can prove it wasn't Rose's potion.'

The next day, Mary ushered Justice Estcourt into her still-room, providing a suitably magisterial chair on which to seat him. Rose was in shackles, led in by the same constable and watchman who had dragged her out of this room the week before. Scanning the gleaming collection of vessels, Mary took heart from the spotless state in which Rose had left the still-room, only a scatter of hyssop leaves upon the floor. As the officers sniffed nervously at the herbs and minerals that scented the air, the magistrate directed them to remove Rose's chains, then waved them to stand aside.

At Mary's instruction, Rose recreated the steps she had taken to prepare the concoction she had supplied to Toby. Paging through Lady Catherine's remedies that addressed stomach ailments, she located the one she had used and prepared the ingredients, reading them aloud as she combined them in a pot of water heated by the sand bath of the furnace. 'Peppermint leaves steeped with crushed garlic, combined with syrup of elderberry and one drop of tincture of birch leaf', this last supplied from a small stoppered bottle, producing indrawn breaths from the onlookers.

After the infusion had steeped, Rose poured it into a cup. Mary raised the cup to her lips and drank it down in full, then chewed and swallowed a mouthful of fennel seeds under the magistrate's critical gaze.

'I have demonstrated my complete confidence in Rose Commin's prescription in front of you as an eyewitness. Surely there is nothing more you need to know.'

But Justice Estcourt was shaking his head. 'Expertise is no proof of innocence, my lady. Indeed, the reverse.' The straw Mary had grasped was, as she had feared, too slender to rescue Rose from the dark water. She had failed her.

The judge turned to Rose and eyed her soberly. 'As the daughter of an impeached witch, your parentage alone would be sufficient to support the charge. Drawings in your own hand that picture a world not visible to mortal eyes supply further evidence against you. The man you treated is dead. Having reviewed all the findings of her ladyship, I find no reason to overturn the maidservant's accusation of murder by witchcraft.'

Rose remained erect, her eyes ablaze. It was Mary who trembled now.

'The trial by water will proceed immediately.'

Mary gasped, but Rose's clear voice rang out.

'I ask to see my accuser.'

The magistrate had raised his hand in a gesture to the constable to take her away. Now he paused.

'That is your right,' he replied with a sigh.

White-faced and shivering, Alice was brought into the still-room. A guilty conscience, was Mary's first thought. Rose looked her accuser over thoughtfully, and then requested the use of chalk, pen and paper.

'You may address your accuser directly,' Justice Estcourt instructed her. But she simply bent over the still-room desk, covering the paper with quick, sure strokes. The others watched in silent curiosity, none more so than Alice herself.

When Rose had finished, she handed the drawing to the girl, who gazed at it wonderingly.

'Is that me?' she asked. 'Alice?'

A large vine-wrapped letter 'A' filled the sheet, arching over the figure of a girl asleep and dreaming, suffused with contentment. Above her, in the triangle of the letter, curled a tiny infant swaddled in leaves, while around the crossbar of the 'A' twined a merry spirit, holding the babe in a gentle embrace.

'You don't need Toby.' Rose's voice was kind. 'All you need is within you.'

Alice released her breath in a long sigh, followed by a river of silent tears. 'You see me,' she whispered. And at length, turning to the magistrate, 'She's no witch.'

CHAPTER THIRTY-NINE

Rose, 1611

Bound and blindfolded at the riverside, I sat in the rowing boat while the rough hands that had seized me prepared to cast off. Strangely, what I longed for most at that moment was the sound of my lady's voice. And then, there it was.

Halt these proceedings immediately! I didn't believe my ears, and when the next sound that came was the beating of wings, I thought I must already be dead and led to heaven by a flock of angels. Then my lady's voice again, bringing me back to earth.

I have returned to Wilton to repudiate this charge against my trusted friend and companion. At those words, I thought my heart would burst. My lady herself removed the blindfold, and her gaze held me like a lifeline. It was her faith that gave me the confidence, a week later in the still-room, to trust my eye and reach out to Alice's heart.

When the magistrate required an explanation, the whole story came out. Toby had bedded Alice repeatedly on the strength of drunken promises that he would look after her and any baby that might result. And it did – but he didn't. Once she told him of her condition, he relapsed into habituating the tavern. When he died, Alice panicked and confessed everything to her aunt. Sarah told the bereft girl that I had employed witchcraft and murder to get rid of Toby so I could have Cicely all to myself.

The magistrate was still not satisfied. 'This drawing itself could be evidence of witchcraft. What is the meaning of that image?'

Lady Mary drew a breath, almost wearily. 'Its meaning, sir, is that this girl is pregnant. The baby is Toby's doing. Rose has helped her see that a false accusation will not bring him back, and that her care now is for the new life growing within her.'

The judge was looking at her, hard, still undecided. Lady Mary drew herself up and fixed him with her most imperious glare.

'The accusation is withdrawn, and there is no evidence there was even a murder. You *must* dismiss the charge.' Dowager or no, she was Countess of Pembroke still.

With a sigh, Justice Estcourt nodded.

I was free.

The next afternoon, I returned to the still-room to tidy it. I swept the workbench clean of the remnants of peppermint leaves, stored the garlic in its pot by the window, returned the elderberry syrup to the shelf above the workbench, and opened the cabinet of remedies to replace the birch-leaf tincture. That was when I noticed the phial of turbith, that bright-yellow distillation of quicksilver and acid. It was lying on its side on the top shelf, half empty.

My own voice echoed in my head as I remembered showing it to Cicely, along with the other potentially poisonous substances in the cabinet. *Beneficial in extreme cases and small doses, lethal if misused.*

I breathed deeply, once, set the phial upright, and locked the cabinet.

When Cicely came to my room that night and took me in her arms to welcome me home, I asked no questions. But she had something to tell me.

'Me first babe, lost to miscarriage – that was Toby's doing too.' Shocked, I searched her face. 'I had thought about what tha said to me, that I didn't have to marry him. I told him then I didn't know if we were suited to one another. He begged me to stay with him, promised he loved me. When I wouldn't speak to reassure him, he went a bit mad. There was always some crack in him that could scarce be seen unless he was mithered.'

She turned away, and I could see she was reliving the moment in her mind.

'He threw me against the wall, and the next moment he was sobbing in me lap. And then the babe was coming, too early. He ran away, and tha came and cared for me instead, Rose. I lost the babe, but didn't leave him after that. He told me I was his only hope for happiness in this world.' Her head was bowed, her last words soft. 'For too long I let his story be me own. 'Til the end.'

I saw again the phial of turbith on its side. I wondered, with some part of me, if I had instructed Cicely so carefully in the still-room because I had hoped for this, without daring to think it. When she took my face between her hands, I knew she had drawn on the resolve I had lacked.

'Thou hast been me best hope, Rose,' she whispered. 'Always thee.'

If Toby had not raised a hand to Dorcas, he might still be alive. I shivered at the thought. I was ready to claim the future we shared. The double ouroboros.

Lady Mary smiled when I unveiled my *Rosa Mundi* painting. 'I'm surprised they didn't accuse me of witchcraft as well, seeing my face in that rose.' She touched her gold serpent ring to the silver seal that hung from my neck. 'We have both lived through stages of transformation that we'd not care to repeat. The difference between us is that you've been able to see the ouroboros for both of us when I could not. Thank you for completing the circle.'

I left my service at Wilton at the end of that year, with my lady's blessing, and purchased a cottage in Amesbury with my savings from the shillings and sovereigns my drawings had earned over the years. It was a small, bright house at the other end of the village from where I'd grown up, nestled at the edge of a meadow and boasting a large garden plot, long-neglected and completely overgrown. I had plans for that quarter-acre – a herb garden that was worthy of my mother's vision and also honoured my two mistresses. Looking over the patch the day I moved in, I remembered the rainbow hues and fragrances that greeted me when I first came home to Amesbury from Wilton – blue borage starflowers, golden rounds of tansy and mugwort, pungent scents of ginger and sage, thyme and rosemary.

Soon, Cicely would join me. We planned to start a business, with a stall in the marketplace – like Da – selling the flowers and herbs we'd grown and the herbal distillations we'd made – like Mum – and guided by the stars and planets, like the man whose role in my life I had finally accepted. Mayhap the stall would also offer my drawings of the flowers, herbs and stars – but without the peeping spirits. Not all have the eyes to see.

After I cleared the garden, I planted a rose bush in the centre. At its base I buried my astral ring. I had no more need of it.

CHAPTER FORTY

Mary, 1612

Mary had no living daughters, but she believed that there was someone to carry on the Sidney legacy of creating new heavens and new earths. Her niece and goddaughter, Mary Sidney Wroth. She had marvelled at Rose's insistence, after the performance of *Antonius*, that her niece loved her son. William was preoccupied with the thrust and parry of political advancement, seeking occasions where he might show himself to best advantage, at court and in public. By contrast, Mary's namesake lived inside her head, reading and writing to make sense of her world, as Mary herself did. Mary Wroth was a frequent participant in the Circle. She often shared passages of the prose romance she was composing, following the path opened by her uncle Philip's *Arcadia*. Mary feared that her son might destroy not only her niece's marriage, but her dreams.

'Don't underestimate the power of a woman who lives in her mind,' Matthew told Mary when she confided her apprehensions. 'Your niece might be more resourceful than you give her credit for. Consider the example of her godmother.'

But Mary knew that her own example as a mother was all too flawed. William was proof of that.

How could she counsel her niece and goddaughter when she herself had failed so abysmally at mothering her children? But when Mary Wroth's closest sister, Kate, died – another Kate! the losses only multiplied – the Countess seized the opportunity to reach out to her goddaughter, in her own way.

Crossing out more lines than she saved, she laboured for most of a day to write the letter. Finally, after penning the fair copy, she folded the paper, lit a candle, and sealed the wax with the ruby-eyed head of her ouroboros ring.

Dearest Mary,

When I lost my sister, as you have now lost yours, I wanted my life to be over. And for many years it was.

Married to a man I had not chosen, unable to love my children as they deserved, cut off by death from my brother – the only man with whom my mind had fully come alive – I might as well have been dead myself. Until my labour in the still-room helped my sister-in-law to conceive her first child.

You, my goddaughter and namesake, are the fruit of that labour, more precious than any Philosopher's Stone.

Trust your voice, Mary. I do.

* * *

'I want to build you a house.' They lay abed in the spring sunlight, limbs entwined. Matthew's lips brushed Mary's ear. 'A dwelling we can share for the rest of our lives.'

'That sounds ominous,' Mary said with a playful smile. But she wasn't really jesting. She didn't want to think about *the rest of our lives* with a lover ten years younger than she, who was likely to outlive her.

'I envision a country manor house, like King Basilius's woodland lodge in your brother's *Arcadia*.'

Mary rolled off his shoulder and sat up. 'Certainly not.' Her response burst out with no forethought. She was dismayed to see the hurt in his eyes, but she knew he was prepared to hear whatever she said. 'I don't want to live in a romance, Matthew. I want to live in the real world.'

Now she let thoughts she had previously stifled pour forth. 'For so long I escaped from my circumstances into verse and tales, constructing worlds more beautiful and coherent, even in loss, than anything I had experienced. Working with Will on *Antony and Cleopatra*, I was satisfied to imagine a true love that ended in tragedy, because at least while it lasted, it conjured heaven on earth. But I'm finished with that. I want to live my dreams now instead of writing them.' She looked down at him and smiled. '*Here is my space.*'

'No romance, then,' he agreed, with his quirky grin. 'But a nice view.' When she raised her eyebrows, he explained, 'Your property near Ampthill in Bedfordshire affords magnificent vistas of the countryside. I have an architect working on the design. Inigo Jones. I hope you'll like it.'

The notion was delightful, and so like Matthew to quietly conceive an original plan. Why, then, was she so unsettled? By the terms of her husband's will, they could never marry, but why not share a dwelling that was theirs alone and not an inheritance? She realised, now, that sharing a household with a husband had represented confinement for so long that the very prospect of binding herself in that way seemed dangerous. Entering into such new, unmapped territory – for thinking, for grieving, for loving – she had feared losing her bearings.

Then, unexpectedly, Mary laughed aloud. With liberty and relief. Their trip to the Continent had offered a vision of a shared life that could continue after they returned, whether in a new house or not. She was fifty-one. Whatever *the rest of our lives* held in store, she knew she wanted to share it with this man.

The next day, word came that Will Shakespeare had retired from the stage and departed London for his home in Stratford-upon-Avon. On the heels of the news came a letter, addressed in a familiar script, simply marked *Epilogue*.

There was no message, only lines from one of his sonnets – one Mary knew well.

As an unperfect actor on the stage,
Who with his fear is put beside his part,
So I, for fear of trust, forget to say
The perfect ceremony of love's rite.
O learn to read what silent love hath writ:
To hear with eyes belongs to love's fine wit.

To hear with eyes was Rose's gift to her. And Will's words were, indeed, the perfect ceremony of Mary's partnership with the playwright. Her own words for Cleopatra in their play completed the circle: *fire and air.*

In the nine years since he had come to Wilton, Matthew had never been inside the cathedral in Salisbury, by far the most prominent structure in the region. As the family and servants generally worshipped in the parish church, the cathedral was reserved for ceremonial occasions such as weddings and funerals. Mary's husband was buried there, beside her firstborn daughter.

On a bright May afternoon, a year after their return from the Continent, Mary ordered a carriage and rode with Matthew to the cathedral. But not to mourn.

Outside the Gothic facade, a delicate lacework of white stone, they paused and looked at each other in silence. Their love, Mary was learning, needed few words. They entered the cathedral together. In the purse at her waist she carried the gift she had secretly commissioned.

Craning her head upward to point out the soaring vault to Matthew, Mary was swept by dizziness. This beauty was indeed *past the size of dreaming.* Impossibly high, the arched ceiling progressed the length of the nave along orderly ribs of stone supported by towering pillars and walls punctuated by gleaming stained glass. Gazing with Matthew at the timeless wonder of the sanctuary, Mary heard her own words echoing back to her. *Life is too short for half-measures.*

Standing by the altar and drawing him close, Mary spoke

softly but clearly. 'I take thee, Matthew, for my wedded husband.'

Matthew looked startled, then amazed, then joyful. He took Mary's hands in his. 'I take thee, Mary, for my wedded wife.'

They spoke the next words together. 'To have and to hold, from this day forward.'

From her purse Mary withdrew a ring and slipped it onto Matthew's finger. Around the gold band, in a never-ending circle, a pair of snakes entwined.

CODA: THE STONES

Mary and Rose

Over the ages, alchemists have pursued the Philosopher's Stone, a substance with the power to produce perfection from flawed materials, seeking to transmute base metals into gold.

That has never been Mary's goal. She has long understood perfection to be beyond her reach. The goal she seeks is not perfection but metamorphosis, not completion but continuation. Each experiment a chance to begin anew.

So when Rose invites her to visit the Stones on the winter solstice, to watch the sun set, she declines. Why observe another ending?

But Rose insists. She knows her former mistress has more to learn from marvels that can't be encompassed in words. And she wants them to share the sight.

They arrive breathless from the uneven trek. Rooks wheel

overhead. To Mary, the irregular circle of Stones seems more rubble than marvel. More aspirational than complete. An imperfect experiment. Until the sun begins to sink in the sky.

'Look, my lady.' Rose takes Mary's hand. 'In winter, the sun sets where it rises in summer, at the top of the circle.'

Mary thinks of her own Circle, of her life's irregular orbit, its broken shards and piecemeal stitching, and suddenly she sees the Stones in all their lopsided perfection. Moved by the vision, she begins to speak.

'*Wholeness may arise—*' At Rose's sharp intake of breath, Mary stops and turns to her.

'*—from fragments pieced together aright.*' Rose completes the truth. Both women smile in surprised recognition.

The moon is rising now, as if catapulted into the heavens by the departure of the setting sun. White and full, speckled with darkness, bursting with light.

The companions stand side by side, opposites yet equals, washed in moonlight.

AUTHOR'S NOTE

Mary Sidney Herbert (1561–1621), one of the earliest women authors in Renaissance England to publish under her own name, successfully forged a place for herself in a man's world. An influential literary patron as well as author, the Countess of Pembroke has been celebrated by historians for convening a literary salon of cutting-edge writers in early modern England, while her published play about Antony and Cleopatra is believed to have influenced Shakespeare. A member of one of England's leading families, she carved out space for herself as a daring and often controversial figure in a royal court riven by jealousies and intrigues.

In *Imperfect Alchemist*, the fictional Mary Sidney Herbert is mediated through my knowledge of her real-life circumstances and her writings. She was also a scientist, practicing alchemy in her private laboratory to prepare chemical and herbal remedies. Although the Countess was a well-regarded alchemist, no manuscript records of her alchemical recipes or experiments survive. I have drawn on historical accounts documenting the detailed practices of other female alchemists of the period in order to present an authentic, if conjectural, account of her scientific work.

Authors such as Edmund Spenser, John Donne and Ben Jonson, interested in testing the limits of literary forms, participated in the Countess's writing circle. Responding to her known patronage of women authors such as Aemilia Lanyer and her goddaughter, Mary Wroth, I have imagined some of these women into the Countess's Circle, their interaction with the male authors inspiring visions of new possibilities. My account of Mary's collaboration with Shakespeare is another fiction that is not beyond the realm of possibility (nor is the theory that she was the secret author of his works, though I don't subscribe to it).

My primary invented character, Rose Commin, is based on accounts of servants and country folk of the period. Fear of witchcraft was common, and that strand in the story incorporates historical examples of the treatment of women accused of sorcery. Looking at the world through Rose's as well as Mary's eyes has enabled me to broaden both characters' perspectives and their intersecting lives beyond the historical facts.

Apart from Rose's family, the Pembroke servants and a few others, most of the characters in the book are fictional renditions of real historical figures, whose roles combine elements of their actual lives with my own inventions. As well as the authors in the Wilton Circle and the courtiers in Mary's life, they include the court painter Marcus Gheeraerts the Younger; the physician, naturalist and poet Thomas Moffett; the Countess's alchemist associate Adrian Gilbert; the proto-feminist Marie de Gournay; and John Dee, the most prominent occultist of his time and astrologer to the Queen. Simon Forman was a Wiltshire-bred, London-based astrologer and herbalist who was apprenticed in his youth to a cloth merchant named Commin. Matthew Lister served the Dowager Countess as family physician and was rumoured to be her lover.

The Countess's pioneering literary and scientific experiments challenged many of Renaissance England's established conventions – one of the things that most strongly drew me to her. Another was her role as mentor to a cohort of women writers and patrons, including Mary Wroth, Aemilia Lanyer, Elizabeth Cary and Anne Clifford, as well as Queen Anna of Denmark, all of whom I plan to include in a projected series of novels, *Shakespeare's Sisters*. This novel ends in 1613, eight years before Mary's death in her sixtieth year. The year that the Countess died, her niece and namesake, Mary Wroth, published the first love sonnets and prose romance by a woman in early modern England, for which she was labelled a 'hermaphrodite' by courtiers in the circle of King James.

The most significant source for my knowledge of Mary Sidney Herbert's life was the late Margaret Hannay's meticulous biography, *Philip's Phoenix: Mary Sidney, Countess of Pembroke* (Oxford Univ. Press, 1990), while my quotations from her works are drawn from the Oxford University Press editions of her poetry and prose.

A guiding principle has been to avoid contradicting historical facts, but I have sometimes adjusted the timing of actual events by a couple months or years, in order to serve the story and the narrative flow. My aim has been to tell a story that imagines the perspectives of historical women in a world that encompasses both known facts and imagined possibilities, illumining the historical record without being limited by it. I like to think that the real Mary Sidney Herbert, who reinterpreted the Psalms with her brother Sir Philip Sidney, resurrected his *Arcadia*, and reinvented the figure of Cleopatra in her *Antonius*, would appreciate my transmutation of her own story.

ACKNOWLEDGEMENTS

This novel feels both unexpected and inevitable, a product of sustained labour and a miracle. My acknowledgements and thanks, consequently, are manifold.

With my students at Smith College, who have journeyed alongside me in exploring the works produced by Shakespeare's Sisters – the early modern women authors whose voices were first heard by Shakespeare and his contemporaries – I share the ongoing joy of discovery. I express special appreciation to Mary Ruth Robinson, whose extraordinary honours thesis on 'The Countess of Pembroke's Cleopatra' deeply informed my understanding of Mary Sidney Herbert's play.

To my colleagues at Smith College – particularly Ruth Ozeki and Carole de Santi – whose advice and encouragement have helped clear the way for my creative work, I extend my thanks. I'm grateful also to my enthusiastic and supportive friends and colleagues in the burgeoning interdisciplinary field of early modern women and gender studies, many of whom contributed constructive responses to my fiction along the way – Diane Purkiss and Marion Wynne-Davies, Katie Larson and Lisa Walters, Ilona Bell and Mary Ellen Lamb, Susan Frye and Naomi Yavneh, Mihoko Suzuki and Gweno Williams, Paul Salzberg and Gary Waller, Annie Jones and Sharon Seelig, Alison Findlay and Georgianna Ziegler. My grasp of the possibilities of biofiction has been illuminated by the work of Michael Lackey, as well as by my co-editors for a forthcoming collection of essays on biofiction about early modern women, James Fitzmaurice and Sara Jayne Steen.

My first and greatest debt in the field of scholarship on the Sidney family women goes to the late Margaret Hannay, whose two biographies, on Mary Sidney Herbert and Mary Sidney Wroth, have given life to my efforts, from bone structure and lineaments to beating hearts, grounding my inventions in the historical record.

This novel owes much to scholars of early modern women scientists and alchemy, as well as to historians of women's lived experiences and voices in the early modern world, whose expertise has provided the tincture in which my story has steeped.

On location, I have benefited from the expertise of the docents for Penshurst Place, Wilton House, Ludlow Castle and Cardiff Castle. I'm thankful also to the current owners of Ivychurch Manor and Tickenhill Manor, whose generosity enabled me to visit locations central to Mary Sidney Herbert's life that are not open to the general public. Houghton House, her final residence, is now a stunning ruin, while Baynard's Castle long ago burnt to the ground, its location commemorated in the name of the Castle Baynard ward of the City of London. Grants from the Smith College Faculty Development Fund supported my research at those locations.

I thank my agents – Jacques de Spoelberch, whose belief in my fiction and in the arc of the *Shakespeare's Sisters* series has supported me from the start, and Charlotte Seymour, who found a wonderful home for *Imperfect Alchemist* with Allison & Busby. Lesley Crooks has been a generous and thoughtful editor, helping me to realise my vision for the novel. Thanks to Lesley's colleague, Daniel Scott, for a review of the Yorkshire dialect. My thanks also to Susie Dunlop, Kelly Smith, Kirsten Munday and Christina Griffiths.

I have been heartened by encouraging words from novelists whose historical fiction about female figures in particular I have long admired, including Geraldine Brooks, Emma Donoghue, Sarah Dunant, Rachel Kadish and Philippa Gregory. And I have often been carried forward by the faith and love of my close friends – Laurel and Paul Foster-Moore, Anna Jonson and Mary Ann Kelly, Lynn Newdome and Carol Stoddard, Laura Vogel and Jane Yolen. Particular gratitude goes to Jenny Critchlow, whose faith in my creative vision during an early research trip to the UK renewed my own confidence and resolve.

My four children offered unflagging support and enthusiasm during this novel's extended period of research and writing. Since the publication of my first book, *Changing the Subject*, about Mary Wroth – dedicated to Fiona, Isaiah, Damaris and Elias – their presence in my life continues to put everything in place. And my sister and best friend, Marcia Ishii-Eiteman, has always been in my life and at my side. Her enduring love and generous appreciation of my voice as an author has sustained me since our shared childhood, when I would put handwritten tales into her holiday stocking as sister-gifts.

Without my helpmeet and heartmate, my first reader and most rigorous editor, this novel might never have come to be. Chris Rohmann's keen eye and nuanced ear for language complements his directorial sense of each scene. His ability to pare away the extraneous and highlight the essential has supported an illuminating process of transmutation. As my central characters in the novel learn, *Wholeness may arise from fragments pieced together aright.* My thanks to Chris, always, for piecing together my fragments aright.

Naomi Miller is descended on her mother's side from a Japanese shogun of the late 1500s, and on her father's side from Dutch-English settlers who arrived in America at the time of the *Mayflower*. She is a professor of English and the Study of Women and Gender at Smith College, Massachusetts, where she specialises in Shakespeare and his literary 'sisters' – women writers of the Renaissance. *Imperfect Alchemist* is her first novel.

naomimillerbooks.com